The Mano

The Manor House

Jane Holland

First published in Great Britain in 2022 by Orion Dash,
an imprint of The Orion Publishing Group Ltd.,
Carmelite House, 50 Victoria Embankment,
London EC4Y 0DZ

An Hachette UK Company

1 3 5 7 9 10 8 6 4 2

A CIP catalogue record for this book is
available from the British Library.

ISBN (Paperback) 978 1 3987 1059 7
ISBN (eBook) 978 1 3987 0839 6

Typeset at The Spartan Press Ltd,
Lymington, Hants

Printed in the UK

www.orionbooks.co.uk

For my husband, Steven Haynes.

Chapter One

Years have passed. You haven't changed.
Same river, same boots, different fish.

— From 'There' in *Estuary*

Nobody had asked him the most important question of all.

Stunned by this astonishing oversight, Eleanor glanced about at the intent, forward-facing profiles of those around her.

All these clever people, she thought in disbelief, and not one had yet formulated the question that had been burning a hole in her mind even before she came here tonight. The question that had brought her to this poetry reading, despite it being forbidden, despite the risks, despite everything...

Still, she sat quietly, as she had been taught, waiting and listening with barely suppressed impatience to the sometimes rambling, sometimes erudite questions from other members of the audience, and the clear, natural, deeply reasoned responses of the man on stage.

His performance impressed her more with every word he uttered. There was something about his measured tone, the way he weighed each question and approached it on its own terms, however slight or inapposite, that filled her with a deep sense of admiration. To engage with such a mind...

I

But the one question she needed to have answered never came, and the omission was simply maddening.

Eleanor began to fidget as the lengthy question and answer session wore on, first chewing on her blonde hair and then playing with the gradually unravelling sleeve of her drab green cardigan.

Surely, she thought, somebody must ask him soon?

But nobody did.

She was still in a fever of expectation when the compere rose from his seat at the end of the first row and held aloft his clipboard to indicate that the session was at an end. He was short and sweating, with a little moustache and an indulgent expression on his round face as he briefly consulted his clipboard before launching into his vote of thanks to their guest speaker.

'I think I speak for everyone when I say that tonight's guest speaker, a young Cornishman of no little repute, has given us much to think about,' he began, pausing for a hearty round of applause. Then he began to list what he felt had been among the highlights of the evening's meeting, to more scattered applause and general comments of agreement.

Something burst in her chest; a floodtide of emotion suppressed too long swept through to demolish her inhibitions.

Eleanor abruptly thrust her hand in the air.

The compere faltered, catching the movement out of the corner of his eye. His voice tailed off, and he turned slightly towards her.

'It seems we have one last question from the audience, Mr Chance,' he said, and glanced at the man on stage. 'Will you accept it?'

'Gladly.'

The compere nodded in her direction, once again indulgent but now fatherly as well, as though conferring a very great favour on her. 'Yes, miss? What would you like to ask our guest?'

Eleanor stared at him, suddenly mute. Her brain had not thought beyond the revolutionary act of putting her hand in the air.

Many other male eyes now turned towards her, a mind-numbing sea of faces gazing back at her through the dense, smoky air.

She felt her cheeks flush scarlet, adding to her confusion. Her mouth was dry and could not seem to utter sounds. She half-expected one of the men to jump up and demand that she leave the hall at once. 'Fraud!' 'Imposter!' 'How dare you?' And maybe they would be right.

She wasn't a student or an academic. She'd never even been to school. Well, not a proper school like everyone else. She was also a woman, and young.

But none of that was her fault.

The man on stage was also waiting. She didn't dare look up at him to find out. His silence was as eloquent as his speech.

'Stand up, miss,' the compere urged her with a gesture, impatient now. 'So we can see you.'

Reluctantly, Eleanor rose to her feet, clutching her hand-bag, and the chair legs scraped on the wooden floor in the narrow space. It was an ugly sound and made her shudder. She found herself quite unable to look up at the stage, so cleared her throat and addressed herself to the back of the seated man's head below her, who mercifully was still facing front.

'Thank you for coming tonight, Mr Chance,' she began. 'I can't tell you how much it meant to hear you read your poems the way they're supposed to sound. I've only ever read verse in a book before, you see, so ...'

3

A rumble of laughter made her stop and stare about herself.

'Do you have a *question* for the speaker, miss?' The compere glanced at the wall clock with undisguised significance. 'We're already running over time.'

'All right, I'm getting to it,' she said defensively.

Again, the men around her laughed.

They found her silly and ignorant, she realised, her heart thumping hard. She wished she'd never stuck her hand up. But there was no escape from it. Not now.

'I just wanted to know,' she rushed on, finally daring to raise her eyes to the man on stage, 'if your poems are true.'

More laughter. Louder this time.

They had not understood what she was asking, she thought, and felt a stab of anger. What gave these people the right to laugh at her?

But the man on stage had understood. He was staring at her fixedly. 'What's your name?' he asked.

She had not expected such a question, and blinked, temporarily flustered by it. She did not dare give her full name. Not here, in front of everyone. She thought for a guilty moment about lying, giving a false name instead. Or telling him she was called Nell, the nickname her mother had always used for her.

His intent gaze would not permit her to lie.

'Eleanor.'

He had thick, springing dark hair that fell in a ramshackle manner across his forehead; he'd had to brush it back occasionally as he read his work to them, afterwards replacing his hand in one trouser pocket in a careless manner, rather like a schoolboy. His shoulders were broad and so was his chest, but he seemed agile enough when he moved.

There was a kind of smouldering restlessness and intensity

about him that pleased her, and she guessed instinctively that he would understand and appreciate her own tempestuous moods.

The poet was younger than she'd expected, however. She doubted he was even thirty. Yet already he had two books of poetry out; they'd been well-received by London reviewers, and the first had won a national award, as the compere had pointed out in his introduction.

It was unnerving to consider how much this man had accomplished in such a short period of time, for he himself had admitted earlier that he'd only begun writing verse at the age of twenty. One year younger than her own age now.

'Well, Eleanor,' Mr Chance said, with an almost infinitesimal pause after her name, 'that rather depends on how you define the truth.'

She waited, confused, in the hope that he might elaborate. But Mr Chance merely looked away and lit a cigarette, his air casual, dismissive, as though the matter was over.

Was she supposed to have given him her definition of the truth before he could answer fully? All she had really wanted to know was whether his poetry was based on real life. If the mysterious 'lady' mentioned in some of his more recent poems, for example, was a real person or a figment of his imagination. But she had not dared ask such a personal question.

The compere inclined his head with a relieved smile, indicated that she should sit down again, and returned to his vote of thanks.

People began to applaud. The evening was over.

Disappointed, Eleanor dragged on her coat and knotted a patterned headscarf under her chin, making her way to the door with the rest. Someone had already started noisily stacking seats at the back of the hall. There was a queue to get out. Now that it was over, and she had not got what she came for, she began to fret about the lateness of the hour. The meeting had gone on far too long; she would be in trouble.

One man glanced at her knowingly, impudently, and she lowered her gaze to the shoes of the person in front. It was dark outside and raining softly, but she had not set her hair, so there was no need to worry…

'Eleanor?'

Her name made her turn, startled. She'd known his voice immediately. The deep timbre that shook her to the core, the oddly out-of-place rustic accent on the ends of words.

'Mr Chance?'

'Lyndon, please,' he corrected her, and put out his hand like a test. His eyes were dark and seemed to devour her. 'It's my father who's Mr Chance.'

She stepped out of the queue, aware of others staring at her again, and shook his hand awkwardly, her handbag crooked in her elbow.

He had a fearless handshake, the kind where all four fingers curl around to grip you firmly and the thumb lies along the top. Pointing to the heart, her father would have said.

'I'm sorry to have given you such a cryptic answer back there.' Lyndon Chance held her gaze with dark, hypnotic eyes.

There was something leonine about him up close, but earthy with it. He didn't seem to have noticed her shabby clothes and shoes, or the cheap headscarf. Instead, he made her feel as though she were the only woman in the room. The only woman on earth, perhaps.

'It was a question that deserved a longer answer than we had time for,' he explained, adding, 'Some of us are heading

6

to the pub down the road. Perhaps I could buy you a drink? Make a better stab at answering you properly?'

Have a drink in a pub? With a real poet?

It would mean getting home late, Eleanor thought warily, and no doubt smelling of smoke and alcohol, too.

'I'd like that, thank you.'

Later, on her walk home, her low heels clacking in the darkness, Eleanor felt herself sway and knew she ought not to have agreed to another drink. She never drank alcohol. And Lyndon had lit a cigarette at one point and passed it to her, and she hadn't refused it, although she didn't smoke either. It had all seemed so natural, even the way Lyndon had spoken to her, focused on her face, the two of them sitting far too close in the snug at the back of the pub, so that their thighs brushed from time to time …

Her cheeks flared with heat again.

She hardly dared recall what they had discussed. Though what a conversation it had been!

Lyndon had deftly turned aside her questions about his poetry, speaking instead with glowing pride of Cornwall, the duchy where he'd been born and still lived occasionally when he wasn't travelling or studying. It sounded wonderful, an idyllic place compared to the dreary, smoky streets of the towns where she'd lived, so many of them, ending up at last here in tiny Cirencester.

He had a twin brother named Oliver, which was something she couldn't imagine; to meet someone on the stair with the same face as oneself and an entirely separate life … So intimate and yet so different.

She'd laughed and smiled, and spoken utter nonsense, no doubt. Poetry had jostled in her head with alcohol and the thick drifting fragrance of cigar smoke from the compere, whose name was Teddy, and several of the arts committee, who were all fighting for the chance to speak to Lyndon Chance.

But the great man only had eyes for her.

'And what about your family?' Lyndon had asked at last, breaking the spell, his eyes so intent it was hard to look away.

'Oh, well, I have a father, and a brother...' Her voice had died away, and then she'd gathered up her coat and bag. 'But look at the time! It's last orders. I have to go, I'm sorry.'

He'd come to the door of the pub with her. 'Let me walk you home.'

'No, thank you.' She'd been firm, declining his repeated offer to accompany her home. 'It's not far. And it's perfectly safe. This is Cirencester. Nothing happens here.' And she'd laughed, a little too wildly.

Lyndon had followed her along the street a few steps, until the sound of drinkers in the pub had begun to fade, and then caught her elbow, stopping her.

'Eleanor, will you come and visit me in Cornwall?'

She'd stared at him, her mouth open. 'I beg your pardon?'

'You told me you liked Charles Causley's work. I might be able to introduce you to him. And to other Cornish poets I know.'

'Causley?' she'd repeated in awed tones.

'There's quite a lively scene in Cornwall these days. It's not like when I was younger. Betjeman has a house near us, too. Though he's not often there.'

'But Cornwall... It's so far away.'

'There's a railway track runs past our house, all the way along the estuary. I could pick you up at the station in Wadebridge.'

His home, Lyndon had explained, was on the picturesque Camel Estuary in a remote corner of North Cornwall. He'd described the house to her in loving detail, a large Tudor manor house with granite walls and formal gardens, and how he used to look out of his bedroom window as a boy and watch birds break cover from among thick reeds at dawn to skim the pale waters of the estuary.

It all sounded marvellous, a perfect retreat from the world.

But she'd known it was impossible as soon as he mentioned it. Beyond impossible, in fact. They would never permit her to leave.

'I can't, I'm sorry.'

'Give me your telephone number at least,' Lyndon had persisted, not letting her go. 'Or your address. I could write to you.'

Lyndon Chance, writing to her?

It was everything she had ever dreamt of.

But the thought of her father intercepting his telephone calls or his correspondence had terrified her; accusations and vicious punishment would inevitably follow such a discovery. She'd shaken her head, staring at him, numb with yearning, and he'd finally given up, backing away with a strange, bitter desperation in his face.

'I'll be at Green's Hotel until nine o'clock tomorrow morning,' he'd told her, his eyes locked with hers, 'if you change your mind. You can drop a note in at reception. I'll check there before I go.'

Then he'd left her.

Eleanor walked and swayed, oblivious to her surroundings, and dreamed about how her life would be on the far-off Cornish coast...

But reality was waiting for her.

Before she could even fit her key to the lock, the front door jerked open and her father stood there, large in the doorway.

'It's almost midnight,' he spat, then grabbed her in off the doorstep and slammed the door. 'Don't you care what the neighbours think?' Then her father sniffed her, and his face darkened still further. 'You've been drinking. And smoking.'

His voice shook with fury. 'What have you been doing all this time? As if I need to ask … I can smell the stink of sin on your body. My God, you little whore!'

His arm swept up, the back of his hand catching her hard across the cheek, and she fell clumsily into the hat stand, knocking it over.

Her father stood over her, panting heavily.

A door opened upstairs, light spilling out onto the dark staircase, and then her brother Fred came thumping down in his pyjamas.

He was only three years older than Eleanor, but her father treated him like a man and her like a child; a child whose job it was to stay home and clean up after them and cook their meals. Because, since her mother's death, there had been nobody else to do it.

'Where's she been, Dad?'

'*Who* has she been with?' her father growled, correcting him. 'That's the real question. And I intend to find out.'

Eleanor rubbed her cheek, trying not to cry. It would only encourage him to be crueller. Her instincts also warned her not to volunteer too much information about where she'd been. In the past, her father had turned up at places where she'd made friends and made it impossible for her to ever go there again.

'I … I was at a meeting,' she stammered.

'What kind of meeting?' Fred looked incredulous. 'Do you mean a political meeting? Or a church meeting?'

'A meeting that went on until such a late hour? And you stinking to high heaven of smoke and booze? What do you take me for? A fool? No, you've been to some filthy pub or night club. With someone you shouldn't have been with.' Her father would hit her again if she argued with him, she knew, so she stayed silent. 'Get up and go to your room.'

Her father watched while Eleanor picked herself up, neither man offering her a hand. She staggered towards the stairs, her cheekbone aching. He followed after her, waited while she cleaned herself up in the bathroom, and then shoved her into the bedroom, locking the door after her.

He then went downstairs, presumably to talk to her brother where she couldn't hear their conversation.

Taking care not to make too much noise, Eleanor knelt on her bedroom floor and peeled back the drab brown carpet at one corner. She prised up the loose floorboard beneath and listened intently to the conversation in the kitchen below.

'She's got some fancy man,' her brother was saying angrily. 'She must have, to be out so late. What are you going to do, Dad? You can't let this go.'

There was a long silence.

'Only one thing we can do,' her father said in the end. 'Take her back to her grandfather's place in Plymouth. She'll be kept tight there. Otherwise, whoever this man is, she'll find a way to see him again. Soon as my back's turned.'

'I don't want to leave Cirencester. I like my job.'

'You don't have to leave, son. I'll go with her and come back once she's safely stowed.'

'Who's going to clean for us until she comes back? Cook for us?'

'I may have to marry again.'

Her brother said nothing to this, except, 'Bloody girl.'

'She's unnatural, that one. Just like her mother. But my father will see to her, all right. He knows how to keep a woman in line. When I married your mother, he told me:

spare the rod, spoil the bride. But I didn't listen. More's the pity.'

'Maybe Grandad could find her a husband. Someone in the Brotherhood.'

'That's my thought, too.' Her father gave a short sound like a laugh under his breath. 'This could be useful to us, boy. If she marries someone high up, someone with influence. She's not a bad looker, for all her ways.'

'When will you leave?'

'We can't risk her getting away,' her father said decisively. 'I'll pack a bag tonight and drive her down to Plymouth myself first thing in the morning. That will sort her out, you'll see.'

Eleanor dropped the bedroom carpet back into place, and rolled over onto her back, staring up at the stained ceiling.

Go back to live with her grandfather in Plymouth?

No, never.

The man was vile, a brute and a bully who wielded his belt for every tiny or imagined transgression. Last time she'd been left with her grandfather, as a rebellious young teenager, she'd come away black and blue all over, barely able to walk for weeks afterwards.

Now she was twenty-one, God only knew what they'd do to her as punishment for her 'sins'. Not that her father cared about that. So long as she meekly agreed to be married off to whomever they chose.

She's unnatural, that one.

Her brother had not asked what Dad had meant by that.

She fingered the tender skin over her cheekbone and wondered if there'd be a bruise there in the morning. Though it hardly mattered. Not where she was being taken.

What on earth was she going to do?

★

It was a little after six-thirty in the morning.

Eleanor was crouched behind a small van in the car park of Green's Hotel, with nothing but an overnight bag containing a few clean clothes and a spare pair of shoes, and her handbag.

Her ankle hurt, for she'd twisted it slightly when dropping out of the first-floor window into the flowerbed below. In the glimmering dark before dawn, she'd limped across the back lawn and groped along the fence for the place where a panel had come loose, and from there climbed out into the alley that ran behind the houses.

Once clear of the alley, she'd made her way through various back streets to Green's Hotel, which stood silent and dark at that early hour, and hidden away in a corner to wait.

She needed to escape Cirencester unseen. But she had no cash of her own for the bus, despite a Post Office savings book with a few pounds in the account. Besides, the bus station would be the very first place her father would look for her. And she had few friends; she'd call most of them acquaintances rather than friends, and of those only two or three were not members of her father's church.

Her father had discouraged friendships outside church circles and kept her at home most of her life. Indeed, it was only in the past year, since turning twenty, that Eleanor had begun to rebel, slipping out of an evening to go to the pictures on her own, pretending afterwards that she had been for a long walk. She could think of nobody who would willingly accept her into their home. Especially once she admitted that her irate father and brother might turn up at any minute to hammer on the front door.

The time passed intolerably slowly.

After several hours crouched behind the van, she was tired and stiff, and beginning to despair. But seeing Lyndon

Chance's tall figure cross the car park, Eleanor straightened and moved hurriedly to intercept him.

'Hello.' Her voice was high and breathless with nerves. 'I'm so sorry, but is there any chance of a lift out of town?'

She'd had plenty of time to consider what would happen if the poet refused and was terrified by the prospect. Yet, somehow, she managed not to let it show.

Lyndon Chance stopped dead and stared at her. He held a battered-looking suitcase in one hand, a leather briefcase in the other.

Just as last night when she'd stood to ask her question, he seemed almost stunned by her approach, his gaze fixed on her face.

'You.'

'Yes, me again. Sorry to be a nuisance.' Embarrassed by her situation, Eleanor glanced at the sports car he had been heading towards. 'Is that your car? How marvellous. It looks awfully swish. I … I just need a lift out of town. I won't get in your way, I promise.'

'A lift out of town,' he repeated mechanically, and unlocked the boot of the sports car. He put his cases inside. She got the feeling he was playing for time. 'Where are you going?'

'I don't mind. Er, are you heading towards Exeter?'

'Of course. I can drop you in the city centre.' He held out his hand for her bag. 'It may be a bit of a squeeze to get that in the boot, but I'll try.'

'Thank you.'

He eyed her bruised face as he opened the passenger door for her, a frown in his eyes, and she steeled herself for some awkward questions.

But to her relief he said nothing.

Within minutes, they were motoring out of Cirencester

14

on the Bristol Road. Lyndon had pulled on suede gloves and settled a tweed cap low on his forehead before heading off, and she had no qualms about his driving abilities, for he seemed confident and didn't even bother to consult the map. There were still rainclouds to the east, but thankfully they were heading west, where a few glimpses of blue sky could be seen in the distance.

Eleanor sat beside him in a state of trembling wonder, not quite able to believe she had carried it off. All these years of captivity. And now she was escaping her family.

At last, at last . . .

Then, on the very outskirts of Cirencester, she nearly choked.

'Oh my God,' she whispered, staring bolt-eyed at the road ahead, her stomach lurching with fear.

'What is it?' he asked, glancing at her quickly.

'My dad . . . That's his car.'

The large old Ford was moving slowly and inexorably down the road towards them, her father behind the wheel in his best black overcoat, the one he wore to church meetings. He was pausing at every side road to look up and down, hunting for her, and then driving on.

She could tell from the way he was hunched over the wheel that her father was incandescent with rage, without even being close enough to see his expression.

To her relief, Lyndon didn't demand an explanation, but nodded grimly. 'Better get your head down, then.' As she ducked, he dragged a tartan blanket through from the back seat and draped it over her. 'Keep still. We'll be past him in a minute.'

Bent almost double, with her head in the footwell, Eleanor waited in the stuffy dark under the tartan blanket.

She felt sick with apprehension, shivering at the thought

of her father stopping Lyndon's car and making her get out. Though that public humiliation would be nothing compared to what he and her grandfather would do to her later by way of reprisal.

'It's all right, he's gone. You can come out again.' He plucked the blanket off her head and watched as she sat up again, her hair dishevelled. 'Bad news, is he, your old man?' His gaze raked her pale face, and then he turned back to the road. 'Is that where you got the shiner?'

'Yes.'

'Want to talk about it?'

Now that he had helped her escape her father's clutches, Eleanor felt a little safer in his company.

Briefly, she told him what had happened when she got in the previous night, carefully leaving out the part about the religious sect they belonged to and her fear of being forced into marriage with one of the other members. She found most ordinary people disapproved of such sects, and she didn't want Lyndon Chance to think poorly of her for having been brought up in one.

'Sounds like a prize bastard,' Lyndon said in a harsh tone. He seemed angry on her behalf, something she'd never experienced before, and which surprised her. 'Small wonder you're so eager to get out of town. But are you sure Exeter is the best place for you? Do you have friends there?'

'No, but I'll soon get a job. I'm a hard worker and there must be jobs available in a city that size.'

There was a slight smile on his face as he asked, 'I take it you've never been to Exeter?' When she shook her head, mystified, his grin widened. 'Then I have news for you. Exeter may be a city, but it's not that big a place. And it's not so very far from Cirencester either. Not as far as London,

I mean.' He studied her face. 'Won't he go looking there eventually, once he's tried Bath and Bristol?'

'I suppose so, I don't know. To be honest, I hadn't thought beyond getting out of the house this morning.' The terrible enormity of what she'd done suddenly hit her. 'Oh God, what have I done? Dad's going to kill me when he catches up to me.'

'Then we'd better make sure he never does,' Lyndon said, an edge to his voice. He glanced at her again, and his expression, which had become surprisingly fierce, softened. 'Hey, don't cry. You're safe with me. I won't let him touch you.'

'Thank you,' Eleanor managed to say.

Lyndon drove in silence for a while, staring fixedly at the road ahead, his gloved hands gripping the wheel. Then he turned his head to smile at her. 'Look, you said you wouldn't mind coming to visit me in Cornwall this summer. Why not bring that plan forward a little, and let me drive you down there now?'

She was amazed. 'Sorry?'

'You can stay as long as you like, we've got plenty of room. Our place is pretty inaccessible, too, right on the north coast and a good few miles from the nearest main road. Your father would never think to look for you there, I guarantee it.'

A distant alarm bell rang softly in her head. Something in the tone of his voice, perhaps, or his light smile. But she ignored it.

With any other man, she might have felt uneasy, agreeing to such an outrageous idea out of the blue. Motor all the way down to Cornwall with him? Stay in his family home?

They had only met last night, for goodness' sake.

But this was Lyndon Chance, a well-known published

poet, not some random stranger who'd picked her up from the side of the road.

Still, she ought to be cautious.

'I say, that's awfully kind of you,' she said hesitantly. 'And I'd love to say yes, of course I would. It sounds heavenly. But it does seem a bit intrusive, me just turning up out of the blue. I mean, won't your family mind?'

'Not even remotely,' he assured her.

Chapter Two

Camel Estuary, North Cornwall, present day

> Spirit was her battle dress –
> Bold and precarious,
> Like a calf's first tottering steps
> Into April frost.
>
> – From 'Habit' in *Estuary*

Taylor knocked the last tent peg as deep as she could into the dusty ground and checked the guy rope for adequate tension. Then she straightened up, hammer in hand, conscious of a job well done.

Directly ahead, looming over the smooth blue dome of her tent, was a large but somewhat ramshackle manor house, its earliest structures apparently dating from Tudor times. It was set in sloping gardens that must once have been quite fine but were now a mass of overgrown shrubs and cracked stone steps. There was a kind of malevolence at work there, she thought, studying the house. And yet a fierce happiness, too, a determination to be free.

If only she'd been tidier as a girl, more punctual, more obedient, he might not have lost his temper quite so often…

Beyond the manor house lay the Camel Estuary, a broad current of water that swept through the nearby picturesque town of Wadebridge before rolling steadily on, widening as it meandered towards the Atlantic Ocean.

Taylor shielded her eyes, looking west into blazing afternoon sun; the old manor house was nothing but a grey, forbidding outline of slate roofs and tall chimneys, the estuary beyond shrouded by reed marsh and tangled patches of whip-thin cord grass, today looking more like the South of France than Cornwall, on one of the hottest days of the year so far. One of the hottest days since records began, she suspected, increasingly glad of the total sunblock she'd applied before getting out of the van to erect her tent.

But then, every summer's records now seemed to exceed those of the year before, just as every winter saw ever colder weather, freak storms and so-called 'natural' disasters.

Humanity was on a downward slope, she thought grimly, and someone had stupidly tampered with the brakes.

Someone long before her time, of course. But Taylor was aware that she and her descendants, if she should ever produce offspring, would reap the unhappy results of that mess.

Was it too late to make a difference to the climate emergency? She had to hope it wasn't. Because otherwise, what was the point of it all?

Disturbed by the increasingly morose direction of her thoughts these days, she walked back to her van in the lane and returned the hammer to her toolkit, hearing her university tutor's voice in her head: 'Don't give up on this planet just because everyone else has, Taylor. One person can still make a difference.'

She could only hope Dr Chang was right.

'Hello.' A man's voice brought her round in surprise. 'Did you get permission to camp here?'

'Of course.' Taylor shielded her eyes again as she peered at the man standing before her in the lane.

It was hard to make out his face, the sun being at his back, but his voice was smooth and cultured, not as hostile as his question. He looked to be wearing waders and a fisherman's jacket, and sure enough, was holding rods and a bucket of bait.

Was this her host?

'At least, I was told it wouldn't be a problem,' she added. His question left her uncertain of her welcome though. 'Mr Chance?'

'God, no.' The man sounded amused now. 'I have about a decade on Julius Chance, more's the pity. Besides, he's out at the moment.'

'Oh.'

'It's a Friday, so I imagine he'll have taken his grand-mother into Wadebridge to do the shopping. That's their usual routine.' The man looked her up and down, perhaps reassessing her. 'The family don't like people camping on their land. Actually, they don't like people, full stop. But if they're expecting you ...'

'Actually,' she admitted guiltily, 'I have got here a few days earlier than planned. I was hoping Mr Chance wouldn't mind. I certainly don't intend to disturb the family if I can help it.'

Taylor looked about at the river, the insect-rich fields and woods, and drew a deep, exhilarated breath, unable to contain her enthusiasm at being here at last.

'This is such a wonderful place, isn't it?' she said, still shielding her eyes to look at him. 'Utterly glorious.'

'I couldn't agree more.' The man smiled, moving at last out of line with the sun, and she saw the good-humoured, weathered face of an outdoor type, somewhere in his mid thirties, fair-haired and with a twinkle in his deep-set brown eyes. 'I'm Rob Mackenzie, by the way. But everyone calls me Mack.'

'Taylor Pierce,' she said promptly.

She often thought of people as colours; it was an odd thing to do, apparently, and her friends at university had always laughed at her for it, but it felt real to her.

In her view, everyone came with their own innate colours hovering around them, a bit like a halo. Someone had once told her it was called an 'aura'. It might be eccentric, but she often used her special perception to judge people, some auras being brighter and friendlier than others.

Rob Mackenzie's aura was a ruddy orange, with a shiny white intensity at the outside edge. She instinctively trusted it, and him.

'Good to meet you, Taylor. I would shake your hand, but ...' He gestured with his fishing tackle, and grinned. 'Sorry.'

'Not a problem.'

'Look, I'm renting a little riverside cottage along the lane there, just for the summer. Feel free to drop round for a chat. It can get lonely out here on your own.'

'Oh.' Taken aback by this offer, she was instantly suspicious, despite his trustworthy air. 'Thank you, I'll bear that in mind.'

A shout made them both turn.

Weaving towards them out of the flat scrublands beside the lane was a spindly boy of about nine or ten, with a fair thatch and lively eyes, dressed in shorts and a blue T-shirt.

It wasn't hard to work out who he was. Talk about a chip off the old block, she thought, glancing from man to boy.

'Dad!' He ran past Taylor with barely a glance for her, and skidded to a halt before his father, breathless and holding out a closed fist. 'Look!'

Cautiously, the boy opened his palm, and the large grasshopper, which he'd been shielding against escape, leapt straight off his hand and into a clump of untidy grasses in the verge. The insect hopped rapidly from one green-brown stalk to another and was soon lost from view.

'Wow,' the boy said, laughing wildly. 'Did you see that? The funniest thing...That was a huge jump.'

'Yes, an astonishing distance. Though I've told you before not to disturb any of the wildlife. Which includes trapping them.'

'It was only a grasshopper.'

'All the same ... Live and let live, yes?' Mack seemed to remember her presence and turned his son to face her. 'This is my son, Davie.' He tousled his son's fair hair affectionately. 'Davie, this is Miss Pierce. Say hello.'

'Hello,' Davie repeated obediently, and displayed a missing tooth as he grinned. His curious gaze shifted to the new structure in the field – if it could be called a field, when it was really just glorified scrubland – and his eyes widened. 'Is that your tent? It looks rather small.'

'Well, it's a one-man tent. Or one-woman, in this case. I don't take up much room. And I have my van for storage space. I hope to be camping here a good few weeks. Maybe until the end of the summer, if Mr Chance doesn't kick me out before then. So we'll be neighbours for a while.'

Davie looked pleased. 'You must come and visit us at the cottage. I've been making an ant nest between two sheets of glass.'

'I'd like to see that. If you're sure your mum won't mind?'

A common wasp, slightly dozy in the warmth, buzzed about her head and she flapped it away. The boy stiffened as it flew towards him, and shrank back behind his father, his smile vanishing. His aura, which had been a bright, glowing white before, turned abruptly dark.

'It's OK, Davie.' His father put an arm about his narrow shoulders and glanced up at Taylor, no doubt feeling he needed to explain the boy's behaviour. 'He's allergic to wasp stings.'

'Oh God, how awful.' She nodded sympathetically at the boy. 'I'm allergic to strawberries. I ate one in a fruit salad last year by accident, at a friend's house, and my throat swelled up like a bullfrog's. I couldn't breathe; it was terrifying.'

Davie nodded as though he understood exactly how that felt. 'What's a … a bullfrog?'

Briefly, she explained the difference between a frog and a bullfrog. Father and son listened to her explanation with fascination, though she felt sure Mack already knew everything she was saying and was merely being polite.

'And the grasshopper you captured?' She smiled, warming to her subject. 'That was a Meadow Grasshopper. You can tell by the all-green body and little dark stripe. The males have this odd growling noise they make by rubbing their legs against their wings, basically to attract the females.'

'You know a lot about wildlife,' Davie said, looking impressed.

'That's because I'm a conservationist,' she told him, and pointed to the University of London logo on her T-shirt. 'At least, that's what I want to be. I'm still a student, really. I'm doing a master's degree. That's why I'm down here, in fact. To study the estuary for my research dissertation,' she nodded to the water behind them, 'including its flora and fauna. And particularly the land around Estuary House.'

'And you're happy to stay here?' Mack raised his eyebrows. 'The stories we've heard about the Chances don't paint a very flattering portrait … Murder, mayhem, and so on.'

24

She had a good idea what he was talking about but decided to play it dumb. After all, if she was supposedly there as a conservationist, she would hardly know that much about the family history.

'Murder?'

Mack grinned, looking round at her, the twinkle back in his eyes. 'I'm sure most of it is nonsense. But there's Lyndon Chance ... You've heard of him, I take it?'

'The poet, yes.'

He was going to say more but stopped, looking sharply towards Wadebridge, and she turned her head, too, listening.

A car was coming.

Even if she hadn't been able to hear the throaty rasp of its engine, she would have spotted the cloud of dust spiralling in its wake as the car chugged out of town along the country track that ran beside the estuary.

'Sounds like Julius on his way back.' Mack called to his son and gave her a fleeting smile. 'I'm sorry, we have to go. The family don't like us hanging about.'

She wondered why, but said nothing, merely nodding. 'Goodbye, then.'

She raised a hand in farewell to Davie, who waved back cheerfully before setting off at a trot along the winding, tree-lined lane, followed by his father.

Within another minute, they were out of sight.

Just in time too, for a battered green Land Rover appeared from the opposite direction as she was locking the van and pulled up next to her with a screech of brakes.

A young man in his twenties was behind the wheel; he looked out at her with suspicion, one tanned forearm stretched along the open window.

Julius Chance was the antithesis of the mild-mannered Mack, she thought, having turned with a carefully prepared smile only to be confronted by a hostile stare that left her feeling vulnerable and exposed.

Instinctively, her fingernails curled into her palms.

Perhaps if she hadn't hidden under the bed that day, stifling her sobs behind shaking hands, but had run to their neighbours for help ...

Taylor sucked in her breath, pulling back her shoulders at the same time as though to gain extra height. Pointless, of course, for she was a mere five foot two and this man looked lean and lanky, his head nearly brushing the roof of the Land Rover.

She had thought Julius Chance abrupt and uncommunicative in his emails. But the look on his face was a whole new level of unfriendliness.

He was also uncomfortably attractive.

Sleek, inky black hair fell to his shoulders in a studied, hippyish way, with eyes to match under dark brows set in an angular face, and a mouth that looked grim enough to be almost savage.

Taylor gazed into that face and fought a strong desire to recoil. He looked like someone who'd spent his formative years stranded on a desert island, fending for himself with nothing but a sharpened stick to hand and a rabbit-skin coat, and was now being forced to learn how to be 'civilised' again, without the slightest desire to do so.

'OK, who the hell are you?' His cold stare shifted from her to the ancient van. She saw his lip curl with distaste. 'This is private land,' he told her. 'No camping allowed.'

Wow, she thought. So Mack had been right about the lack of hospitality.

Her first impulse was to pack up her tent, jump back in her van and escape. But she'd driven a long way, and this visit was the culmination of a long-held dream. Nobody was going to chase her away from Estuary House. Not without a fight.

'Mr Chance?'

His eyes narrowed but he said nothing.

'How do you do?' Taylor held out her hand, determined not to be intimidated by his manner. 'I'm Taylor Pierce from the University of London. We exchanged emails a few months back. I'm here to do a conservation study. Maybe you remember?'

He still neither replied nor shook her outstretched hand, so she pressed on regardless, pinning a bright smile to her face.

'In your last email, you agreed that I could camp in the field behind the house. You said I wouldn't be disturbing anyone up there.'

There was an elderly lady in the passenger seat of the Land Rover. She was presumably his grandmother, Mrs Chance.

This woman leant forward and studied Taylor with an inscrutable expression. In comparison to his darker-than-midnight blue aura, which pulsed and crackled with menace, her own was a faded golden white, tattered and fragmented about her head, mingling with wisps of silvery white hair.

'Are you the investigator?' the old lady asked.

'Gran, just leave it, would you?' Julius Chance flashed a warning look at his grandmother, who sat back, facing front with a sigh. His head swivelled and he glared at Taylor again. 'Look, I need to take my grandmother up to the house and unpack her shopping. Then you and I will talk.'

'I'd be happy to help with the unpacking,' she offered.

But he'd already revved the engine and accelerated away, leaving her choking in a cloud of dust from the spinning tyres.

The investigator?

Taylor grinned. That was one way of putting it, she supposed. Though she doubted that was what Mrs Chance had meant.

A wooden gate with Estuary House painted in black letters on a cracked white background stood about thirty feet away. The Land Rover barely slowed for the turn into the gate, and then took the narrow track marked Private at a ridiculous speed, the old vehicle lurching in and out of deep mud ruts, before finally vanishing round the other side of the vast house. Soft dust fell like rain afterwards, drifting slowly back across the overgrown formal gardens at the front of the house.

'Welcome to Cornwall,' Taylor muttered to herself, and leant her back against the warm panels of the van, wishing again that she could just pack up and leave.

The busy, crowded streets of London in the middle of a heatwave had never seemed more inviting. But of course, she'd given up her student accommodation for the summer and would be unlikely to find anywhere else to stay. Not in London, at any rate.

Murder and mayhem, and so on.

Mack was mistaken if he thought whatever had happened here in the past would put her off Estuary House.

Lyndon Chance was the reason she'd come here this summer. The infamous, long-dead Cornish poet was why she'd chosen this lonely stretch of saltmarsh and intertidal mudflats as the focus for her conservation thesis, rather than a dozen alternative areas of special interest around the British Isles.

And she had no intention of leaving.

Chapter Three

Dark roots, deep as teeth, gave up ungodly stench.
Like old drains, blocked
By a severed head.

— From 'Estuary at Dusk' in *Estuary*

It was early evening by the time Lyndon's sports car finally swept through the town of Wadebridge, passing over a bridge with a generous river flowing beneath, and turned down a narrow, bumpy lane a few miles beyond the town. Being September and close to the Cornish coast, the air was damp and a little chilly. Eleanor dragged her trusty green cardigan out of her bag and pulled it on for extra warmth. The sky was darkening minute by minute, its gloom a little intimidating.

Yet it was so magical to be driving through unfamiliar countryside, far from the restrictive grasp of her family and church, that she welcomed even the dusk as somehow friendly and exciting.

They'd broken their journey at Exeter earlier in the day, wandering about the cramped, medieval streets for an hour, and then standing to admire the cathedral with its high ornate pinnacles and its flying buttresses, which apparently dated from the fourteenth century. Lyndon had insisted on steering her into a side street restaurant where they'd eaten a very tasty meal of braised shin of beef served with herby dumplings and vegetables.

He'd paid for Eleanor's meal, too, which had embarrassed her. But without any money of her own, she'd had no choice but to accept.

Still, she was enjoying his company tremendously, and had listened intently to every word he'd said about Cornwall and the Camel estuary where they were headed. Though part of her wondered what her father would say if he could see her now, sitting down to 'break bread', as he would put it, with a man she barely knew, in this strange city, as bold as brass.

While Eleanor might not know exactly what her father would say, she knew with quivering certainty what he would *do*. Beat her within an inch of her life, most probably, and then drag her off to her grandfather's place for more of the same.

'Hey, you all right?' Lyndon asked, glancing at her as he slowed the car for a tight bend in the road.

'Just a little chilly now it's getting dark.'

Eleanor drew her cardigan closer, uneasy about telling him a fib, but sure he wouldn't want to hear all about her personal woes.

Though, in fact, it was such a wonderful, novel experience, talking to a man like Lyndon, with nobody about to overhear their conversation or forbid her to speak her mind, that Eleanor began to face even the thought of her father's wrath with equanimity.

She was tasting freedom for the very first time in her life, and it was better than she'd ever dreamed it could be.

'Not far now,' he assured her.

The hills flashed a gloomy grey-green in the twilight, rising and rolling and dropping sharply away at times to reveal a glimpse of ocean in the distance.

'Oh look, the sea!' she exclaimed at one point, staring towards it, and though Lyndon said nothing, he grinned. She was curious. 'Don't you love the sea?'

'I suppose I'm just used to it.'

'I'm not.' She hugged her shapeless cardigan close to her body, peering eagerly ahead in case another pale stretch of ocean became visible through a sudden dip in the hills. 'We lived by the sea near Weston when I was, oh, probably six or seven. I don't think we were there very long. My mother was still alive in those days.' She was aware of him listening with interest and tailed off. 'Ever since then, it's been all smoky towns or cities — nowhere exciting.'

'You've moved about a fair amount, then?'

'We've had to, because of my father.' Again, she baulked at admitting that he was a minister for their church, and often involved in what they called 'missions', meaning he would move into an area to gather new believers and 'seed' a new church there. 'Because of his work, I mean.'

'What does your father do?'

'He's a … a salesman.' There, no lie necessary. What her father sold was God and redemption, and a more conservative way of life. But she still felt unhappy talking about her family and pointed hurriedly ahead as the car crested a hill, beginning the steep slope downwards. 'Is that the estuary? It's lovely.'

A broad, shimmering sleeve of pearlescent water lay nestled between mud flats, alternately grey as the twilight around them and white as the passing clouds. As they came closer to the estuary, the sky itself seemed to open up, everything somehow clearer than in the hedge-bound lanes they'd been navigating so carefully for the past half an hour. Seabirds minced about on sandy banks or rose wheeling grey-winged out of the leggy reed marsh, the mudflats exactly as he'd described them to her.

There was a decidedly exotic air to the place, a sense of magic conjured up out of the dusk…

'What do you think of it?' he asked, glancing at her.

He had slowed as they began to descend the hill towards the water, his own gaze fixed on the broad grey estuary, his mouth tightening, as though experiencing something similar to her, but deeper, sadder, years of familiarity and nostalgia mixed up with the beauty of it all, and the faintest hint of bitterness.

'How could you ever bear to leave such a place?' she asked in awe.

He gave a harsh bark of laughter. '*L'enfer, c'est les autres.*' He glanced at her face, which she imagined must be blank. 'Sorry… It's French, a quotation from a play by Jean-Paul Sartre.'

She had never heard of that name and knew very little French, only a few words she'd gleaned from a secretly borrowed library textbook. Her father had insisted she had no need for foreign languages and the strange ideas they put in people's heads.

'What does it mean?'

'Hell is other people, I suppose.'

She understood immediately. Or thought she did.

'Your family?'

Lyndon nodded. 'My family.' Those two words seemed to be dragged from him most unwillingly, and he laughed again afterwards, as though to lessen their impact. 'But don't worry, they're not ogres. Or at least they'll be kind enough to you.'

'Because I'm not you.'

His mouth crooked, he shot her a shrewd look. 'Clever little thing, aren't you?'

'I have a family, too,' Eleanor said simply.

He turned a thickly wooded corner with careless speed, as though not expecting to meet anyone coming the other way, and she saw a large, rambling cluster of buildings ahead of them.

The manor house had been built side-on to the estuary below it and sat gloomily in a field near the base of the hill. It was both taller and broader than she'd expected from his description, at least three storeys high and with several wings, though some of the tiny, latticed windows suggested a dimly lit interior.

She studied the sagging slate roof he'd so lovingly described, and the grey granite walls that held it up, darkened virtually to black in some patches, mossed and lichened in others. Some windows had been almost completely obscured by gleaming swathes of ivy and other climbing plants that clung indomitably to the stone. To its sloping front was a steep gravel drive that weaved through once-formal gardens, dotted with steps and stone urns and low hedges, and even what looked like a decaying wooden beehive. Surrounding the manor house and gardens, stood a number of low, unexceptional outbuildings, most of them newer and in rather better condition than the main building.

The place reeked of quite terrifying antiquity, she thought, staring at its forbidding outline against the sky, more used to Victorian terraced houses or modern builds than anything this old and historic.

The house seemed to be waiting for her.

It was a dreadful suspicion, and one that made Eleanor clutch the seat and wish she'd never come.

Still, it was rather too late to change her mind now, she told herself. The deed was done, and she could not escape. Or if she needed to, it would have to be on foot.

That worried her.

The nearest town of Wadebridge had been quite a drive from here, and they hadn't passed a village or even so much as a hamlet for some time either, meaning it would be a tiring and lengthy walk back to civilisation. She suspected the nearest bus route couldn't be less than a two or even three-mile walk, she felt sure.

In other words, if she decided to leave but Lyndon refused to drive her back to the nearest town, she could be stranded here.

Oh, stop thinking up worst case scenarios, Eleanor told herself crossly, and tried to study the house with optimism instead.

But its grim, grey stone walls didn't exactly combat her feelings of unease. Only the thinnest smoke issued from one of the three vast chimney stacks, suggestive of a fire burning down to nothing, and she could see no lights inside.

'Nobody home?' she asked him, half-hopeful he might give up and turn around, though she knew that was unlikely.

'It doesn't look like it,' Lyndon agreed, and gave a careless shrug. 'But not to worry. That smoke is from the range. I imagine they've left it to burn low. Which suggests they'll be back soon enough.'

'Do you have a key to get in?'

'No need. The place is never locked.' He laughed at her confusion. 'This is rural Cornwall. Nobody comes out this far. And what would be the point of locking the doors against Mr Nobody?'

'I suppose you're right.'

'Besides, Mrs Barclay is probably around somewhere. The housekeeper.'

Eleanor swallowed. 'Your parents ... They have a house-keeper, do they?'

'It's a big place.' Again, he seemed to pass this off as unimportant. 'And Mrs Barclay's late father was a tenant of my grandfather's, back in the day. A colourful character, by all accounts, though I never got to know him. He knew these wetlands like the back of his hand. A real estuary man.' He sounded wistful.

'So you have tenants?'

'Not as many as the family used to have. Dad's been forced to sell some of the larger properties. But we still own ...' Lyndon described a wide arc with his arm, encompassing many of the hills and fields behind the house and much of the land below it as well. 'Well, quite a lot of land hereabouts. I know the new boundaries. But it would be easier to show you on a map.'

Lyndon slowed on the lane below the house, which was just a narrow, muddy track by now, and pulled in close to the hedge. Apart from a rusting tractor a few hundred feet away, nestled on some scrubby-looking grass under a tree, there were no other vehicles in sight.

He paused, peering out at the dusk. 'There's a yard behind the house, but I'd rather not announce our presence just yet, so the lane will do for now.'

'You don't want anyone to know you've arrived?'

'It's complicated. Look, you'd better hop out first,' he told her, an odd note in his voice. When she hesitated, unsure what he meant, he added, 'I need to get out on your side. I don't want to block the lane for when the others come back.'

Eleanor obeyed, taking a few steps away while he climbed out and went to fetch the luggage from the boot.

The first thing that struck her on getting out of the car was the heavy, almost oppressive silence, which seemed to clog up her throat and lie heavy on her lungs, taking away her ability to speak.

Despite the looming proximity of the granite-walled house, it felt like a lonely place, utterly devoid of people and human activity. And yet the landscape thrummed with life beneath that silence. The ground itself struck a deep note that vibrated up through her feet and ascended her spine, bone by bone, until it came to her brain, and set that jangling, too.

Sacred.

That was the word, Eleanor decided.

It was a *sacred* place.

The house had been built on the lower part of a slope, only a short walk down through sparse woodlands to the long, pale stretch of mud flats below, the estuary waters gleaming beyond them, a broad expanse that culminated in another bank of mud flats on the opposite side, and the steady white-green rise of land, ruffled with dark-headed marsh reeds and feathery pampas grasses.

Eleanor stood with her senses ablaze, tuning into the cries of gulls along the estuary, the melancholy bleat of hill sheep in the distance, and the rustle of an autumnal breeze through the trees, their leaves already on the slow turn from green to vibrant yellows and reds.

Lyndon came up beside her, awkwardly juggling their luggage, his driving gloves off but with his tweed cap pulled low over his forehead.

'So, what do you think?' he asked again.

It really seemed to matter to him what she thought of the place. She liked that about him. He cared about her opinion; she wasn't used to men doing that.

Eleanor cleared her throat, half-expecting to find it silted up, and was shocked to hear her voice again.

'It's miraculous.'

'That's one word for it.' He grinned, looking up at the old

house from under dark brows. 'Though a better one might be decrepit.'

'Oh no!'

'Oh yes,' he insisted with a short laugh, beginning to trudge up the lane towards the gate, with her by his side. 'We'll go in the side way. It's quickest.'

Beyond the gate, she could see a faint grassy track that led up towards a porched side door, bypassing the once-grand formal gardens just visible to the front of the house. A tiny brook ran bubbling through the grass not far from the track, the ground muddied around its meandering path.

'What a marvellous house,' she said, straining to see it through the dusk.

Again, he laughed shortly. 'No mains electricity, no telephone, and no water except what we pump from the spring.'

'I don't mind any of that. In fact, I think it's charming.' Eleanor glanced uncomfortably at her bag, tucked under his arm. 'Can I carry something?'

'Of course not. I can manage.'

He was such a gentleman, she thought with quick approval, and then realised that it also made her suspicious of him. She couldn't imagine her brother Fred behaving so gallantly towards a woman, though her father could occasionally put on a good show when he wanted to impress the ladies in a new town. But perhaps other men were polite and friendly. Perhaps it was only that she knew so few men that his behaviour surprised her.

Yet she was wary, all the same.

There was something Lyndon wasn't telling her, she was sure of it now. Ever since he'd first mentioned Estuary House to her, Eleanor had felt a lie in the air between them, its horrid, disjointed energy like a crackle of static under his words.

All her life she'd been lied to; she knew the signs and intonations, the ugly gaps where truth had been bled out long ago.

But what could Lyndon Chance possibly have to lie about?

The narrow side door was followed by a short flight of steps that led into an entrance hall, which was vast and dark, its dank air giving off an impression of faded grandeur. There were large gilt-framed paintings on the walls and displays of crossed swords at intervals, but she couldn't see any details. To her relief, they didn't linger there. Lyndon led her straight out of the hall and through a corridor-like room with a low beamed ceiling and dark slate flags polished by time and the constant passage of feet.

She could see the touch of the housekeeper on the clean, latticed windows and gleaming floors, and yet everything felt somehow disorganised. In fact, as they moved through the ground floor, things became increasingly chaotic. There were old wooden chairs stacked up in a corner, coats draped over the banisters, shoes and mud-flecked boots deserted in odd places.

Eleanor didn't mind a bit of chaos. She wasn't that keen on housework herself. But Estuary House had a sullen air of neglect developed over many years, not a cheerful lived-in messiness.

It struck her that this Mrs Barclay couldn't be a particularly hard-working housekeeper. But if her father had always enjoyed a rapport with Lyndon's family, perhaps her lack of attention slid by without comment.

Still, it did seem odd.

'Wait here, I won't be long,' Lyndon said in an offhand manner, and disappeared upstairs with their bags.

While he was gone, Eleanor wandered silently from room to room in gathering gloom, taken aback by the sheer scale of the place. She had somehow imagined his 'Tudor manor' would turn out to be a glorified farmhouse with a few antique features. But this was both much grander and even more ramshackle, and the countless number of rooms was a little intimidating.

She peered into the large, empty kitchen, a surprisingly cavernous space dominated by a rack of hanging steel implements and a scrubbed pine table. Dried herbs had been tied in clumps and dangled from an oak beam above the table, giving off a faintly aromatic scent. There was also an elderly range along one wall, its gentle warmth somehow reassuring.

In what was presumably a living room, she found a large oxblood Chesterfield sofa and two matching winged armchairs with sagging seats, alongside a sturdy black wood burner – dark and unlit – and three walls of disordered bookshelves, books piled up in untidy heaps, large hardbacks and tatty paperbacks jumbled together, dust jackets lying abandoned on the floor, and no sense of a guiding intelligence.

Glancing up, she realised the ceiling had been painted with a fresco at some point in the past, showing the estuary winding through a lush green landscape, with the great house itself dominating the left bank of the river. Though the paint was dirty and marred in places, it was still rather an impressive undertaking, and turned an otherwise drab sitting room into something magnificent, she thought.

The seemingly endless shelves of books were also impressive. Never having seen so many in one place before outside of a public library, Eleanor stood a moment, trying to read some of the faded titles on the spines but unable to make them out properly in the gloom.

She tried a door that opened onto dark stairs and presumably led down into the cellar, popped her head round a handful of other doors only to discover narrow pantries and a below-stairs storage cupboard, and then abruptly found herself back in the entrance hall with the huge paintings.

Turning on her heel to examine the hall, her eyes now accustomed to the gloom, she realised it was a handsome wood-panelled space with stone floors and a high ceiling, gilt-framed paintings on the walls, and a massive fireplace, large enough to roast a pig in.

Unnerved by the way her shoes clicked noisily across the vast hall, she chose another corridor to escape down, almost at random, and then another, which ended in a low arched doorway that opened onto a small study.

This room was rather tidier than the others; a large mahogany desk with a bottle-green leather top and a leather swivel chair drew her eye immediately, followed by more shelves of books, this time kept in a more orderly manner. She found several books of poetry on the desk, one of them with several pages marked with dried flowers, and wondered with a sudden flush of enthusiasm if Lyndon used this room to write in. There seemed to be a fine view down across the formal gardens to the riverfront, and she could just imagine him looking out across the estuary as he wrestled with his next line ...

By then, it was too dark to see much of the view or to make out any titles on the bookshelves, so she retreated into the corridor, only to realise that she was hopelessly lost.

A tiny sound somewhere nearby made her stop and listen, suddenly spooked by the loneliness of the old house.

Was somebody there?

'Lyndon?' She felt her heart begin to thud. 'Is ... Is that you?'

Silence.

The short hairs prickled on the back of her neck. She took another step, and then turned abruptly, aware of somebody watching her from behind.

A door she hadn't noticed before had swung open, and a woman stood in the doorway, a faint light behind her. It was impossible to make out her features, but her long dark hair had been piled up in a beehive style, emphasising a shapely throat and profile.

'Hello?' Eleanor felt ridiculously panicked. Could this be Lyndon's mother? 'I'm so sorry if I disturbed you. I'm with Lyndon. He's just gone upstairs to—'

But the woman held up a hand as though to silence her and Eleanor stopped, backing away. To her relief, she heard Lyndon coming along the corridor.

'Sorry I took so long,' he said, and then saw the woman standing in the doorway and almost flinched. 'Oh, Mrs Barclay. I thought ... Well, never mind.' He seemed to shake off his hesitancy, raising his chin with a defiant air. 'Where are my parents?'

The woman came forward, studying him calmly. 'Hello, Lyndon.' Her voice was low and musical, with a West Country accent. 'Your parents have gone into town. But they should be back soon. Is your mother expecting you home? She didn't mention it.'

'That's because I didn't tell her. This is my home; I don't need to ask permission to turn up.'

'Of course not,' the woman agreed, 'but a little forewarning is always appreciated, especially when bringing an extra guest. I'll have to go shopping again tomorrow if we're to have enough food on the table come dinnertime.' Her gaze shifted curiously to Eleanor, and then widened. 'My goodness. Who on earth gave you that nasty black eye?'

'None of your business,' he said shortly, and pulled Eleanor away. 'Come on, darling. Let me show you upstairs.'

Darling?

Eleanor flushed and let him lead her away down the corridor. But she felt the other woman's gaze on her every step of the way, and knew she was not welcome there.

Chapter Four

A bright, brassy eye, peering up at us
Out of the dirt …

— From 'Yellow Oxeye' in *Estuary*

Waiting down by the gate to Estuary House for Julius Chance to return from unpacking his grandmother's shopping, Taylor plucked a long, whippy stem of grass from the verge and chewed on it for sustenance as she walked a few steps further along the lane to study the impressive façade of Estuary House.

Her stomach rumbled, reminding her that she hadn't eaten in hours. Taylor shoved the thought away impatiently. Who could think about food at a time like this?

She was looking at the very house where Lyndon Chance had been born and brought up, one of the finest Cornish poets of his generation, a man whose fascination with ecology, decades before climate change had become the overriding concern of her generation, had fuelled her own obsession with conservation from an early age.

She imagined the young poet-to-be wandering the rolling green hills behind the house as a boy, maybe wading out into the estuary shallows with a fishing rod, or swimming in the cool water, or capturing insects just like young Davie had done. All those activities found a mention here and there in his poems, especially the powerful and deeply nostalgic *Estuary*, an award-winning book-length poem sequence set almost entirely in this place, his childhood environment. Lyndon Chance had written *Estuary* in the last year of his life, and she had a pet theory – which she'd kept safely to herself, for fear of being mocked by other academics – that this final poem sequence contained a code, perhaps a key to the mysteries that had mired his reputation, especially among women.

Head to one side, Taylor considered the row of gloomy first-floor windows with interest. Had any of those front-facing bedrooms been Lyndon's?

He'd given a magazine interview once where he'd discussed how much he'd loved these views of the estuary as a boy, always out somewhere fishing or tramping the marshes. But she tried to imagine him in later years, too, rising in the dawn light to stare down towards the milky currents of the river, still half-asleep, haunted perhaps by ghosts from his troubled past.

As though in response, a face appeared at the middle window to stare down at her, pale and somehow blurry behind glass.

Taylor gasped and recoiled, staring up at the indistinct face. Her heart jumped and accelerated wildly.

'What the hell …?'

Slowly, a hand came up, palm flat against the pane, fingers spread wide in a kind of greeting.

She ought to have told someone, of course. A teacher, the police, maybe even the school nurse … But she hadn't realised that some things weren't normal.

Taylor caught her breath, and then lifted a hand in instinctive response. What an idiot she was.

It was the old lady, of course.

44

Mrs Chance.

Not the accusing ghost of… She didn't even know who or what she was thinking of. God, what was going on with her? She was nervous as hell today, jumping at nothing. It had to be all that talk of murder and mayhem earlier; it had touched a raw nerve inside. Yet she had no idea why. It wasn't as though she hadn't heard it all a thousand times before, and often in far more lurid terms.

Murder was what most people thought about when they heard the name Lyndon Chance. Those who knew his story, at least.

Most poets of the sixties weren't household names. But most of them also hadn't led private lives that still sparked as much prurient interest as Lyndon Chance's. She herself had read so many magazine and newspaper articles about his personal life, delved into dozens of official and unofficial biographies, and listened to endless theories about what he was supposed to have done, some of them frankly crazy, others more subtly persuasive.

His widow had never uttered a word about her husband's past, nor given a single interview about her life with him. Yet people still dragged her into the debate, all the same. The woman had to know *something*, didn't she?

The hand wavered and fell. The pale face disappeared from the window.

A door slammed shut.

Taylor, with difficulty, lowered her gaze in time to see Julius Chance striding swiftly down the drive towards her.

She was reminded of a hurricane.

'I'd forgotten you were coming,' Julius admitted before even reaching her, thrusting a hand impatiently through his dark hair. He addressed Taylor without looking directly at her, which was rather disconcerting. 'I'm afraid it's a little

45

inconvenient for you to be here right now. My grandmother isn't in the best of health, and we need some privacy.' He paused. 'Why don't you come back another time? Say, late autumn?'

Stunned by his arrogant demeanour, Taylor struggled to know how to respond without sounding angry. But really, what a nerve!

'I'm very sorry to be putting you out, and obviously I don't want to intrude on your privacy,' she said with restraint. 'But no, I can't come back in the autumn.'

The cold stare swivelled back towards her face, his expression disbelieving. 'Why not?'

'As I said in my email, this is the only time I can be in Cornwall all year. I have to work on my thesis during the autumn and winter terms. I put the summer aside for research, and this is the best season for it, frankly.' Taylor saw the heavy frown in his eyes and folded her arms; she felt defiant now, done with wary politeness. 'Besides, you can't seriously expect anyone to camp out here for four or five weeks in the autumn. The weather will be atrocious.'

'Oh, not in Cornwall,' he said, with a dismissive wave of his hand. 'It's always mild down here in autumn.'

'Not when you're in a *tent*, Mr Chance.'

His gaze warred with hers; Taylor got the feeling he would not be happy until she'd got back in her van and driven back to London. It was tempting to keep battling. But she recalled an old saying about catching more flies with honey than vinegar. It was worth holding her nerve, at any rate. She wanted to stay here on the Camel Estuary. Had to, in fact.

'Look,' Taylor added, carefully softening her tone, 'I can see this is an inconvenient time for you. But it would be more than inconvenient for me if I had to leave without doing my research. To be blunt, it would be a complete bloody disaster.'

'How so?'

'This research is for my final dissertation. Without it, I can't get my master's degree.'

'I see.'

'Plus, I've gone to considerable personal expense over this trip, even subletting my digs in London. So, I've got nowhere else to live until September at the earliest. And I did give you plenty of warning. You can't bail on me now.'

His brows knit together. 'Are you always this difficult?'

'I can stand up for myself.'

'So I'm learning.' Julius Chance grimaced, looking from her to the van in the lane; she got the impression he was resigning himself to having an eyesore parked outside his house for the rest of the summer. 'Oh, very well. You can stay ... since you're here now.'

'Thank you, Mr Chance.' She could not suppress a tiny grin at the victory, and saw his eyes narrow on her mouth.

'Call me Julius,' he said curtly. She thought he still looked suspicious though and wondered why he had such an issue with her. 'But I won't have my grandmother bothered, do you hear? She's fragile. Not up to entertaining visitors.'

'Understood.'

'Hmm.' He turned on his heel, studying the blue dome of her tent up in the field beside the house. 'That doesn't look very sturdy. Are you sure it's water-tight?'

'I should hope so, for the price.'

'It can't be comfortable though. Not for several weeks on end.' He glanced back at her speculatively. 'Wouldn't a bed and breakfast be better? I'm sure there must be something still available in Wadebridge. I could recommend one or two places.'

47

'I couldn't possibly afford a bed and breakfast. Besides, I don't mind roughing it. And I can always sleep in the van if the weather deteriorates.'

'Fine, if you insist on doing things the hard way ...' He sounded irritable but looked vaguely amused by her refusal. 'So, I imagine you have things you'd like to ask me.'

'That can wait.'

'But I have a few things to say to you, Ms Pierce. If we're going to be neighbours this summer, I need to set out some ground rules for your stay.' Julius paused, removing a large pair of sunglasses from the top pocket of his open-necked shirt and putting them on as though to hide his eyes. 'Shall we walk down to the Camel together?' he asked, indicating the river below them.

'I'd like that, thank you.'

They walked down the lane together, stopping beside a majestic beech in full spread that shaded an old, lichened wooden stile. She felt awkward when Julius held out a hand to help her over the stile, as though she wasn't perfectly capable of negotiating it herself.

Still, Taylor decided it wouldn't be a good moment to press her feminist credentials on him, taking his hand instead with a perfunctory smile and a muttered, 'Thanks.'

Beyond the stile was a steep bank, brambly and labyrinthine with nettles, which she negotiated carefully, dislodging a stone here and there. At its base was the Camel Trail, a popular tourist attraction, as she'd learned online while researching the estuary and its environs. Nobody was about at that hour of the day, though she'd spotted numerous cyclists passing to-and-fro in the sunshine earlier, plus several dog walkers and families with young children.

She could understand the attraction. The coastal air was fresh and tangy, the countryside quiet as a churchyard, far from the noisy flow of traffic across the bypass flyover at Wadebridge.

And then there was the glorious wildlife.

As they walked across the trail, a flock of herring gulls, their cries loud in the silence, swooped low over the estuary on their way down towards Padstow and Rock, two resort towns perched either side of the river mouth where it broadened generously into the sea.

'This used to be a busy railway line,' Julius commented, glancing up and down the empty trail path. 'North Cornwall was quite popular with the Victorians. Seaside holidays at Padstow were all the rage once. Buckets and spades, donkey rides, bathing wagons, and so on.'

'I've always fancied trying out a bathing wagon myself.'

'I can imagine that.' Julius gave a short laugh. 'But I guess this part of the coast must have fallen out of fashion after the Second World War, because they closed the line in the sixties. Now we get ramblers and cyclists along here instead of steam trains.'

'Yes, I believe John Betjeman was quite scathing about the closure of the branch line to Padstow.' She hesitated, then added impetuously, 'And he wasn't the only writer up in arms about it. There are several poems in *Estuary* that reference the old branch line.' She smiled. 'Dazzling work by your grandfather.'

'You're a fan?'

There was something unsettling in his voice ... Almost like hatred.

Taylor became wary. 'I think he was an excellent poet.'

'I see,' he said, almost blandly, and she was thrown, wondering if she'd imagined the caustic tone. 'Yes, I know the sequence you mean. The steam trains, the branch line, and the estuary. My grandfather loved all this ...' He gestured

49

about them at the hills behind them, the water and the silent roadway where trains used to run daily. 'The Camel Estuary was his special place. His sanctuary from the world.'

Again, that odd note in his voice. Perhaps it was bitterness against those who had made his grandfather's life unbearable.

'And you?'

'Me?' Julius looked at her, clearly surprised by the inference. 'I'm only here to keep tabs on my grandmother, who refuses to leave. I envy you living in London. A world away from this.'

'It certainly is.'

After leaving the trail, they pushed through a cluster of ten foot high, feathery grasses that rustled thickly about them, and once free of those, picked their way warily over hole-pocked mudflats down to the damp and gritty foreshore. Bright-green glasswort sprouted in clumps here and there, and deep pools glistened with tiny, jewelled creatures stranded by the last high tide.

It was breezier down by the water. Occasional warm gusts snatched at her hair and clothes, then subsided just as quickly into quiet and peace again.

The glassy waters of the estuary lay ahead.

Taylor stood a moment on the soft, crumbling edges of the mudbank and looked out across the rolling expanse.

The River Camel.

Months of dreaming and planning, and saving every penny she could, and here she was at last. She'd made it.

A movement caught her eye; she lowered her gaze to the water at her feet, suddenly entranced.

Small, narrow-bodied fish and other creatures darted shyly through the sunlit shallows, scurrying back and forth through puffs of mud cloud or from deep under rocks, only to disappear when Julius came to stand next to her, his long shadow brushing the cool surface and no doubt frightening them away.

She raised her head again, studying the opposite bank of the river; it was a good distance away and wilder-looking than this side. That would be one of her places of exploration, she decided. It was a place that figured prominently in Lyndon Chance's final poems, and if she was to get to grips with the mysteries of that opaque last book of his, she would have to investigate the reed-thick wilderness that lay opposite Estuary House, not just its charming environs.

'Such a beautiful place,' she said.

'I suppose so.'

He didn't sound enthusiastic. Was familiarity breeding contempt or did he genuinely not care about his surroundings?

She couldn't imagine ever getting so used to this view that she dismissed it as uninteresting. Though there were tiny black midges in the air, which she kept having to wave away from her head. And the smell of the mudflats was definitely more pungent here, a sharp hint of salt in the mix, too. But she breathed the air in gladly, more relaxed now that Julius Chance had agreed that she could stay.

A world away from London.

Yes, it was, and she had no desire to drive back to the hot, sticky, relentless churn of the metropolis.

This was heaven, and it was all hers for the next five or six weeks. But she must make the most of her time. Not waste a single second of it.

'So, what are you here for?' Julius asked lightly. 'I mean, really?'

'I don't understand.'

'Oh, come on, Ms Pierce – I'm sorry, I've forgotten your first name.'

'Taylor.'

'Taylor, thank you.' He turned to her, removing his sunglasses. His gaze was intent. 'Let's have a little honesty. You said this was a research trip.'

'It is.' She faltered, taken aback by his sudden alarming scrutiny. 'Conservation—'

'Yes, I read your emails. Several times, in fact. Both when they first arrived and just now up at the house. That isn't what I'm talking about.'

'You'd better explain it to me, then,' she said bluntly. 'Because I don't have a clue what—'

'Lyndon Chance.' He nodded grimly at her embarrassed silence. 'You're here to research my grandfather, not the estuary.'

'That's not true,' she protested.

'What do you take me for? A fool?'

'Of course not.'

His eyebrows rose steeply. 'So, you seriously expect me to believe that your interest in my grandfather's poetry is purely coincidental to your choosing this part of the country for your conservation research?'

'I happen to like some of his poetry, that's all. I'm into poetry. So what? That doesn't mean …' He held up a hand, and her voice tailed off. Her cheeks were burning. 'What?'

'I asked for honesty.'

Taylor dropped her gaze before the searing look in his and hunted for the right words to reassure him. But what could she say, after all? He wasn't so far wrong that she could just deny it.

'Fine, OK,' she muttered, thinking fast, and stared rigidly down at the mudflats they were standing on. The sandy brownish goo was oozing around her white trainers as her feet began to sink gently in the mud; if she stood here much longer, they'd be ruined. 'I ... I would like to tie some of my conservation research into my interest in Lyndon Chance's poems. You see, my idea is to explore the impact of wild and remote places like this,' she added hurriedly, sensing him about to interrupt again, 'on the human psyche. Given the influence of his surroundings on your grandfather's poetry, the Camel Estuary was an obvious choice.'

'Exactly as I suspected.' Julius Chance looked savage again, his good humour vanished. 'You're one of *them*, aren't you?'

She stared, bewildered. 'One of who?'

'The crazed horde of women who come down here every year on the anniversary of his death,' he said furiously, 'tramping our property without permission, defacing my father's headstone at the parish church, chanting their slogans at the gate, and upsetting my grandmother.'

Taylor was shocked.

She knew there was a small, hardcore group within feminist literary circles who denounced Lyndon Chance as a woman-hater, picking over rumours of 'dark secrets' in his past and pointing to lines in his poems, which they claimed were misogynistic. What she hadn't known was that they ever actually came down here to trouble the family. And as for defacing his headstone ...

Even though she had no connection to those women, Taylor still felt ludicrously guilty over their actions.

Her mother had been a huge fan of Lyndon Chance's. In fact, that was partly why she'd come down here this summer: to feel closer to her mum in some intangible way, by toting around her much-thumbed paperbacks of Chance's poetry and walking to places he described in his *Estuary* collection, the poems her mother had loved best.

Mum had mentioned the haters to her once, saying she

53

didn't believe for a moment that Lyndon Chance had ever murdered anyone, let alone a woman.

'That's nothing to do with me,' she told him carefully. 'But I'm sorry you and Mrs Chance have had to put up with such appalling behaviour.'

He didn't seem impressed by this apology, his mouth twisting cynically.

'Very nicely put. So why don't I believe you?'

'I have no idea,' she said frankly.

'Right, that's it.' He glared at her. 'I want you to pack up your tent and leave my land, Ms Pierce. Your behaviour has been downright unprofessional. Criminal, even. I've a good mind to make a complaint against you to the university. Coming down here under false pretences, lying to me about your true aims, bothering my family ...' He stopped, frowning. 'Are you even listening to me?'

Taylor, becoming hot and flustered under this torrent of unjustified wrath, had turned her gaze upon the cool estuary waters as an escape. Which was when she'd seen a woman on the opposite bank, standing perfectly still on the fringes of the green–brown reed marsh, looking straight at them.

The woman seemed almost as old as his grandmother. She was wearing a dingy, dove-grey tracksuit, its top zipped up to the neck as though she was cold. Her face was wraith-thin, cheeks pinched inwards. Silvery-grey hair straggled about her face, some of it piled high on her head and secured with what looked at that distance to be black ribbons.

She seemed to project an aura of black laced with silver, like smoke trailing away on the wind.

The old woman's head was tipped to one side as she stood there like a wild bird in the reedbeds, listening and watching. Not that anyone could hear what they were saying across such a broad stretch of the river. But perhaps she had been out walking, and the sound of Julius's voice, raised in anger, had caught her attention. Which was an embarrassing thought.

Julius had followed her gaze, and now made a strangled noise in his throat. 'Oh God,' he said thickly.

The woman raised her arm and pointed stiffly with one finger.

Not at Julius, but at Taylor.

Then she turned and walked away, her figure fading like grey smoke through the gently waving reeds until she was lost to sight.

'What on earth ...?' Taylor looked round at him, confused.

His jaw worked silently for a moment, then Julius slid his sunglasses back on.

'You can stay,' was all he said.

Chapter Five

Locomotive god, it spilt
Its gleaming, evangelical innards as it flew.

– From 'Last Train to Padstow' in *Estuary*

The dark stairs were broad and sweeping, easily wide enough at one point for three to walk abreast. Eleanor felt bewildered, clinging close to Lyndon and wishing they had brought a torch. But he had been in such a hurry to get away from that woman, there simply hadn't been any time to suggest it. And now she felt quite lost. The landing was long and gloomy, with many closed doors and a sense of immense space around them, as though the house stretched on forever.

'What did you say to Mrs Barclay?' Lyndon whispered urgently as soon as they were out of earshot.

'Nothing.'

'You're sure?'

'Of course. I just turned a corner and found her standing there in the dark, watching me ... I nearly jumped out of my skin. Then you appeared.'

'Good.'

'Why? Lyndon, who is she?'

'The housekeeper. I told you about her, remember? She loves to stick her nose in other people's business where it doesn't belong. I'm glad you didn't tell her anything.' He stopped, looking down at her. 'What were you doing anyway, wandering about down there without any lights on?'

'You said … no electricity.'

Lyndon gave a short laugh. 'I said, no mains electricity. My father had a generator installed in one of the outbuildings years ago.' Turning, he snapped on a wall light. The corridor was flooded with a soft golden glow that illuminated dark green flock wallpaper punctuated by framed paintings and etchings of Cornish landscapes and churches, along with the occasional starchy-looking Victorian relative in a sepia photograph. 'Better?'

She felt stupid. 'Much, thank you.'

'We may live in the back of beyond, but we're not savages.'

'I'm sure you're not.'

She tried to smile, though her heart was still thudding, and she felt uneasy. Lyndon was hiding something, she was sure of it now. Why had he spoken so roughly to the house-keeper? And why on earth had he called her 'darling' in front of that woman? He had quite deliberately made it sound as though they were lovers.

'I told you to wait for me,' he said.

'I know, I'm sorry; I was curious.' Hurriedly, she tried to distract him. 'Your family has so many books. It's like a public library down there.'

'My late grandfather collected most of them. Poppa – that's what we called him – was a big reader and an even bigger thinker.' Lyndon paused. 'I was very close to him.'

She wondered at the loss in his voice, for she could never imagine being that close to her own grandfather. Grandad was too ready with his belt or the back of his hand.

'Your grandfather sounds like an interesting man.'

'More than you can know.' Lyndon frowned, studying her face. 'Hey, you look exhausted. It's been a long day, hasn't it?'

'I am quite tired,' she admitted, adding with an embarrassed laugh, 'And I could do with a wash.'

'Then let me show you the bathroom first.' He turned to the left where the corridor branched into two, the way ahead once more shrouded in darkness. 'I've been putting clean sheets on the bed in the guest room. That's why I was such a long time. Probably made a complete mess of it, but ... Well, at least it won't be a bare mattress. And while you're freshening up, I'll check with Barclay if there's something we can scrounge for supper, shall I?'

Eleanor nodded, secretly relieved by the words 'guest room', having started to fear he intended her to share his bedroom – and maybe his bed, too. Yet again she was surprised by his chivalry. He'd made the bed up for her. She had never heard of a man doing such a thing.

'Thank you,' she said, feeling a bit better. 'Though you seem to be doing all the work so far. And for a mere stowaway as well.'

'Hardly a stowaway, Eleanor.' His smile reassured her. 'I asked you to come with me, remember? You didn't curl up in the boot of my car.'

'All the same, you should let me prepare supper.'

'Good God, whatever for? Barclay will do any cooking required. That's her job. Besides, it will probably only be bread and cold meat at this time of night.' He held out his hand. 'Come on, let's get you unpacked and sorted. Before my parents come back home and spoil everything.'

That seemed an odd thing to say, Eleanor thought, instantly suspicious again. But then she remembered what he'd said earlier about hell being other people, and suddenly felt that she understood him *perfectly*. Which was absurd, given that they'd only known each other about twenty-four hours in total.

Eleanor wondered what her own father and brother were doing right now, and whether they'd stopped looking for her yet.

She doubted it.

Lyndon showed her the bathroom, a cool, high-ceilinged room with a white enamelled bathtub on legs in the middle, and an uneven floor that sloped towards a lavatory with a huge wooden seat and a tiny arched window above it. The room overlooked the estuary, she realised, peering out through thick, greenish glass.

'My father had the toilet put in about ten years ago,' he told her before turning off the light again. 'The west wing has a late Victorian bathroom with a lavatory,' he added hesitantly, 'but the roof isn't sound, and would cost too much to repair. So, we tend not to use that part of the house.'

The west wing?

This house was far grander than he'd made it sound back in Cirencester. She felt awkward, unsure that she belonged in such a place. What would his parents make of her?

'That's a shame.'

'Land rich, cash poor, that's us.' There was an odd note in his voice. 'Your bedroom's this way.'

It was a very large but sparsely decorated room, with dark shutters at the window, an intricately woven Turkish rug laid across bare wooden boards, and a vague smell of mothballs in the air. But as well as an old-fashioned wardrobe and dressing table, it also held a four-poster double bed with lace drapes, exactly like something out of a Gothic novel, a sight that delighted her beyond words. Eleanor had never seen a four-poster bed before, let alone slept in one.

He turned on the overhead light. 'What do you think?'

He'd not only made up the bed, she realised, but placed her bag beside it, ready to be unpacked.

Gingerly, Eleanor put her handbag on the dressing table, and sat on the bed; the mattress was lumpy but not uncomfortably so. The dark wooden headboard was a little dusty from lack of use, but the rest looked perfectly charming. It was like walking into a fairy story, she thought, playing with the pink ribbon that held the white lace bedcurtains open.

He watched her, an amused smile on his face.

Eleanor asked, quite entranced by her surroundings, 'Do all the rooms have old-fashioned beds like these?'

'God, no. This was my grandparents' room. Personally, I hate all this chintzy old stuff myself. It's like something out of a Hammer horror film.' When she looked up at him, puzzled, he gave a short laugh. 'Don't tell me you've never been to the pictures?'

'Oh no, I've been to the pictures.' Only a few times, but she didn't want him to think her a complete bore.

'But not to see horror films, I imagine?'

Eleanor shook her head.

The unmistakable sound of a car engine in the distance killed Lyndon's smile. He went to the window and unbolted the shutters, and she got up from the bed at once, wondering why he seemed so grim. It was almost dark outside now. But a thin shaft of light illuminated the lane below the house, touching the scrubby bushes beyond it for a few seconds before a vehicle came lurching round the corner and floundered to a halt beside his sports car.

The engine could clearly be heard turning over in the quiet of the evening.

'Damn,' he said curtly, staring down towards the lane.

'Your parents?' she asked, her heart beating hard, despite the fact that she was there legitimately.

Lyndon nodded abruptly and slammed the shutter closed again, as though to disguise their presence there in the bedroom.

Perhaps his parents wouldn't approve, she thought, and was not surprised by that. Her father would have torn seven strips off her for having a man in the house, let alone in her bedroom. And would never have let her forget it either.

For a moment, Lyndon said nothing, gazing blindly at his hand, still flat on the shutter. Then he turned, coming towards her. Something in his face frightened her.

'What is it?' she whispered, shrinking a little.

'All right, Eleanor,' he said in a changed voice, suddenly low and urgent, 'listen, here's the thing.' Lyndon thrust a hand in his trouser pocket and used the other to brush back his hair with a nervous gesture. Then he raised his eyes to hers, his expression almost desperate. 'We're married, understand?'

'*Married?*'

'You and me; we didn't just meet last night. We've known each other for ... I don't know, three or four months. A whirlwind romance, that kind of thing.' He locked gazes with her. 'Come on, you know what I'm saying.'

Blood was drumming wildly in her ears. 'You want me to tell your parents that we're married?'

'My parents, my brother if he's here ... Whoever asks.'

Her mouth was dry. 'I can't.'

'Why not?'

'It would be a lie.'

'For God's sake! What does that matter?'

'Because I don't understand why you want me to say that we're married. Would your family be shocked otherwise? You and me, travelling together, but not married? Is that it?'

Eleanor saw him hesitate, and pressed on, 'Surely the truth would be easier than such a huge lie, Lyndon?'

'No,' he said doggedly.

'But they'll see at once that we're not ... intimate.' She fought against the urge to look back at the bed. 'And what about later? I can't stay here forever. Won't they wonder what's happened to your "wife" when I leave Cornwall?'

'None of that is important right now.'

'It's important to me.'

'I hear what you're saying.' He put his hands on her shoulders, gently enough, though she still felt under his control. 'But you need to look past the conventions of right and wrong, and just follow your instincts. Can you do that for me?'

Eleanor shook her head, deeply uneasy now. There was a wildness about him she hadn't seen before, though had suspected a few times on the journey here. Something in his eyes ...

She stepped back and he released her without protest. 'I'm sorry,' she said with wary dignity, 'you've been very kind. But I think I'd better go. Perhaps if I walk back to the main road—'

He held up a hand, and she fell silent.

From below, she could hear a door opening and closing, and raised voices calling his name, alongside the excited barking of a dog. His family were returning from wherever they'd been tonight, and had no doubt recognised the sports car in the lane.

'If you don't do as I say, I'll ... I'll have to let your father know exactly where you are,' he said. 'I'll drive up to Wadebridge tonight and speak to the police. I'll tell them you're not in your right mind, that you need to be looked after by your family.'

'What?'

Eleanor stared at his dark, forbidding face, and her skin crept with horror as she realised how she had been lured to this remote house, her fears lulled by promises he'd never intended to keep…

She had run from home this morning, thinking to make a new life for herself away from the oppression of her zealous family, and had stupidly trusted Lyndon Chance to help her escape. Instead, the poet had brought her here and now intended to compel her to do his will.

'You wouldn't do that to me,' she whispered, hoping she was right. 'You're not capable of such cruelty.'

'Come down and tell my parents that you're my wife, or you'll find out exactly what I am capable of,' Lyndon said softly. 'Your father could be here on the train as early as tomorrow evening.'

Her eyes widened. What kind of monster was he?

'I'll run away,' she told him fiercely. 'I ran away from home. I can run away from you.'

His jaw tightened. 'I don't want to be your jailor, Eleanor. But I'll keep you locked up in this room until he arrives to collect you, if that's what it takes.'

Eleanor was shocked by this threat. Would he really lock her in? The implacable look on his face convinced her that he would.

She couldn't go back to Cirencester, not after this taste of freedom. Having finally escaped her father's iron control, she would almost rather die than go back to him.

'All right.' With a sudden shiver of fear, Eleanor hugged herself. 'I'm not happy about it, but I'll do what you say. I'll pretend to be your wife. Just please don't tell my father where I am.'

'That's the spirit.' Lyndon looked her up and down. 'No

time for you to change your clothes. But do you have any makeup to hide that shiner?' When she shook her head, he grimaced. 'Maybe we can cook up a story to explain it. I don't want anyone thinking I've been knocking you around.' He paused. 'Meanwhile, I'd better find you a wedding ring. Because my mother doesn't miss a trick.'

Chapter Six

The last dim view of the dead
Through a wind-blown mandala.

– From 'Iris' in Estuary

The old lady was beckoning to her, Taylor decided.

Mrs Chance was standing at the wall that separated the manor house from the fields behind it, looking straight at her and definitely beckoning. It had taken several minutes of mystification, watching Mrs Chance's odd fidgets and gestures without knowing what to make of them, until the hand-waving became frantic and could no longer be ignored.

Surprised, Taylor put down her sketchpad and scrambled up from the grassy hillock where she'd been sitting to work.

She'd been sketching out a rough outline of where Estuary House stood in relation to the Camel Trail and the foreshore, with the wide expanse of the bay in the distance towards Padstow. Her skills as an artist were not particularly brilliant, but all she needed was a basic idea of location for her notes. There was her camera, of course. But photographs couldn't always capture the relationship of one thing to another, she had found, especially when dealing with a complex landscape like this, with so many different strata to it.

'Hello,' Taylor called out. 'Good morning!'

Mrs Chance, peering over the ivy-clad wall in her

direction, smiled. Not waving now but making a kind of 'We come in peace,' sign. She didn't say anything, but simply nodded enthusiastically at Taylor's acknowledgement.

The woman was Lyndon's Chance's widow, of course. It was well-known that she never gave interviews or consented to speak about her husband or his work, any more than her grandson did. And from what Julius had said about the crazy protesters who came here every year to mark the anniversary of his death, that was hardly surprising. So it was odd to be beckoned to in such a friendly fashion, when he must surely have told his grandmother that her reasons for coming here were not purely linked to ecological research.

Curious, Taylor tucked her sketchpad and pencil back into her rucksack and headed down the field towards the house.

On her way, she stopped briefly to check that the tent flap was zipped up, keen to keep insects out after two nights spent hunting for what had sounded – and felt, getting up in the morning to find several bites on her arms – like a particularly persistent mosquito.

She'd barely seen Julius Chance since her arrival two days ago, her only interaction with the family having been a twenty-minute dumbshow as his grandmother hung out her washing on the back line, occasionally stopping to wave a hand at the sky and then at her in a mysterious manner. But she knew he was out at the moment, having heard his Land Rover bumping along the lane earlier that morning before gunning up the hill towards the main road.

She approached the house with a cheerful smile. 'Is everything all right, Mrs Chance? Do you need any help?'

'Oh, yes please.' Nodding, Mrs Chance unlatched the back gate, dragging it open across a thick clump of weeds that really ought to be cleared, and waved her inside. 'I hear that you've come to investigate.'

So, Julius had told his grandmother, after all.

'I'm sorry,' Taylor began awkwardly, but was interrupted.

'No, no, don't apologise. It's a good thing. We need an investigator.' Without explaining that cryptic remark, Mrs Chance nodded emphatically for her to come through into the back garden. 'Don't be shy. I've been waiting for you.'

Taylor was bemused. 'You have?'

'Oh yes, for ever so long.'

Taylor stepped past her into the garden, looking up at the dark outline of the house against the sky. 'Is Julius still out? I saw his car go past.'

'Julius is always coming and going.' Mrs Chance turned to fiddle with the gate. 'It's the house. It drives him away. He can't stand it.'

'Oh dear.' Taylor wondered for the first time if Mrs Chance was suffering from a touch of dementia; her comments seemed disconnected from reality. But maybe she was just an eccentric old lady. 'Do you know when he'll be back?'

'Could you shut this for me? I can't seem to ...'

'Hang on, let me.' Taylor fastened the latch on the gate, and then gave her a quick smile. 'Is that right?'

'Perfect, thank you. Now, forget about Julius. He's an unbeliever.'

'Sorry?'

'If he were here, he'd shoo you away. Like a little dog.' Mrs Chance flapped her hand in quick demonstration. '*Shoo, shoo!*'

Taylor suppressed a grin.

'He's gone to Truro for the whole morning, so you can come inside and ask me your questions. No need to worry about interruptions.' Mrs Chance led her down the overgrown path, glancing back with a worried frown as they reached the back door. 'Only three questions, mind. Any more would be cheating. Promise?'

'I promise.' Taylor had no idea what she was talking about. But she was dying to get a peek inside Lyndon Chance's birthplace, so it was probably best to play along. 'Three questions. Not a problem.'

She followed Mrs Chance through a narrow stone doorway at the back of the house, and along a bewildering number of passageways, peering curiously down other corridors or into rooms they passed without entering, seeing ramshackle furniture and decaying splendour everywhere.

Still, the interior of the old manor house smelt faintly exotic, the air full of spices and the rich tang of beeswax.

'This way, keep going, left, right, and left again,' Mrs Chance muttered when Taylor paused too long, her attention having been caught by something shadowy in the distance. 'It's a big house. You don't want to get lost.'

'Sorry.'

Taylor hurried on. But her senses were in overdrive, soaking up the atmosphere and trying to take in as much as she could during this brief visit. She might never get another chance to look around the manor.

Her first impression was of a dark husk of a house whose walls seemed to curve in places, cupping them inside. The ornate wood panelling creaked from time to time like a ship at anchor, and although it was probably her imagination that the floor tilted and sloped in some corridors, it still left her a little seasick. Yet the house warmed and shone, too, in an almost friendly fashion wherever the sun touched a wall or floor through tiny, latticed windows.

It was also disorienting.

Sunlight bounced glaringly off a convex mirror, hung on a sharp bend in the passageway to show people coming the other way; Taylor gave an involuntary gasp and flung up an arm to shield her eyes, momentarily blinded.

If only she hadn't dawdled that day; night had already fallen by the time they got back, the front door opening to a dark, bulky silhouette with the light behind him ...

Taylor had the disconcerting sense of being trapped inside a honeycomb; even the slate flags under her feet had a dull yellowish sheen in places, the stone worn down into rough, uneven circles and semi-circles, like a pattern of overlapping moon phases.

Houses could have auras just as human beings did.

Estuary House had a conflicting aura. It seemed to pulsate in some places with an almost raw, unadulterated evil. And yet in others, it glowed with warmth and understanding. Like two personalities in the same body.

It made the place hard to read.

They came to a vast entrance hall at the front of the house, but Mrs Chance didn't stop.

There was a huge stone fireplace opposite the front entrance; the hearth was cold, with half-burnt logs lying amid the ashes from a previous fire. The place smelt damply of woodsmoke and neglect. Beside the fire were two highbacked armchairs facing each other, and a dark wooden settle that gleamed with polish like the stone flags. It seemed somebody was looking after the place to a certain degree, though she couldn't imagine either Julius or his ageing grandmother doing the housework.

There were large, gilt-framed paintings hanging on the wood panelling, and Taylor paused to study them.

There was one of a tall, fashionable young woman in eighteenth century dress, probably Georgian. Her gown had panniers, making her hips look enormous, and her white-gold wig was elaborate. She wore a striking, rather masculine gold ring on her right hand, like a signet. The woman's smile was enigmatic, a beauty spot beside her mouth. Looking up at that face, Taylor could not help smiling in return, as if at a shared joke, though she didn't really know what or why.

In the background to the woman's portrait stood Estuary House in full sunshine. It looked rather grander than it did now, she thought, mentally comparing the house in the painting to the one she had seen on arriving the other day. The house façade was free of clinging ivy, and the formal gardens were elegant and well-maintained, the stone steps blanched white in the sun. There was even a peacock strutting between the low hedges. Purple verbena, rosemary shrubs and catmint sprawled softly over gravelled paths, while the summer bedding plants stretched under a china-blue sky in a riot of red, pink and yellow flowers.

At one of the front windows, she could have sworn she saw a face looking out, just as she'd seen Mrs Chance at the window on that first day.

She moved closer to have a better look, craning her neck to look up at the painting, which was roughly eight foot high.

From behind, Mrs Chance said, 'That's the Lady Elizabeth, one of the more infamous daughters of the family. She fell in love with a pirate and ran away with him.'

'Goodness.' She recalled some passing mention of the Lady Elizabeth in a few of Lyndon Chance's poems and decided she would have to study them more closely.

'Oh, it was a huge scandal. Her father never stopped looking for her. But she was right to run away, if you ask me. He was a cruel man, her father. Three wives, and they all died young of mysterious causes.'

Taylor shivered.

For once she was not alone in her instinctive reaction to

such tales of injustice from the past; Mrs Chance seemed affected in the same way. She gazed up at the lady with a fearful look on her face.

'Nobody ever heard of the Lady Elizabeth again, poor girl. Probably came to a sticky end out on the high seas. But I imagine she had fun before ...' The old woman paused, seeming to have lost the thread of what she was saying, and eventually shook herself. 'Well, we'd better get on. It's down this way, follow me closely.' She gave a cracked little laugh. 'I still get lost all the time.'

They passed a narrow window that overlooked the river, and she thought of the strange woman she'd seen on the far shore of the estuary. The woman's fleeting gesture before she walked away, her finger pointing directly at Taylor.

Immediately afterwards, Julius Chance had capitulated on letting her stay. The two things had to be related. But how, she had no idea.

'Here we are.' Mrs Chance came at last to a plain, wooden door at the end of a long corridor and stopped, looking back at her. 'This is my sitting room,' she explained, adding shyly, 'My sanctuary. Not even Julius comes here.'

'I'm honoured.'

'We need to talk where we won't be *disturbed*.' Her voice had dropped to a whisper on that last word.

Surprised by this, Taylor glanced over her shoulder. But the corridor was empty. 'Is someone else in the house today?'

'Nobody living,' Mrs Chance said promptly, but then tapped her nose as though to indicate a secret. 'Two left.'

Taylor was thoroughly confused by this exchange.

'Two ... Sorry, what?'

'Two questions left, of course.' Mrs Chance opened the door and gestured her inside. 'It's like the Ouija board. You can only ask three times. After that, the spirits get restless.'

'That wasn't meant to be one of my questions.'

'I explained the rules.'

'Yes, but ...' Taylor's shoulders slumped as she realised the futility of arguing with her host. 'Fine, whatever. Two questions left.'

Taylor went inside, heading instinctively for the window first. It was automatic for her to check out the exit points in every new room she entered, mindful that she might at any minute need to get out quickly. A hangover from her childhood, her therapist had said.

The room was snug and cosy. A threadbare red rug lay over the stone flags, while a cream two-seater sofa and mismatched green fabric armchair dominated the small space. There was a thin black cat curled up on the armchair, who didn't stir even when the door closed. A sideboard stood against the wall, littered with bits and pieces, framed photographs half-hidden by debris, as though anything Mrs Chance couldn't find a better home for had ended up there.

Beyond the latticed Tudor-style window, clusters of trees and tall grasses stretched down to the muddy estuary foreshore. Out in the middle of the current, a small yacht was sailing downstream, fleeting glimpses of its white sails just visible through green branches as it passed like a gull on the wing.

Lyndon Chance must once have stood here, she thought, at this very same window, looking out at the same view. Her mother would have been so thrilled to be in her shoes today. The thought made her sad. So much promise snatched away in a moment ...

Taylor looked down to the estuary and felt the same bittersweet sense of idyll and exile Lyndon had expressed in many of his poems. The yearning, the nostalgia, the regret.

The only difference was that he'd been a gifted poet, able to spin such experiences into literary gold, and she ...

Well, she wasn't a poet.

'Sit, please sit.' Mrs Chance scooped up the unresisting cat and sank into the armchair with it on her lap. The animal instantly sat up and began to purr with a deep throbbing note, kneading at her dress with hooked claws. 'Julius told me I wasn't to talk to you.'

'Oh.'

Taylor, perching on the edge of the sofa opposite, was unsure why she'd been brought here if Mrs Chance didn't intend to say anything.

'So,' the old lady continued blithely, 'you should feel free to ask whatever you like. I'm all ears.' She held up two fingers. 'But you only have two questions left, mind. No exceptions.'

She seemed to be treating this like a game. Except Taylor had no idea what kind of game it was or what the rules were.

What did she want to ask Mrs Chance?

So many things ... What it was like being married to such a great poet; what kind of man Lyndon had been; and whether the darkest rumours about him were true.

Her gaze fell on an old black-and-white photograph in a frame, placed on a low table beside the hearth.

The photograph showed Lyndon as a young man, possibly before he had even met his future wife, standing on the estuary foreshore with a woman of a similar age. Lyndon was unsmiling and the young woman was looking away from the camera, shielding her eyes against the sun so that her features were obscured. The wind whipped long, thin hair about her face and flapped at her pale, sleeveless summer dress. She was tall and angular, with jutting hip bones and skinny arms, and

73

clearly not Mrs Chance, who looked to be built along very different lines. Yet there was something oddly familiar about the woman all the same.

'Who's that?' she asked, unthinking.

'Ah!' Mrs Chance gurgled and pointed at her, almost with delight. 'Only one question left.'

'That's not fair. I didn't mean to ask that as a question. I ... I wasn't ready.'

Mrs Chance looked at her, brows raised.

'Damn,' Taylor muttered.

The old lady moved the cat, rose slowly and picked up the framed photograph. 'That's Lyndon when he was a lad,' she said, peering down at the two sunlit figures with the glittering waters of the estuary behind them, 'and that,' she tapped the glass, 'is Iris.'

'Who's Iris?'

Mrs Chance studied the photograph for a moment in silence before handing it to Taylor. 'Lyndon's sister.'

Taylor took the photo frame and stared down at it in wonder. 'His sister? Of course, how stupid of me. I remember reading about her in one of the Lyndon Chance biographies, but there weren't many details. One of his biographers said she just kind of ... disappeared. I assumed he meant she got married young and moved away.'

'Oh no, she never married; she's still Iris Chance.'

'Still?' Taylor's voice was high with disbelief. 'You mean she's alive?' Hurriedly, she added, 'If you'll allow me another question.'

But to her relief, Mrs Chance seemed to have forgotten her game of three questions. There was a faraway look on her face as she answered simply, 'Iris was Lyndon's younger sister, by three years. They were very close. Very close indeed. At one time, I thought ...' She stopped dead and gave her head a little shake. 'Well, all water under the bridge. A long time ago now, isn't it?'

'Where does she live?'

'Here, of course.' Mrs Chance drifted towards the window, waving her hand about vaguely. 'Iris haunts this place.'

'Sorry?'

'Ever since Lyndon's death. Because it was so sudden, per-haps. He had a heart attack, you know. She wasn't prepared to lose him so soon.' Her eyes softened. 'None of us were.'

'But you said ...' Perplexed, Taylor put the photograph back on the low table. 'I'm sorry, I'm confused. I thought you said Iris was still alive. How can she be haunting you?'

'Iris is always hanging around. Even when she's hiding in her little bolthole across the river or it's pitch-black, I still know she's out there.' Mrs Chance was gazing out of the window; her fingers brushed back and forth across the latticed pane as she muttered, 'Staring at me from across the water like she's accusing me of something.'

Taylor, joining her at the window, suddenly sucked in a breath. 'Of course,' she whispered, understanding. 'The woman in the reed marsh.'

'You saw her.'

Taylor nodded. 'The other day, Julius took me down to the foreshore, and there was a woman watching us from across the river. About your age, I suppose, but it was hard to tell at that distance. Anyway, this woman pointed at me, and Julius said ...' Taylor hesitated. 'Well, he'd been telling me I had to leave Estuary House. Then this woman appeared, and quite suddenly he changed his mind.'

She scoured the banks opposite, but there didn't seem to be anyone there today. The leggy reeds waved enthusiastically in the breeze, stretching a long way inland, and the mudflats along the river's edge were deserted, sunlight glinting off rivulets and deep pools and spongy-looking green patches of what was probably samphire.

'So that was Lyndon's little sister,' Taylor said slowly.

'Stay away from her.'

Taylor was taken aback by the sharp tone. 'Why? Is she dangerous?'

The old lady hesitated, then abruptly waved her hand. 'No more questions now. You're all out of questions.'

'I'm sorry. I didn't mean to—'

'He'll be back soon. Julius can't find you here. He'll know we've been talking.' Mrs Chance gestured to the door; her voice rose, panicked. 'Leave. Now.'

Taylor closed the door quietly behind her. Confused, she hesitated in the semi-darkness of the wood-panelled corridor, peering up and down, trying to recall which way they had taken to get here. Should she turn left or right?

As she stood there, she became aware of a presence in the shadows to her left, and deliberately did not look that way.

She often felt 'things' like that.

But in her experience, it was better not to make it obvious she'd noticed.

Mrs Chance was talking to herself behind the door at her back, pausing occasionally as though having a conversation with somebody whose replies were unheard.

'Yes, I know. But she wouldn't stop asking… It's not my fault. Don't blame me. I told her she could only ask three questions.' The woman gave a frightened cry. 'But I thought it was what you *wanted*!'

Finally, she subsided into angry muttering, too low for Taylor to make out.

Could she be talking to someone on the phone?

It was possible, though Taylor hadn't seen a telephone

handset or mobile in the room. But it was either that or Mrs Chance was hearing voices.

After dithering for a moment, Taylor turned right and headed for a faint source of light, threading her way delicately through various look-alike corridors until she found herself back in the stone-flagged entrance hall with the vast, medieval-looking hearth. Again, she had that odd, prickling sensation of being observed but paid no attention. Though she noted a curious urge, hard to resist, to glance up at the portrait of the swashbuckling Lady Elizabeth.

He always felt braver after the sun went down. Darkness was when the bad things happened ...

Somebody flung open the front door and walked straight in, surprising her in the act of crossing the entrance hall.

'Ms Pierce? What the hell are you doing here?' Julius Chance stopped dead so that the middle-aged woman scurrying in at his heels almost collided with him. 'How dare you enter this house without permission?'

'Mrs Chance said—'

'You've been talking to my grandmother, too? I told you she wasn't to be bothered.' He looked Taylor up and down, anger and frustration on his face. 'You people never respect boundaries, do you? I want you gone by tonight or I'm calling the police. Do you understand?'

Chapter Seven

Light falls ruinous
Over Neptune, a tuning-fork in Scorpio …

— From 'Ecliptic' in *Estuary*

Lyndon found her a heavy wedding ring that he said had belonged to his grandmother, which made her feel even more awful about deceiving his family. But he didn't seem to notice her shudder, merely nodding in satisfaction when it fitted her ring finger perfectly. Then, her nerves jangling as though she were being taken to her execution, Eleanor consented to be led downstairs and into the untidy, book-lined sitting room to meet his parents.

Lyndon's father stood by the wood burner, which had just been lit, no doubt to take the autumn chill off the room. He was a vast, untidy man in a tweed jacket and a pair of green corduroy trousers. The lapels of his shirt collar were well-worn, but his black brogues had been polished, only marred by a few flecks of dirt. He looked to be in his late sixties, with a receding hairline, bulging eyes, and the mottled flush of a habitual drinker, something Eleanor knew about from various members of their church whose drinking had occasionally caused her father problems.

Mrs Chance was at least fifteen years younger than her husband. Seated on the oxblood sofa, one leg crossed over the other, she was unclipping her earrings, one by one, and grimacing as she did so. She had a tidy figure and was dressed conservatively in a cream woollen dress with matching sleeveless jacket and shiny shoes. Her auburn hair, lightly streaked with grey, was set in neat waves, apart from one rogue curl that hung over her forehead like an inverted question mark.

'Ah, the prodigal son returns,' his father drawled, stooping to stroke a huge, hairy Irish wolfhound that had appeared out of nowhere to greet him, the dog's tail wagging furiously. 'Where the hell have you been, boy?'

'Lyndon,' his mother exclaimed at the same time, staring at him with delight, before her smile faltered on seeing Eleanor behind him in the doorway. 'Oh . . . You've brought a guest home.' Then her smile seemed to freeze in place as Lyndon dragged Eleanor forward, keeping her firmly by his side.

'Not a guest, Mum. She's my wife,' he announced starkly. 'I got married.'

At that unexpected disclosure, his parents shifted their attention to her, considerable shock on their faces. His mother seemed particularly upset by his news, her eyes widening, her mouth opening and closing, with no sound coming out.

Eleanor wished she had the nerve to defy Lyndon and tell them the truth. That she barely knew their son. She hated the thought of lying to them, especially about something so important.

But more than that, she feared the idea of her father arriving in Cornwall to drag her back home. Better to be Lyndon's prisoner than her father's, she reckoned. And maybe he only meant this sham marriage as a practical joke, the truth to be revealed to his parents at a later date.

She hoped so, at any rate.

'What did you say, boy? Your *wife*? You got *married*?' His

79

father pushed the fawning dog away to stare at his son, then swung to study Eleanor. His mouth gaped in amazement as his bleary eyes fixed on her face first, then sought for her wedding ring. 'Good God!'

Eleanor had expected surprise. But his parents' stunned reaction shook her. Was she so very grim and undesirable in terms of a daughter-in-law?

His mother groped for a packet of cigarettes on the coffee table and fished one out for herself. She had recovered her poise but was clearly shocked by his announcement.

She flushed and her lips quivered as she looked Eleanor up and down before turning her gaze on her son for a proper explanation. Her face seemed made to express outrage as a default; her wide blue eyes were bold, her mouth a shade too large, everything about her exaggerated, like a cartoon character.

'I ... I'm sorry, Lyndon, but I don't understand. What do you mean, *married*?' Her voice was not shrill, as Eleanor had half-expected, but husky and low, perhaps due to her smoking habit. An unlit cigarette dangled from between long, red-tipped fingers as she fumbled for an ornate marble lighter. 'Lyndon, darling, for God's sake ... Do stop horsing around. You're not making any sense.'

'On the contrary,' Lyndon said coolly, 'I'm making perfect sense. You told me to sort myself out. Well, I did, and here's the result.'

Having lit her cigarette, his mother slammed the heavy marble lighter down on the table, shaking her head. 'You disappear for bloody months on end,' she hissed, 'and then turn up here without a word of warning, with some tarty blonde in tow—'

'This is my wife, let me remind you,' Lyndon told her with surprising restraint. 'Try to be respectful.'

'How about you try a little truth first?' His mother pointed. 'Did she walk into a door to get that face?'

Eleanor flushed and put a hand to her bruised cheek. So that was why they were so unhappy. She'd forgotten the black eye.

Lyndon ran a hand through his hair, then said doggedly, 'I got into a pub fight. Someone threw a punch at me, and ... Eleanor got in the way. I'm not proud of it. Please don't insinuate that I would ever hurt a woman.' He sounded strained. 'I'm not that kind of man.'

'I'm glad to hear it. Though taking your wife out drinking wasn't a good idea, was it?' His mother drew on her cigarette. 'Married ...' She shook her head. 'No, you can't mean it. You're always pulling my leg, Lyndon. Tell me this is another of your little jokes, and I promise I'll laugh.'

'Laughing at me is all you ever do,' Lyndon said, his eyes flashing. 'It's typical of you not to take me seriously.'

Eleanor wished she could sink through the floor. Or at least be allowed to escape this difficult family reunion. Bad enough being forced to endure her own father's wrath on a daily basis, along with her brother's easy contempt ... But these people were strangers to her. All of them, even her so-called husband.

His father took a step forward, his face belligerent. 'That's enough. Don't speak to your mother like that, boy.'

'I'm not a boy anymore, Dad, remember? I'm a married man. And no, it's not a joke. That's the last thing it is.' Lyndon took Eleanor's hand and drew her to his side, ignoring her small noise of protest. 'I'm perfectly serious. This is my wife, and her name is Eleanor.'

His mother took another deep, urgent drag on her cigarette, and then flicked its grey tail of ash towards the ashtray.

She glared at Eleanor in silence, her lips pursed, making it clear she knew who was to blame for this rushed marriage.

His father was frowning, too. 'Is that my mother's wedding ring she's wearing?'

'Yes.' Lyndon lifted her hand, letting them see the gold ring more clearly. 'We used a cheap one for the ceremony. Needs must, and all that. But as soon as we got here, I gave her Gran's ring instead.' He linked fingers with her and pulled her hand close against his side in a shockingly intimate gesture; it was hard for Eleanor to school herself not to pull away in dismay. 'I didn't think you'd mind. Gran always said it should go to the first of us who got married.'

His father grunted under his breath but didn't comment.

'And where did you meet *Eleanor*?' his mother asked.

'That's not important,' Lyndon told her.

'Isn't it?' Her eyebrows rose. 'How long have you known her?'

'Nearly three months.'

His mother's eyes widened at this disclosure, and Eleanor thought it was just as well she didn't know they'd barely known each other twenty-four hours.

'Are you pregnant?' his mother asked her abruptly.

'Of course not!' Eleanor exclaimed.

'We fell madly in love and couldn't wait to tie the knot, that's all you need to know,' Lyndon said lightly. He slipped an arm about her waist and drew her even closer, ignoring her stiffness and averted face. 'Now that we're here, I want this to be our home. If you're willing to put us up, of course.'

His parents said nothing.

'I hope you'll make my wife very welcome,' Lyndon added. His dark eyes sought Eleanor's face, the glint in them unmistakable. 'She's been looking forward to meeting you both for ages. Haven't you, darling?'

'Oh yes,' Eleanor murmured as his arm tightened about her; she even dredged up a smile from somewhere. 'Ages and ages.'

It felt like she was trapped in a nightmare.

'So, let's start again, shall we? Eleanor, this is my mother, Camilla Chance,' Lyndon introduced his parents with a bland smile, as though they were meeting at a party, 'and my father, Gerard Chance.'

'I'm very p-pleased to meet you both, Mr and Mrs Chance,' Eleanor stammered, aware of Lyndon's sardonic gaze on her face. There was a long silence, into which she added unhappily, 'Thank you for having me.'

His father rubbed his chin and said nothing.

Also without a word, his mother turned away, grabbing at a bell pull that hung beside the hearth. Somewhere far off a bell tinkled.

'I'll ask Mrs Barclay to bring us a pot of tea,' his mother said with her back still turned, the words friendly enough, though Eleanor fancied she could hear a shake in her voice. 'I think we could all do with a drink.'

Was it really such a terrible thing for their son to have married? Or was it Eleanor herself that his parents objected to as a daughter-in-law? Even though the whole thing was a charade, it was hard not to be a little offended by so much undisguised hostility.

'Sod the tea.' His father turned to pour himself a large tumbler of whisky from a drinks tray on the cluttered side-board. 'Lyndon?'

'No, thank you.'

'For God's sake ... Not even to toast your bride?'

Lyndon hesitated, then nodded. 'Just a small one, then.'

'And, er, how about what's-her-name?'

'Eleanor,' Lyndon snarled.

'Sorry,' his father said, drawling again as he poured his son's drink, 'I've only just met the girl. You'll have to give my brain time to catch up.'

'I prefer tea, thank you,' Eleanor said politely.

His father shrugged, handing Lyndon his drink. 'Suit yourself.' He raised his glass. 'To Lyndon and Eleanor.'

Lyndon raised his glass to her in a mocking half-salute, but said nothing, merely drinking his whisky in one swallow and returning the glass to the tray.

His mother looked away, still smoking nervously.

With surprising speed, Mrs Barclay appeared in the hall. She took in the scene at a glance, showing no surprise when Mrs Chance introduced Eleanor as her new daughter-in-law.

'Congratulations,' the woman said to Lyndon and Eleanor in a wooden voice, and then turned back to her employer. 'Would you like me to bring biscuits with the tea, madam?'

'Have you eaten yet, Lyndon?' his mother asked sharply. 'We dined early this evening, because of the meeting.'

'No, and Eleanor is famished.'

'Mrs Barclay, if you could possibly make something quick and easy for their supper, and take it through to the dining room—'

'I'd rather eat in here where it's warm,' Lyndon interrupted. 'No need to stand on bloody ceremony. Cheese on toast on a tray will be fine.'

Eleanor was not consulted but said nothing, still struggling to accept the increasingly surreal events of the evening. She had no objection to make, however, she was, in fact, starving, and cheese on toast sounded perfectly marvellous.

Mrs Barclay merely nodded and slipped away, seeming unmoved by Lyndon's rudeness.

'Let me top up the wood burner, it's getting low.' Lyndon pushed a few sticks of wood into the smoking burner and then slammed the heavy metal door shut again, flames dancing behind the blackened glass. He straightened, reaching for a cloth to rub his dirty hands. 'So, where have you two been tonight? You look smart, Dad.'

'Town hall meeting in Wadebridge. Thought it merited a jacket and tie.' His father slipped a finger under his collar as though it were too tight, and indeed his thick neck did seem to be bulging over it. 'Those environmental idiots ... They're trying to stop us selling our own land now.'

'What land?'

Grabbing her hand, Lyndon sank into one of the armchairs and dragged an unwilling Eleanor down to perch on his knee.

A fiery blush rose in her cheeks as she risked a quick glance at his father. Whatever must he be thinking? Nothing very complimentary, she guessed, judging by Mr Chance's stony expression. But he didn't comment.

'Seventy-five acres up at Shakers' Field, overlooking the bay.' Gerard shrugged and sat down opposite them. 'I've been made a good offer for it. Holiday chalets. They look handsome enough on the architects' plans. Only *apparently*,' he said, with a derisory laugh, 'it'll destroy the natural habitat of ... oh, whatever. Wild beasts, insects, birds, butterflies, even trees ... You name it. They're worth more to these protesters than an honest man's living and the right of city folk to come down to Cornwall and take a breather for a few days.'

'I'm afraid I'm more on the side of the butterflies.' Lyndon looked impatiently at his father. 'And there's no point pretending to be a simple Cornish farmer for Eleanor's benefit.' His voice was unfriendly. 'She's seen over the house.'

'I never said I was a farmer; I'm a landowner, like my father before me, and his father before that.' Gerard pulled a sour face, finishing his whisky. 'A landowner who can't sell his land to turn a profit now, thanks to these bloody protest-ers. What use is that?' He looked at Eleanor with sudden interest. 'You look like a clever young thing, what do you think? A man should be allowed to develop his land how he sees fit, shouldn't he? Or are you one of these *environmental-ists*, or whatever they call themselves?'

'I've never really thought about it,' she said nervously.

'Not a country girl?'

Eleanor shook her head mutely, unsure how much to say about herself or whether she ought to say anything at all. Lyndon had not told her to lie about being from Cirencester, it was true. But he'd blocked his mother's question about where they'd met and she could feel his gaze on her face now, as though silently warning her to keep quiet.

'Well, well.' His father turned his head towards his wife, a significant glance passing between them. 'Married a townie. That's not your usual taste.' He leant back in his chair, his gaze shifting abruptly back to his son's face. 'Does your brother know?'

'No,' Lyndon snapped.

His father gave a grim laugh. 'That's the way the wind blows, is it?' He looked at Eleanor searchingly, his bloodshot eyes squinting. 'Lean forward into the light, girl,' he ordered her. 'Let's have a proper look at you, then.'

There was an old, round-bellied green lantern hanging from a beam above the wood burner, surrounded by a few tiny flies, flitting back and forth in an agitated fashion as though confused not to be outside. She supposed there were often flies indoors here, the house being so close to the estuary and marshlands. The lantern gave off a soft light, spilling a circular golden pool between the armchairs while leaving the rest of the room in gentle shadow.

Hot-cheeked, Eleanor glanced at Lyndon for guidance. To

her surprise though, he wasn't annoyed but seemed almost amused by his father's command. He gave her a slight nod, and Eleanor shifted her weight forward into the lantern's yellow glow.

His mother leant forward, too, stubbing out her cigarette as she looked straight at Eleanor.

For a moment, both his parents studied her intently and unsmiling, like this was a test of some kind. She waited for the verdict, but neither of them spoke. After a moment, his mother sucked in a sharp breath and reclined on the sofa again, and his father merely sighed and leant back, nodding as though some question had been answered.

'Sly work, I call it.' Gerard gave a little jerk of his head. 'But Oliver will find out about her soon enough, mark my words.' He got up and fetched the decanter of whisky, pouring a couple more fingers of golden liquor into his own glass, then glancing back at Lyndon. 'Another?'

'Thanks, but I've had enough,' Lyndon said shortly.

Wordlessly, his father knocked back the whisky in one swallow, and then poured himself another couple of fingers before settling into his armchair.

'What did you mean just now about Oliver?' Lyndon asked him, his voice tight. 'Is he coming home? I thought he was away until Christmas.'

'Ah, well.' His father lifted one large shoulder in a careless shrug. 'You're not the only one in this family who knows how to be sly.'

'What are you talking about?' Lyndon sat up.

'Now, don't get yourself in a tizzy.' Gerard gave him a malignant smile. 'I only meant that Oliver's got himself a woman, too.'

Lyndon audibly sucked in his breath, his body tense. 'A woman? You mean a wife?'

'You can stop sweating. They're not married yet. You've stolen a march on him there. She's a gorgeous looker though. Jamaican mum, British dad. Wants to be a model or an actress or something like that.' His father seemed amused by this. 'I can't see it lasting. He's working in Truro now, got a flat there, and she's a bit of a glamour puss, wanting to be off to London all the time.'

'Oliver managed to get himself a job?' Lyndon's lip curled.

'Some office block near the cathedral. You'll have to ask him about it. Wants to be company director one day, he says.'

'And he will be,' his wife shot at him defiantly.

'Olly's still your mother's pet, as you can see.' Gerard's smile grew more cynical. 'But he won't take kindly to you getting wed. And don't think you can keep it quiet. Not now you've brought your bride home.' He laughed. 'I daresay your mother's itching to run away and dash off a letter to her favourite son. Aren't you, Cammie?'

'Hush,' Camilla told him, her face censorious.

Her favourite son.

That seemed rather mean, Eleanor thought, especially given that Lyndon had told her he and Oliver were twins. She wondered if it was true or merely a joke that their mother preferred one son over the other. Surely no mother could be so cruel?

'It's family news,' Camilla said stiffly. 'Oliver deserves to be told. Of course I shall write. And to Iris, too.'

'Who's Iris?' Eleanor dared to ask.

Gerard frowned at his son. 'You married this girl, but never mentioned Iris to her?'

'Her name never came up, that's all. We had other things to discuss beside my siblings, believe it or not.' Lyndon threw her a look, frustration in his face, and Eleanor knew that she'd made a bad mistake. 'Iris is my younger sister. She isn't here right now.'

He didn't elaborate on that.

Camilla stood up, smoothing down her jacket. 'I'd better ask Mrs Barclay to get your room ready, once she's finished in the kitchen. Did you bring your luggage in from the car yet, Lyndon? Your father can help, if not.'

'Thanks, but there's no need. I already brought our bags in and made up the double bed in Gran's old room.'

Her eyes widened. 'But—'

'The bed in my room is a single,' Lyndon said calmly. 'You can hardly expect me and my wife to share a single bed.'

Eleanor caught a look of anguish on his mother's face, hurriedly extinguished.

'Of course not,' Camilla said faintly, sitting down again. 'You're a married man now. You must do as you wish.'

His father laughed again but said nothing.

A double bed.

Eleanor's stomach clenched with sudden fear, though she dared not look up, sensing Lyndon's intent gaze on her face again. There was no doubt in her mind that he intended to share that four-poster bed with her tonight, so as not to arouse suspicion in his parents.

Exactly how far would this charade of theirs extend?

Chapter Eight

A woman steps out
From the dark cavern of history.

– From 'The Lady Elizabeth' in *Estuary*

Taylor strode through the wreck of the formal gardens at Estuary House, almost running down flights of cracked steps, past moss-covered urns smothered in weeds, and flowerbeds overtaken by coarse grass and low-growing shrubs, never once looking back. Her head was buzzing with conflicting emotions. She felt unsteady, knocked off balance by the way both Julius Chance and his grandmother had spoken to her.

She was unwelcome here. That much was obvious.

'Ms Pierce?'

It was Julius, calling after her in his deep, abrupt voice, but she paid no attention. He could get lost.

'Ms Pierce, I'm sorry,' he said, raising his voice as he began to follow her down through the gardens. 'Please come back.'

How dare he speak to her like that?

Yes, she'd asked his grandmother a few questions without him being there, aware that he would be annoyed by her presence in the manor house. But that was no reason to suggest she'd been trespassing, and then threaten to call the police.

Julius Chance had no idea how to behave in a reasonable,

civilised way. But then, he'd been brought up in privilege, hadn't he? Estuary House might be a little ramshackle, but it was still huge and must be worth a fortune. Why would a man who lived in a house like that ever expect anything other than obedience from lesser mortals?

When he raised his hand, you always knew to duck. And run like hell.

She crunched across the gravel drive without slowing her pace and had almost reached the entrance gate when Julius finally caught up with her.

'Ms Pierce, what I said just now ...' Tall and long-limbed, Julius fell easily into step beside her, only slightly breathless, his gaze on her face. 'It was uncalled for. I apologise, and I take it back. There's really no need for you to leave.'

'Your grandmother invited me in.'

'Yes, she just told me. Gave me an earful, actually. I hadn't understood the situation, you see.'

'You thought I'd broken in, didn't you? Climbed in through a window like a cat burglar, maybe, so I could have a snoop around or interrogate Mrs Chance while you were out.'

'Something like that.' He stepped in front of her, forcing Taylor to stop. 'Look, I'm sorry, I honestly am.' He stuck out a hand. 'Truce?'

She stared at his hand, astonished, and said nothing.

'My grandmother wants you here, and it's obvious Iris does, too.' He grimaced when she looked up, startled. 'Iris is the woman we saw across the river the other day. She's my great-aunt.'

'Yes, your grandmother mentioned her. She said Iris "haunts" the place.'

'That's one way of putting it.' He had still not lowered his hand, holding her gaze intently now. 'Will you accept my apology and stay?'

Suspicious that he suddenly wanted her around after trying so hard to get rid of her, Taylor was nonetheless mollified.

Reluctantly, she shook his hand. 'All right.'

She glanced back at the house; Mrs Chance had wandered out onto the long, ivy-draped veranda near the front entrance. The middle-aged woman who'd followed Julius into the house was with her, talking earnestly while they both stared down the gardens towards them.

'Well, I have some things to do,' she said awkwardly, and Julius moved aside to let her continue walking, but then fell into step with her again.

'My grandmother would like to invite you to dinner,' he said. 'Maybe Friday night?'

She was surprised but eagerly accepted. 'That would be lovely, thank you,' she said, and then added quickly, while he was in a good mood with her, 'By the way, is there any chance I could use your facilities occasionally?'

When he stared at her, she gave an embarrassed grin. 'I love camping, and I brought a portaloo with me in the van. But being able to shower and use an indoor toilet on a regular basis would be nice, too.'

'Of course,' he said at once. 'There's a downstairs bathroom near the side door. The house is usually unlocked during the day, but I can let you have a key for nights.'

'Thank you, that's very kind,' she said, and then asked on a whim, 'Who was that with your grandmother?'

There was a flash of irritation in his face.

So much for a truce, she thought. He really didn't like people knowing his business. But she supposed he couldn't be blamed for that, not when the locals loved to gossip about the Chance family.

'Nobody in particular. She's come to help me with something. A special project.'

Taylor had spotted a small white hatchback parked in the nearby lane, a cheerful red-and-green logo painted on one of its door panels. '*Cornish Moves*. She's an estate agent?' She stopped dead as the truth hit her. 'You're putting Estuary House on the market?'

Shocking as this was, it explained his cagey behaviour. This estate was the birthplace of Lyndon Chance and encompassed large swathes of land along the protected estuary. He must know what it would do to the poet's legacy to sell this place.

'That's none of your business.' Julius took a step back, his hands clasped behind his back, and nodded her through the open gate. 'And if you want to stay here, Ms Pierce, I suggest you keep such ludicrous imaginings to yourself. I'll respect my family's wishes to have you about the place, but there are limits. Be sure not to cross them.'

With that, he returned to the house.

She stared after him, her head buzzing with precisely the kind of wild speculations he suspected her of harbouring.

After heading back to her tent for Lyndon Chance's final collection of poems, Taylor decided to settle her nerves with a stroll down to the river, book in hand. She was still sure there was a message buried in Lyndon's cryptic last sequence, if she could only figure it out, and visiting the various sites mentioned in his poems seemed like a good place to start.

Julius couldn't really be planning to sell up, could he? Especially with his grandmother still living. Her memory might be dodgy at times, and her speech eccentric, but Taylor was sure the old lady had no intention of leaving. And if Mrs Chance actually owned the manor house, which seemed likely, he would find it very difficult to put Estuary House on the market without her permission. And what about Iris?

She crossed the Camel Trail, following the line of the old railway track for a short while – just as she had done with Julius on her first day – before shifting to a narrower path that led through trees towards the broad, rolling river. There, ferns and mosses grew larger and more lush in the shade, spilling onto the track to mingle with red fescue and the occasional patch of sea purslane as the ground grew boggier the nearer she came to the water's edge.

Taylor stopped, bending to snap off a leaf of sea purslane, and sniffed it speculatively. She seemed to recall it was possible to make pesto with purslane instead of the traditional basil. But after a quick nibble on the bitter-tasting plant, she grimaced, chucking it away.

Maybe not.

Opening her mother's much-thumbed paperback of *Estuary*, she flipped through a dozen annotated pages, finally pausing at a poem that had been heavily marked and underscored in red biro.

'Half-Light.'

One of her mother's favourites, it would seem. Otherwise, why all the tiny, scribbled marginal notes and circled words?

Gently, Taylor ran a thumb over the deepest underscoring, noting where the tip of the biro had bitten into the soft paper, shredding it.

'She looked out of place,' she read the highlighted passage out loud, 'that gleaming yacht, sailing/Down the Camel like a young bride in white.'

These lines filled her with sadness and dread, haunting rather than beautiful. Yet she had no idea why.

She peered down at her mother's barely legible scrawl in the margin. *Sense of alienation? Purity/innocence don't belong.*

94

Or only in passing. Sacred marriage of male/female. Atonement? 'Gleaming yacht' wealth/capitalism symbol. Out of place in the natural world.

Maybe the sadness she felt was for her mother. All that intellectual promise, her marriage a sham – a place of domination rather than love – and no chance to show the world her talent.

Strolling on in the sultry afternoon, Taylor reached the end of the marshy, overgrown path, yet still couldn't see the water's edge; there were only trees and a seemingly impenetrable thicket of blackthorn ahead, and everywhere the wild, tangy scent of a tidal river. A spiralling cloud of midges swarmed busily above her head, and she flapped at them impatiently.

A twig snapped somewhere in the undergrowth, close by. Then another. She stilled, listening. Human or animal? Or even a bird?

'Hello?'

There was no reply.

A flash of white through the bushes had caught her eye though. Then the faint sound of voices, growing stronger. A man and boy, chatting just out of sight.

'Mack?'

She guessed he couldn't hear her. But Mack had said the riverside cottage he was renting was somewhere down this way, hadn't he?

She began to push through the thick, rambling shrubs, some of them a good eight foot in height as well as impenetrable in places, half-smiling at the thought of surprising him and Davie with an impromptu visit.

Finally, there was an opening in the thick, glossy-leaved bushes, and she squeezed through it, finding herself on a neatly kept gravel path. Straight ahead was a pretty white building, and beyond it, at long last, the lugubrious, soft-blue crawl of the River Camel under a startlingly azure sky, its waters dotted with sea birds and edged with acres of waist-high green reeds.

It was the old chapel, she realised, squinting up into a too-bright sun at what looked like the bell tower. The place had been converted sympathetically into a holiday let, just as Mack had described it, stained-glass windows set into deep stone walls and flowers sprawling from a range of stylish terracotta pots outside the porched front door.

'Hello?'

And suddenly there he was, ruffling Davie's hair and then watching indulgently as the boy ran down towards the river.

'Mack? It's me, Taylor.'

Mack looked round and smiled at her, raising a hand in quick welcome before waving her to join him. Then he himself went back inside the chapel, not waiting to see if she was coming or not.

Taylor hesitated.

Well, she'd wanted something to take her mind off Julius and his odd, prickly behaviour, hadn't she?

She slid the book of poems into her rucksack, hurriedly shouldered the pack, and started down the path towards the chapel.

Chapter Nine

Twig-thin legs like a medieval cleric's
Under his gown,
He digs down into mud with all the ardour
Of a newlywed.

– From 'Oystercatcher' in *Estuary*

It was already light by the time Eleanor opened her eyes.

She stared up at the unfamiliar lace canopy above her head; the draped white material gathered in a tiny star at the centre, with folds radiating out, soft and billowy. A wedding dress, floating above her head.

Eleanor blinked, utterly disorientated, unable to recall where she was. This was not her grim, cracked bedroom ceiling, nor could she hear the neighbour's dog constantly barking or her father calling up the stairs to demand where breakfast was, despite the light flooding into the room. Her astonished gaze dropped to the four wooden posts of the bed, also draped with white lace tied back with pink ribbons. The lumpy, dough-soft mattress sank beneath her as she shifted.

With a shock that rocked her whole body, the strange events of the past twenty-four hours flashed through her head. Eleanor remembered where she was and, more importantly, *who* she was supposed to be.

Blinking, she jolted upright, thankful to find she was wearing her flannel nightdress, buttoned prudishly up to her neck, and heard Lyndon say with an amused drawl, 'Ah, you're awake at last. I was beginning to think I'd married Sleeping Beauty.'

She'd assumed from the silence that she was alone but realised at a glance that Lyndon was still in the room, seated cross-legged on the floor in his pyjamas, with what looked like a pack of playing cards spread before him. They were not like any playing cards she had ever seen before; these cards were decorated with strange, bright figures in primary colours, and although they were plainly part of a set, no two cards seemed alike.

'Taroc cards,' he explained, seeing her curiosity, and held one up for her. Bordered in red, the card depicted a medieval-looking man with a wand and a cup standing before a rough table. Beneath this image the black-lettered caption read: *The Magician.* 'Have you ever used them?'

Eleanor shook her head, trying not to blush at the sight of him in his pyjamas. Had they really shared a bed last night?

Before turning out the light, Lyndon had shoved a thick bolster pillow between their bodies, his smile enigmatic. 'To protect your virtue,' he'd said, or something like that, and she'd known with a stab of embarrassment that he was mocking her.

Eleanor had lain rigid and cold for the first half an hour, painfully aware of every tiny movement of his adjacent body, listening as his breathing settled into the gentle rhythm of sleep.

She herself had not intended to sleep, curled on her side as close to the edge of the bed and as far away from him as possible.

But eventually, the seeping warmth of a hot water bottle

snuggled against her icy toes, and the weight on her eyelids of sheer exhaustion after a tumultuous day, had got the better of her, and she'd slipped into a deep, dreamless sleep.

'Taroc?' She peered down at the cards, confused. 'I've never even heard of them, sorry. Is it some kind of game?'

'Quite the opposite. They're for telling the future.'

Her eyes widened at this, and she felt her heart begin to thud. 'You mean, they're like the cards fortune-tellers use?' He nodded, and she stared at him, horrified now. 'But why would you even touch such a thing? My father says they're the work of the Devil.'

'Maybe he's right,' he said lightly, and replaced the card on the floor, then began studying the others, arranged in a semi-circle around him. 'God, Devil, spirit, mystery ... What does it matter? There are forces at work in the world that we don't understand, but these cards do. Whenever anything important happens in my life, I like to consult them and study their messages, for good or evil. They help me make the right decisions.'

'Or the wrong ones,' she whispered, her attention caught by a card that clearly depicted the Devil himself, a tall figure with black curving horns and hairy goat legs.

Lyndon laughed, picking up that exact card and examining it without any sign of fear, almost as though he'd noticed her staring.

'Perhaps.'

Eleanor crossed herself, only belatedly realising that she was reacting just as any other member of her father's religious sect would, faced with something they didn't understand.

There was a bath towel draped over a chair back near the bed. She slipped her legs out of bed and made a grab for the towel, clamping it against her chest as she backed towards the bedroom door.

'I need a wash,' she said, half-expecting him to forbid her to leave the room.

'I need to apologise for last night,' he said instead, and she stopped dead, staring down at his averted profile. 'What I asked you to do ... That charade with my parents. I'm sorry, I could see how uncomfortable it made you. I'm not forcing you to stay if you'd rather not.' He placed the Devil card face-down, resting his palm over it as though hoping to draw its wicked energy into himself. 'Though if you choose not to leave, I give you my word I'll never try to force you into anything you don't want to do, again. From what you told me about your father, he's not too big on freedom for women. But you'll be free to do whatever you want here at the manor house. To become anything you want.' He paused, as though waiting for a response. But she said nothing, merely listened, her heart thumping hard. 'I'd like to take you for a walk down to the river after breakfast,' he added quietly. 'Show you how beautiful the estuary is, how its peace and beauty can fill your soul. I can't make up for how I treated you last night, but ... Will you stay?'

'Yes,' she whispered.

'Thank you.' And he bent his head to scribble a few notes in a small black book balanced on his knee.

Still confused by this change in him, Eleanor peeked at his notebook and caught a glimpse of half-lines and odd circlings on the page.

Was he working on a poem while studying his pack of 'taroc' cards? Much of his poetry used strange, exotic imagery, which she now suspected must have come from witchy sources like these cards. Not a comfortable thought, given how often she had recited and even memorised his poems, not understanding their darker references.

Her father would have a fit if he could see her now, in

her nightie, having spent the night in the same bed as a poet who took instruction from demonic cards.

Fifty fits, in fact.

But it answered in part the question she'd asked the first night they'd met – whether his poetry was 'real' or made-up out of his imagination. Even if dreams and visions conjured up by taroc readings made their way into his poetry, Lyndon believed in these cards and what they represented. To him, they were real.

But did that also mean the love scenarios his poems sometimes described, like the 'lady' he'd written of with such yearning and bitter unhappiness, came from the cards? Or was she a real flesh and blood woman? Eleanor had not yet discovered that, though it was clear how passionate and forceful he could be under that cool exterior.

Still, Lyndon Chance hadn't taken advantage of her during the night, she thought, studying the back of his head with faint surprise. He hadn't even tried to touch her. Not once.

The whole thing was very odd.

'Best dress warmly though,' Lyndon added, glancing up as she fumbled for the door handle. He studied her flannel nightdress, his ironic gaze moving from her bare toes to the bath towel clasped to her chest. 'Oh, and you may need to borrow some of my mother's wellies. It's muddy down by the Camel, this time of year.'

After breakfast, with nobody about but the snooty house-keeper, Lyndon found her a pair of over-large, fleece-lined Wellington boots and they trudged down through elaborate gardens to the lane below. A quick hop over a stile, and more trudging through a muddy stretch of grassland, and they reached a thick hedge broken at one point by a low gate.

This gate, bearing an enamelled sign warning of DANGER, led onto the railway.

'The train to Padstow is due to go through in a few minutes,' Lyndon said, stepping through the gate and across the line without any sign of fear. He glanced up and down the track and then checked his wristwatch, his air laconic. 'Four minutes, to be precise. We'll watch the train go past, shall we, and then walk down to the river?'

'Please be careful,' she told him, a little panicked.

'Worried for me?'

'Of course I am.' Eleanor closed the gate behind them with a click, but stayed off the track. 'You might get hit.'

'Don't worry, it's hard to miss it coming, the bloody thing makes such a racket on its way through,' he told her casually, and then spotted her expression. 'Look, as soon as the train's within sight, I'll jump off the track. Honestly, I've done this a thousand times. There's no danger.' Lyndon held out his hand, his smile inviting. 'Come and join me. It's fun.'

'No, thank you.'

Lyndon shrugged, thrusting his hands into his trouser pockets. 'I grew up standing on this track, playing chicken with the trains. We used to come down here all the time, me and Oliver.' He gave her a sidelong look. 'If a train didn't hit me when I was six, it's hardly likely to hit me now.'

Eleanor hoped he was right.

She peered back down the line to where the track curved away in the direction of Wadebridge, but could neither see nor hear any sign of an approaching train. Maybe he'd got the timetable wrong, she thought. Or perhaps the train was late.

The day was bright and cold, and the only sound was of seabirds crying plaintively somewhere out of sight. The hedges were high on either side of the track, but she guessed they must be very near the estuary, tasting salt on the air.

'I'm surprised your mother allowed you boys to play on the line.'

'She had no idea,' Lyndon said lazily. 'Once, we even borrowed Dad's old service revolver and pretended to stick up the train.' He grinned. 'Only someone must have seen us, because Dad came down here the next day, took back the pistol, and walloped the hell out of us.'

A moment later, a loud whistle split the silence, and Eleanor shrank back against the gate.

She'd never stood so close to a railway before in her life; her father had never taken them on train journeys, and although she'd lived near the station at her grandfather's place in Plymouth, she had never been permitted on the tracks.

'I think the train's coming.' When he didn't move, she asked urgently, 'Didn't you hear it?'

He seemed unperturbed. 'Of course I heard.'

'Then get off the line.'

'Why do you care what happens to me?' Lyndon demanded, looking round at her. 'Last night, I forced you to pretend to be my wife. I humiliated you in front of my parents. Made you sit on my knee, even sleep in my bed. Yet now you're afraid I may get cut in half by a train?'

'If the train hits you, it could be derailed. Then I might be killed, too.'

The whistle sounded again, louder and somehow more urgent for being substantially closer. There was steam visible now, grey puffing plumes like smoke rising in the air beyond the distant trees and hedges. The train, she guessed, must be nearing the bend.

Lyndon had smiled appreciatively at her catty tone. 'That's

more like it.' He stepped off the track and joined her. 'Stop looking so frantic. You'll enjoy this, I promise.'

Eleanor hurried to open the safety gate, but he caught her by the hand and pulled her back against him.

'Wait,' he whispered in her ear as the train appeared around the bend in the track, rushing towards them in what seemed like a great hiss of steam. 'I need you to trust me.'

'But we're too close. We'll be killed!'

'Trust me,' he repeated, his arms warm and strong about her. 'Don't look at the train, Eleanor. Look at me instead.'

She turned, raising a panicked gaze to his.

'You believe me, don't you?' he asked, his eyes intent on her face.

'Believe what?'

'That I'm sorry,' he said softly. 'Bringing you here, asking you to lie for me ... There's a good reason for it. I can't tell you the whole story yet. But one day you'll understand.'

'Will I?' she whispered, but the words were lost in another shriek from the train's whistle as the locomotive hurtled towards them. She gave a tiny cry, her heart thumping. 'Lyndon!'

Something changed in his face, and he bent his head to kiss her.

Startled, she gripped his shoulders, paralysed by the touch of his mouth against hers, and the blood drummed violently at her temples until she thought she would pass out.

Her first kiss!

The train whooshed past, dragging at her hair and clothes, and the world turned white with steam all around them, enveloping them in its clammy mist ... And then the train had gone, and Lyndon was still kissing her, his arms cradling her tightly.

Eleanor pushed him away, reeling back as though he'd

struck her. 'No,' she said faintly, and heard her father's stern voice in her ear, warning her of the dire consequences of young women who kissed men, or flirted with men, or let themselves be seduced ...

Her foot in the clumsy Wellingtons caught on the iron track, and she tripped, almost tumbling backwards onto the railway.

'Hey, careful.' Lyndon gripped her by the forearm, preventing her from falling. There was a frown in his eyes. 'Calm down, Eleanor. It was only a kiss.'

Only a kiss.

This man has no idea what my life has been like, she thought, and was more determined than ever not to embarrass herself further.

'I know that,' she said, her chin up. 'I just didn't like it, that's all.'

His eyebrows rose. 'I'm sorry.'

'I don't think I want to walk down to the river today.' Her voice was sharp. 'It's cold. I'd like to go back to the house.'

Lyndon considered her for a moment in silence, a muscle jerking in his jaw, then he said grudgingly, 'There's one more thing I want to show you, if you're willing. You said you enjoyed my poetry.'

'I do.'

'Then come and see where it all began.' He held out his hand. 'It's a very special place, and I think you'll like it.'

Chapter Ten

These worms have no care for a girl
With stars in her hair.

– From 'Ground Zero' in *Estuary*

As soon as she followed Mack through the arched doorway into the converted chapel, Taylor was confronted by a glimmering ball of darkness within. She stopped dead, not sure what she was looking at, and felt a rush of malevolence whoosh past her cheek like bad air escaping.

She stood motionless in the chapel doorway, holding her breath, and waited for her erratic heartbeat to return to a steady rhythm.

Something here had triggered a memory.

He dragged his dark, filthy aura about with him, tattered like the torn edges of a cloak, and if she got too close, it would envelop her, too, in its sooty darkness.

Pushing the past aside, she focused on the evidence of her eyes instead. There were three narrow, arched windows along the north-facing wall that bordered the estuary. Two of them held pretty stained-glass windows picturing saints with halos and pale, mournful faces. The middle pane was of clear glass; through it, she could see timeless clumps of bullrushes spearing upwards and the River Camel beyond them, its deep, swift current reflecting a cloudless blue sky.

The low roof of the chapel arched above her, whitewashed and with exposed beams, the space both cheerful and luminous.

So why this horrible sense of foreboding?

Mack was cleaning paintbrushes in the sink, daylight from the large central window bouncing off his white shirt and open, guileless face. The light shimmered playfully about his head, the sound of the running tap somehow soothing to her frazzled nerves.

'Please, come in,' he insisted, turning to find her still hesitating on the threshold. 'What is it? Is something wrong?'

'No, I just ... This was a chapel, you said?'

'That's right.' He glanced up at the wooden beams, and then around the whitewashed walls, seeming to approve of what he saw. 'I believe it was a private chapel once, back in the day, attached to Estuary House.'

'They had their own chapel?'

'That was quite common, as I understand it.' He grinned. 'Probably too far for the lord and lady of the manor to travel into Wadebridge on a Sunday morning, especially when all the servants had to walk there and back, too. The round trip would have taken them hours. So, I imagine they decided to build their own chapel out here at the water's edge.' Mack followed her gaze out of the window towards the river. 'Beautiful, isn't it?'

'Yes, absolutely.' Taylor struggled to sound enthusiastic. The darkness might have been dispelled, but the sense of malevolence remained. 'So, you rent this place from the Chance family? I thought you weren't on good terms with them.'

'I'm not.' Mack gave her a crooked smile and stood the wet brushes in a glass jar to dry. 'The family sold the place years ago to a Mrs Hibbert who lives further along the estuary. And I rent it from her.'

Taylor gazed about the old cottage, trying to dampen

down her sense of horror. But it was no good; she felt nauseated, her nerves prickling with discomfort. The light seemed too bright, and it was already giving her a headache that felt like it would turn into a migraine if she stayed here much longer.

Yet whenever she looked away from the window, the cottage seemed to darken, turning grim, and there was an offensive smell, too, like something rotting under the floorboards or behind a wall. A rat, perhaps. Or maybe it was sewage she could smell. Like the manor house itself, they must have a cesspit here, so far from the town; maybe it was backing up. Not a nice thought.

To her amazement, Mack seemed unaware of the stench. Or perhaps he was so accustomed to it, he no longer noticed.

Cheerfully, he nodded to a narrow stair that led up to an open plan space, where she could see a bed and wardrobe through a low wooden railing.

'Davie sleeps up there, and I take the sofa bed down here. It's small, but we don't need a lot of space. Davie spends most of his time outside anyway. Like right now.' He frowned, glancing out of the window. 'I hope he's not gone far.'

'I'll see if I can find him,' she said quickly.

He began to protest, but Taylor slipped back out into blessed sunshine as though she hadn't heard, unable to stay a moment longer.

There was a narrow track that led from the chapel doorway down to the mud flats that bordered the river, and she hurried along it, struggling to keep her balance as it grew slippery, eventually turning into a slipway that petered out a few feet from the water's edge.

The sense of release whenever it was time for school. Though some days he'd refused to let her leave, locking the front door and slipping the key into his pocket with a mocking smile.

★

She stood on the riverbank for several minutes, her face upturned, watching gulls wheel and soar on black-tipped wings. Dragging fresh air deep into her lungs, she struggled to rid herself of that all-pervasive sense of... she didn't know what.

She couldn't put her finger on why she felt so off balance. But if she'd ever believed in the genius loci, the spirit of a place, this was it. There was something downright *evil* about the chapel. Or maybe some evil act had been done there once, and the memory of it still clung to the walls.

An evil act...

She'd been ten years old when her father had come home drunk and itching for a fight. Her mother had been helping Taylor tidy her bedroom, the two of them giggling and messing about. When he'd stumbled through the front door, not simply mouthing off as usual, but yelling threats and obscenities, her mother had gone pale. Urgently, she'd whispered to Taylor to hide under the bed and not come out, whatever happened.

Those were the last words her mother had ever said to her. Not, 'I love you,' but, 'Don't move. Don't make a sound.'

Taylor stared across the shining estuary to the distant bank through a cloud of dancing midges that was drifting ever closer. The nagging headache was on the brink of becoming a migraine, she realised, shielding her eyes against the sun's glare to watch a ringed plover. The bird dropped in flight towards the water, a distinctive black ring about its neck. Summer plumage, she thought, and lowered her gaze.

Someone on the opposite bank was watching her.

She got the impression of a lone figure, standing straight among the sunlit rushes and water-logged scrub that fringed the mudflats.

Could that be Iris Chance again?

A motorboat coming down the river at speed distracted her, and when she looked back, the figure was gone. Scanning the opposite bank, excitedly hunting, her gaze finally snagged on something. A dead tree, blanched and bare, its withered trunk thrusting up out of the reed marsh like an old woman's arm reaching to the sky.

Disappointment flooded her. Was that what she'd seen? Not Julius's great-aunt, but a *tree*?

'Hello,' someone said hesitantly.

Taylor turned, startled, and looked down.

Young Davie was there, gripping a rod and fishing tackle.

'Hello,' she replied, her head pounding now with the most appalling pain. 'Your dad's up at the cottage; he's been looking for you.' She saw Davie gazing up at her strangely and realised she must be grimacing. With a supreme effort, she gave the boy what she hoped was a reassuring smile. 'Been out fishing?'

'I've been walking up and down, trying to find a good spot to set up my rod.' He paused, looking troubled. 'I didn't know you were here.'

'Your dad invited me down to look at the cottage. It's a cosy spot for the two of you, isn't it? Are you ...?' Her migraine was threatening to overwhelm her, tiny black spots dancing in front of her eyes so she could barely see the boy properly. 'Are you having a good summer so far?'

Davie nodded, but said with an odd inflection, 'It gets a bit lonely sometimes. I'm glad you've come.'

Taylor gave him a smile, trying to breathe away the pain.

The river rolled massively by under the wide blue of the sky, its surface smooth and serene, untroubled by its attendant midges.

In the distance was the dizzyingly high flyover that marked

the small town of Wadebridge, upriver. She could see the flash of sunlight on tiny vehicles crossing back and forth at speed. Downriver, where the estuary gradually widened like a mouth until it met the open sea, was Padstow, and its opposite number on the other bank, the more upmarket seaside town of Rock with its large, sea-facing, detached properties, most of them rumoured to be holiday lets or second homes.

She'd never visited either Padstow or Rock but would like to. She wondered how long it would take to walk to Padstow along the Camel Trail and decided she should try it in a day or two. She had stout walking boots with her, after all. It would be nice to get a sense of how unspoilt the shoreline was along the estuary, and what the view would have looked like from the steam train when it was still running. There were several poems among Lyndon Chance's oeuvre about the old railway; his work wasn't all about the river and the gorgeous Cornish landscape, or his difficult emotional life.

She could walk the Camel Trail for a full day, to Padstow and back, and check in with his poems at each stop.

Like a pilgrimage.

'Hey, you OK? You rushed out like the devil was at your heels.'

She turned at the first words, the hairs rising inexplicably on the back of her neck, not quite recognising the deep voice. But it was only Mack, coming down to the water's edge with a bucket of bait and some fishing rods in the hazy sunlight.

'Sorry, just a touch of migraine. I needed fresh air.'

'Better now?'

'Much,' she lied politely.

'What are you looking at?' Mack asked, peering across the river.

'Nothing. I thought I saw ...' She shook her head, feeling a bit foolish. 'Nothing.'

'Well, there's a boat, you know. If you ever want to row across to the other bank for a proper look at ... nothing.' He was grinning.

'A boat?'

He pointed upriver to where the marshland curved suddenly inward like a treble clef; the faint, water-logged track along the river seemed almost to lead there.

'Follow the shoreline. You'll find a little inlet with a rowboat moored up in it. Big red stripe along the prow. By all means, borrow it.' He paused. 'Though the current's quite strong in the middle. How are your muscles?' When she laughed, looking ruefully at her skinny arms, Mack laughed, too. Was he mirroring her? 'You'll be fine. What are you hoping to find over there, anyway?'

'I was curious to meet Iris, that's all. Julius's great-aunt. I saw her over there, the very first day I came to Estuary House.'

'Right. Do you know where she lives?'

When she shook her head, Mack pointed, and Taylor turned to follow the line of his arm; he seemed to be indicating the heart of the green sunlit reeds opposite them, roughly where the withered tree stood.

'You should be able to pull the boat ashore on that stretch,' he told her, as though this was the easiest thing in the world. 'Keep walking north, and you'll soon see her shack.'

'Shack?' She raised her eyebrows.

'It's more of a hut, really.' He paused. 'Just be careful, OK? Don't expect a warm welcome.'

'Sorry?'

But Mack wasn't listening anymore. He'd turned to follow his son and was picking his way downstream along the boggy track through thin, tangled patches of cord grass and sea arrow.

'Hang on,' he called after the boy, a strained note in his voice. 'Wait for me, Davie. It's not safe.'

Taylor looked back at the withered tree on the opposite bank, trying to fix its location in her memory.

She was determined to row across to the other side as soon as possible and meet the elusive Iris. And maybe ask her opinion on the *Estuary* poems, assuming she had an opinion.

Had Lyndon been a violent man, like her father? Had he been guilty of the terrible crimes the haters and gossip-mongers had accused him of? Nothing had ever stuck, of course, through a lack of evidence, but she knew about the accusations. And many in the literary community still believed them, the poet's reputation marred by that darkness.

'Lyndon Chance would never have done that,' her mother had once told her, shaking her head as she clutched one of his poetry books to her chest. 'No, I refuse to believe it. Nobody could write such beautiful poetry and be that *ugly* inside.'

The truth was out there somewhere though, and perhaps Iris could lead her to it. But did she really want to find out? If Lyndon Chance turned out to be guilty as charged, could she live with that, knowing her mother's idol had been a murderer and a woman hater?

When Taylor glanced over her shoulder a few minutes later, meaning to ask how long it would take to cross the river, the mud flats were empty.

Mack and his son had gone.

Chapter Eleven

A temple flares
In the dusk. A gong shivers.
From out of the earth's farewell
A burnt offering.

– From 'East of Rock' in *Estuary*

'A chapel?' Eleanor stopped dead, staring in disbelief, and shook her head. 'This is what you wanted to show me?'

Lyndon had told her *this* was where he wrote his poetry. Or where it originated, at least. A place of poetic inspiration. He hadn't explained that it was a chapel though, or she wouldn't have come.

Religious buildings were not among her favourite places. She associated them with hurt and shame and her father ...

'Yes, though it's long since disused,' he said calmly, confirming her suspicions. 'No longer a going concern, as they say. So there's no need to fear us being pounced upon by some ogre of a vicar.' When she still refused to budge, he raised his eyebrows, seeming amused by her reluctance. 'What's the matter? It won't tumble down.' He grinned. 'Not while we're in it, at any rate. It's perfectly safe; I must have slept here, oh, dozens of times.'

'You've *slept* here?' Eleanor turned her stare on him, horrified. 'In a place of worship?'

'Does that worry you? Blasphemy?'

'I don't know. Maybe.'

'Trust me, I mean no disrespect by coming down here, Eleanor. Quite the opposite.' He turned his head to glance at the waters of the estuary, just visible through undergrowth on the far side of the chapel, a secretive half-smile on his face. 'This is a special place for me. The old chapel by the river. I hold it dear to my heart.'

She was suspicious. 'I didn't think you believed in that kind of thing.'

'What, religion? God?' He gave a short laugh. 'I'm not sure I do. Or not the kind of god you mean. I believe in … all this.' He gestured to the wilderness about them, the estuary, the grey Cornish skies like granite glowering down at them. 'Nature, the universe, whatever you want to call it. Things beyond our ken.' He nodded. 'This chapel is definitely part of that. It's a link to the divine. And the divine is what I try to reach when I'm writing. Do you understand?'

'Up to a point, yes.'

'Jack Clemo says it better than I can, of course. One of our last religious poets and a true Cornishman.'

She nodded enthusiastically. 'I have one of his books.'

'In that case, I must drive you over to meet him some time. He and Causley are very big on the local poetry scene. Did you know that Jack's blind? And deaf, too.'

She shook her head, shocked and fascinated. 'Really? That must be so hard. How does he write poetry?'

'I believe he dictates some of it to his mother. God knows what she thinks of it all. Jack's very influenced by Yeats and Lawrence, though he likes to say he isn't.' He searched her face. 'Have you read much Yeats?' When she nodded, he asked eagerly, 'What do you make of his work?'

'I like it, especially his later poems. Though all that Crazy Jane stuff leaves me cold. What does any of it mean?'

'Does a poem have to mean something?'

'Yes,' she said bluntly.

He seemed amused by her answer. 'Well, let me show you inside the chapel. There's meaning in a place like this, if you know where to look for it. And then you can see first-hand what kind of thing inspires me to write. Or some of it.'

Secretly enchanted by the way he had spoken about poetry and the divine, Eleanor allowed him to persuade her down the slippery, moss-covered path to the chapel entrance.

The crumbling walls, daubed with patchy whitewash, were half-hidden by thick creepers and tree branches. The arched door and windows proclaimed its earlier life as a chapel, along with the coloured pane of glass glimpsed through a tangle of spiny thorns growing against one wall. She guessed it had not been used as a chapel for some years though; the overgrown path that led to its door spoke of long neglect, and the sunken slate roof showed signs of collapse.

Ahead was a low arched doorway with a thick wooden door, studded and barred like the entrance to a prison. The door had a rusty handle like the ring that goes through a bull's nose, but ornate, the metal moulded in black twists.

Lyndon turned the heavy handle without hesitation and the door swung open with a grating sound.

Stagnant air rushed out of the chapel. A kind of thin, whistling sound came with it, as though the chapel were a stone flute, and the wind was playing on it.

Eleanor forced herself to follow him inside, wishing she was not such a superstitious creature. But a lifetime spent in her father's devout company, constantly warned of the slippery ways of demons and evil spirits who would lead her astray, and being made to study the Holy Bible and pray for her soul morning and evening, had left her on the one hand wary of anything religious and on the other deeply afraid in case it all turned out to be true.

The ceiling was higher than she'd expected from the outside, with rafters coated in the greyish flecks of bird droppings and the occasional feather. The place felt damp and unwelcoming, and smelt musty, too. Most of the old wooden pews were stacked against the wall, but two had been pushed together to create a makeshift bed, with embroidered kneeling cushions taking the place of bedding and a grim-looking eiderdown draped carelessly over the top.

The chapel had a kind of desolate beauty that appealed to her. She could see why Lyndon wrote here, feeling her own imagination stir in response to this place.

There were three stained-glass windows along the wall that faced the estuary, depicting various Biblical scenes. The middle window sported a hole the size of a cricket ball, roughly where a saint's face should have been, obliterated by some accident in the past. The lead had buckled slightly around the breakage, but the rest of the stained-glass window was intact, its colours surprisingly bright given the muted autumnal light outside.

She studied the red robe and bare legs of the man with the missing face. Presumably the patron saint of the chapel, she guessed, judging by the water flowing behind him – obviously intended to be the River Camel – though she didn't know the names of any Cornish saints. Or many saints at all, in fact.

The Brotherhood frowned on saints, in general. Too showy and ostentatious, too prone to theatrical deaths that smacked of egotism rather than humility and hard work.

'What's that sickly sweet smell?' She wrinkled up her nose.

'I'm not sure. Incense, perhaps? I've been known to burn a few sticks in the past, to get into the mood to write. Or perhaps it's something rotting.' Grimacing, he headed for a mess of burnt-down candles and spent matches on a windowsill beneath the stained-glass; there were dirty glasses beside them, too, and an empty wine bottle. 'I'm not very tidy, I'm afraid.'

'Honestly, though, aren't you worried about ...?' Eleanor glanced about herself and shivered. 'Misusing a place like this?'

'I told you, this hasn't been sacred ground for years. Maybe not since the turn of the century. Certainly, it fell out of use as a chapel a long time ago. But there's something about the light and the solitude ...' Lyndon turned on his heel, tilting his head to take in the dusty rafters and the narrow, stained-glass windows. 'It calls to me.'

'You come here to write verse.'

'Sometimes, yes. Especially when I was younger.' He seemed to shake off that contemplative mood, beginning to tidy up. 'Though most recently, I suppose, it's been a place of retreat.' His mouth twisted. 'I come here to escape. To be by myself.'

She felt that tug of natural sympathy again. They were similar in some ways, she couldn't deny it. And now she'd met his parents and seen the house, she could readily understand his need to get away and clear his head.

'I get that. But to sleep here ...'

'Well, I haven't always been alone,' Lyndon said in an odd tone, and abruptly stopped what he was doing, seeming to abandon the task of tidying up as pointless. 'I may seek sanctuary in a chapel, Eleanor. But I'm no saint.' He looked round at her, his gaze moving slowly from her hair to her feet and back again in a way that made her blush. 'In fact, I'm the opposite. More of a sinner, my mother might say.'

Eleanor felt her heart begin to thud and wasn't sure where to look. 'Perhaps we should head back to the house.'

'Wait.' His stare was intense, unnerving. 'I want to show you something. It'll only take a minute.'

'What is it?'

'Please, come here.' He held out his hand, and Eleanor found herself obeying, unable to resist the note in his voice despite knowing she was his captive here. 'Look through the hole in the glass. What do you see?'

She bent slightly and stared out through the halo of cold air where the saint's head had been, not sure what he expected her to say.

'The river,' she said simply.

'It's not just a river, Eleanor. Not to me. That mass of cold silver on its way to the sea … It's the lifeblood flowing through the ancient veins of Cornwall. Constant, too, like the heart's rhythm. It carries all our hopes and dreams away with it.' His voice dropped. 'Beautiful, don't you think?'

She didn't reply, straightening with her eyes on his face.

'And yet dangerous,' he continued, running a hand across his brow. 'So dangerous. The river brings us death as well as life.'

'Lyndon,' she began, but he ignored her.

'I see it in my dreams. It's part of me. I grew up with this river. And I expect I'll die with it, too.' He made a strangled noise under his breath, adding thickly, 'Or by it.'

Eleanor blinked. Her vision was blurred from the sharp, cold air by the river, or maybe there were tears in her eyes. She wasn't sure which. The light in the chapel seemed so pure and hard, she couldn't bear it. It felt as though they were standing in the eye of a storm.

They stared at each other in silence.

Then the door to the chapel flew open, the sound of its violent grating like a thundercrack, and she turned, startled.

A man stood framed in the doorway. His eyes blazed in a dark, familiar face.

'My God!' the man cried hoarsely, and took a hasty step towards them, his gaze devouring her face. 'I didn't believe them when they said ... I thought it was a joke ... But it's true.' His voice choked on the words. 'It's true.'

The man looked exactly like Lyndon.

Eleanor didn't know why she fled, but she had no choice. Something inside her broke and she desperately needed to be outside, to escape the strangeness of the disused chapel and breathe the cool air again.

She hesitated, then chose not to turn towards the River Camel. Not after the way Lyndon had described its deep, rolling waters.

Beautiful but dangerous.

That was the last thing she wanted right now.

Instinctively, she headed back towards the grassy track, catching the echo of raised voices behind her in the chapel. Two men arguing, throwing bitter insults at each other ...

He must have been Lyndon's twin brother.

Oliver Chance.

Seeing him in the doorway, looking so exactly like Lyndon, she had been frightened for a moment. As though he were a ghost or some other supernatural being, which was ridiculous. But that was what came from being raised in a family that believed in the Devil as a real person, stalking the world with horns and a tail, hunting for victims ...

What an idiot she was, running away like that.

Somehow, in her distress, she missed the path Lyndon had

used, finding herself instead in a tangled jumble of overgrown bushes and stunted, misshapen trees. She was stumbling and scrabbling her way through these, low-hanging branches whipping her in the face, when abruptly they fell away, and she realised she had hit the grassy lane at last.

She turned, disorientated and breathless, and almost slammed straight into somebody, swerving at the last moment in shock.

'I say, watch where you're going ...' It was a man, who sounded as surprised and off balance as her. As she staggered sideways, he held out a hand. 'Careful now, you don't want to fall. Is anything the matter? Are you hurt?'

The man was tall and lean, with distinctive reddish-blond hair under a tweed cap; he was wearing long black waders and a fisherman's waxed jacket.

'No, I'm so sorry,' she stammered, her cheeks flaming with embarrassment.

He held a fishing rod in one hand and was carrying two trout in the other; their dead, glassy eyes stared sideways at her, almost accusing.

'Excuse me,' she said awkwardly, and hurried on down the lane, head down, before the stranger could ask for an explanation.

All she could focus on was what had happened back in the chapel.

Oliver Chance hadn't seemed terribly happy at the sight of her, his brother's apparent wife. More shocked and horrified, in fact. And what on earth had he meant by, *I didn't believe them*? What had his parents said about her? She shouldn't let any of this touch her. But Oliver's obvious revulsion had wounded her.

First his parents. Now his brother. It was eating away at her. She wasn't a great beauty, it was true. No doubt they thought her unworthy to marry into the Chance family. But none of that explained their vehement reactions. After all, she was hardly a monster.

What was it that made them all loathe her so much?

Chapter Twelve

The moon shrugs, sometimes shining,
Sometimes dark. Love
Keeps on shovelling dirt, regardless.

— From 'Translation of Light' in *Estuary*

A few days after her visit to Chapel Cottage, Taylor packed her rucksack and walked along the sunny foreshore until she found the red-striped rowboat, more or less exactly where Mack had told her it would be.

An inner-city kid, she wasn't exactly at home on the water. But she'd taken a canoeing course in her first summer at university and felt confident enough to face the short trip across the estuary with equanimity. All the same, she was taken aback by the raw strength of the river currents, which were like nothing she had ever experienced before. She almost turned back as water eddies brutally shoved the small rowboat around in circles, leaving her rowing exhaustedly against the tide, unable to wrest back control.

'For God's sake …'

As the boat spun, she caught a quick dizzying glimpse of someone back on the foreshore watching her.

Mack?

She couldn't raise her hand to acknowledge him, and the watcher didn't wave either, standing motionless under a dark hood pulled far over his face. Unlikely to be Mack, she decided, and turned her focus back to rowing. He didn't strike her as the type to wear a hoodie.

She had to fight to keep the boat on the right heading, rowing furiously until she was past the worst, muscles aching from the unaccustomed exercise. After that, it was simply a question of manoeuvring the boat past island stretches of sand bars, keeping her gaze fixed on the marshy inlets until she saw a reasonably hospitable place to come ashore.

By the time she'd dragged the boat free of the water and straightened, whoever had been watching from the opposite bank had vanished. A tourist, perhaps.

She'd seen plenty of summer visitors on the Camel Trail today, hiking and cycling the scenic route between Padstow and Wadebridge. Though most had been families with young children, and few tourists ever ventured onto the boggy mudflats that fronted the estuary.

Taylor paused a moment to get her breath back, wiping wet, sandy hands on her jeans.

She could see the whole of the cottage from where she was; it was smaller than she'd realised, a low whitewashed building set perilously close to the bank of the river, with a rather charming bell tower above its arched entrance. But the place had been a chapel once, she recalled. No doubt the bell had called the faithful to mass; she wondered if it was still intact, and when it had last been rung for that purpose.

Still, she hadn't enjoyed the awful sensation of foreboding that had forced her to flee the cottage the other day.

It wasn't unusual for her to get 'bad vibes' from places she visited; such head-trips were all part of her irritating sensitivity to people and things. But she'd never experienced anything that visceral before.

The front door of the cottage was invisible from where

she stood, that side of the house shrouded by greenery, and there was no sign of Mack or his son today. But as she stood looking across the estuary, a cloud scudded briefly over the face of the sun, darkening Chapel Cottage so that it looked almost ruined, and for that moment she thought she heard voices on the wind, perhaps even somebody crying.

Then the sun brightened again, and all she could hear was the soft lapping of water at the marshy shore and children's voices raised in play somewhere upstream in the direction of Wadebridge.

Taking a sip from the water bottle strapped to her rucksack, Taylor turned determinedly away from the silky, shining scarf of the river, its mudflats and wading birds, to face the hinterland.

Reeds grew tall and thick in every direction, rustling in the summer breezes that swept in gusts down the widening channel of the estuary as it headed for Padstow and Rock. At first, she could see no obvious path through them. Then, after careful scrutiny, she pinpointed the blanched trunk of a withered tree in the distance and, in a direct line with it, a gap in the bristling army of reeds. That had to be the same withered tree she'd seen from the other bank. The one that Mack had said marked the way to Iris's shack.

Taylor settled her rucksack on her back, crouched to tighten her boot laces, and then made for the gap in the reeds.

Once there, she discovered a rough sort of track, narrow and green-shaded, leading away in the direction Mack had suggested. She spotted several unfamiliar butterflies on her way and stopped to take photos on her phone; someone on Facebook would be bound to know the species and whether they were rare.

After following this path for several minutes, she caught

sight of a dilapidated building ahead – an old wooden hut, or perhaps a summer house – set in the midst of reeds and riotous undergrowth, everything green and sprawling and wild.

Iris's 'shack', presumably.

At her approach, birds rose in alarm with a sound like clapped hands, and she stopped, adjusting the pack on her back and listening carefully before creeping forward a few steps at a time.

This far from the river, there was nothing much to hear, apart from reeds rustling in the breeze. The place had an unearthly quiet about it. Taylor listened intently but heard no voices, no music, no laughter, no footsteps. Only the hut itself, which made a gentle creaking sound from time to time, like an old swing twisting in the wind.

After a moment's uncertainty, Taylor circled the wooden hut or shack, which at least showed signs of being inhabited – there were clothes hanging out to dry on a makeshift line to one side: faded jeans, and two long, tie-dye shirts, along with some grey-looking underwear – and approached what appeared to be the front door.

'Hello?'

There was a small porch with three wooden steps up to it. It housed an assortment of dirty old buckets and tools, and a torn sack marked POTATOES. A handwritten invoice had been stapled to the top of the sack, and though it was largely illegible, she could just make out the words, *I. Chance*.

Emboldened by this, she marched up to the door and knocked. 'Hello, is anybody at home?'

She cleared her throat, and waited, but there was still no sound of anyone stirring inside. All the same, the hair prickled on the back of her neck, and she felt like she was being watched.

'Miss Chance?' she continued. 'I'm a conservationist. My name is Taylor Pierce. I'm staying across the river at Estuary House, doing some research.' Warily, she glanced over her shoulder, but there was nobody in sight. 'I'm sorry to disturb you like this, but I was wondering if I could talk to you about the estuary and ... and about your brother, Lyndon.'

There was still no response.

She turned on her heel and gazed about the place, wondering if Iris was watching her from somewhere among the waist-high reeds. But she couldn't see anyone. Maybe the woman was out walking along the estuary and would soon return.

There was a gravel track, mostly grassed-over, which she guessed must lead towards the main A-road between Wadebridge and Truro. Some of the grass was flattened in one area and showed a dark oily patch where she suspected a vehicle was usually parked. But it was empty at present, and a mass of wild, overgrown grasses and scrub blocked her view of what might lie beyond.

The idea that Iris might own a car intrigued her. Somehow it didn't fit ... And yet she lived so far from civilisation, a car must be essential. Unless Julius picked her up from time to time, which she supposed was also possible.

Could Iris have driven into town for supplies, perhaps?

Unwilling to go back without even leaving a note for this last elusive member of the Chance family, Taylor checked her rucksack and found a pen and notebook. She wrote a note for Iris, including her mobile number – on the off chance that the wilderness-dwelling Iris might possess a phone or have access to one – and tore the sheet from the book.

Too late, she realised there was no letter box.

She tried wedging the note in the doorframe, but it

kept fluttering in the breeze and then dropping out. And it wouldn't quite fit beneath the frame either.

In the end, exasperated, she wondered if she could simply leave the note inside, and rattled the handle, finding the door unlocked.

It swung slowly open.

'Hello, Miss Chance?' she called into the shack, which was a dim and musty-smelling one-storey affair, with only one visible window at the back, shuttered against a view of the estuary. 'I'm sorry, the door wasn't locked. Is anyone in?'

There was a low bed in one corner of the main room, thankfully unoccupied, and some rough furniture. The place had a wood burner with a metal chimney stack pushing through a rough hole in the roof, plus what she decided was a kitchen area, though it only boasted half a bucket of water, a couple of gas rings for cooking, and an assortment of dirty cups and plates heaped on the counter.

There was also a cat, she realised belatedly, spotting a movement out of the corner of her eye.

The cat was black, staring at her malevolently from inside a tatty, newspaper-lined cardboard box beside the bed. A sibling of the skinny black cat that belonged to old Mrs Chance, perhaps?

Taylor crouched, saying softly, 'Hey, you're a cutie; what's your name?' But the cat spat at her furiously, and then darted out of the shack before she could try to stop it. 'Oh no, good kitty! Please come back ...' She straightened, chewing on her lip as she regarded the half-open door. 'I hope you're allowed outside or I'm in big trouble now.'

She had been planning to leave the note in a prominent position, but then decided Iris might not be happy about her trespassing and letting her cat out. It was a disappointment, but maybe she should simply come back another day instead.

As she was backing out, something caught her attention. 'What on earth...?'

The wall behind the low bed – which she hadn't seen properly on first entering, her eyes not having adjusted yet to the darkness – was dotted with torn scraps of paper and picture cards, all pinned or stuck to the wooden wall.

Taylor took a few steps towards the bed and stopped.

There were a few tarot cards pinned up on the wall, overlapping each other. She guessed they'd been taken from several packs, for the cards seemed to have differing design styles, and there were several of the same card by different artists.

Having dabbled with esoteric practices in her teens, Taylor was able to identify most of the cards taken from the Major Arcana – The Lovers, of course, and The Wheel of Fortune, The Tower, The World, The Hanged Man, and The Magician – but she struggled to understand their significance, especially to Iris.

Lyndon Chance had been obsessed with the tarot, of course. But it seemed that obsession had rubbed off on his sister, too...

There were excerpts from poems, too, written out in a confident hand but showing a few crossings-out, as though during the act of composition.

Taylor stiffened, recognising the handwriting.

Excitement made her breathe faster. Could these fragments be from Lyndon Chance's notebooks?

She leant over the low bed, peering closer for confirmation. Sure enough, the torn scraps of lines and stanzas were familiar.

'*Forever, like the sea, like the river,*' she whispered, reading aloud.

She reached out and touched one scrap of notepaper, her

hand trembling. The ink, once black, was faded almost to obliteration by exposure to light and damp over many years.

They appeared to be originals of some of the poems from his final book, *Estuary*, or at least very early drafts of them.

'These should be preserved,' she said out loud, fury rapidly taking the place of excitement. 'Kept under glass in a museum. Catalogued and copied. Not left here to rot.'

The rattle of an old diesel engine drew her round.

'Shit.'

Taylor hurried outside, pulled the door shut behind her, and quickly jumped down from the porch.

A battered white Transit van was already in sight, bumping up and down on the grassy track as it crawled towards her. Behind the wheel was the straggle-haired woman she'd seen in the reeds that day with Julius Chance, though she was now wearing large, round-framed sunglasses that consumed much of her face. Her lips were moving in speech; from the occasional flash of teeth and the way her long-fingered hands clutched the wheel, Taylor guessed she was not happy.

About a hundred yards from the house, the van stopped, though the engine kept running.

Iris Chance leaned over for a moment, as though reaching for something low down in the passenger well. Then she straightened and climbed slowly out of the van.

'I'm so sorry if I'm trespassing,' Taylor began as the elderly woman headed towards her, moving stiffly and with a set expression, and then her voice tailed off into horrified silence.

Iris Chance had a shotgun, and it was pointed right at her heart.

He was careful never to leave marks. Or not where they'd be visible to others. But he always wanted to go further, to hit harder; she'd seen it in his face, a kind of greed for pain, a madness that would take hold of him some nights.

'Wait, don't shoot!' Taylor thrust her hands up in the air in an age-old gesture of surrender. 'I'm a friend of your sister-in-law's,' she added. 'My name is Taylor Pierce, and I'm staying over at Estuary House.'

It was a little white lie. She was hardly a friend of Mrs Chance, and she was camping beside the house rather than staying in it, per se.

But right now, she preferred being a liar to being shot.

Iris stopped, but said nothing, still pointing the long-barrelled gun at her. It was impossible to tell what she was thinking with those sunglasses on, but Taylor got an impression of fury mingled with fear.

Still with her hands in the air, Taylor continued quickly, 'I'm a research student. I'm studying the estuary and its effect on the local inhabitants. I ... I just wondered if I could talk to you about this place, that's all. And maybe about your brother, too? Lyndon Chance wrote about the estuary in his poems. His poetry forms part of my research.'

She thought it best to admit to that straight away. Julius had guessed it, anyway, and Mrs Chance had seemed to know by intuition.

'That's my place, that is. My private place.' Iris did not lower the gun. Her accent was very Cornish, but also clipped and authoritative, like Julius's. 'What the bloody hell were you doing in there?'

'I came to see you. The door was unlocked. I'm sorry, your cat got out. If you like, I can help you find her. Or him.'

Iris dragged off her sunglasses and stared at her intently, as though only just seeing her for the first time. Her face was weather-beaten, with many deep-etched lines about her eyes and mouth, and a constant frown. She had a strong look of her brother.

131

'I know you,' she said, jerking the sunglasses towards Taylor with an aggressive air. 'Don't I?'

'Maybe, yes. You saw me across the river last week. I was with Julius. Your nephew?' Cautiously, Taylor kept her hands in the air. 'You pointed at me. Do you remember?'

Iris gave a kind of grunt. 'Uh, that's right,' she said, and reached up to settle her sunglasses on her white hair, the shotgun barrel wobbling as she did so. It looked like a very old gun but cared-for, the barrel gleaming in the sun. 'You were with Julius. That stupid boy ...' She bared her teeth. 'Thinks he knows better than me what the house wants. What *Lyndon* wants. But he's wrong.'

'What does Lyndon want?' Taylor asked swiftly, and regretted it as soon as she saw Iris's face close up. She glanced over her shoulder at the shack, hoping to distract her. 'It's amazing, this place. Beautiful, but quite lonely, I expect. You live here all year round? It must be cold in the winter.'

'I've got a wood burner.'

'Of course, that makes sense.' Taylor caught sight of a small black, whiskered face watching them from among the reeds. 'Oh look, your cat's over there. I'm sorry she escaped.'

'It's a he.'

'Right.' Taylor hesitated, keeping an eye on that menacing shotgun barrel. 'Should I help you get him back inside?'

Iris threw back her head and laughed. 'You can't make a cat do nothing he don't want to do. Not a damn thing. Like me, see?'

'Yeah, I get that. And I'm very sorry for disturbing you, Miss Chance. I can see now it was a mistake to come here.' She started to edge away, hands still raised. 'I'll leave.'

'Hold on. You were inside, weren't you? In my house.' Iris took another step towards her. 'What were you looking for? What did you *see* in there?'

Taylor thought of the tarot cards she had seen, of the broken Tower, its smashed stones and lightning bolt, the tumbling bodies ...

'Nothing, I swear.'

'Those are *my* things in there. The only things I got left.'

'I'm sorry.'

'Sorry? I'll make you sorry, my girl.'

Another vehicle was coming fast along the grassy track, thumping up and down on the uneven ground. Light flashed off a dark windscreen. Iris blinked and swung to face the approaching car, the barrel of her shotgun jerking up as though about to fire.

It was Julius Chance, racing towards them in his battered green Land Rover.

Chapter Thirteen

Taroc-packed, Greek letters dancing, it sings
This far and no further.

– From 'Hierophant' in Estuary

Eleanor halted in the doorway to the empty dining room and stared in, unsure what to do or where to go. It had to be about six-thirty by now, which she'd been warned was suppertime. Yet nobody seemed to be about, although the grey wolfhound lying in the entrance hall had raised his head to stare at her when she came downstairs, his tail thumping the stone in an uneven rhythm.

On returning from the old chapel and running up to her bedroom, she had seen only Lyndon, who had come in with barely a look in her direction and told her curtly to change for dinner.

Then he'd disappeared and not returned.

So far, they'd been taking their meals in one of the cosy side rooms off the entrance hall. Tonight, she'd been told, they would be sitting down to eat in the formal dining room.

The massive dining table had been laid for six people, though it could easily seat twelve or even fifteen, she guessed. Draped in white linen, the table had been dressed with sparkling glassware, cutlery, and a floral centrepiece, wreathed about with ivy tendrils. The flowers gave off a deep, heady aroma that she didn't recognise, or perhaps the candles lit about the table were scented, she couldn't be sure.

She'd never seen anything so elaborate in her entire life, and the sight was a little intimidating.

There was jazz music playing somewhere in the room, a radio, perhaps, or a record player. She knew it was jazz but was not used to hearing music – her father had never allowed a radio in the house, and once, memorably, had given her the strap for humming the tune to a hymn on a Sunday afternoon. 'Music belongs to the Devil,' he'd snarled at her.

Eleanor stood in the doorway, staring in at the glittering dinner table and listening to the jazz in a kind of dream state ...

Her gaze drifted around the dark, wood-panelled room. Above the sideboard, a large, gilt-framed oil painting portrayed a battlefield scene: men in scarlet uniforms fought and died in thick mud, fallen horses gasped their last, velvety-dark rain clouds swept in above a distant vista of trees.

Eleanor looked up at the painting gloomily. So much death. She doubted she'd be able to swallow a single mouthful of her supper with that thing glowering down at her.

'Waterloo,' a man said from behind her, and she jumped, turning in surprise.

'Sorry?'

It was Gerard, Lyndon's father, smiling at her in a knowing way; he tipped the contents of a whisky tumbler to his lips.

'The great battle that finished off bloody Napoleon and his forces. One of my ancestors fell there, fighting for this country. They say he split a French officer in half before he died. Good man.' His face was flushed, his eyes glassy. 'You like it?'

'Not really.'

135

He laughed, looking her up and down. The word 'insolent' came to her mind. 'Forthright little thing, aren't you? Not like the other one.'

Eleanor was puzzled. 'What other one?'

'Dad,' Lyndon said sharply, appearing out of the shadows at the far end of the corridor that led back to the entrance hall and main stairway.

He had washed his hair, she realised, and donned a fresh white shirt. He was also wearing a tweed jacket and tie. She thought he looked like a country gentleman, a stranger.

He was regarding his father with hostile eyes. 'Drinking already?'

Gerard ignored this barb, merely heading into the dining room to refill his glass from one of the decanters on the sideboard. 'Seen your brother yet?' He sounded almost malicious, though Eleanor couldn't imagine why. 'Oliver and his little tart arrived while you were out. I sent him down to the river after you.'

'He found us.'

Little tart.

Eleanor glanced at his father, frowning, but said nothing. Why did he have to be so rude and disrespectful towards women?

'And the girlfriend?'

'He was alone.'

'Pity.' Gerard sloshed a healthy dose of whisky into his glass and added a splash of soda from the siphon. He was slurring his words, she noticed. 'Quite a dollybird, she is. Can't remember her name, but he said she wants to be a model. Probably make it, as well. A dusky beauty like that. Whatever else you may say about your brother, you can't fault his taste in women.'

'Dad, for God's sake.'

'What?' The bleary eyes slid past his son's angry face to Eleanor. 'Oh, right. Yes, sorry. Forgot about her.'

She looked away.

Gerard came over, and cleared his throat, his smile embarrassed. 'Sorry, my dear. Did I offend you, er ...?'

'Eleanor,' Lyndon supplied irritably.

'Eleanor, that's it. I'm afraid you'll have to forgive me, Eleanor. I'm not as well-educated as my son. Marlborough School, that's as far as I got. Never bothered with Oxford and all that. Books and reading were more my father's line. Lyndon takes after his grandfather, of course, but the apple fell a bit too far from the tree as far as I was concerned. Came back from school and spent the rest of my life here in North Cornwall, tramping the fields with a gun.' He sipped his whisky, studying Eleanor. 'So I never learnt any bloody manners, or so my wife is forever informing me.'

Someone called for Lyndon from outside the dining room, a woman's voice, and he excused himself with a dark look at his father.

'Back in a minute,' he told her. 'Why don't you sit down, Eleanor? Let my father get you a drink.'

'I'm fine with water,' she said, but he'd already gone.

'Water? Don't be ridiculous.' Gerard poured her a glass of white wine and waved her towards one of the seats at the table. 'Go on, pull out a pew. You'll be on my wife's left-hand side, I imagine, with Lyndon opposite. She wants to talk to you.'

Eleanor sat down in the allocated place, feeling queasy. His mother wanted to talk to her? What about?

She wished she had the nerve to state baldly that she was not married to Lyndon. That she barely knew him, in fact. But as much as she dreaded speaking to his mother and possibly giving herself away, the prospect of her father appearing to drag her away was more powerful. Until she had worked out a method of escape from this isolated place without Lyndon coming after her, perhaps in a towering rage, she would have to play his bizarre game.

Though perhaps it wasn't so bizarre, she thought, uneasily aware of how closely Gerard was hanging over her. Lyndon had a reason for pretending to be married, and after his brother's reaction this afternoon, she had a good idea it was not just to avoid his parents' disapproval of them coming down here together.

'Try your wine,' Gerard said cajolingly. 'It's an excellent Burgundy.'

'Maybe later,' she said politely, and reached out to pour herself a glass of water instead from the jug.

'No wine?' His eyes narrowed on her face, and then he smiled. 'In the family way, are you? I suppose you can't stand the taste. Well, Camilla was much the same when she was expecting.' He backed off, giving her a wink. 'Got to look after the succession.'

Eleanor flushed. He still thought she was pregnant, despite their denials.

'No, really, I'm not … We're not …'

'Say no more.' Gerard made his way to the head of the table and sank down into his high-backed seat, lounging there with a wolfish grin. 'I have to admit, I'm impressed with Lyndon. To have snagged you with such speed, I mean. No shilly-shallying about with a long engagement like last time. But then, why would he, with so much at stake?'

She stared, her attention caught. 'Last time?'

'Olly must be sick to his boots, poor lad,' Gerard continued as though he hadn't heard her, 'to see his brother rally like this and beat him to the finishing line.' He put down his whisky, suddenly eyeing her intently. 'Did Lyndon ever tell you about our little bet?'

'Dad!'

Eleanor turned, ridiculously thankful for Lyndon's return. She didn't know what to make of what his father had been saying, and had become distinctly uncomfortable, alone in his company...

Except that Lyndon wasn't alone, she realised with a kind of numb internal shock.

His spitting image stood at his shoulder, accompanied by a tall, immaculately dressed girl in a clinging white dress and matching heels that showed off the honey-dark colour of her skin. Her hair was a cloud of wild and wispy black, clustered about her head. Shockingly, the hemline of her dress was thigh-high, while her only concession to a draughty old house in autumn was a crocheted cardigan slung over bare shoulders.

But Eleanor was more interested in Oliver Chance; she felt her cheeks flush, and her eyes widen as their eyes met for the second time that day.

Oliver.

His brother.

More than that, she thought, staring avidly. *His twin.* It was eerie, looking from one man to the other, and seeing almost no difference in their faces.

If they had been wearing the same clothes, Eleanor doubted whether she could have picked Lyndon out from his brother. Luckily, she already knew he had come down to dinner in a tie and tweed jacket. His brother was dressed more casually in a black sweater and slacks; his hands jiggled in his pockets as he studied her in return, an unfathomable look on his familiar-unfamiliar face.

Lyndon cleared his throat, and his brother stirred.

'You must be Eleanor. I'm sorry if I startled you earlier, down at the chapel.' Oliver came over at once, holding out his hand in a friendly manner. 'I thought for a moment you were someone else, that's all.' They shook hands; his grip was firm, his smile surprisingly open. 'I'm Oliver, Lyndon's brother. We're twins.'

'So I see.'

'And this is Jeannie.'

'Nice to meet you,' said Eleanor politely, getting up to shake hands with the dark-skinned girl, who looked to be about her own age and was really quite beautiful. 'I'm Eleanor.'

Jeannie said, 'Nice to meet you,' in a husky voice. She put a hand up to her thick black halo of hair, just a quick push as though to give it extra bounce. Her dark intelligent eyes skimmed over the bruise on Eleanor's cheek, and then she looked away, seeming embarrassed. 'Hello again, Mr Chance,' she said, addressing Lyndon's father instead. Her mouth curved into a smile. 'Is there anything to drink?'

'Is the Pope Catholic?' Lyndon's father looked delighted. 'But call me Gerard, please. Happy to wet your whistle, dear girl; what's your poison? And how about you, Olly? What will it be tonight? Wine or whisky?' He didn't bother asking Lyndon, Eleanor noticed, who was in any case helping himself to some water.

While the others talked drinks, Eleanor sank down into her seat again, once more feeling out of her depth.

I thought for a moment you were someone else.

That didn't seem very likely, did it? Not after the way Oliver had stared at her earlier, bolt-eyed, choking out some horrified exclamation ... Unless he, too, had been looking at her black eye and wondering if his brother had done it. Though what had Gerard meant when he'd mentioned a 'bet'? Lyndon had interrupted his father before he could elaborate, and she was pretty certain he'd done so deliberately, to stop her learning more.

The clang of a dinner gong sounded somewhere in the distance.

Almost at the same time, Camilla wafted in on a cloud of perfume and hairspray, wearing a pale pink linen suit, her hair set in well-ordered waves as always.

'Olly, my darling.' His mother kissed him on the cheek, barely glancing at Lyndon, who was standing near the diamond-leaded window now, staring out at the thickening dusk. 'I've missed you so dreadfully. I do wish you'd come home to see us more often.' Her hand gripped his shoulder almost convulsively. 'But I'm glad you seem to be settling down at last.' She bestowed an approving smile on Jeannie, and only then seemed to notice that Eleanor was already seated at the table. Her smile became oddly fixed. 'Oh, er, have you been introduced to Lyndon's ... wife?'

The curious, delicate emphasis she placed on the word 'wife' made the hairs prickle on the back of Eleanor's neck.

'Yes, Mother, we've met.'

A significant look seemed to pass between mother and son, and then Oliver came around the table and drew out the chair next to Eleanor's. 'I think this is my seat,' he murmured, sitting down next to her with a flickering smile.

Lyndon sat opposite Eleanor, a grim expression on his face, and Jeannie took her place next to him, with the two parents at either end.

'Well, isn't this lovely?' Camilla said, beaming at them all, and laid her white cloth napkin across her lap.

Lyndon looked at Oliver across the table, unsmiling, and Eleanor shivered, wondering if the two brothers had quarrelled again. If they had, she could only hope it had not been over her. She was embarrassed now about the rash way she'd behaved at the chapel, pushing past Oliver in that hysterical way and simply running off. But at the time she'd felt trapped and under attack, the subject of some cruel, impenetrable joke.

Mrs Barclay came into the room as though on cue, pushing a hostess trolley with warming plates on both levels, the dishes topped with domed metal lids to keep the food hot.

'Ah, Mrs Barclay. I hope you girls like roast chicken.' Camilla played with her rings, of which she wore several on both hands, turning them round and round. 'Not a terribly exciting dinner, maybe. But Mrs Barclay has done her best with what we had in the pantry. I'm afraid we weren't expecting a houseful tonight.' She smiled down the table at Oliver again; Eleanor thought she looked almost desperate to please him. 'Though you're very welcome. I couldn't be more pleased, in fact. All of us together again.'

'Not all of us,' Lyndon said tightly.

There was a short, awkward silence. None of them looked at each other. Gerard knocked back the last of his whisky and then reached for his napkin, shaking it out.

'I'm sorry not to have given you more warning, Mum,' Oliver said calmly. 'But as soon as I got your note, I had to drive over and meet Lyndon's blushing new bride, didn't I?'

Not all of us.

Eleanor wondered fleetingly who could be missing from the table, and then remembered the sister that had been mentioned in passing when she first arrived. Iris?

'There you go, Mrs Chance.' The housekeeper placed a gold-edged white plate in front of her; it contained thin slivers of chicken in a fragrant gravy, artfully arranged. '*Bon appetit.*'

Mrs Chance.

That was supposed to be her, Eleanor realised with a start, and belatedly thanked the woman, aware of Lyndon's sardonic gaze on her face.

She gazed down at her plate, suddenly starving.

Having handed out the chicken, Mrs Barclay then made her way about the table, carefully serving them all one at a time from bowls of steaming vegetables – carrots, broccoli, cauliflower – and then delicate creamy slices of potatoes baked in a dish with cheese on the top. The dinner smelt delicious, and it was all Eleanor could do not to tuck in before the others.

Her father and brother had never adhered to any formal table manners, but she knew it wasn't the done thing in polite circles to eat before everyone had been served, so she sat with her hands in her lap, listening as Oliver described some amusing encounter with a sheep during their moorland drive from Truro.

After the main course, there was a small bowl of tinned fruit topped with a thick, sweet, white concoction his mother told her was 'Cornish clotted cream', followed by a platter of cheese and biscuits.

Simple fare, as Camilla herself acknowledged several times. But Eleanor devoured everything with great enthusiasm. Her father didn't believe in desserts, considering such delights a luxury and sheer wanton extravagance. And he couldn't stomach cheese, so they never had it in the house.

'Shall we play a game after dinner?' Oliver asked as Mrs Barclay was serving them all coffee. He turned to her with a smile. 'Would you like that, Eleanor?'

She stared at him, unsure what he meant by 'a game' or what she was supposed to say in reply. She knew no games, except perhaps card games like Patience, which some of the older ladies at her church sometimes played at gatherings.

'Oliver,' Lyndon said in a kind of warning growl. 'Leave my wife alone, would you?'

His brother ignored him, his gaze still fixed on Eleanor's face. 'Have you ever used a Ouija board?'

The others were all looking at her now, too, she realised. Eleanor took a quick sip of her coffee to mask her nerves. There was something about such intent scrutiny that made her fearful of doing or saying the wrong thing.

'I … I don't know what that is,' she admitted.

'Olly darling, please don't start all that nonsense again.' Camilla gave a theatrical shudder. 'Ghosts and ghouls, and God knows what else. I have no idea why you young people should find it so amusing to commune with the dead.'

Eleanor felt her hand tremble and set her cup back down on its saucer with a jerk. 'Sorry? Did you say … *the dead*?'

'No need to fret, girl, it's only a bit of fun,' Jeannie told her lightly, though she'd barely spoken at all during the meal, and produced a packet of Benson and Hedges 100s from a smooth plastic clutch bag. She placed one of the long, elegant cigarettes between her lips, and at once Gerard leant forward to light it for her. He was rewarded with a smile and a flutter of eyelashes heavily tipped with black mascara. 'Thank you, Gerard.'

'Mum's right,' Lyndon said, addressing Oliver. 'It's not a good idea.'

'Scared?'

Lyndon raised his brows at his brother's taunt. 'Me?' Coolly, he accepted a cigarette from Jeannie, who also offered the packet to her boyfriend and then to Eleanor, too, almost as an afterthought. 'Don't be ridiculous.'

Aware of everyone still watching her, Eleanor took a

cigarette. She waited for Lyndon to lean across and light it for her, even managing a smile for him as he did so.

They were supposed to be married, after all.

But when she tried to emulate Jeannie's husky, 'Thank you,' and her inviting smile, she inhaled too deeply, not being used to smoking, ended up coughing and spluttering, and had to down half a glass of water under their amused eyes. 'Sorry.'

'I say we set up a Ouija board in the den and take our drinks through after coffee.' Oliver turned his head. 'Barkers, is the wood burner going in there?'

'Not *Barkers*, Olly,' his mother muttered, lighting one of her own pink cigarettes with a gold lighter. The packet said *Sobranie Cocktail*. She sucked hard, and then blew smoke furiously out of her nostrils, like a steaming dragon. 'Please say, "Mrs Barclay". For Mummy's sake, yes? How many times do I have to tell you?'

'Sorry, "Mummy",' Oliver replied with an ironic grin.

But Mrs Barclay, clearing away the remains of the cheese platter, threw the young man a warm smile.

It seemed the housekeeper, too, had a soft spot for Oliver.

'Yes,' Mrs Barclay told him, 'the wood burner is lit. I always keep the den warm when you're home. But I'll bring in another basket of logs, shall I? You lot will need plenty of fuel if you're going to spend half the night in there.' The housekeeper laughed when he protested, her look indulgent. 'Oh, I know what you're like, Master Oliver. You and your brother have been the same since you were young. Any excuse to avoid going to bed.'

Eleanor glanced across at Lyndon in silent query, but he shrugged, meeting her eyes with an odd expression.

This awful séance business must be going ahead, she realised.

Suddenly, the coffee tasted lukewarm and bitter, and she stubbed out the smouldering cigarette before she could make more of a fool of herself.

Set up a Ouija board. Commune with the dead.

Her heart thumped unpleasantly. Too much coffee when she wasn't used to it. Or the noxious tobacco fumes, perhaps.

She kept her face carefully blank. But all her father's dire warnings over the years came back to haunt and terrify her, warnings – once laughable, now somehow horribly real – about those who played games with the Devil and got what they deserved.

Chapter Fourteen

Stripped, stunned, sluiced-out, shot – their bones,
Eclipsed by mud, shine
At the flood tide, the full moon of the river.

– From 'Earth Song' in *Estuary*

'What did you think you were doing back there?' Effortlessly, Julius Chance manoeuvred the Land Rover down the narrow, bumpy track through bristling walls of reeds. 'Apart from trespassing once again, that is. All this is Chance land, both sides of the river. And I don't recall ever giving you permission to speak to my great-aunt.'

Iris Chance, though still armed with her shotgun, had not stopped Taylor from running to the car and throwing herself into the passenger seat. She'd merely watched with a sour expression.

Julius had not spoken to his great-aunt. He'd merely raised a hand in greeting, and then thrown the vehicle swiftly into reverse, turning it through one hundred and eighty degrees with a twist of the wheel, and heading back towards the main road.

Out of breath, Taylor shifted in her seat to watch Iris over one shoulder. But the wild-looking woman remained in the same spot, holding the shotgun in a now lax grip, her gaze fixed on the car until they were out of sight.

'Yes, sorry about that, it was an accident,' she told him, facing front again. She'd decided a lie would be better than the truth, though she seemed to be telling rather a lot of lies these days. 'I came across the river to do a little exploring on this side and found her shack. Does she really live there? Why doesn't she live up at the house?'

'Never mind that. You're lucky I happened to see you out in the rowboat earlier. I thought you might have trouble rowing back across. The currents are incredibly dangerous if you're not used to them.' He shot her a look. 'You stole our boat.'

'Your boat?'

'Who on earth did you think it belonged to?'

She opened her mouth to explain about Mack, and then changed her mind. Mack had told her quite explicitly that he and Julius Chance were not friends, so she doubted Julius would be too happy to know she'd been spending time with him and his son.

Mack must have lied to her, she realised. Or not been clear enough. She'd assumed he was saying it was his rowboat and she had permission to take it out. But he hadn't actually used those words.

'I'm sorry,' she said slowly. 'It was a misunderstanding.'

'I see.' Julius slowed as the track ended at a rough crossroads, and then turned right. Ahead, she could see the constant buzz of passing traffic on the A-road. 'So, you're admitting you stole it.'

'I prefer *borrowed*. It's not like I was planning to keep the boat. But whatever. I suppose you intend to frogmarch me to the nearest police station now?'

Having reached the A-road, Julius Chance halted at the stop sign; he was looking round at her rather than at the traffic. He no longer seemed angry.

148

'You don't like me much, do you?' he asked lightly.

Taylor resisted the urge to agree.

Julius added, 'I expect Iris will bring the boat back across at some point. I'll text her later, if you're able to give me a rough idea whereabouts you left it.'

She stared at him. 'Iris has a mobile?'

'My great-aunt may have chosen to retreat from the rest of society, but that doesn't mean she's living in the past.' Julius glanced in the rear-view mirror, but the road there was still empty; he looked down at his hands on the steering wheel, his lashes masking his expression. 'Tell me, exactly how did you know where to find her hideaway?'

'Sheer luck, I guess.' She still judged it wiser not to drag Mack into this mess, even if it made Julius angrier with her. Then added a shot in the dark, 'Plus, something your grandmother said the other day.'

He nodded, taking this without comment. 'I do wonder at your bloody nerve in pinching our boat like that,' he continued after a short silence, 'but no, I won't be accusing you of theft. I do advise you to stay away from my great-aunt in future. As you saw back there, Iris has a gun and a bad temper. Not a healthy combination.'

'I imagine the police would be interested to know that,' Taylor said, wondering if that was the real reason he wasn't planning to press charges. 'I thought she was going to blow my head off.'

'Unlikely.'

'Does she even have a licence for that thing?'

'I have no idea. Probably not.'

She stared at him, astonished. 'This is the south-west, Mr Chance. Not the Wild West.'

His mouth twisting in a grim smile, Julius turned out into the traffic and headed for Wadebridge. She assumed he must be taking her back to Estuary House, but after a moment, he asked, 'Hungry?'

She was hungry actually, she realised. All that exertion with the rowboat, and then getting chased with a gun ...

She'd been scared before, of course. She'd often run and hidden. That's why she agreed to hide that day. Nobody could blame her for that. Except herself.

'Fairly, yes.'

'In that case, let's have lunch in Padstow.' Without waiting for her to agree, he swung right at the roundabout and headed down into Wadebridge. 'My treat,' he added softly, with a swift glance at her face, 'given that you're an impoverished student.'

Taylor was astonished by this offer, and suspicious, too, that he must have some ulterior motive, like a half-hearted attempt at seduction now that threats had not worked. Or maybe he really was concerned she might make an official complaint about his great-aunt threatening her with a shotgun.

She made a show of checking her phone, half-tempted to bite his head off with a snappy refusal.

She'd been on the back foot ever since arriving at Estuary House. This felt like an opportunity to turn things in her favour. Julius was a difficult, prickly man, and she wasn't entirely sure she could trust him to tell her the truth. But he was also the closest she had found to a living relative of Lyndon Chance who might have something coherent to say about the man and his poetry.

'Thank you,' she said with a fake smile. Putting away her phone, she settled back in her seat to enjoy the drive to Padstow, which admittedly she was keen to visit. 'Sounds like a great idea.'

From the knowing look he shot her, Taylor got the

impression he knew exactly what she was thinking and was determined not to play her game.

But she didn't care.

She'd dealt with men like him before, men who always got what they wanted, and it would take more than his skilful, aggressive manoeuvring to get under her skin.

Padstow, a town just along the coast at the mouth of the Camel Estuary, was even more picturesque than her online research had suggested. They wandered together through the seaside resort, through narrow winding streets and along the sunny inner harbour, while Taylor took multiple photos with her camera phone and stopped to peer into quaint old shops. Julius pointed out a few places of interest, and patiently answered questions she asked about the local history of the town. But she often caught him watching her with a speculative gaze, and knew he was trying to work her out.

Julius clearly had suspicions about her research project and just how closely it involved his grandfather. But he never asked her directly and Taylor was careful not to give anything away, aware that her stay on his property would be short-lived indeed if he realised just how intimately her final thesis would seek to connect the estuary with Lyndon Chance's life and work.

They had lunch in a charming French bistro with a red-and-white awning, set a few streets back from the harbour. It boasted free wi-fi, so she rather sneakily took the opportunity to upload all her photographs and notes to the cloud for free, something she'd not been able to do since arriving in Cornwall.

Ravenous, she ordered moules-frites: mussels in a creamy wine sauce, served with crisp golden fries on a side plate.

Julius ordered steak baguette with Dijon mustard and a

green salad, and ate this with his fingers while listening to her talk about the ecology of the Cornish coast, occasionally chiming in with anecdotes about beach cleans and various disappearing species of birds along the estuary, especially rare waders.

'Dessert?' he asked at the end.

'Just coffee will be fine.' She turned to the waiter. 'Black, no sugar. Thank you.'

'Same here.'

While they lingered over their black coffees, Julius finally seemed to unwind a little, even going so far as to describe his earliest memories of his grandfather.

'Lyndon Chance was quite an intimidating man,' he told her, 'and I don't just mean physically. He had a real presence. You always knew when he had walked into a room, because the air almost stilled. Though I suppose with all the dark things that had happened to him...' He glanced out of the window at a passing couple, deep in conversation, his gaze distracted. 'When he passed away, my grandmother shrank into herself. For the first year, she barely ever came out of her room and didn't speak to anyone outside the family. It was awful. And not long after Lyndon died, my father also passed away.'

Lyndon's son, Philip Chance, a fashion photographer and a rather profligate character by all accounts, had dropped dead from a brain aneurysm in his early forties.

That kind of deep, shattering loss left traces on a child, as she knew only too well.

She remembered reading about his mother, too. Alice Chance had been very beautiful in her teens and early twenties, an actress and model who'd given up work to settle at Estuary House with Philip and their son. A lot younger than her husband, she'd eventually grown bored with life in the country and started taking work in London and Hollywood again, absent from the family home for long intervals.

'And your mother?' Taylor asked, though she'd looked through online newspaper archives and knew the basic story.

She didn't want him to think she'd been creepily reading up on his parents; it had merely formed part of her general research into Lyndon Chance and his family.

'She left about a year after Dad died. Moved to the States and remarried. I imagine she's still there, though we haven't stayed in touch.' He shrugged, as though his mother's abandonment meant nothing to him. Taylor recognised that instinctive rejection of pain and understood it only too well. 'Couldn't take the pressure. All that media attention, the usual rubbish about a Chance family curse. Plus, a sense of guilt, perhaps.'

She frowned. 'Guilt?'

'She was partying in London when my father died,' he explained. 'A big photo shoot for Vogue, followed by the usual circus. She called home to say she'd be staying longer than expected, and they had a fight on the phone.' His voice faltered. 'Dad got blind drunk that night. There was never any evidence that it precipitated what happened, but ... my mother blamed herself at the time.'

'How old were you?' Taylor asked softly.

He sipped his coffee, still not looking at her. 'Sixteen.'

'I'm so sorry.'

'I was away at boarding school when she left for the States.' That he considered this an act of betrayal was obvious from his tone, though he passed no comment on it. 'Gran started looking after Estuary House with my great-aunt's help, but Iris ... Well, you've met her. It was obvious my grandmother needed proper help. As soon as I'd graduated from university, I came home for good and started trying to hold the estate together.' He leant on one elbow, staring down into the cup. 'An impossible task, of course. My father had already sold the most valuable land to pay for my mother's plastic surgery and their endless foreign holidays.'

Taylor saw a darkness settle about him as he talked about his parents, a decades-old bitterness in his heart. She knew what it was like to despise a parent; how it could still destroy you even years later, long after they were dead, the sheer weight of all that disillusionment ripping you apart.

'I'm sorry.' On impulse, Taylor reached across to touch his hand, and felt him jerk under the contact.

'Thank you.' Julius looked down at her hand in surprise, even confusion, and she removed it awkwardly. 'Though I shouldn't have said any of that. Forget it, would you?' He cleared his throat, straightening his back. 'How about you, anyway? Any tales of childhood woe to add to the pot?'

'My mother died when I was ten.' She swallowed before adding as quickly as she could, almost in a mumble, 'She was murdered.'

'Oh God, Taylor.' He looked genuinely stricken. 'I ... I don't know what to say. That's appalling, I'm so sorry.'

She said nothing, but stared fixedly at a stain on the table-cloth, the words going round and round in her head as she wished them unsaid. Whatever had possessed her? Outside her occasional therapy sessions, she had never told anyone about her past before.

Abruptly, he knocked back his coffee and stood up. 'I'll pay the bill and we'll head back, shall we?'

As they walked back towards the car park, Taylor spotted a copy of Lyndon Chance's *Estuary* in the window of a second-hand bookshop.

It was the same paperback edition she kept in her rucksack

for easy reference, the same one her mother had annotated and underlined, but in much better condition.

'Oh, look,' she said, forcing a smile.

'What is it?' Julius glanced at the book before saying, 'Oh,' and walking on, his long strides hard to match.

Surprised by this dismissive behaviour, Taylor followed more slowly, catching up with him when he stopped at the corner.

'It's a difficult legacy, I imagine,' she ventured, curious to understand his odd reaction on seeing the book. 'Are you not interested in your grandfather's poetry?'

'I used to be. I read his poetry collections cover to cover when I was a teenager. But now?' Julius continued walking, his face averted. 'I don't have time for poetry anymore, frankly. It's nothing to do with real life.'

She didn't know how to answer that.

They'd reached the sunlit harbour at last, and the place was humming with life: crowds of summer visitors with dogs and small children in tow, painters with fold-up easels and stools, and hoarse-voiced men advertising ferry rides across the narrow channel to Rock or trips up and down the Camel Estuary on a pleasure boat.

Discreetly, Taylor decided to change the subject, pointing out a stunning white catamaran sailing into the harbour.

But she'd seen the sudden yearning in his face at the sight of Lyndon Chance's book in the shop window and didn't believe a word of it.

Chapter Fifteen

You couldn't sleep that night, your brain mercurial,
   rolling the hours
Backwards …

   – From 'Retrograde' in *Estuary*

The Ouija board was every bit as mysterious and unnerving as Eleanor had feared, and yet oddly innocuous, too. It was a large yellow-and-black rectangle, with the alphabet set out in two rows of capital letters across the middle, a row of numbers beneath, one to ten, plus a large black YES and NO opposite each other at the top of the board. At the very bottom, was the word GOODBYE.

But what she found even more frightening than the Ouija board was the utter seriousness of the other three as they took their seats about the table, Lyndon even placing a pad and pencil at his right elbow. 'For noting down messages from the spirit world,' Jeannie explained to her in a whisper.

Oliver's girlfriend seemed excited by the prospect of conjuring the dead, her eyes glowing as she watched the two brothers set up the Ouija board for their séance. But perhaps Jeannie didn't fear the spirit world as she did, Eleanor thought, sitting with her hands in her lap and struggling to suppress her rising sense of panic.

She herself had been brought up to believe in the occult

as something real and dangerous that must be shunned at all costs, for it could cost a sinner his or her soul. As she'd grown older, of course, Eleanor had started to question those beliefs and even distance herself from them, though it was never possible to discard them completely. Her father had seen to that, insisting that she be 'churched' in the claustrophobic fold of the Brotherhood where her continuing obedience could be monitored.

All the same, it was hard not to feel the weight of the situation.

The small room was gloomy, lit only by a table lamp and a few candles that Jeannie had lit and set about the wood burner. A cold wind had sprung up outside, blowing so gustily that the glass rattled in the window frame. As the candle flames flickered, the shadows grew longer, dancing violently about the room. If ever there was a moment for Eleanor to believe in spirits, and the ability of those who had passed over to return and speak to the living, this was it.

Oliver glanced at Eleanor's face, and then poured her a large glass of whisky and soda. 'Here, drink this. You look like you need it.'

'Thank you.'

Eleanor gulped down a large mouthful without thinking, her throat was so dry. It was repulsive. Somehow, she managed to conceal her instinctive recoil, not wanting them to think her gauche and inexperienced. But she took care to take a more measured sip next time, relieved to find the whisky and soda slightly less grim second time round.

'Look, are we ready to start?' Lyndon demanded with a kind of suppressed violence, shooting them both a sharp glance. 'Or are some of us just messing about here?'

'All right, brother mine, keep your hair on.' Oliver murmured.

Jeannie gave a gurgle of laughter.

Picking up the pointer, Lyndon showed it to Eleanor. 'This is called the planchette. It's used to point at the letters and numbers that the spirit wants to spell out to us. We all place our hands on it, and … Well, you'll see how it works.'

Eleanor nodded without speaking. But his outburst had worried and surprised her. They weren't really married, so Lyndon couldn't possibly be jealous of his brother's attention towards her. Could he?

Jeannie patted her hair and lit another cigarette, her air coquettish. 'You haven't done this in months, have you?' she said, addressing Oliver. 'I remember what you told me. Let's hope it doesn't end the same way it did last time …'

'What, with the planchette flying off the table just as we were getting to the interesting part?' Oliver grinned, reaching across Jeannie and helping himself to one of her cigarettes. He offered the packet to Eleanor, who took one with a shy nod of thanks. 'I still say it was Lyndon, pushing the damn thing. Only he pushed a bit too hard.'

'Not true,' Lyndon said.

'Oh right, my mistake. It must have been a very bad-tempered spirit, then.' Oliver lit his own and Eleanor's cigarettes with an elegant silver flip-top lighter. 'Though I'd be pretty bad-tempered, too, if somebody kept dialling me up after I'd passed over, asking me to play a game of Ouija with them. I expect the dead have better things to do than listen to our endless questions about the afterlife. *What's your name?*' Putting on a deep, hoarse voice, Oliver gripped his girlfriend's arm, who shrieked with laughter. '*How did you die? Do you have a message for anyone here?*' He laughed, too, and reached for an ashtray. 'Spooky.'

Despite Oliver's air of mockery, there was a distinct tension in the room, and not just from Lyndon.

Did the two brothers always rub each other up the wrong way, she wondered uneasily, or had they argued recently? Lyndon hadn't mentioned before that he didn't get on well with his twin. But perhaps he didn't like strangers to know about it.

Eleanor could understand that reticence. She was used to smiling politely when asked about her father and brother, never letting on how much she feared and loathed her own flesh and blood. Most people could never appreciate how and why she felt that way, instinctively blaming her instead for being an unnatural sister and daughter.

Eleanor, noting Lyndon's silence and averted face, discovered in herself a bizarre impulse to defend her pretend husband. Especially bizarre given that she was only going along with his pretence under duress. 'But, Oliver,' she pointed out, 'you were the one who suggested we play this game in the first place.'

Oliver stilled, not looking at her but drawing on his cigarette. Already the small room was wreathed in faint blueish-grey smoke.

'Quite right, Mrs Chance, so I did,' Oliver said after a brief pause, and then sat up, the mocking smile falling away. He looked around at them all, a challenge in his eyes. 'Let's start the séance, shall we?'

Mrs Chance.

She was sure she hadn't imagined a flick of bitterness behind those two words. Was Oliver angry about their 'marriage'?

That might explain why Lyndon had been so insistent she pretend to be his wife. Because he knew that Oliver, in particular, would be upset to learn that he'd married, and for some twisted reason Lyndon wanted to press his brother's buttons.

★

'Turn off the lamp,' Lyndon said, and Jeannie, after a quick glance at Oliver, swayed elegantly across the room to snap off the light.

The room was plunged instantly into the most eerie, flickering gloom, illuminated only by the wood burner and Jeannie's scented candles...

Eleanor sat stiffly, hugging her sides, looking at each of their faces. It struck her that she could be in danger here, that these people were essentially strangers to her. She knew their names, but little else. What did she even know about Lyndon, after all, except that he was a poet? What did she know about any of them?

Jeannie and Oliver put two fingers each on the planchette, and then looked expectantly toward Lyndon.

He set down his pencil, took a sip of his drink, and then carefully placed two fingers on the planchette, too. 'Eleanor?' His voice was deep and commanding, allowing her no chance of escape. 'Come on, darling. Your turn now. Fingertips only.'

Resisting the urge to run from the house and never come back, Eleanor focused on that word instead. *Darling*. Even if Lyndon didn't mean it, the way he'd said it was somehow comforting.

'Like this?'

Stretching out her arm, Eleanor set the fingertips of her middle and index fingers on the smooth, yellow planchette, copying what he and the other two were doing exactly.

'Perfect,' Oliver told her, jumping in before Lyndon could reply. He smiled at her lazily. 'You're a natural.'

To keep their hands in that position, they were all leaning into the board together, an enforced intimacy that brought her almost as close to Oliver as she was to Lyndon. She

160

smelt whisky on their breath, and saw a bristling shadow on Oliver's chin where he had not shaved for a day or two; candle flames danced in Jeannie's lively dark eyes, as though she were on fire ...

'We call on you, spirits,' Lyndon spoke loudly, seeming to address the air above them, 'to speak through us, and let us know your will. We are open and receptive. Speak then and guide our hands so we may hear your message.'

The others began to move the planchette in circles with their fingertips, and Eleanor's hand was pulled along with them.

'One, two,' Jeannie counted in a high, breathless voice as their hands revolved clockwise about the board, ending on, 'three!'

The planchette stopped moving.

They waited.

'Is anybody there?' Lyndon closed his eyes, head tipped to one side as though listening. She thought he looked unhappy, shadows playing on his cheek and jaw. 'We are ready and waiting to hear you.' He paused and opened his eyes, but all that could be heard was the crackle of logs in the wood burner and the rising howl of the wind outside, rattling the window. 'Is there anybody in the room with us?'

Abruptly, Eleanor felt a tugging under her fingertips.

The yellow planchette moved up and to the left, with all their fingertips still resting on it, and pointed towards the word YES.

'Yes,' Jeannie repeated aloud, her eyes sparkling with excitement. 'Oh yes, yes!'

'And we have a winner,' Oliver drawled.

'Hush, both of you.' Lyndon stared down at the board, his brows jerking together in a frown. 'We hear you, spirit. Now tell us your name.'

Nothing happened.

Jeannie clucked her tongue with sheer impatience.

'Can you spell your name out to us, spirit, using the Ouija board?' Lyndon asked. 'Let us know who you were in life.'

Still nothing.

Eleanor stiffened when Oliver's warm fingers brushed against hers on the planchette.

Automatically, she glanced his way in surprise and found him gazing at her, mockery in his eyes. She shifted her fingers over, to break contact, and saw his smile broaden. Then he followed, moving his own grip slightly across until he was touching her hand again.

Devious wretch!

She was tempted to kick him under the table but was worried she might hit Jeannie by accident. That would be hard to explain, besides being unfair to his girlfriend, and would probably only amuse Oliver even more.

The planchette slid down the board, much to Jeannie's delight and apparently of its own volition. Its sharp tip pointed to the capital letter E.

'E,' Lyndon said.

The planchette moved again, swinging wildly.

'L,' Jeannie said breathlessly.

Again, Eleanor felt her fingers tugged sideways.

'I,' Lyndon read out.

As it dropped violently to the end of the alphabet, pointing at the letter 'Z', she stared down at the planchette, partially hidden now by their covering hands, and reminded herself that it wasn't moving on its own. One of the other three must be moving it, for it wasn't her.

However much she feared the supernatural was real, she found it hard to believe they had actually managed to summon somebody who had passed over, simply by calling on the spirits. It seemed too easy to be true.

Gradually, the planchette spelt out ELIZABETH, and they stopped while Oliver lit a new cigarette and Lyndon wrote down the spirit's name.

'Elizabeth,' Jeannie repeated in a puzzled tone. She glanced at Oliver. 'Do you know anyone of that name? Anyone who's passed over recently, I mean?'

Oliver shook his head, expressionless.

'All right, let's find out more about our visitor.' Lyndon put his fingers back on the planchette, locking gazes with Eleanor. The intimacy of his stare gave her an odd little quiver inside, as though her tummy had turned over. 'You OK?'

'Of course.'

His brows rose in patent disbelief, but his smile was encouraging. 'Just say if you're not.'

Silently, Eleanor nodded.

He was right not to believe her, of course. She didn't want to appear foolish in front of the others by showing it, but she felt far from comfortable. Still, she took immense pleasure in his concern for her, and the warmth of his finger pressed against hers on the planchette. Lyndon was so very handsome, and when he smiled at her like that, she felt as though she would do anything for him, follow him anywhere ...

Once all four of them had contact with the planchette again, Lyndon breathed in and out several times, and then bent his head as if in prayer. After a short pause, he said in a deep voice, 'Elizabeth, we welcome you to our gathering tonight.' The wind gusted again, rattling the glass in the window frame. 'Are you able to tell us how you died?'

The planchette was still.

Then, it swept up to the word YES.

Lyndon, raising his head to see the answer, gave a slow, understanding nod. He looked round at them all, his face grim. 'Did you die of a sickness, Elizabeth?'

This time, the planchette veered across to the right.

NO.

'Did you die of old age?'

NO.

'Was your death accidental?'

NO.

Lyndon paused, his face unreadable.

Eleanor shivered, wishing she had never agreed to play this game. There was a curious numbness at her back, like a draught had come creeping through the long, dark corridors to stroke her spine with chill fingers. She checked over her shoulder, but the door to the den was still shut fast. Far from being comforted, she thought the small room felt even more claustrophobic, almost tomblike, a sliver of ice embedded in the heart of the great house.

To her right, his gaze fixed on the Ouija board, Oliver drew deep on his cigarette and blew a perfect, shimmering smoke ring that slowly dissipated above his head.

In the velvet smoke haze and flicker of candlelight, Eleanor thought he looked like a shadow image of Lyndon. A demonic version of the man on her other side, intent on his next evil deed. Though it was ridiculous to polarise the two brothers in such black and white terms as good and bad; she did not know either of them well enough to make such a distinction. For all she knew, it was the other way around.

As though aware of her observation, Oliver's gaze swivelled to her face, hard and interrogating, and Eleanor looked swiftly away.

'Elizabeth,' Lyndon asked softly, 'were you murdered?'

For what felt like a full thirty seconds, the planchette sat still beneath their poised fingertips. Then it shot violently to the top left.

YES.

'Oh my God,' Jeannie whispered, her eyes wide.

The wind moaned.

Lyndon took his fingertips off the planchette with slow deliberation. They all looked at him expectantly, but he said nothing.

Instead, he, too, lit a fresh cigarette and offered the packet to Eleanor, who shook her head silently. Dragging on the cigarette, he wrote the word MURDERED under the spirit's name, and then glanced at his twin.

'You want to go on, Oliver?' Lyndon asked, almost as though goading his brother. 'Or would you prefer to call a halt?'

'Oh, I think we should keep going,' Oliver said lightly. 'Find out who the wicked murderer was. Don't you?'

Lyndon's eyebrows rose in a kind of dark, contemptuous flash at this, as though he could think of several reasons why they should stop. But he didn't comment. Instead, he got up and poured himself a generous top-up of whisky, offered the decanter around, and then took his place at the table again.

'Elizabeth, when did you die?' he asked in a deep, sing-song voice. 'Can you give us a year?'

The planchette moved restlessly about the board under their fingertips, and for a moment Eleanor thought nothing would happen. Perhaps whichever of them was secretly directing it to move had tired of their game, or else couldn't decide on a date.

At last, the planchette dropped to the row of black numbers, and began painstakingly pointing at four numbers in turn.

1, 7, 9, 3.

Jeannie gasped, 'The eighteenth century. That's so spooky!'

Oliver gave a short laugh but said nothing.

'Just to be clear, Elizabeth, you're saying you were murdered in the year 1793?' Lyndon asked.

YES.

Again, Eleanor felt that strange coldness on her spine and glanced back, but there was still nothing there. Only smoke haze and the long threat of shadows draped around the doorway.

She shuddered.

'1793.' Lyndon sat frowning for a moment, glanced at them all in turn, and then asked the air, 'Spirit, are you the Lady Elizabeth whose portrait hangs in Estuary House, where we sit tonight?'

YES.

'Who's that?' Jeannie whispered urgently to Oliver. 'Who's the Lady Elizabeth?'

'Hush,' Oliver told her.

'But the spirit said she was *murdered*. Is she one of your ancestors, Olly? What do you know about her?'

'Be quiet, would you?'

Jeannie glared at her boyfriend but fell into a resentful silence.

'What was the name of your killer, Elizabeth?' Lyndon had his eyes closed. 'Can you tell us?'

Another long hesitation.

Then the planchette began to move again, spelling out a word.

'B,' Jeannie said, watching it shift across the board. 'R. O. T. H. E. R.' Her eyes flew wide as the inference became clear. 'Her own *brother*? That's awful. It can't be true.' She looked around at the others. 'Can it?'

Eleanor felt her chest constrict as though a weight were upon it, pressing hard against her heart so she could hardly breathe.

'No,' she whispered, shaking her head without really knowing why.

'Spirit, you have spelled out the word *brother*.' Lyndon looked up at last. He gazed into the dark, into the murky shadows that lay beyond the half-circle of candles and the dying flames of the wood stove. His voice seemed to come from a long way in the distance. 'Are you saying you were murdered by your own brother, my lady?'

YES.

'Oh my God.' Jeannie withdrew her fingers from the planchette and clasped her cheeks. She looked shocked. 'No, no, no. I can't do this anymore. It's not right.'

'Put your hand back on the planchette,' Oliver told her, his tone brutal. 'We're not finished.'

But Jeannie refused, stumbling away from the table. 'Sorry, I need the bathroom,' she whispered, and left the room.

There was a long silence after she'd gone.

'Murder.' Lyndon took a sip of whisky, watching his brother over the rim of the glass. 'A nasty business.'

'Make-believe,' Oliver snapped.

'If that's what you think, why did you choose to continue?'

'To see how far you'd go.'

'Me?' Lyndon looked surprised. 'I don't know what you mean.'

Oliver opened his mouth to reply, and then shut it again, shrugging. He stubbed out his cigarette but lit another one straightaway. Then his restless gaze, which had been roaming about the dark room, shifted to Eleanor's face.

'What do you think, Mrs Chance?' Oliver asked, almost flippant now.

'Of what?'

'This bloody game.' Carelessly, he flicked ash across the board. 'Do you believe in all this nonsense? I mean, is it really the Lady Elizabeth speaking to us from beyond the grave, or one of us moving the planchette?'

'I don't know.'

'*I don't know*,' he mocked her, putting on a breathless voice as though in mimicry. 'Is there anything you do know, *Mrs Chance*? How much do you know about your husband, for instance?'

Eleanor looked away.

'More than is good for you,' Oliver continued relentlessly, 'if that black eye is anything to go by.'

'How dare you?' Lyndon said, a muscle jerking in his cheek. 'Leave my wife out of it. This is between you and me.'

'Oh no, where would be the fun in that? Besides, a third party is always involved in our little spats, brother mine. And very enjoyable that involvement is, too.'

'Not this time.'

'Let's ask the lady first, shall we?' Oliver grinned. 'She might prefer me to you. As they so often have in the past.'

Lyndon jumped up so violently, he knocked his chair over. The table rocked wildly, too, spilling a little whisky. Oliver snatched his cigarette from the ashtray just as the board was knocked askew and the planchette slid to the floor with a startling clatter.

Eleanor hurriedly left the table, putting some distance between herself and the two men before their row could become physical.

'Oh dear, look at the mess, you shouldn't have done that,' Oliver told him, a sneer in his voice. 'Terminating the game before we'd said goodbye to the Lady Elizabeth? That's bad luck. She'll be so angry now, poor lady ghost. Whizzing about the house with nowhere to go ...'

'Get lost,' Lyndon said through his teeth, still breathing hard. But he seemed to have regained some control. Unclenching his fists with a visible effort, he looked round at Eleanor. 'I'm sorry if I frightened you. Are you OK?'

Eleanor managed a nod, though she felt far from OK. 'I ... I think I'll go and find Jeannie,' she said in a small voice, and fled.

It was paralysingly dark in the corridor outside the den. Eleanor stood there a moment, listening to the heavy silence of the house. At least the brothers were not shouting at each other, she thought, unable to hear their voices through the thick door.

She didn't know which way Jeannie had gone, but there was a glimmer of light to her right, so she decided to try that direction, hoping it might lead her back to the entrance hall and the grand stairs. Perhaps if she could find her way upstairs to their bedroom, she could sit and read until Lyndon came to bed. Though it had to be after midnight by now and she was weary enough to sleep.

She groped her way along the wood-panelling at shoulder level, hoping to come across a light switch.

Some tiny sound alerted her that somebody else was in the corridor, near to her. She couldn't hear anyone breathing, but there was a subtle change in the air. A kind of shift as though the temperature had dropped, perhaps because a door had opened somewhere.

She shivered, staring into the darkness.

'Hello?'

Abruptly, she saw a pale shape a few feet ahead, the vague

outline of something that could have been a woman in a long shimmering gown.

She screamed.

Seconds later, the door to the den flew open and the light in the corridor was snapped on.

'Eleanor?' It was Lyndon.

Eleanor blinked, peering over the arm she'd flung up in self-defence.

At least she had not imagined the new arrival.

But it was no ghost.

A flesh and blood woman was standing directly in front of her, rake-thin, with long dark hair hanging wildly about a pinched face with hollowed-out cheeks, wearing a white robe that looked like it ought to belong to a nun.

Eleanor guessed her to be somewhere in her mid-twenties.

'Christ, what the hell are you doing, wandering the house at this hour?' Lyndon demanded of the newcomer. 'I didn't even know you were back.'

'I just got home,' the woman replied coldly.

'Well, a little warning would have been useful. You scared Eleanor half to death.' He put his arm about Eleanor's waist, playing the part of the protective husband as he looked down into her face. 'You look washed-out, darling. Playing Ouija tonight was clearly a bad idea. I'd better take you back to our room.'

'Who ... Who was that?' Eleanor whispered as he led her away, trying to look back over her shoulder. 'She came out of nowhere. I thought she was a ghost.'

'You mean, the murdered Lady Elizabeth come back to haunt us?' Lyndon shook his head, his mouth twisting. 'Nothing so exciting, I'm afraid. That was just my sister, Iris.'

So that was his mysterious sister. Eleanor felt like an idiot for screaming. And from the way Iris had looked at her, his sister probably thought she was an idiot, too.

But really, the way she'd appeared in that long white robe…

'What was she wearing?'

'Her habit. She wears it everywhere. Didn't anyone think to warn you?' He gave a grim smile. 'Iris found God when she was nineteen. Her dearest wish is to take holy orders and become a nun.'

Chapter Sixteen

Like fresh-killed rabbits in a sack, blood-warm.

– From 'Under A Dead Tree' in *Estuary*

Taylor walked up through the dusty formal gardens in the warmth of the early evening and dragged on the old-fashioned bellpull at the front entrance to Estuary House. From that height, she was looking right across the estuary, the river glimpsed in gaps between tree clusters to where armies of thick, greenish-brown reeds bristled along the water's edge. Beyond that she could just see the slanted wooden roof of Iris's shack, and further still, the lush farmlands of North Cornwall rising in steady increments towards the soft, faded, yellow-blue tinge of the horizon.

All wild nature out there.

Here, beside the dry-edged front lawn, in the shadow of the great house, the air was sweet and heavy with the formal scent of climbing jasmine and summer stocks. Mrs Chance's thin black cat sat grooming in the shade, it had barely bothered to lift its head as she'd passed, her trainers crunching on the gravel.

It ought to be idyllic, she thought, aware of her own nagging sense of discomfort. Estuary House was such a far cry from the grim, inner-city tenement blocks where she'd grown up; she could never hope to belong here, breathing this rarefied air of beauty and history and legacy. She would always be a tourist, an outsider. But perhaps for tonight she could pretend this was her world.

Julius opened the door in smart trousers and an open-necked white shirt, looking her over in a way that made her wonder if he disapproved of her dusty blue shorts and vest top, an old cardigan slung about her shoulders.

Had he expected her to dress formally for dinner?

'I'm glad you were able to come,' was all he said though, standing back to allow her inside. 'My grandmother is expecting you. This way.'

She followed him through the large and gloomy entrance hall, its high windows too narrow to admit much light from the evening sunshine, and along an equally gloomy corridor. As before, she tried to peek into any rooms with open doors, but Julius seemed to sense her doing so, turning every time with such a forbidding look that she didn't quite dare stop for a proper nose around.

All the same, she was deeply conscious of a sense of awe – that she was walking where Lyndon Chance had once walked, that he had passed these open doors or entered these mysterious, unoccupied side rooms, that he must have owned at least some of the books upon the many shelves in view, that he had felt love, hate, despair, and unbearable grief here.

It was probably her imagination, but it seemed as though she could feel his presence, as though Lyndon Chance was still somehow at Estuary House. Still lingering in these rooms, unwilling to leave while the mystery of his life remained unsolved.

It was almost as though she could push one of these doors open wider and discover the poet there, perhaps writing furiously at a desk, or standing with his back to her, head bent, book in hand, or gazing out over the estuary, turning over a line in his mind.

The dining room was huge and austere, with a moulded ceiling, wood-panelled walls, and a vast, gilt-framed painting of a battle scene on the wall opposite the door. Waterloo, clearly.

Mrs Chance was already seated at the dinner table but clapped her hands when she saw them. 'You're here, you're here.' She pointed to the high-backed seat beside her. 'Dear child, do join me.'

Julius poured her a glass of wine, handing it to Taylor with a half-smile. 'I'll leave you two to talk. I have to get back to the kitchen.'

Taylor was astonished. 'Are you cooking?'

'Who else?' His gaze flicked to his grandmother's glass, but she didn't seem to have touched her wine, so he replaced the bottle in the chill bucket. 'We have a cleaner who comes in once a week to keep things ticking over. And there's John, who pops in most months to see to the gardens and do a few odd jobs. But otherwise, it's just the two of us. We usually eat in the morning room, but since we have company tonight...'

His brows rose at her surprised expression. 'What? Did you think we had a multitude of servants hiding below stairs, poised to bring us cocktails or prepare five-course meals as soon as we ring for them? I'm afraid the estate is in rather poor health these days, so we've been left to fend for ourselves. Sometimes all we have for supper is beans on toast.'

'I love beans on toast,' Mrs Chance declared.

'I know you do, Gran.' Julius touched her shoulder before leaving the dining room. 'Go easy on the wine, OK?'

'Wait ... Do you need a hand?' Taylor called after him hastily.

But he'd already gone. 'Stay. Talk.' His voice drifted back

to her on a mocking note. 'That's what you're here for, isn't it, Ms Pierce?'

A dying soldier stared down at Taylor from the vast oil painting, his eyes rolled up white, his face a grimace of pain ...

'You met Iris,' Mrs Chance said.

'Yes.' Taylor tried to smile but found her mouth twisting. She wanted to be positive about the poet's eccentric sister, but the memory of a gun barrel pointed at her head wasn't helping. 'Is she really happy living in that ... that shack of hers? It doesn't look very comfortable.'

'Gerard and Oliver built that place years ago,' Mrs Chance remarked, as though this would answer her question. 'It was a storage hut at first. The family were planning to expand things over that side of the river.' She fiddled with her cutlery. 'But they never did, in the end.'

'So Iris chose to move in there instead of living at home?' Taylor was bewildered.

'You don't like her, do you?'

'I didn't say that. We barely spoke, in fact. Iris wasn't very open to having a conversation. Maybe another time.' Taylor frowned. 'Do you mind me asking how you know I'd spoken to Iris?'

'Ah.' Mrs Chance took a cautious sip of wine, and then another; she made an appreciative noise. 'Mmm. That's good. I only have a glass or two when we have company,' she admitted. 'Do you like wine? I was never allowed to drink when I was young. Alcohol, that is. But I made up for it later.' She stared into the distance. 'Everyone did back then. No shame attached to it. We were all drinkers.'

Taylor looked away, thinking of her father, and then picked up her own wine glass and took a deep gulp of the cold, dry white.

'What did you see across the river?' Mrs Chance asked suddenly. 'Does she still keep that filthy old place as a shrine to him?'

Taylor turned to her, astonished and eager. 'Is that what it's meant to be? A shrine to Lyndon Chance?'

'Oh hush.' Mrs Chance put a finger to her lips. 'Hush, hush.'

'I'm sorry, I don't understand.'

'It's her penance,' the old lady whispered. 'Iris believes in doing penance. She always wanted to be a nun, did you know that? Only they wouldn't have her at the convent. And who can blame them?' Mrs Chance tapped her forehead. 'She's not right up here, poor Iris. Never has been.'

Confused, Taylor tried to nudge her back towards the shrine idea. 'Iris has tarot cards pinned to the wall above her bed. Scraps of poems, too. Handwritten. Some of Lyndon's original early drafts, by the look of them. Do you have any idea why she would have done that, Mrs Chance?'

'They'll be Lyndon's.'

'Wait, those were your husband's tarot cards? His own personal pack?' Instantly, Taylor was fascinated, leaning forward on her elbows. 'I don't know much about tarot, I'm afraid. But I know Lyndon believed in all those esoteric practices ... Tarot, astrology, divination.'

'Oh yes, he was a believer.'

'Some of them looked almost apocalyptic. Maybe I was reading the situation wrong. But I got the strangest feeling, just from the way the cards were arranged on the wall, that they were ... Well, telling a story.'

Mrs Chance looked at her sideways out of small, bright eyes, but kept her mouth firmly shut.

'Here we are.' Julius came into the room, set a plate of

hot food in front of his grandmother, and then offered one to Taylor, too.

Lemon-dressed trout with almonds and a side salad. She thanked him politely, aware of her stomach rumbling.

Apart from their recent lunch in Padstow, the majority of her meals since coming to Cornwall had been perfunctory and uninspiring. Bacon, sausages, mushrooms, along with endless tins of beans, bought in Wadebridge and heated over a gas stove outside her tent. Typical camping fare, and hearty enough to keep her energy levels up, but she'd grown weary of it.

Julius disappeared again, returning shortly afterwards with his own plate, and a large bowl of steaming fusilli pasta for them to share.

'Please, eat,' he said, sitting opposite her. 'Don't wait for me.' This was clearly aimed at Taylor, as Mrs Chance had already started eating. Julius poured himself a large glass of wine, then glanced up at her from under dark brows. 'It's thirsty work, cooking.'

'You deserve it. Thank you for this – it looks amazing.' Taylor tasted the trout; it was cooked to perfection, its soft flesh flaking delicately under her fork. 'Tastes amazing, too.'

'No need to sound surprised.' His mouth twisted, but she thought he seemed pleased. 'So, what were you two gossiping about?'

Taylor glanced at Mrs Chance. 'Tarot cards.'

He groaned.

'I take it you don't approve?'

'Doesn't *believe*,' his grandmother muttered between mouthfuls. 'Thinks it's all rubbish. But he doesn't know, does he? He didn't see. He wasn't *there*.'

Julius shot his grandmother an exasperated look. 'Wasn't where, Gran? Didn't see what?'

'She understands.' Mrs Chance jerked her fork towards Taylor and nodded vehemently. 'Ask her.'

Julius looked at Taylor with raised brows. 'Well?'

'Me?' She shook her head, not wanting Julius to think she was keeping secrets from him. 'We were talking about the old days, that's all.'

'Oh, those.' With a dismissive shrug, Julius began to eat. 'Hmm, this is good.'

Taylor wasn't entirely sure what Mrs Chance meant. But she understood one thing; Iris had done something in the past that made her feel she needed to do penance. The tarot cards and scraps of handwritten poems on the wall were part of that. And that was why Iris chose to live across the river from the big house, cut off from civilisation, all alone in the marshy wilderness of the estuary. It was a deliberate act of self-ostracisation.

'Mrs Chance,' she said carefully, 'do you remember the girl that was at the centre of all that trouble, back in the day?'

Mrs Chance had her head bent, trying to capture a cucumber slice with her fork. 'Hmm?'

'What was her name again?' Taylor paused, watching her closely for any reaction. She'd done her research back in London and knew everything that had been reported in the newspapers at the time. But not the inside story, the intimate details to which only family members would be privy. 'You presumably never knew her. Before your time, of course. But did the family ever talk about what happened?'

Silver head bent, focused on her salad, Mrs Chance showed no sign of having heard that either.

But Taylor refused to give up. 'Did Lyndon discuss her with you after you were married, for instance?'

'Don't you get lonely camping on your own, Ms Pierce?' Julius asked, abruptly interrupting this line of questioning.

'After life in the big city, I mean. All this countryside, hardly anyone about, no traffic noise for miles. It must be disorienting.' He studied her face. 'Were you born in London?'

Reluctantly, Taylor gave up trying to winkle information out of Mrs Chance. She wasn't surprised by their reticence, of course. The family had always been notoriously tight-lipped about the affair, anyway. The newspapers had reported the young woman's death as an accidental drowning. But her body had never been found, and some researchers had speculated that a crueller fate had befallen her.

That, she felt sure, was what Mack had been talking about on her very first day at Estuary House.

Murder, mayhem, and so on.

Maybe that was what really drew her to the 'myth' of Lyndon Chance. The dark history that had always driven him and his poetry to extremes.

She knew all about such darkness.

Taylor nodded and then also bent her head over her meal so she wouldn't have to look up and meet those too-intelligent eyes.

'City girl through and through, that's me.' She shovelled in a large mouthful of pasta, adding as she finished it, 'But I'm not entirely alone out here, as foolish townies go. There's Mack and his son, too.'

'Who?'

Too late, Taylor recalled that Mack had specially asked her not to mention him to the Chance family. He'd claimed they didn't see eye to eye. But she couldn't see what harm it would do to admit she'd spoken to him a few times. Not now the cat was out of the bag.

'Mack,' she repeated reluctantly. 'He's down here for the summer with his son.'

Julius looked at her blankly. 'Staying locally?'

'That's right. I thought you knew him.' Disconcerted by his stare, Taylor glanced sideways at Mrs Chance, hoping she would back her up. 'He's renting a little cottage just below the trail, close to the river. A local woman called Mrs Hibbert owns it, I believe.'

'Mrs Hibbert.' His grandmother had stopped eating, a distant look on her face as she repeated slowly, 'Mrs Hibbert.'

Julius glanced at her. 'You know this woman?'

'Yes, indeed. But she's dead now.' Mrs Chance seemed uneasy. 'Mrs Hibbert died … Oh, years and years ago.'

Taylor did not know what to say to this, but decided it was better not to pursue it. There was no point upsetting her host.

'The trout was truly delicious,' she said to Julius, changing the subject with a quick smile. 'Do you enjoy cookery?'

His twisted smile and raised brows told her Julius knew exactly what she was doing. But he played along, describing in a witty, sparing manner his first few attempts at a cheese soufflé while still at university, while his grandmother once again turned her gaze to the macabre battlefield painting above them, an expression akin to fear in her eyes.

Chapter Seventeen

> He bent his chill bow
> And let fly.
> But, oh, the arrow
> Hit her by
> Disaster, by error.

— From 'North Wind' in *Estuary*

As darkness fell over Cornish hills, the car snaked through narrow, high-hedged lanes towards Bodmin on the edge of the high moors. Eleanor clutched her handbag on her lap, risking occasional glances at Lyndon.

'What is it?' Lyndon was braking at another tight bend. 'Nervous about tonight? I thought you wanted to meet other poets.'

'I do,' she agreed. 'But Causley ... He's a legend. And Clemo, too. What's he like?' She didn't wait for a reply, but rushed on eagerly, 'Will they read some of their poems?'

Lyndon laughed. 'I expect so. But tonight's really about Treviathan. It's his new chapbook they're launching, after all.'

'Right, yes.'

'A chapbook is a short pamphlet, rarely more than twenty-odd poems,' he explained carefully after a pause, although she hadn't asked for clarification. 'Poets tend to put them out between longer books. Usually with small presses.'

'I know what a chapbook is.'

'My apologies.' Lyndon gave an odd laugh. 'I'm too used to my mother and sister, I suppose, who know next to nothing about poetry. I keep forgetting it's a passion of yours.'

He wasn't wrong. But the way he emphasised 'passion' made her shiver. Something in his voice . . .

Lyndon braked again as they swung past a commemorative white clock and into the town of Bodmin, passing rows of tall, thin houses with net-covered windows and scrubbed doorsteps. It was nice to be in a town again, she thought, and to see people about.

'Where's this launch taking place?' she asked.

'In a room above a pub.' He caught her surprise, and grinned. 'What did you expect? This is Cornwall.'

He parked the car and they headed uphill on foot to Fore Street. Heads turned as they entered the small, smoky pub where the poetry reading was to take place, and a hush descended. It was nothing like the friendly, crowded pub he'd taken her to in Cirencester; she was the only woman there, Eleanor realised, and hung back, embarrassed.

Lyndon seemed oblivious to her discomfort. 'Come on, let's go upstairs. I'll get you settled first, and then sort out the drinks.'

On the first floor, a long, narrow room, with a performance area under the old-fashioned leaded front windows, had been set with tables and chairs. Men in suits or tweed jackets, and more than a few younger men in shirtsleeves, stood about arguing and laughing. Several had their noses in books, checking something or other, and pointing out lines of poetry to each other with apparent excitement.

One of these men spotted Lyndon coming up the uncovered stairs, and suddenly they were surrounded, men shaking Lyndon's hand and all talking at once.

'I say, old man, where on earth have you been?'

'Back home at last, Chance? Thought you were too good for us now.'

'Congratulations on the new book.'

'What's this we hear about a wife, you sly dog?' Then they saw Eleanor, half-hiding behind Lyndon, and fell silent.

'Gentlemen,' he said, turning to usher her forward, 'may I introduce my wife, Mrs Chance?' His arm came about her waist, drawing her close to him. 'She's a civilised creature and not accustomed to meeting poets. So, none of your wild behaviour, do you hear?'

There was general laughter, and a few sheepish looks. One of his friends pulled out a chair for Eleanor, even dusting it for her with his sleeve, and she sat down, smiling awkwardly up at the young man.

'I won't be long,' Lyndon told her before disappearing down the stairs to buy their drinks.

Eleanor risked a quick glance about the smoke-filled room, trying not to catch anyone's eye, her heart thumping.

'Hello.' One of the tweed-clad men stood directly in front of her, blocking her view. He had slicked-back hair and an easy smile. 'I'm Charles,' he said, and shook her hand. 'Friend of your husband's.'

'Oh.' Eleanor realised who he was. Her breath caught in her throat, and she found it difficult to speak above a whisper. 'You ... You're Mr Causley, aren't you?'

The famous Cornish poet dropped into the wooden seat beside her and leant forward, frowning; no doubt he hadn't heard a word she'd said. Which was not surprising, given the hubbub of busy male conversation in the room.

'I'm sorry, Mrs Chance. I didn't quite catch that.'

'I said, you must be Charles Causley, the poet.' She was

still holding his hand, Eleanor realised, and hurriedly released him.

'For my sins,' he agreed cheerfully.

'It's so nice to meet you.' She dragged her handbag closer on her lap, horribly nervous. 'I ... I very much admire your poetry.' Belatedly, she recalled the book of his poems she'd brought with her, and dragged it out of her bag, stammering, 'In fact, would you be so kind as to sign this for me, Mr Causley?'

'Call me Charles, please,' he said, and took an ink pen from his top pocket. 'Which of my books did you bring? Ah, *Union Street*. A good choice.' He hesitated, his head bent over the book flyleaf, glancing up at her. 'Should I sign it for Mrs Chance or ...?'

'Eleanor,' she said, her cheeks glowing.

For Eleanor, he wrote, and then signed his name with a flourish, dating the signature and adding *Bodmin* afterwards.

'There,' Causley said, handing it back to her with a smile. 'I hope you've been enjoying the poems. I'll be reading a few of those tonight.'

'I love them.'

Still smiling, his gaze rose above her head and changed slightly, becoming almost wary. She wondered why until the poet stood up, nodding. 'And here's your husband. Congratulations, Lyndon.' He stuck out a hand. 'I didn't know you'd got hitched. And to a poetry lover, too.'

'Yes, sorry about that. We tied the knot in London, just a few weeks ago. No time to let anyone know or put a notice in the papers.' Lyndon put down the beers he'd brought up, shook Causley's hand in a friendly fashion, and then glanced about the place. 'Did Jack Clemo make it? My wife would like to meet him.'

'In the corner with his mother. I believe he's planning to give us a poem or two later.'

So there was one other woman here, Eleanor thought thankfully. She peered past them and caught a glimpse of Jack Clemo's mother, a formidable-looking elderly woman in a soft, brown hat pulled down over wavy hair. Lyndon had already told her that Jack Clemo, deaf and blind, needed to have the proceedings 'spelled' out to him on his palm, using a code his mother had devised. Despite being unable either to see or hear, he was still able to write powerful poetry about Cornwall's 'clay pit' country. She admired the man tremendously.

Eleanor would dearly have loved Lyndon to introduce her to Jack Clemo right away. But the evening had already begun, and people were finding their seats.

'Smoke?' Lyndon lit a cigarette for her and handed it across, then sat back to listen.

John Treviathan, the young Bodmin poet who was launching a chapbook, got up to speak first, and for the next two hours Eleanor sat entranced, listening to work that shook and excited her. Lyndon stood up to read two new, unpublished poems, and she had never felt prouder or more special than when he came back to sit beside her while they were all still applauding his work. She was not really his wife, of course. It was all a sham. And yet, just for that moment, their marriage felt real. She even leant across the table to mouth, 'Well done,' and was rewarded with one of Lyndon's rare smiles and his hand briefly covering hers.

There was an interval, with more drinks fetched up from the bar and lively conversation. She was introduced to Jack Clemo at last, a stocky man in a flat cap, and shyly communicated to him, via his mother's code, how much she admired his poetry. Charles Causley asked if she wrote poetry herself, like the late Sylvia Plath had done, and she was almost shocked. 'No,' she told him, but afterwards caught herself wondering why not, and if she ever could. Poetry was still so vast and mysterious to her though, she felt overwhelmed by such a suggestion.

Someone stepped in and took a photograph of them all standing together, the flash dazzling her. 'For the local paper,' he explained.

Then more poets got up to read.

Lazy, blue-grey smoke from pipes and cigarettes wreathed the narrow upstairs room, obscuring the men's clever, intense faces as they read, and the strong local beer made Eleanor's head spin, but she didn't care. She was in love. With poets and poetry, with the musicality and power of it all...

'Ready to go?' Lyndon asked, leaning over her, and Eleanor jerked back to full awareness, staring about herself as the room emptied of people.

'How do you do it?' she asked as they walked back to the car together in the chill night air. 'Write poetry, I mean.'

Lyndon didn't answer for a while. Then, as they reached the car, he said in a sombre voice, 'I can't help but write, I suppose. If I couldn't write, I'd probably die. Being a poet is who I am, Eleanor, first and foremost. Poetry is all I think about, day and night.' He paused, studying her, and his expression changed. 'That, and... *this.*'

He bent his head to kiss her, and she clung onto him as though drowning, her arms about his neck, their bodies pressed together. It was a different kiss from the one they'd shared down at the railway line. This was hungrier, driven by urgent physical desire and the memory of tonight's poetry. And so primitive, too. She could taste beer on his lips, and smell cigarette smoke.

She was kissing Lyndon Chance, she kept thinking dizzily.

She was kissing a great poet whose work would last forever. And not just that.

He wanted her.

And she didn't know how much longer she could resist him.

Eleanor sat curled up in a large armchair in the den a few days after their visit to Bodmin, reading the book of poems by Charles Causley that the poet himself had signed for her. Or trying to read it, for every time she heard the slightest creak or distant sound in the manor house, she would look up, half-expecting the door to open and Lyndon to appear, demanding to know why she was hiding from him.

Though she wasn't hiding from him, of course. Not really.

But Lyndon had looked so gorgeous that morning, his body warm and muscular, lying close beside her in their fairy tale bed, that she had stammered, 'Good morning,' as his waking gaze turned towards her, and had fled to the bathroom.

She'd washed and dressed there as quick as she could, afterwards escaping downstairs rather than returning to their bedroom, afraid to find him still there, waiting for her.

The kisses they'd shared were beginning to work their magic on her; all she could think about was when he might try to take things further, and what sleeping with him might do to her, emotionally. The growing intimacy between them was both wonderful and terrifying. She feared falling in love and getting her heart broken, for she knew Lyndon was only amusing himself with her while he played this bizarre trick on his family.

Men didn't have the same feelings about physical intimacy as women, did they? For him, those incredible kisses had probably represented little more than an idle flirtation.

Swift footsteps in the corridor made her tense, sitting up in sudden flustered agitation and excitement. Had Lyndon finally tracked her down?

The door opened, and Lyndon stood there.

'Well, well, if it isn't Mrs Chance.' He strolled into the room, closing the door behind him. He was wearing an immaculate white roll-neck sweater with dark trousers, and smelt faintly of citrus aftershave, his chin showing signs of a recent shave. He was quite impossibly good-looking, she thought, and felt her hands clench on her book. 'All alone? That's not very kind of your new husband. Aren't newly-weds supposed to spend every waking moment together?'

That was when she realised with a shock who he was and sucked in a thankful breath.

It wasn't Lyndon, but his twin brother, Oliver.

'He … I left him sleeping.'

'Wore him out, did you?' He laughed at her expression. 'No need to blush, Eleanor. Or may I call you Nell? It's not your fault; I know what my brother's like.'

She didn't quite understand what he meant by that, though she could guess, and looked away, biting her lip in embarrassment.

Going to the window, Oliver gazed down towards the estuary for a moment, and then turned to smile at her. 'What's that you're reading?' She showed him the cover of Causley's *Union Street*, and his eyebrows rose steeply. 'Good God, that's a bit erudite for a young bride. But then, you've married a poet, haven't you? Probably best to bone up on his stock-in-trade. Though I feel it's my painful duty to point out, Lyndon won't be too happy to find you reading his rivals.' He met her blank astonishment with a wink. 'Causley. He's a Cornishman, too, you know. Never the twain shall meet, and all that. Or not in the same pub, at least.'

'I've always liked poetry,' she said, a little defensive. 'And actually, Lyndon took me to a poetry reading in a pub the other night. I met Mr Causley there. And Mr Jack Clemo, too. I very much enjoyed Mr Clemo's second collection, *The Map of Clay.*'

'Dearie me.' Oliver flipped open the gold cigarette case he was carrying and held it out to her politely. 'Smoke?'

'No, thank you.'

Taking his time, he lit one for himself and then placed the cigarette case on the windowsill, staring out across the estuary. He stood very still, and smoke wreathed about his head in the silence.

'What's Lyndon told you about me?' Oliver asked suddenly.

'Nothing.'

His dark gaze dropped to hers with a shock. 'You wouldn't be telling me fibs, would you, Mrs Chance?'

'No,' she whispered, 'and please don't call me that.'

His brows drew together. 'Why not?' Oliver searched her face. 'Don't tell me you don't enjoy being married to my brother?'

For a few terrible seconds, Eleanor was tempted to tell Oliver everything. She felt so alone and unsure of herself, and badly needed to confide in someone. But then she imagined how angry Lyndon would be and feared he might even follow through on his threat to tell her father where she was.

'Don't be silly,' she told him, and closed the book of Causley's poems, throwing it aside. 'Maybe that séance the other night unnerved me. All that guff about the murdered Lady Elizabeth. Was it you who moved the planchette?'

'A magician never reveals his secrets.'

'That sounds awfully like a yes.'

'Does it?'

'Perhaps I will have that cigarette, after all.' Eleanor rose, glancing at the gold cigarette case on the windowsill. 'That's lovely. Was it a gift?'

'My mother gave it to me last year.' Oliver flipped it open again, waited until she'd selected a cigarette, and then lit it for her, studying her face. The flame of the lighter danced briefly in his dark eyes. 'A birthday present.'

Her favourite son.

'You and your mother seem very … close.'

Dragging warily on her cigarette, she blew the acrid smoke straight out of her mouth; she didn't want to inhale, unwilling to make a fool of herself again by coughing and spluttering.

'Why do you think I don't live at home anymore? I've never much liked apron strings.' He drew on his own cigarette; his gaze dropped, admiring her figure. 'Well, not on my mother, at any rate.'

Was he flirting with her?

Then she realised with a tiny shock that he might well consider she was the one flirting with him. She had got up out of her seat and asked for a cigarette, hadn't she? And now she was smiling at him …

'Have you listened to the record player yet?' Oliver asked abruptly, turning away without waiting for her reply. 'My father bought it in Truro this summer. It's rather good.'

There was a vinyl record already on the turnstile, with a stylish gold and black label that stated boldly Parlophone. As soon as he switched it on, the turnstile began to spin, and he bent over it, settling the needle into the first groove.

After a brief crackle, a startlingly loud pop song came through the front speaker. It was fast with a strong beat; instinctively, she began tapping her foot.

'Who's the band?' she asked.

Oliver stared at her, an arrested look on his face. 'The Beatles, of course.' He held up the album cover, which showed four young men leaning over a balcony and grinning down at the camera.

'I've never heard of them.'

'Never heard of them?' he repeated slowly.

She'd made another mistake, she realised. Now he was looking almost suspicious; she needed to work harder to appear normal, like any other girl, so nobody realised the strict religious upbringing she'd had.

'We couldn't afford a record player at home.' She studied it admiringly. 'This one looks like it cost a fortune.'

'You don't listen to the radio?'

'I'm afraid not. My father doesn't like music, you see. Or anything modern, really. So we've never had a radio in the house.'

'Good God, he sounds like a complete bore.' He frowned. 'Is that why you married my brother? To escape your dad?'

She blushed, not answering.

His eyes narrowed on her face, no doubt sensing a weakness. 'Where did you two get married, by the way? Which parish? What date?'

'Goodness, what a lot of questions you ask. Though I suppose it's only natural to be curious. Lyndon must have surprised you, turning up here with some unknown woman on his arm.' Eleanor picked up the album cover he'd shown her; she pretended to study it, her head bent, but really trying to hide her hot cheeks from his too-clever gaze. 'The Beatles. What a funny name. I like their music though. Catchy, isn't it?'

He stubbed out his cigarette in the ashtray, and then silently took hers away and extinguished it, too.

'All right ... You don't like me asking questions, Mrs Chance. But do you dance, at least?'

Realising his intention too late, more struck by the internal rhyme he'd used – Chance, dance – she took a hurried step backwards.

'Oh, no. I ... I can't dance.'

'That's OK, I'm a good teacher.'

He took her in his arms, pulling her close, and she held herself stiffly, gazing down at their shoes, now awkwardly toe-to-toe.

Oliver put a finger under her chin and raised it until she was looking at him; his smile was persuasive. 'Relax. You're my sister now. Dancing is allowed.' He released her and headed back to the record player. 'Let's start with the twist.'

Expertly, Oliver scooped up the needle, flipped the record over, and then carefully resettled the needle on the vinyl.

'OK, watch my feet.' Oliver showed her the step, which involved twisting on the spot, his foot grinding back and forth on the stone floor. 'Hips, too.'

Eleanor watched for a moment, and then tucked her hair behind her ears before trying to copy him, a little ungainly at first, but then finding it easier to do than she'd realised.

'Like this?' she asked shyly.

'Yes, but use your shoulders to get more of a twist.' Oliver lifted his shoulders up and down in an exaggerated fashion as he twisted, grinning at her expression, and laughed when she copied that as well. 'That's perfect. You're a natural.'

She was laughing, too, when the door opened and she looked round to find Lyndon there, glaring.

Lyndon went directly to the record player; he jerked the needle off the record and tossed it back onto its cradle.

Oliver swore. 'Be careful with that, would you? You could scratch the record.'

'I don't give a damn.'

Seeing Eleanor poised to flee, Oliver grabbed her arm. 'Oh no, you don't, Mrs Chance. First time I've seen you with a decent smile on your face. Don't let my brother scare you into running away.'

'Get your hands off my wife,' Lyndon snarled.

'Stop it, just stop it, both of you,' Eleanor said sharply, and shook her arm free from Oliver's grasp. She glared at the two brothers. 'What on earth is wrong with you? I'm not a toy for you to fight over. Leave me alone.'

She left the room, her face hot, and stormed blindly down the corridor, tears in her eyes.

Before she'd gone a few feet, a ghostly figure appeared to block her way, all in white, just like the other night after the séance. Except this time it was daylight, and she could clearly see that it was a young woman, not a ghost, dressed as before in her nun's habit, though without a wimple, her hair flowing long and dark over her shoulders.

Hardly the best moment for an introduction, Eleanor thought, hurriedly wiping away her tears with the back of her hand.

'Hello,' she said awkwardly, forcing a smile. 'You must be Iris, is that right?' She stuck out her hand. 'I'm Eleanor, Lyndon's wife.'

'I know who you are.'

Her cold response threw Eleanor, but she kept smiling. 'I was just going to see if there's any breakfast tea left in the pot. Would you care to join me? We could get to know each other.'

Iris looked at her coolly, her face expressionless. Then she walked away, her long white habit swishing over the stone flags. 'Has he told you about Diana yet?'

Eleanor turned to stare after her, bewildered. 'Diana?' she echoed. 'Who's Diana?'

But Iris had already gone.

Chapter Eighteen

The moon came limping past. The stars
Smote it with atomic hammers,
Pulverised it to a prayer.

— From 'Detriment' in *Estuary*

It was coming up to noon when Taylor, who had risen at six and set out along the Camel Trail while the dew was still fresh on the ground, rounded a bend in the path that took the line of the abandoned railway track and saw the grey rise of Estuary House peeping above treetops in the distance.

The familiar sight cheered her.

She wasn't tired; she enjoyed rambling about the country-side, and even such a long walk was hardly challenging in this flat, leisurely stretch between Estuary House and Padstow. But she was thirsty, and her water bottle had run dry about a mile back.

Before she arrived in Cornwall, it had been one of her ambitions to walk the trail with her mother's old paperback of *Estuary* in hand, trying to associate lines in his poem sequence with the picturesque views and local landmarks along the River Camel.

She'd achieved that ambition now, albeit with little success.

One particular section of *Estuary* had felt like the most important and pertinent to her search; she'd highlighted a few lines in neon yellow and scribbled more notes in the margin to accompany her mother's commentary. *Look for the church*, for instance, in response to repeated poetic references to a bell tolling across the estuary, sunlight through stained-glass, saints' faces like 'burnished gold in the darkness' and a 'wild altar among the woods'.

The old chapel, perhaps, now converted to a holiday cottage?

Yet even that wasn't definite, for those lines had been coupled with references to tombs, headstones and bones. And she was fairly certain there was no graveyard at Chapel Cottage, and never had been. Not unless they'd relocated the graves when the place was converted, a possibility that was both gruesome and unlikely.

No, she felt sure a larger church must be what Chance had been thinking of in those lines. Somewhere along the path into Padstow, perhaps, or one of the dour-looking Victorian edifices she'd seen during a brief visit to Wadebridge. Though the church would need to be close to the water, too, according to his descriptions. Which led her back to Chapel Cottage.

Then there were the lines to do with 'bad blood, and a harvest of rotten fruit'. Some academics had speculated that these referred to various tragedies and scandals that had rocked his family over the years. Especially darkly witty, aphoristic poems like, 'River Crossing' or the metaphorical, 'Execution' that mentioned a life lost in the 'seething cold' of the estuary. But where were the specifics? It all seemed so vague and hard to pin down to any one person or event. Yes, some of the lines mentioned the river that had 'drowned many souls' and 'dark hills, peering vengefully down at the unwary traveller', and some poems held place-names that allowed her to pinpoint exact locations.

But that was about the extent of her success.

Taylor drew a deep breath and stopped walking, closing her eyes instead.

It was time she faced the truth.

Despite days spent on the Camel Estuary, exploring the very places where these poems had been written, or which had at least inspired them, she was none the wiser about Lyndon's past. She was every bit as blind to the true meaning of his work as she'd been in the city, studying his poetry in the hushed university library or listening to old recordings of Lyndon Chance, his voice speaking to her alone through headphones while she cycled to and from tutorials, or sat rocking on the tube through long, flashing tunnels.

That hadn't changed her basic stance, however. She still refused to believe the terrible things people accused him of doing.

Maybe that was naïve of her, as the daughter of a murdered woman. But she desperately wanted to prove Lyndon innocent. Firstly, for her mother's sake, who had idolised him. But also to prove to herself that not all men were like her father, if that wasn't too much like something out of her abuse survivor group online chats.

He used to gloat, saying, 'One day, I'll kill you. I'll kill you and hide your body where they'll never find it.' And she'd believed him. She'd known he was capable of anything. Capable of murder.

Someone was whistling, she realised, and opened her eyes again, turning her head to listen.

Chapel Cottage lay a little way to her left, shrouded by glossy, overgrown shrubs and bushes, only the pale flash of its bell tower visible on the slope down towards the water's edge.

She could hear splashing and boyish laughter now, and grinned. It sounded as though young Davie was having a swim in the peaceful shallows near the cottage slipway. And there was that whistling again.

His father, presumably.

Her smile died as she considered how Mack had deceived her the other day. He'd pointed her towards the inlet where the rowboat with the red stripe had been moored, and she'd blithely assumed it must be *his* property, when in fact it belonged to the Chance family. Taking their boat without permission could have destroyed the fragile trust she'd been building up with Julius and his grandmother. She was lucky that Julius had slipped into a mellow mood after rescuing her from Iris and her shotgun, and hadn't sent her packing.

Taylor let herself through the gate and walked down to the cottage. She could just see Davie down at the water's edge, a pale, slender figure in trunks messing about in the shallows. The boy was diving gracefully in and out of the water, surfacing occasionally with some treasure from the murky depths to show his father – a shiny pebble or piece of debris from the river's past.

Mack was standing on the mudflats, baiting a hook.

'Hello,' she said, approaching the pair.

Davie glanced round at her, his expression one of vague disinterest, and then disappeared below the water again.

Mack did not appear to have heard her, focused on the bait, which looked like a wriggling worm or grub of some kind.

Ugh, she thought, and looked away.

An elegant white yacht was sailing by them on the estuary, out in the middle of the current, its ghostly reflection shimmering in the water. Taylor got out her mobile phone and snapped a few quick shots of the yacht. She saw Mack staring and shrugged. 'I take photos of everything,' she told him sheepishly. 'My food, my friends, anything that moves, really.'

He turned back to the fishing rod without saying anything.

Surprised, she hesitated.

Maybe she was unwelcome, and ought to leave.

The boy resurfaced with a gasp, a little further out in the river; he slicked back his dripping hair before shaking himself like a dog, water droplets flying everywhere.

'I know, how about a selfie? You, me and Davie?' She adjusted the app to take a selfie, held up the phone and leant towards him, making sure she got Davie in the shot, too.

'A little higher,' Mack said softly behind her.

Smiling, glad he was at least talking to her now, Taylor tipped the phone up until the whole of the estuary behind them was also in the shot, then took the picture.

Click.

Below them in the water, Davie gave a sudden, sharp cry of pain. Taylor spun, startled. The boy splashed towards them, clutching his bare shoulder.

'I ... I think I've been stung,' he gasped, and fell clumsily onto the bank, half-slipping backwards into the water. 'A ... a wasp.'

His father jumped into the shallows, his jeans instantly soaked up to mid-thigh, and dragged his son back onto the mudflats. Swiftly, he knelt to inspect a small red mark on the boy's shoulder and swore under his breath.

'You're right. It does look like a wasp sting.' He tried to get his son to sit up, but the boy was already gasping for breath. 'Davie? How do you feel? Where's the pain? In your chest?'

Taylor, horrified, recalled Davie telling her that he was allergic to wasp stings.

Davie had collapsed in his father's arms, shuddering. His face was turning an awful colour, and he was struggling to breathe.

Mack swung to her, fear and panic in his face. 'Help me, please.'

'Do you have an epi pen? Up at the cottage, maybe?'

'No ... I ...' He tried shaking his son, but it was clear that Davie was already losing consciousness. 'Breathe, Davie, please try to breathe. It's going to be OK. You hear me? Dad's going to fix this.'

Swiftly, she checked her phone, but there was no signal. They were in the middle of nowhere here, close to the open sea, and there were many network blind spots along the estuary.

She swore under her breath. 'No signal. What about yours? Mack? Where's your mobile phone? We need to call an ambulance.'

But he didn't seem to be listening.

'Look, I'll get my rucksack,' she said, struck by a sudden idea. 'I left it by the cottage. I've got an epi pen in my first aid kit.' She turned and ran. 'Two minutes, OK?'

Taylor raced up the uneven, overgrown path back to Chapel Cottage. Her rucksack was still where she'd left it on the stone slab outside the cottage entrance. Seizing it, she spun around and ran back to the shore while scrabbling inside for the epi pen in the first aid kit. But her mind was running as fast as her feet.

If only she'd found a weapon that night, a heavy weight of some kind, she might perhaps have hit her father, managed to beat him off. But she'd hidden instead. 'Don't move. Don't make a sound.' She'd squeezed into that dark narrow space under the bed like the coward she was, both hands clamped over her ears.

When she got back to the mudflats, panting and sweaty, there was no sign of Mack or his son where she'd left them.

'Mack?'

She trod out gingerly across the oozing mud, gasping for breath, the epi pen in her hand, and stared wildly up and down the foreshore and across the water, which was empty of boats now. Even the graceful yacht was almost out of sight.

'Mack? I've got it,' she called desperately, 'I've got the epi pen.'

There was no reply.

Where the hell had they gone? Was it possible that Davie made a miraculous recovery in the two or three minutes she'd been gone?

Or perhaps – which seemed more likely – Mack had carried him further along the shore to the thick reedbeds where the rowboat had once been tethered. He might have seen someone hiking there and gone to fetch help. Or maybe he'd thought of rowing Davie down to Wadebridge and a doctor, though he must have known such a journey would take far too long. An allergic reaction needed to be treated in minutes. Seconds, preferably.

She walked a few minutes in that direction, still calling, 'Mack? Davie?' at intervals but saw nobody.

Hurriedly retracing her steps, Taylor put away the epi pen, returned to the mudflats where she had last seen them, and stared out across the flat waters. The estuary seemed to mock her with its loneliness and silence, nothing but the distant cries of seabirds to be heard.

Perhaps the situation hadn't been as dire as she'd feared. They must have somehow got past her, maybe taking a different route through the scrubland, and had returned home to the cottage now.

She had to check. Even if Mack didn't want her around anymore, she had to know for sure that the little boy was OK.

Trudging back up the slipway to Chapel Cottage, a gloomy shadow seemed to move across the face of the sun, and she raised her head to find Julius Chance there, blocking her path.

'What are you doing down here?' she asked, surprised.

His brows rose. 'I could ask you the same thing. This is Chance land, in case you weren't aware of it.'

'Maybe once upon a time. Now it belongs to Mrs Hibbert.'

'Not her again,' he said wearily, thrusting both hands into his jean pockets. 'I told you, I never heard of the woman.'

'OK.' She waved a hand impatiently. 'Look, it doesn't matter. Have you seen Mack? The guy I told you about at dinner, the one who's renting Chapel Cottage for the summer? This is urgent. His boy had an allergic reaction, and I ran to get him an epi pen, except he's vanished. No sign of either of them anywhere.'

Julius was staring at her strangely. '*Chapel* Cottage?'

'Yes, you just passed it.'

'There's no cottage on the foreshore.' He frowned. 'Not this close to the river, at least. It wouldn't be safe.'

'Please don't be ridiculous. It's an old chapel converted into a holiday let, you can't have missed it.' She hurried past him, pointing extravagantly up the path. 'Look, there it is. Chapel Cottage.' Except all she could see ahead was a tangle of overgrown bushes and trees, and above them, a dirty, ramshackle bell tower. 'Oh.'

Falteringly, she took a few more steps until she was past the bushes and could see the building properly.

The pretty, renovated cottage with its terracotta urns of flowers and welcoming, sunlit porch was gone.

In its place, was the shell of an ancient, ruined chapel. Its moss-covered roof was half caved-in, its riverfront walls a mouldy grey from repeated floodings, and there was a patchwork of holes in the chapel's dull stained-glass windows.

'Are you OK?' Julius caught up with her. 'Hang on, you said there was a boy. An allergic reaction?'

'Davie. He was stung by a wasp. Couldn't breathe.' She moved away from him, heading doggedly for the chapel's entrance. 'Mack? Davie?' She was raising her voice, just in case they were inside and could hear her. And yet, the rational part of her mind was telling her not to be an idiot. 'Where are you? I've got the epi pen if you still need it.'

Reaching the doorway, she peered inside at damp, foul-smelling walls and a muddy interior, the whole place cluttered with what looked like flood debris. Where she'd stood in the kitchen area and looked out across the estuary was a jumble of broken, water-stained pews and a row of narrow, stained-glass windows with missing panes and peeling lead.

It made no sense.

'I don't understand,' she whispered as Julius joined her in the doorway. 'There was a ... a kitchen area.' She pointed. 'I stood right there, talking to Mack. He's been staying here all summer. He and his son, Davie.'

'Taylor, nobody's been living here,' Julius said firmly. 'Nobody's ever lived here. The place is derelict.'

'I must have taken the wrong path, then.' She blinked, her head buzzing as she tried to make sense of what she was seeing. 'Is there another chapel? A little further along the shore, perhaps?'

Silently, he shook his head.

Taking a few steps back, Taylor stared up at the sagging

roof and crumbling bell tower, and then turned to study the slipway that led down to the shadowy estuary, its waters turning slowly sombre as the sun began to set.

'But I watched while Davie swam in the shallows,' she said, looking at the mudflats. 'Less than an hour ago.' She looked back inside the ruined building and felt a sudden chill; she drew her jacket closer. 'This is impossible.'

'Come inside and see for yourself,' Julius said, holding out a hand.

'But Mack—'

'I don't know any Mack.'

'He's a real person,' Taylor told him angrily. 'So you can stop looking at me like that. His name is Robert Mackenzie. But he prefers Mack.'

'Robert Mackenzie.' He was frowning.

'I met him on my first day here. We've talked several times. I like him.' She swallowed, turning away. '*Liked* him.'

'OK, I believe you. But he's not here now, is he? So why don't you step inside and take a proper look around the chapel?' His tone was persuasive, but she didn't respond. 'What is it? Are you scared?'

'No.' Taylor glared at him.

'Worried in case the ceiling falls on your head, then?' Julius shot an ironic glance indoors. 'I think it's safe enough so long as we don't disturb anything structural.'

'I remember smelling something in there,' she whispered, standing on the threshold, her heart thumping. 'It was a really bad smell.'

'I'm not surprised. The river must have washed all sorts of muck in here over the years.'

She was surprised. 'You've been here before?'

'Of course. I told you, this place belongs to my family. I often played here as a boy, despite being warned not to by my grandmother. Came down a few times in my teens, too.' He grinned at her expression. 'It was somewhere to listen to music and smoke the demon weed where my parents wouldn't catch me.'

Taylor let out a long-held breath, and then nodded, trying to calm down. Whatever she had or hadn't seen in here, none of it was his fault. And if she kept pushing, he might start to think she was crazy.

'Were you a rebellious teenager? I can't imagine that.'

His smile twisted. 'You have no idea.' Standing back, he gestured for her to explore the tiny chapel. 'After you.'

Slowly, Taylor picked her way down what was left of the central aisle, staring in disbelief at the wrecked spines of pews, wads of damp rubbish, and other cobwebby debris lodged in a tide of thick black mud peppered with stones and shingle.

'The river did all this?'

'I'm afraid so,' he agreed, watching her. 'There used to be flood defences in the old days, back when the chapel was in regular use. Mud banks, and so on. The defences were pretty intact up until the fifties or sixties. But then the river levels started rising, and it all just washed away over the years. Now, whenever the river floods, I have to walk down here to check it's still standing. I'm always amazed it hasn't tumbled down completely. But it's a tenacious old building, I'll give it that.' Julius glanced towards the altar end, where a low dais still housed a stone slab, now askew and half-buried in mud. 'And rather beautiful in its own way.'

She turned to look around. A faint light shone through the stained-glass that remained in the central window, a few shards of yellow and red and blue leaded glass, much of it cracked, the whole structure riddled with holes. Cool air blew through the gaps, and she caught glimpses of the silvery river rolling along on its way to the sea, inexorable.

Taylor remembered looking out across the estuary from this window, watching Davie's fair head bob up and down in the water. She thought of Mack chatting and laughing with her. And yet it had never happened.

Mack didn't exist, she told herself, and caught her breath in shock.

The body had seemed so unreal afterwards. Limp and staring. She had stood over it, and then crashed out of there, running and running as hard and fast as she could so her heart would burst and she, too, could escape into darkness, like her mother...

Had she stood here, amidst the mess and chaos of a disused chapel, and imagined the whole thing? Imagined Mack and Davie? All their conversations together? Davie's wasp sting, too, and his rattling breath that had sent her dashing back up here to grab her bag and the epi pen? Had she even imagined the terrible smell that had made her visits here so short and unbearable?

She could smell nothing in the chapel now except damp wood and stone, and fresh salty air.

'You're sure nobody's ever lived here?' Taylor whispered, almost afraid to raise her voice. 'It's never been renovated? Never used as a home?'

'Absolutely not.' Julius turned on his heel to study the rotting walls and beamed ceiling. 'Though my grandfather used to come down here to work on his poems; he called it his "sacred space". He never permitted anyone to redecorate or move a single pew, even though it must have been in quite a state by the time he died. I suppose he thought fixing the place up would spoil it in some way.'

'I didn't know that.'

'Given his status as a poet, the family should probably have made more of an effort to keep the chapel in reasonable condition after his death. Renewed the flood barriers, mended the stained-glass, cleared the path of all that undergrowth.' He was frowning, an odd note in his voice. 'My grandmother was always against it though, as I recall; I assumed she didn't want to waste the money.'

His mobile phone buzzed. Groaning, Julius dragged it out. The screen gleamed bright in the dim space.

'Gran.' He threw her an apologetic look. 'It must be important; she hardly ever uses the phone. Sorry, do you mind if I answer this? I'll have to go outside for better reception.'

Julius strode outside, heading a few feet down the slipway before stopping. She caught a flash of him through one of the broken panes of stained-glass, and heard him on the phone, that gentle, endlessly patient voice he always used with his grandmother.

Frowning, she checked her own phone. Sure enough, she had one bar now. Down at the river, there'd been no mobile signal.

Or had she simply imagined that, too? Like Mack, Davie, the allergic reaction ... This chapel as a renovated cottage, when it had never been anything but a damp and derelict wreck.

It had all seemed so real to her.

She looked up at the central stained-glass window in its stone arch, studying the broken saints and fragments of holy scenes. The window must have been lovely once, back in the days when Lyndon Chance considered the chapel a 'sacred space' for writing. Now it just looked sad and lonely, like the rest of this shambolic place.

She was standing on a broken floor slab. It tipped to one side under her weight, and she rocked on it thoughtfully.

Without warning, the stone gave way, sinking several

feet below ground level as though the earth beneath it had subsided.

With a cry, she tumbled into a deep hole or crevasse under the floor, finding herself on her knees in mud and rubble, staring up at the stained-glass window from a crooked angle.

A saint stared back at her, floating, bodiless, on empty space.

'Ouch.'

Painfully, Taylor began to struggle back to her feet, groping around in a pit of damp, stony mud for a purchase. That was when she realised she was holding something in her hand.

'Oh my God...'

Something long buried under that cracked stone. Something that must have been exposed when the earth subsided under her feet.

It was a bone.

A smooth, mud-covered, but undeniably human bone.

Chapter Nineteen

Venus sleeps on the hot coals of the heart,
Smouldering.

— From 'Exaltation' in *Estuary*

Eleanor fastened her stockings before wriggling into the stylish pink twinset, complete with matching skirt, that she'd borrowed from Mrs Chance. Lyndon had fabricated some tale of missing luggage to explain her meagre hoard of clothes, so his mother had reluctantly offered the use of her wardrobe, since they had similar builds.

It had been such a luxury to take her time in the bath, more accustomed to squeezing in a wash between household chores or Bible studies, or their never-ending visits to other members of the Brotherhood, where she would sit with the women of the family while her father 'ministered' to the men in a separate room.

The water had been hot, too, not teeth-chatteringly cold, and she'd even thrown in a handful of Mrs Chance's lavender-scented bath salts.

And now she was alone in the bedroom, Lyndon having left her there soon after lunch, an odd smile on his face.

'Dad's asked me to take a walk along the river with him,' Lyndon had said with an air of excitement, grabbing his jacket on his way out. 'Wish me luck.'

'Good luck,' she'd replied automatically, and had only thought to ask him why once he'd gone.

Perched on the window seat, Eleanor rummaged for a comb among her few possessions and was just dragging it through her damp hair, tugging on the tangles, when she caught sight of a dark head in the formal gardens below, and realised it was Oliver.

She shrank back out of sight, and then realised how foolish that was; it was unlikely his brother would spot her from that distance.

Besides which, Oliver was turned the other way, standing at the top of a flight of mossed stone steps, gazing down through winter trees towards the estuary. The collar on his dark leather jacket was turned up against the cold, his head tilted back as though he were trying to see the opposite bank of the river, which might just be possible from that vantage point.

Watching him warily, she found herself half-smiling, and caught her breath at the realisation that she found Oliver attractive.

And yet, why shouldn't she?

Eleanor laughed at herself, getting up to return the comb to her dressing table. 'Idiot.'

She lingered there, studying herself in the mirror, not sure whether to be pleased by what she saw. For a few seconds there, she'd believed Lyndon's lie that they were married, man and wife, and had berated herself for fancying his brother. And she did look the part of a young wife, dressed in his mother's smart, feminine clothes, the weight of a gold family wedding ring on her finger. But there was a faint flush in her cheeks and a wild look about her eyes that must tell everyone who looked at her how innocent she was ...

She was still a virgin. That fact surprised her. Lyndon

could have taken advantage any time he chose since bringing her here. They were sharing a bed, for goodness' sake.

Yet he hadn't seduced her.

Perhaps Lyndon didn't find her attractive. Early on, she'd assumed he must do, asking her to travel down here to Cornwall with him, and later, to pretend to be his wife. He had stared at her so hard that first evening in Cirencester, his eyes narrowed against the pub's thick smoke haze, and she had thought ...

Well, she had thought exactly what her father had drummed into her head for years. But if there was any lust in Lyndon's heart, it was well under control. And as for having his way with her ... No such luck.

After the poetry reading, she'd been convinced that Lyndon would try it on with her. But when they'd gone to bed that evening, he'd merely said a soft, 'Goodnight,' and rolled away from her as usual, a cold, stodgy pillow between their bodies to keep them apart.

Was she disappointed?

A little, yes. She knew it was dreadfully sinful, given that their marriage was a sham, but ever since her first night in Estuary House, she'd been wondering what it would feel like to be Mrs Chance for real. To have him love her as a husband.

Lyndon had returned from his walk along the river and was standing at the bottom of the flight of garden steps, glaring up at Oliver. Their father was nowhere to be seen. But she could hear raised voices; the two men were arguing, Lyndon's face dark with fury.

Eleanor unlatched the old-fashioned window as quietly as possible and pushed it open a crack, leaning close to hear what was being said.

'Does she know?' Oliver asked, his voice indistinct, for his back was still towards the house.

'Know what?'

'Why you married her? Why you trapped her here? Does Eleanor know the real reason behind this whirlwind romance of yours?'

'You don't have a clue what you're talking about,' Lyndon said bitingly. 'But if you keep pushing, so help me, God—'

'What? You'll thump me? Beat me to a pulp? Defend her honour?' Oliver was laughing. 'You don't have it in you. You're a failure, Lyndon. I've seen the way she looks at you. You haven't consummated the marriage, have you?'

'Leave Eleanor out of this.'

'It's not just Eleanor though, is it? You were the same with Diana. She wanted it, brother mine. God, she wanted it so bad.' Oliver stuck his hands in his pockets. 'But you weren't man enough to give it to her, were you?'

'Shut up,' Lyndon bit out abruptly, violence in his face.

'Oh, you can't help it, Lyndon. *A fault in nature*. That's what your precious Shakespeare would call it. Your tragic flaw. Madly attracted to the Muse but unable to stick it to her like a real man.'

'You have a filthy mind.'

'I've got red blood flowing in my veins, that's what I have. I'm not afraid to take what's put in front of me. I may not have fancy airs and graces like you or know how to write a bloody sonnet. I'm a Cornishman though; I get the job done. And Dad knows it.' Oliver gave a mocking bow and flourish, taunting his brother. 'That's why he's going to leave this place to me and my descendants.'

'Ah, but that's where you're wrong, Oliver.' Lyndon's eyes glittered, and his mouth crooked in a triumphant half-smile. Then the flash of humour abruptly vanished, his expression stony again. 'Dad's changing his will. He's going to leave Estuary House to me. The land, too. Lock, stock and barrel. He just told me.'

There was a sudden silence; a trio of pale-bellied geese flew overhead on their way to the estuary, widespread wings cracking the air.

Almost flinching at the sound, Oliver looked up at the geese wildly, and then back at his brother.

'Impossible,' he stuttered. 'You're lying.'

'Go ask him yourself if you don't believe me.' Lyndon jerked his head back towards the river. 'I left him walking Caesar.'

Oliver paused, and then ran lightly down the steps. Lyndon stepped aside, his face wary, body tensed as though expecting a fight. But his brother hurried past and through the gate at the bottom of the formal gardens.

There was a man walking along the lane, wheeling a bicycle, a tweed cap on his head, scarf wrapped about his neck to keep out the cold.

Oliver burst out of the gateway, almost colliding with this stranger. There was a muffled expletive, and then Oliver ran on.

The man pushed back his cap to stare after him. She recognised him at once as the same man she'd bumped into once before, down near the waterside chapel. A young boy, who'd been trotting by his side, stopped and looked up at the house enquiringly. She could see the boy clearly through the open gate. Fair-haired, open-faced, curious.

As soon as his brother had gone, Lyndon swung back to the house and looked straight up at their bedroom window, as though aware she'd been listening to every word of that bitter exchange.

Eleanor ducked out of sight. But she knew he must have seen her. Her heart was racing.

Does Eleanor know the real reason for this whirlwind romance of yours?

It must have something to do with their father changing his will in Lyndon's favour. Was that why he'd brought her here, demanding she pretend to be his bride?

She didn't understand. And she doubted Lyndon would ever explain it to her. He liked to keep his secrets close.

Madly attracted to the Muse but unable to stick it to her like a real man.

No ambiguity there. Her cheeks burnt with embarrassment, and she clasped them with cold hands, breathing fast.

Was that why Lyndon never touched her at night?

Oliver seemed to be insinuating that his brother was impotent. No, he'd done more than insinuated. He'd said it as though he knew for sure.

Because of this Diana, whoever she was.

Her predecessor?

Lyndon had lost this Diana to his brother, by the sound of things. Perhaps he'd brought her here to Estuary House, much as he'd brought Eleanor, and Oliver had spoiled everything by seducing her behind his back. Just as he'd tried seducing her the other day, flirting madly over the record player, asking her to dance, almost kissing her...

I get the job done.

She'd seen Lyndon's face change when Oliver said that. For a split-second, he had looked so still and ashen, like a marble statue, caught out of time into a memory so terrible that his whole being had frozen.

The door flew open.

Lyndon stood in the doorway, staring across at her; she'd

still been crouched by the window, trying to cool her hot cheeks, but jumped up at his entry.

'I'm sorry,' she said quickly. 'I couldn't help overhearing. He was speaking so loudly.'

'Forget it,' he said crisply, and held out his hand. 'Come here, I need to tell you something.'

Surprised, she let Lyndon draw her towards him. 'Is it about your father leaving you the house?'

'You heard that, too?' He searched her face. 'Look, ignore all that. My brother is a bastard. Not literally, of course. More's the pity.' His smile was humourless. 'Though that would make me one, too, wouldn't it? The curse of twins. Wherever he goes, I have to follow. And vice versa.'

'Which of you was born first?'

'I was.' He saw her expression and laughed shortly. 'No, that doesn't make me automatically his heir. It's my father's house. He can leave it to whomever he chooses. And he chose Oliver a long time ago.'

'Is that why you wanted me to pretend we were married? To persuade your father to leave you the house, rather than him?'

He gave a curt nod. 'Partially, yes. You won't tell the others? That we're not married, that is.'

'I won't tell.'

'Thank you.'

His gaze moved to her mouth and paused there. She felt a thrill move through her and almost drew back but forced herself not to move. This was her future now, she told herself fiercely. It had to be a path of her own choosing, not the one her father had insisted upon.

'I hope this sudden change of heart isn't just to save you from being returned to your father's keeping.' He hesitated. 'I shouldn't have threatened you with calling him, it was a low thing to do. I'm sorry. I would never really have done it; I hope you know that.'

'You were desperate.'

'Not that desperate. It was because ... Well, I'll tell you about that another time.' There was a rolled-up newspaper tucked under his arm; he drew it out and shook it open, clearly reluctant. 'Here, look at this. Dad picked it up in town this morning.'

It was a report about the poetry reading they'd attended in Bodmin. She nodded, smiling. 'You got a mention,' she said, scanning the story swiftly.

'No, this.'

He tapped the grainy photograph that accompanied the story, and she studied it dutifully. There was Jack Clemo and his mother; Charles Causley; the young poet, John Treviathan, proudly holding up a copy of his chapbook; several other men she vaguely recognised from that night; and Lyndon himself, standing next to Eleanor.

'Oh, what a dreadful picture of me,' she said automatically, grimacing. 'I look drunk.'

'The caption, Eleanor. Read the caption.'

'Well, it's just our names, and ...' Then she read out the words he was pointing at silently, '*Along with newly-weds Lyndon Chance and his bride, Eleanor.*' She bit her lip, seeing what he meant. Telling family and close friends he was married when he wasn't was one thing, but having it printed in the newspapers was much more serious. 'Yes, that's unfortunate.'

'It's more than unfortunate. This is the Western Morning News, and it's got quite a wide circulation in the West Country.' Lyndon paused. 'Maybe I'm over-reacting. But isn't it possible that someone who knows your family may recognise you from this photograph, and get in touch with your father?'

She opened her mouth to deny that as a possibility, and then shut it again, remembering her grandfather. He lived in Plymouth in Devon. She'd seen him reading the Western Morning News many times; he might already have seen this, in fact.

'Oh God.' Her heart was thumping so violently she felt sick.

'Are you OK?'

Eleanor couldn't seem to focus on what he was saying. Wrapping both arms about herself, she glanced over her shoulder to see if the window was still open. She was so cold, her skin was covered in goosepimples.

'Perhaps we should do it for real,' he said roughly, watching her.

'Sorry?'

'Go to church. Get married.'

They were standing very close. She put a hand, daringly, on his chest, and felt the rapid thump of his heart.

'I'd be trapping you.'

'But isn't that exactly what I've done to you, Eleanor?' There was remorse in his face. 'I brought you down to Cornwall to escape your father, but then wouldn't let you leave. You walked out of one prison and straight into another.' His voice was gruff. 'Don't think I'm not aware of that irony.'

'I came here of my own free will.' She raised her gaze to his. 'Yes, that first night, you threatened to tell my father where I was. But that feels like a hundred years ago now. I'm not a damsel in distress, and you certainly don't need to rescue me with an offer of marriage.' She managed a smile, though her chest was heaving, her mouth dry. 'I could have walked out any time I wanted.'

'Why didn't you, then?'

Their eyes met.

'Can't you guess?' she whispered.

Lyndon gave a muffled groan, and then bent his head to kiss her. His arms came about her, seeming to be everywhere at once, touching her, stroking her intimately, moulding her body against him.

She gasped and let her head fall back, not merely acquiescent but trembling with desire. She didn't care anymore that she was going to burn in hell. Not if Lyndon Chance was twisting in the flames with her . . .

Fiercely, he kissed her mouth, her neck, even pushing the soft woollen jacket and blouse aside to kiss her bare shoulder.

'I need you so much,' he muttered against her skin.

She gripped his shoulders for support, stumbling, almost falling, her body unbearably hot and out of her control.

They staggered backwards in each other's arms, the floorboards creaking in protest under their feet. The door was still ajar; with a fierce gesture, Lyndon kicked it shut before scooping her up and carrying her to the four-poster bed with its dainty lace curtains and pink ribbons. The whole structure creaked under their combined weight, and then he jumped up again, a frown in his eyes as he looked down at her.

'No, I can't, this is wrong . . .' Lyndon said, and ran a hand over his face. 'There are so many things you don't know about me. And you're a complete innocent; it would be unforgivable.'

Eleanor lay on her back on the soft eiderdown, staring up at him, wide-eyed and breathless. An incredible and shocking boldness took hold of her, and she realised she didn't care anymore what he thought, or indeed what anyone might think of her behaviour.

Slowly, she pulled up her skirt, displaying the bare skin above her stocking tops in silent invitation, and saw his eyes darken.

'Christ, Eleanor,' he said thickly, pausing only to remove his jacket and kick off his boots before stooping to kiss her again, his mouth hungry. 'You're sure? You're not going to change your mind? Because I don't want you to say afterwards that—'

'I'm sure.'

Chapter Twenty

A slovenly mouth, deep in the belly of the boat,
Spits out her destiny like ticker tape.

– From 'River Crossing' in *Estuary*

'I'll have to secure the chapel for tonight,' the woman officer, whose name was Leah, told them apologetically after calling back to police headquarters for advice. 'I'm sorry it took us so long to get out to you. But there's a music festival going on at Week St. Mary and we're being stretched pretty thin. And there won't be a forensics team available to exhume the remains until tomorrow morning at the earliest.' She paused, watching her colleague pick through some of the damp rubbish on the far side of the chapel, and then turned back to them. 'Now, you're sure you didn't know about these remains before you entered the chapel?'

'Like I said before,' Taylor repeated their agreed lie, 'I'm down here on a research trip for my thesis. We were taking a walk along the river when I told Mr Chance I was interested in looking inside the chapel. The ground gave way under my feet … and there it was. A human bone.' She cleared her throat, her voice suddenly croaky. 'When we dug down a little deeper, we found the others and realised we had to call you.'

Between the two of them, after realising there could be

a whole skeleton buried under the chapel, they'd decided not to mention her encounters with the ghostly Mack and Davie to the police, and to describe their visit to the chapel as purely coincidental. Julius had thought mentioning ghosts would only make the police think she was crazy, and Taylor, made uncomfortable by the woman officer's intent stare as she gave her statement, was secretly inclined to agree.

Leah turned to Julius, politely lowering her torch beam. 'I understand this chapel belongs to your family, Mr Chance?'

'That's right.' Julius stood over the hole, his face unreadable in shadow. 'But I haven't been in here since last autumn, when the river rose after a week of prolonged rainfall, and I came down to check for flooding.'

'You didn't notice anything unusual at that time?'

'Not even remotely.'

Her colleague Jim came back, his torch beam bouncing over the stained-glass, briefly illuminating saints and bright, gleaming halos. 'So, do you have any idea who these remains belong to or when they might have been buried here?'

'I'm afraid not.'

Jim crouched, shining his light into the hole. 'There's no chance this is a bona fide burial, where the headstone's simply been removed? It's a very old chapel. Must have been here a good hundred years, at least.'

'Rather longer than that,' Julius said ironically. 'But I'm not aware of any burials ever having taken place on this land. This was a private chapel, intended for services only. Family burials always took place at the parish church. Though you may want to reach out to whoever keeps the parish records, just to be sure.'

'Okey-dokey.' Leah opened her kit bag and rummaged about inside, no doubt planning to secure the chapel for the night with police tape. 'You two should go back to the house now. It's pitch-black out there but I'm sure Jim will escort you, make sure you get home safely.' She looked at her fellow officer. 'Jim?'

'Ready whenever you are.' Jim waved his torch.

Taylor followed Julius and the officer up the narrow, over-grown path back to the Camel Trail. It was a misty evening, a low-hanging cloud having descended across the river during the evening, and as they walked, they could hear every sound in the darkness. Every twig crack, every rustle in the bushes of a wild animal scurrying for cover.

On the wooded slopes above the disused railway, Estuary House stood dark and silent, except for a light in one of the upstairs windows.

Mrs Chance's bedroom, Taylor guessed.

She shivered, wondering what the old lady would make of the news that human remains had been found under the family chapel.

According to Julius, he hadn't told his grandmother what was happening when he spoke to her earlier, only explaining there'd been a collapse at the chapel and the police needed to be called to secure it.

They reached the gate into the formal gardens, the evening air warm with the lingering scent of jasmine.

Jim bid them a surprisingly cheerful, 'Goodnight,' and dis-appeared back into the gloom, leaving them alone together.

'Taylor, why don't you stay in the house tonight?' Julius asked. 'I know you like to be independent, but you've had quite a shock.' She couldn't see his smile but heard it in his voice. 'I could even rustle up a pot of tea and some bacon sandwiches.'

'That's very kind. But I'm bushed and I'd just like to get some sleep right now. Like you say, it's been one hell of an evening.' Taylor desperately needed to get away and clear her head, which was buzzing with unanswered questions, not to mention the cruel, psychic impact of handling those long-buried human remains. 'Thanks for the offer though.'

'I'd like to know whose grave that is,' he said.

'Me, too.'

Taylor started to turn away, but Julius said deeply, 'Wait,' and when she glanced back, surprised, he bent his head and kissed her on the lips.

She froze, not sure what to do or say.

'Goodnight,' he said huskily, and waited at the gate into the field until she reached her tent and unzipped it. Only then did she hear him walk up through the formal gardens to the house, both of them listening to the other in the misty night silence.

At first light, the cars and vans had started to arrive, deep engine notes breaking the accustomed peace of the estuary.

Taylor, who'd been unable to sleep for more than a few hours anyway, got dressed again in the cool, misty light of dawn, pulled on her boots and hurried back down to the chapel. She saw lights on in the great house as she walked past, and soon after arriving at the river spotted Julius down there, too, talking to the officer in charge; his arms were folded, and he was looking pale and unshaven.

She guessed he hadn't spent a very comfortable night either.

The forensics team passed her, clad in protective gear, carrying their equipment into the old chapel. She peeked through the door; they'd already set up mobile lights and erected a white tent over the site where they'd unearthed the bones.

All she kept thinking was that it must be Mack's skeleton that she'd found in that sunken grave. Mack's or perhaps

Davie's. Why else had she seen them around the chapel so much? Two people she now knew didn't exist. Or didn't exist any longer.

Mack had woven a fantasy for her, inviting her down to the chapel, making her see a renovated cottage instead of a tumbledown ruin, talking to her about the Chance family.

It had all felt so real to her. The cottage, his bicycle, his young son. Utterly real and tangible.

And yet the chapel was ruined, its roof sagging, its walls dark and blotchy with damp: incontrovertible proof that she had imagined all of it. Or been tricked in some way.

Were the dead able to inhabit the present so seamlessly they could appear a part of it? she wondered. Or perhaps those we lost never really went away after death, but remained in the stream, omnipresent, drifting silently through time along with the living, yet separate, too. Until one of them chose to make themselves seen, that was. To become part of life again, even if only briefly and for one particular person.

But why her?

Why had Mack chosen *her*, of all people, to find those bones under the chapel, and not somebody else?

She knew the answer to that but wished she didn't. Because she'd always been too close to that dividing line between life and death, between now and the hereafter. Because she saw auras like halos around people and objects, and felt things nobody else could sense.

That terrible night had come back to her so many times, it was hard to be sure now what was a real memory, and what was merely the memory of a memory, each vision inlaid upon another, the whole thing built up like tiers of a cake. Only the truth of what happened remained, and her own gnawing sense of inadequacy, of guilt ...

'Hey.' Julius put a hand on her shoulder, startling her. 'You didn't need to come back down here.'

'I know.' She turned, her quick smile at the ready. The one that kept most people at bay. 'But I couldn't stay away. It's just so weird. Don't you think? And unsettling.' She saw his wary expression. 'I swear, I didn't know those bones were down there. I was as shocked as you.'

'I believe you. And I hope you didn't mind not mentioning Mack in your statement. Obviously, if you'd rather be completely straight with them, that's your choice. But—'

'But they'd think I was mad,' she supplied for him, nodding. 'Honestly, it's fine. I told them I was a research student, that's all.'

'Did you tell them you were investigating my grandfather?'

'No, of course not. I said it was ecology. Which it is,' she added awkwardly. 'With a bit of poetry on the side.'

A young man was snapping photos of the exterior of the chapel, even taking a few sneaky shots inside the porch, maybe hoping for a glimpse of the body itself.

One of the police told him to move along, and the man said defensively, 'I'm a member of the press,' but headed back up the path to the Camel Trail anyway, looking satisfied as he checked through the photos he'd taken.

'Creep,' Taylor muttered, watching him go.

Julius took a deep breath. 'Apparently, the police may be on site here several days, making sure they haven't missed anything.' He stood to one side as another white-clad forensics person tried to pass them on the narrow track. 'Let's leave them to it, shall we?'

'I guess.' She fell in beside him, burning with curiosity. 'Anything new?' When he shook his head, she asked, 'How's Mrs Chance taking it?'

'I'm not sure.' Julius hunched his shoulders, pulling his

jacket collar closer against the morning air. 'Gran barely said a word last night when I told her what we'd found. But she looked frightened.'

'I'm so sorry.'

'The police will want to speak to her, of course, as the owner of the land. My great-aunt, too. I'd better drive over later and pick Iris up. She may have to stay at the house for a few days, until all this blows over.' He saw her curious glance and looked embarrassed. 'That hut of hers. It's not exactly a registered dwelling place, if you see what I mean. The police are pretty *laissez-faire* down here. But I wouldn't want them to find out she lives there full-time. It could become awkward.'

They reached the willow tree near the old wooden stile. Julius climbed over first and then turned to give her a hand, though she didn't need one. It was eerily quiet, apart from the ubiquitous birdsong. The lane lay empty and still in the hazy morning sun, the police vehicles having approached the chapel along the nearer Camel Trail.

Above them, Estuary House rose like a monolith, still partially in shadow. The windows watched them silently.

'I wonder who those bones belong to,' she said, voicing the question uppermost in her mind, the one that had kept her awake most of the night.

'That's the million-dollar question, isn't it?' Julius walked on a few steps, and then stopped dead, suddenly grimacing. 'God, this is a mess. I won't be able to keep Gran out of it for long, that's for certain. Once the newspapers find out about those remains, and they will find out—'

'I'm so sorry. This is all my fault.'

'Don't be absurd. You weren't to know what was under the chapel floor. But what if that body turns out to be ...' He cut off that sentence and ran a hand through his dishevelled hair. 'Well, I'm sure you did your research before you came here. You must know the worst stories about my grandfather.'

'Yes, and I don't believe any of them.' A horrible thought struck her. 'Julius,' she whispered, grabbing his sleeve as he turned away. 'What if it's Oliver?'

'Sorry?'

'Those bones in the grave. What if they belong to Oliver Chance?'

'Impossible.'

'But he disappeared, didn't he? He left Estuary House soon after Lyndon married and never came back. That's what I've read, anyway. Nobody ever heard from him again.'

Julius looked baffled. 'Because he went abroad.'

'You know that for sure?'

'Iris told me he did. And my grandmother, too.' He paused and shrugged. 'I don't have any proof, of course. But everyone always assumed he left England after a row with my grandfather.'

'And never came back? Not even after Lyndon died, to try and claim the house and land for himself?'

Julius rubbed his forehead, his brows knitting together. 'No,' he agreed slowly. 'But absence of proof isn't proof either. The fact that he never came back doesn't mean he was murdered.'

'Where is he, then? What happened to him? Why has Oliver never been back in touch with the family?'

'Good God, you're incorrigible. You and your wild imagination.' Julius sounded at the end of his patience with her. 'All right, tell me this. Who on earth would have wanted to murder my great-uncle?'

Unable to answer that question, Taylor fell into silence, following him through the gardens to the front entrance of the great house.

Mrs Chance must have seen them coming from a distance; she had opened the door in her dressing gown and stood now on the threshold like a figure in a Greek drama, wringing her hands, her eyes wide and scared in a white face.

There were roses growing in a tangle over one of the garden archways, a few red petals scattered on the gravel as they passed beneath. One stuck damply to the edge of her trainer; she glanced down at its bruised scarlet, fragile as tissue paper.

Taylor remembered the short final poem in the *Estuary* sequence; its invocation to the gods to punish those whose evil deeds go undiscovered.

And the tarot cards pinned to the wall in Iris's shack.

The Lovers.

The Hanged Man.

And The Tower, its ruins struck by lightning, dead bodies tumbling down along with its broken stones.

'Lyndon might have done.' She was filled with a terrible sense of foreboding, as though the house were about to fall on her, and maybe the sky, too. She grabbed his sleeve, whispering urgently, 'Maybe Oliver was finally going to tell everyone the truth about what happened to that dead girl ... so Lyndon murdered him and buried him under the chapel.' She swallowed. 'In his *sacred space.*'

Chapter Twenty-One

The river, a hanged man –
Stone-still and heavy, waiting to be let down briskly
Into his grey shroud.

– From 'The Hanged Man' in Estuary

Everything had changed, Eleanor thought to herself, and yet nothing whatsoever had changed. It was an unsettling realisation.

She felt hollow inside, unsteady on her legs, and a little sore in places. She also felt ordinary, as though something quite commonplace had happened, something that needed no comment or regret. Sex had been uncomfortable and embarrassing, and yet wildly enjoyable at the same time. And she still hadn't accepted his offer of marriage, though he'd repeated it several times afterwards, almost begging her to take his name.

She'd done it, and out of wedlock, too. The ultimate act of defiance against her father.

Nor was Lyndon impotent, as his jeering brother had insinuated during their row.

He was very far from impotent.

All the same, it hadn't been the thunderous, soul-shaking event she'd expected after years of being warned that, unless she were properly wed, devils would emerge from hell at the sinful moment of her undoing to drag her below the earth with dreadful shrieks. Of course, she'd never believed in all that apocryphal nonsense her father had spouted during his bible-thumping sessions. But she'd anticipated feeling different somehow when she rose from the crumpled bed after their lovemaking.

Instead, the same anxious face looked back at her from the mirror, and when she hurried into the bathroom, it was the same pale, uninteresting body she washed, albeit with a few tell-tale marks here and there where he'd gripped her in passion ...

At dinner that evening, where she had steeled herself for verbal fireworks between the two warring brothers, it seemed nothing much had changed there either. Nothing was said about the argument earlier, nor about their father's change of heart over who should inherit the property.

But perhaps, Eleanor thought, watching them covertly as she devoured her dinner, hellishly starving, the inheritance wasn't as settled as Lyndon believed. Either way, the two brothers studiously avoided speaking to each other, except in curt monosyllables, and to her surprise even Mr Chance confined his conversation to recent flooding, which was causing problems with drainage to land they owned on the opposite bank of the river.

'I'll row across there with you tomorrow morning,' Oliver said promptly. 'Take a look at the situation.'

'No, Olly, you stay here. Lyndon can go with me this time. We'll take the car, go the long way round.' Their father reached over to spear another dripping piece of roast beef from the dish in the centre of the long dining table. 'He hasn't seen the improvements we've made to the west meadow yet. Or the new storage hut. Time he did.'

Oliver said nothing. But his gaze, cold and resentful,

flicked to Eleanor's face, almost as though blaming her for his father's change of heart.

It was not a comfortable thought.

'May I come, too?' she asked.

Everyone looked at her, his father frankly astonished, Lyndon with his eyebrows raised.

'You?' Mr Chance scratched his head, then shrugged. 'I don't see why not. Though I doubt you'll be interested.'

'Whatever interests Lyndon must interest me now,' she said bravely, and met his gaze across the table. 'I'm his wife.'

Oliver made a snorting noise.

Eleanor had worried that she'd made a bad mistake, asking to go across the river with them. But Lyndon's faint smile reassured her. He approved of her boldness, just as he'd approved of her that night in Cirencester, standing up in front of all those clever, educated people to ask her question.

Besides, she'd taken a man into her bed, and the sky had not fallen. She mustn't be such a mouse in future, she determined, but would speak her mind.

'Where's Iris this evening?' she asked their mother, having noticed the girl's absence at the dinner table and hoping to change the subject.

Camilla picked up her wine glass and drank deep, not looking at her. 'Iris is having one of her prayer and abstinence evenings. No food, no drink, no contact with other people. I daresay it's good for the soul, but it must be absolute hell on the knees.' She put down her glass, exchanging a warm smile with Oliver when he generously topped it up again. 'Thank you, darling. More lovely wine for Mummy.' She looked down at Jeannie, seated beside Lyndon; the girl's head was bent, her expression preoccupied as she studied her meal. 'And how are you enjoying your visit here, my dear?'

'It's amazing,' Jeannie said with genuine enthusiasm. 'I love this house. And the gardens. All those palm trees. It's like the Caribbean.'

'You and Oliver shouldn't wait too long before tying the knot,' Camilla told her with a persuasive smile. 'I know you probably feel you're too young and there's plenty of time to get married. But the longer you wait to start a family, the harder it gets.'

Jeannie was staring at Camilla in dismay. 'Sorry? Get married?'

'Lyndon's already beaten his brother to the altar, of course. Such a shame. But a baby would be the real clincher. I'm sure Oliver's keen to do the right thing and propose.' Camilla gave a tinkling laugh, seeming to find this rather inappropriate discussion entertaining, but Oliver looked away, a hard tinge of red in his cheeks. 'He must really love you. Otherwise, why bring you all the way here to meet the parents?'

Jeannie smiled faintly, saying nothing. But as soon as Camilla's attention turned elsewhere, she threw a questioning look at her boyfriend, who studiously ignored her.

After they'd finished dessert, Mrs Barclay came in to clear the dishes, and told them the Ouija board had been set out again in the den, apparently on Lyndon's instructions.

As soon as Mr and Mrs Chance had left the table, by mutual consent the younger people drifted into the den, drinks in hand, to listen to the record player and amuse themselves by calling on the spirits of the dead.

'What was all that about at dinner?' Eleanor whispered to Lyndon as soon as the other two had their backs turned. 'Your mother was practically goading Oliver to propose to Jeannie. I didn't even know he was that serious about her.'

'I doubt he is,' he said, with a dismissive lift of his shoulder.

'Pay no attention; my mother's obsessed with the succession, that's all.'

'She must want a grandchild very badly.'

'Yes, perhaps.' Briefly, his gaze met hers, and then drifted to his brother. 'Look, do you want to play Ouija again or not?' he asked in a raised voice, spinning the little yellow planchette with one finger.

'Yes, if you're keen.' Eleanor also glanced across at Oliver and Jeannie, who were talking intently as they flipped through a rack of album covers, heads bent together, presumably trying to agree on which record to play, though it looked to her as though they were secretly arguing. Over what his mother had said at dinner, no doubt. 'But only if the other two agree. It'll be no fun with just the two of us.'

His eyes shifted back to lock with hers. 'Sure about that?'

Eleanor blushed.

He trailed a finger down her cheek. '*Girls blush, sometimes, because they are alive,*' he quoted softly.

'Is that ... "Aurora Leigh"?'

Lyndon nodded, an odd smile still flickering on his lips. 'Elizabeth Barrett Browning.' Then his smile died, and he turned away, strolling towards his brother instead. 'We're going to play Ouija. You two want to join us?'

Lighting a cigarette, Oliver glanced round at the board. 'More of your games? I thought you'd be done with that, after last time.'

'It's not a game, Oliver, talking to the dead.' Without looking at his brother again, Lyndon lit a candle and brought it to the table in a glass container. 'Besides, we were interrupted last time. You said it yourself – it's bad luck not to finish the conversation.' He sat down at the table. 'Bad manners, too.'

'And will your wife be joining us?' Oliver drawled.

'Oh, I don't mind,' she said, breathless as a schoolgirl, her gaze on Lyndon's face.

'That's settled, then.' Lyndon's voice was lazy; he, too, flicked open his lighter and lit a cigarette, passing it to Eleanor as she took her place beside him. 'Here you go, darling.'

She accepted it with a shy smile, very aware of his fingers brushing hers. It reminded her they were now lovers and had lain in bed together for almost an hour earlier while he touched her in the most intimate places, teaching her about sex, whispering instructions in her ear as she boldly touched him in return.

If they carried on like that, it might not be long before they had a pregnancy to announce to the family, she thought, and felt a nagging anxiety at the prospect. Would Lyndon stand by her in that event? While she thrilled at having defied her strict upbringing by taking a lover without being married, she didn't like the idea of trying to raise a child alone, nor the disadvantages her child might face without the support of its legal father.

'Come on, hurry up,' Lyndon addressed the other two, his tone sharpening. 'Turn the music down and the lights off. Let's do this properly.'

'Hang on, man, would you? So impatient…' Jeannie, bending over the record player, changed the stylus and swapped the dance 33 she'd originally chosen for a classical 78 instead. 'There,' she said, laughing, 'that's a bit spookier. You need to get the atmosphere right, you know?'

Eleanor didn't know the composer, but the soft, lilting strains of violins accompanied by a melodious piano seemed eerily perfect as the room sank into a flickering, candlelit darkness.

It had turned wet again earlier in the evening, and a hard rain now beat inexorably at the windows. Eleanor recalled what Mr Chance had said at the dinner table about local flooding and imagined the River Camel swelling with the excess rainfall, rising higher and higher, until it lapped at the doors and windows of the ancient, ivy-swathed manor house.

As before, they all reached into the intimate little circle of four, setting their fingertips to the yellow planchette.

'Is anybody there?' Oliver called, a hint of laughter in his voice as he glanced about the shadowy room. 'Are the spirits with us tonight? Or are they on holiday?'

'For God's sake,' Lyndon growled at his brother, 'take it seriously or leave the room.'

'Olly, hush now,' Jeannie said, wagging a finger at him. 'You promised to behave.'

Oliver shrugged but fell silent.

'Spirits of Estuary House,' Lyndon called after a moment's pause, 'hear us. We call you through the dark and the rain, through the years and down the centuries. We who are the living, and you who are the dead, hear us, we beg of you.'

His eyes glittered in the candlelight as he looked at each of them in turn. 'Are you there, spirits? Speak now. Let us know that you are with us.' Lyndon drew in a sharp breath. 'Is anybody there?'

The planchette plunged upwards to the word, YES.

'Oh goody,' Oliver muttered.

'Welcome to our house,' Lyndon continued, a deep resonant note in his voice that made the tiny hairs rise on the back of Eleanor's neck. 'Will you give us your name, spirit?'

They waited in silence for what felt like ages. A log popped in the wood burner. Behind the shutters, rain pattered in the empty flowerbeds outside the window. The clock on the mantelpiece began to chime ten.

The planchette moved.

'D,' Jeannie chanted, as though none of them could read the letter it was pointing at.

'Well, well,' Oliver murmured.

Lyndon said nothing.

After a long pause, the planchette jerked to the right, and stopped at the letter I.

'I,' Jeannie said, watching avidly as it left the letter I and began to move again.

Lyndon's face was set in granite.

Eleanor's heart began to thump. She had decided she didn't much like this game. It was too frightening.

'A.'

Could it be Jeannie manipulating the planchette?

It was possible, Eleanor decided, glancing at her face. Jeannie was certainly enjoying the game the most, her eyes lit up with excitement. But why would she do that?

By far the likelier culprit was Oliver though, whose eyes were fixed grimly on the planchette as it slid to the letter 'N'.

'N.' Jeannie sucked in her breath, looking round at them all. 'D. I. A. N.... It must be spelling *Diana*.'

Before she even said the name, Lyndon jumped up with a muttered curse, knocking his chair backwards as he did so. He stalked towards the door and then stopped abruptly, running a hand over his forehead as he turned and stared back at them, his eyes suddenly wild.

Eleanor withdrew her fingers from the planchette, which sat there inert and innocent on the board.

Diana.

The same name Iris had mentioned to her in the corridor.

'How dare you?' Lyndon demanded, glaring at his brother.

'I know you're angry over the inheritance. But *this*?' He choked over the words. 'You must be sick in the head.'

'I didn't suggest we played Ouija again,' Oliver replied coldly. 'Just as I didn't make the planchette point out those letters.' He picked up his cigarette, which had been burning away in the ashtray. 'Does it occur to you that this could be real, Lyndon? That Diana is genuinely trying to communicate with you from the afterlife?' His voice became mocking again. 'Or are you so obsessed with getting this house, you'd rather believe it's me tormenting you than Diana really being here and wanting to talk to you?'

'She's not here,' Lyndon said flatly.

'Sorry, who is this Diana and what's she got to do with you two?' Jeannie looked from one brother to the other. 'I take it she's dead?' Nobody spoke. 'OK. So how did she die?'

Eleanor gripped the thin edge of the table, fighting the urge to run away. She looked up at Lyndon, awaiting his reply, fearful but secretly relieved she wasn't the only one there who didn't know who this Diana was. Especially given the powerful effect this dead woman's name seemed to have over everyone.

'Lyndon?' she whispered.

He didn't reply, staring down at his twin with a terrible rage in his face, as though he wanted to kill him.

'Good God, now doesn't that beat all? I can't believe you still haven't told Eleanor about Diana.' Oliver took a fresh cigarette from the packet and lit it off the back of the one still smouldering. 'So, will you tell your wife who Diana was,' he asked, sounding almost bored at the prospect, 'or should I?'

At this, Lyndon finally stirred. He came back, letting out a long-held breath and sat down at the table. Eleanor noticed that he didn't look at any of them, gazing instead at the motionless planchette, still pointing towards the letter N.

'Diana Farthing was a local girl,' he said slowly, in a voice that Eleanor didn't recognise. 'The daughter of one of my dad's tenants, a farmer. About three years ago, we were engaged to be married.'

Jeannie gave a little gasp and covered her mouth with her hand. She shot a scared glance at her boyfriend but said nothing.

'And?' Oliver prompted him softly.

Lyndon did not reply at first. He took a new cigarette from the packet and lit up; his hands were steady despite the macabre nature of the discussion. Then he put the lighter down, glancing at Eleanor. 'And you look a bit like her,' he added in an offhand way.

'*A bit?*' Oliver gave a laugh that grated at Eleanor's nerves.

'All right, she looks a lot like Diana,' Lyndon snapped, and dragged deeply on the cigarette before muttering, 'The two of them are ... *were* strikingly similar.'

His brother shook his head. 'Similar?' He turned to Eleanor. 'Don't take this the wrong way, but apart from your fashion sense, you and Diana could almost have been twins. Not quite like me and Lyndon, but maybe in a certain light ...'

'I don't understand,' Jeannie whispered.

'Well, I think I do,' Eleanor said, and angrily stubbed out her cigarette before rising.

'Eleanor, don't go, please.' Lyndon leant forward, a pleading look on his face. 'Listen, I never meant for any of this to happen.' She heard his words slur and realised he was only talking this way because he'd been drinking. 'It wasn't planned. You have to believe me.'

Things had begun to crystallise in Eleanor's head. His

bizarre behaviour when they met, the way he'd persuaded her to accompany him down to Cornwall, and then his urgent insistence that they pretend to be married. Then he'd even offered to marry her for real.

She'd been so flattered.

Yet none of it had been about *her*. It had all been about this other woman he'd been in love with three years ago, this dead fiancée she apparently resembled.

No wonder the housekeeper and his parents had been so horrified that first night. It must have been like seeing a ghost.

He'd made a fool out of her.

'How did she die, Lyndon?' Eleanor repeated Jeannie's earlier question. She sat down again, staring at him. 'No more lies.'

'I've never lied to you,' he burst out.

'*How did she die?*'

'She drowned,' his brother cut in with frightening calm.

The record came to an end, and Jeannie jumped up to remove the needle. Outside, the rain had stopped now. It felt to Eleanor as though the house and grounds were listening to them, and the estuary, too, the unseen river rolling between black banks under a moonless sky.

'Diana drowned,' Oliver repeated, his voice turning husky, 'out there on the Camel Estuary. Three years ago last summer. And nobody regrets her death more than I do.'

'*You?*' Eleanor didn't understand.

'Diana was with me at the time, you see. She'd had a nasty scrap with Lyndon and needed some time away from him. So, I took her sailing on my yacht for the afternoon.' Oliver paused, staring fixedly down at the Ouija board. 'We dropped anchor in the bay, had lunch on board, and a few drinks. The water was a little choppy that day, with a strong current, though nothing I couldn't handle. I was just turning the boat when Diana went overboard and was drowned.'

'Oh my God,' Jeannie said, her eyes wide with horror.

'I jumped in after her, of course. Dived under the water, hunted for her everywhere. Even under the boat. But it was no use.' Oliver stubbed out his cigarette, staring at Lyndon with hard eyes. 'Your husband still blames me for it, as you can see.'

Eleanor studied Lyndon's profile. He looked so cold and austere; it sent a chill through her. 'Her body was never found, you mean?'

'Not to this day,' his brother told her. 'They dragged the river but it's tidal. Her body would have been swept out to sea within a very short time after she went into the water. In the end, the coroner ruled it death by misadventure. But everyone knew the truth.'

'Stop lying,' Lyndon ground out.

'The truth?' Eleanor stared from him to Oliver. 'What do you mean? I thought you said she went overboard.'

Oliver gave her a direct look. 'I told you, she'd had an argument with Lyndon the day before. She swore it was all over between them, that he didn't love her anymore.'

Lyndon jumped to his feet and strode to the door, leaving the room without another word.

In confusion, Eleanor stood, too, not sure if she should follow, but Oliver stopped her, saying, 'No, let him go. There's more. Only Lyndon doesn't want to hear it.' Accepting another lit cigarette from Jeannie, he dragged on it deeply. 'Diana didn't fall into the river by accident; she was far too experienced a sailor to be so careless.'

'What are you saying?'

'Like I told the police, she was distraught that day, weeping...' Oliver looked at Eleanor with an unfocused gaze, as though lost in the past. 'To my mind, there's only one explanation for what happened that afternoon. Lyndon had tossed her aside like she meant nothing, so Diana threw herself into the water deliberately. She killed herself rather than live another day without him.'

Chapter Twenty-Two

She looked out of place, that gleaming yacht, sailing
Down the Camel like a young bride in white…

> – From 'Half-Light' in *Estuary*

Two days after the police had taken away the remains under
the chapel, the weather broke, and the heavens opened. Rain
pattered down relentlessly for hours. It even permeated the
double lining of Taylor's so-called 'waterproof' tent, leaving her bedding damp and forcing her to move everything
into the central compartment, far enough away from the
rainwater coming in drips off the side panels to stay dry.

She spent the morning inside the tent with the front flap
propped open for ventilation, typing up notes on her tablet.

It was difficult to concentrate, and not just because of
the rain.

Julius might think her crazy. And she could hardly blame
him. First, she'd been seeing people who weren't real in
a cottage that had never existed. Chatting with them, too,
which was somehow worse. But that didn't mean she was
wrong in her suspicions. And she couldn't shake the awful
fear that Lyndon Chance – the poet she admired more than
any other in the world – had murdered his twin brother, and
that she had found the unfortunate man's bones. Thanks to
a non-existent Mack and Davie, whose every move seemed

to have been designed to draw her attention towards that chapel. Not to mention that appalling smell of something rotting.

A little after noon, she heard boots squelching through the mud, and looked up to find Julius Chance looming large in the opening to her tent. He was wearing a tweed cap and a long-line waxed jacket, its collar turned up against the rain.

'Come up to the house, for God's sake,' he said gruffly. As he tipped his head, rain poured from the brim of his cap onto his chest, and he grimaced. 'You can't stay out here in this downpour.'

'I'm fine,' she lied.

'Look, I've just been watching the weather report. This rain has stalled above us. Won't clear for several days. Don't be stubborn about it.' He peered impatiently into her damp tent. 'Come up to the house. I've sorted out a room for you. Unless you enjoy being a martyr to your camping fetish?'

She gave a half-laugh, tempted to say yes. But she didn't want to push her luck either. Not with the Chances. Mack might have been some kind of vision, but he'd made a lot of sense when talking about Julius and the family. They didn't take kindly to strangers.

'I don't want to impose—'

'You won't be imposing. In fact, you'll be doing me a favour.' He ducked his head and lurched into the tent, crouching low with one wary eye on the roof. 'Iris had a visitor last night. A local journalist who wanted her take on the bones under the chapel. Apparently, she was completely freaked out by him. So, she's back at the house again, staying with us until the media feeding frenzy has died down.'

'Then you won't want two guests at the same time,' she pointed out.

'Iris is one of the most difficult women I know. And she

blames me for this whole circus. Thinks I'm carrying on the family curse. Having you there, too, may take the edge off her angst.'

Taylor closed the cover on her tablet. 'I don't like the sound of a feeding frenzy. What does it entail?'

'Phone's been ringing on and off all morning. I've unplugged the bloody thing. I've had emails, too, dozens of them. Even offers of money for an "exclusive" interview.' He gave a crooked smile. 'I could do with the money, but not the bad publicity.'

'I thought the police were keeping a lid on the story.'

'This is rural Cornwall. We don't get many dead bodies in this neck of the woods, so news of them tends to get out pretty quick.' He raised his eyebrows. 'Now, will you please pack a bag and come back to the house with me?'

'Give me half an hour. I'll be there.'

He grunted, but she could tell he was pleased. 'I could organise some lunch for you, too, if you'd like?'

'Sounds perfect, thank you.'

When he'd gone, Taylor gathered together all her key books, papers and notes, and carefully photographed them – in case of loss – and then packed them in her rucksack, along with a change of clothing and her night gear, plus slippers, washbag and a few other essentials, including her tablet and charger. It would be good not to have to use the petrol generator in the van to keep her devices charged, at least for a few days. She tucked her phone in the back pocket of her jeans, pulled on an anorak, swung the rucksack over one shoulder, and left her tent, zipping the whole thing up in case of invasion by wild animals during the night.

It felt strange, walking into Estuary House and knowing it would be her home for the next few days at least. She wiped her damp boots in the front porch, hung up her anorak, and then stood waiting in the echoing entrance hall, staring about at the vast oil paintings and crossed sword displays on the walls.

The Lady Elizabeth stared down boldly from her gilt picture frame, a hint of laughter in those lovely eyes. Her gold signet ring seemed to glint as though real enough to reach out and touch.

'Admiring the most infamous daughter of our house?' Julius asked, appearing at the top of the staircase.

'She is rather eye-catching.'

'The artist was very talented, wasn't he? A Cornishman. Died young though, so never became famous.' He paused. 'You know her history, I presume?'

'Some of it, yes. And your grandmother filled in a few details I hadn't been aware of. Ran off with a pirate and came to a sticky end on the high seas. Though how anyone would know that, I can't imagine. Unless,' she added dubiously, 'she sent a letter home after eloping with her swashbuckling pirate?'

'Seems a bit out of character, I agree.' He came to stand beside her, and they both stared up into the Lady Elizabeth's rouged and powdered face. 'Quite a stunner, isn't she? A real handful, too, by all accounts. I would have thought she could do better for herself than marry some smelly old pirate.'

'You have no sense of romance.'

'Perhaps not.' He looked at her coolly. 'But people did smell in those days. Even the young ones. Quite dreadfully, in fact.'

'How would you know? You weren't alive then.'

'Well-known fact. No deodorant, no dentists, and hardly anyone ever took a bath. Stands to reason that they smelt bad.' He held out a hand for her rucksack. 'May I take that upstairs for you? Might as well show you the room before we sit down to lunch. I've given you an en-suite.'

'Very posh. But thanks, I can carry this myself.' She paused, frowning. 'Hold on. An en-suite? Is that a hint? Are you saying I smell?'

His eyes glinted. 'No self-respecting host would ever suggest such a thing to a guest. But lunch won't be for another hour at least. Mainly because I'm preparing it myself and I haven't even made a start yet. So ... plenty of time for a shower, if you should feel so inclined.'

Her cheeks burnt. 'God damn you.'

'Very likely.'

She followed him upstairs to a pretty room with a view over the estuary, a large pine-framed bed covered by a pristine white duvet cover with matching pillowcases, and a vase of fresh-cut flowers on the bedside table. The wallpaper was a subtle pattern of rosebuds on a white background, and here and there hung typed and framed poems by Lyndon Chance, some accompanied by hand-drawn animals and estuary scenes in the margins, all covered with glass.

Exclaiming in delight, Taylor studied each poem in turn while he waited, watching from the doorway. They were all taken from Lyndon's famous last collection, *Estuary*. The paper was faded in places, perhaps by long exposure to the sun, but the tiny marginal sketches of animals and trees were still perfectly sharp and delicate.

'These are marvellous, Julius. Who made them?'

He hesitated, then lifted a shoulder. 'That would be me. A project in my youth.'

'You drew *all these*?' She tapped the glass on one of the poems, peering closer at the image of a badger before turning to stare at him, open-mouthed. 'These little pen-and-ink sketches are all your own work?'

'Guilty as charged.'

'But you're a natural artist. These are beautiful. And so well-executed.' She stared at him. 'Do you still draw?'

'Occasionally.' He looked embarrassed.

'I'd love to see your sketchbooks sometime.' She saw his instinctive recoil and threw up her hands. 'Unless you'd rather not share them, of course.'

'I'd rather not.'

'Fair enough.'

She knew how it felt to harbour a secret talent and fear its disclosure to the world. She dabbled in poetry herself at times, but never showed anyone. It would kill her to have someone read her private scribblings and laugh. Or worse, damn her with faint praise.

'My mother would have loved this room, you know.' She looked round and grinned at the surprise on his face. 'Mum was a huge fan of Lyndon's. She had copies of all his poetry collections and used to annotate them. Underline her favourite quotations, write cryptic comments in the margins, that kind of thing. She absolutely adored him.'

'Is that why you like his work so much?'

'I don't know, maybe. Studying my mum's annotations, reading his poems from the same copies she owned ... Yeah, it helps me feel closer to her. But I enjoy his poetry in my own right, too.' When he didn't say anything, she hugged herself, embarrassed at having revealed so much about her private life. 'Look, thanks for the room. But I'd better take that shower now.'

'The en-suite's through there.' Julius pointed to an open doorway on the other side of the room. 'I've left you some towels and shower stuff, too. Just in case you need any.' He disappeared, closing the door with a muttered, 'See you downstairs.'

To Taylor's surprise, Iris was also at lunch. She had brushed her straggling grey hair and tied it up with a hairband, and was wearing a clean shirt and jeans; she looked almost civilised, especially in that setting. She sat opposite Taylor in what they called the 'morning room' – a large, well-lit room overlooking the back gardens, dominated by a vast Welsh dresser stacked with decorative plates and teapots and chinaware from down the ages – and picked at a beetroot salad without much interest, her curious stare mostly on Taylor's face rather than her plate.

'Bones in the chapel,' Mrs Chance said out of nowhere, and pointed her knife at Taylor.

They all looked at her.

'So you found the bones?' Iris asked through a mouthful of beetroot and lettuce, her tone grudging. '*You?*'

'For my sins,' Taylor said, 'yes.'

'All have sinned and fallen short of God's law,' Iris replied, no doubt taking her reply as a sign that they were kindred spirits. She leant forward on her elbows, her face intent. 'It's what you do afterwards that counts. What kind of *penance* you undertake.'

Taylor wasn't sure how to respond to that.

Iris added fervently, 'He who sows of the flesh reaps only corruption, while he who sows of the Spirit will reap eternal life and salvation.'

'I'll bear that in mind.'

Julius rescued her with a sharp hike of his eyebrows. 'Pass the salt, would you, Aunt Iris?'

'What?' Iris turned her head vaguely to look at him, then her gaze fell on the salt cellar in the middle of the table, an elaborate design in silver, though sadly old and dented. 'Oh.' She passed it along to him, muttering, 'And he said, "Bring unto me a fresh bowl, and put salt in it." So they brought it unto him.' She swung her head, looking back at Taylor with a sudden, fierce frown. 'For Moab shall become as Sodom, and the Ammonites as Gomorrah, a land sown with salt and overgrown with nettles, and a wasteland forever.'

'Quite,' Julius agreed. 'This beetroot is delicious, isn't it? Makes a change from bread and cheese for lunch.'

His grandmother made a grunting noise under her breath. 'Turns your pee red though,' she complained, sipping from her water glass. She made an odd face afterwards and smacked her lips. 'Mmm, too bland. Why can't we have lemonade?'

'Because it doesn't agree with you, Gran,' he told her calmly.

'But I like the bubbles.'

'Maybe at dinner.'

Mrs Chance seemed to accept this, smiling benignly down the table at Taylor. 'This is nice,' she said, gesturing at their plates. 'Quite like the old days. Everyone around the table.'

'How did you know where to look for the body?' Iris asked Taylor. Her direct gaze had not wavered all that time.

Taylor glanced at Julius, who shook his head almost imperceptibly. *No ghost talk, thank you.*

'The ground gave way while I was standing there. It wasn't deliberate.' She looked hurriedly towards Mrs Chance, hoping to change the conversation. 'You were talking about the old days ... How many people lived here when you first came to Estuary House?'

'Oh, well, let's see. It was quite a crowded house that first summer.' Mrs Chance put down her knife and fork, and began to count on her fingers. 'There was me, Lyndon, Iris.' She hesitated, blinking. 'Their parents, of course. Barkers ... She was the housekeeper, Mrs Barclay. And Oliver, Lyndon's twin brother.'

'Did you ever know Diana Farthing?' Taylor ventured.

She'd recently been re-reading her research notes on Lyndon's background and double-underlined the name of the young woman that he was supposed to have driven to suicide.

Diana Farthing was someone she needed to ask the family about, not least because hardly anyone seemed to mention her. That in itself struck her as suspicious.

Mrs Chance stilled. 'Who?'

'Diana was before her time,' Iris said at once, frowning darkly. 'I only met her once myself and can't remember a damn thing about her. So no point asking me either.'

'What I remember,' Mrs Chance continued dreamily, 'is that Oliver had a girlfriend with him that summer. Such a beautiful girl. Jamaican descent. She had the most fabulous Afro. I think she wanted to be a model. Or was a model, perhaps. But I can't for the life of me...What was her name?'

'Jeannie,' Iris supplied, playing with her salad.

'That's it. Jeannie.'

'Don't get yourself worked up, Gran.' Julius topped up her water glass. 'Or it'll be a very long afternoon.'

'I'm not getting worked up, dear. I liked Jeannie, that's all. She was a nice girl, and you really couldn't blame her, she wasn't to know.' Mrs Chance stared out of the window, smiling with faint regret. 'Poor, poor child. I never got a chance to say goodbye, you know. Funny the things you remember.'

'What happened to her, Mrs Chance?' Taylor was fascinated.

'Who?'

'Oliver's girlfriend, Jeannie. You said you never got a chance to say goodbye. I just wondered what happened to her.'

Mrs Chance was silent for a moment, staring at her with

sudden intensity, as though she'd only just realised what they were discussing.

Then she picked up her knife and fork again.

'Oh, nothing,' she said vaguely, 'nothing happened to her at all.' She speared another cube of beetroot with a wavering hand. 'Just life.'

Chapter Twenty-Three

The ritual closes, not with a prayer
But a flint-cold wind, chipping away at us.

— From 'Elementals' on *Estuary*

In the morning, Eleanor woke to the sound of birdsong to find Lyndon gone again, and cold daylight streaming in through the open window.

After washing, she dressed in her own clothes, shabby as they were, and trailed reluctantly downstairs, driven by hunger. But Oliver and Jeannie were already sitting down to breakfast with Mr and Mrs Chance, and after last night's dreadful scenes at the séance, she couldn't face speaking to any of them.

After what Oliver had said, it was hard not to wonder if the 'lady' in some of Lyndon's darker poems was not a poetic fiction but in fact Diana Farthing, the woman who had drowned in the estuary. Judging by those poems, he must truly have been in love with her. But if so, why had he ended their relationship in such a heartless manner?

Perhaps it had all been a misunderstanding, she decided, unwilling to think him capable of such deliberate cruelty. Only Diana had taken his rejection to heart and drowned herself before he could take it back. And Lyndon had never recovered from her death. That would certainly explain the anguished yearning in his poems about her, and the aching sense of loss ...

Pushing such unhappy thoughts aside, she slipped into the cavernous, old-fashioned kitchen and asked Mrs Barclay if she knew where Lyndon had gone. She had to speak to him about this, she couldn't simply pretend it had never happened.

'For a walk by the river, most like.' The housekeeper looked her up and down, not bothering to hide her contempt. 'You'll be wanting to visit one of them fancy dress shops in Truro soon, I daresay. Mrs Chance told me about your luggage, how you "lost it" on the way down. Bit odd, that.'

'Yes, thank you,' she said coldly, and let herself out of the back door. There was a porch there, containing Wellingtons, among other things. She selected a pair that seemed the right size, checked inside them for spiders, and then squelched down towards the river.

On the other side of the railway line, she met the fair-haired man in the tweed cap again. He was out walking with the same boy she'd seen him with yesterday, a child of about ten years old, presumably his son.

'Hello again.' The man stopped, looking round at her, so that she had no option but to stop as well and speak to him. He removed his cap and gave her a courteous nod, almost as though she were the lady of the manor. 'I didn't introduce myself last time we, er, bumped into each other. But you seemed in a bit of a hurry.'

'I'm sorry about that.'

'Oh, no need. It's all very informal here. I'm Robert Mackenzie, but everyone calls me the damn Scot. Bit of a standing joke among the Cornish, though I've never even been to Scotland. Born and bred right here on the estuary.'

He had a weather-beaten face and cheerful blue eyes, a little creased around the edges; she guessed his age to be somewhere in his mid thirties. 'I live a couple of miles down the railway line towards Padstow. You must be the new Mrs Chance.'

She shook the hand he was holding out, feeling like a fraud. 'Yes,' she stammered. 'How do you do?'

'How do you do?' he responded politely.

'And is this your son?' She smiled at the boy, who was really quite charming-looking, with ruddy cheeks and a broad smile. 'I say, have you been collecting acorns? Those are very fine.'

The boy looked sheepish, stuffing a handful of oak leaves and acorns into his pocket. 'They're not bad. We got better ones last week though.'

'This is Davie, my lad,' Robert Mackenzie said, putting an arm about the boy's shoulder.

'Not at school?'

A cloud seemed to pass over the man's face. 'He's not well enough. Asthma, you know. Had a few bad attacks recently. I'm keeping him at home with me until he's on the mend.'

'Poor boy, I'm sorry to hear that. It must be a lot of work for your wife though, having him at home all day.'

Again, he hesitated. 'My wife is … She's dead.'

'Oh no. Sorry, I'm such an idiot.'

'You weren't to know. We're still learning to muddle by on our own, aren't we, Davie?' He gave his son an encouraging smile, but the boy merely hung his head, staring down at his scuffed boots. 'Well, look, it was good to meet you properly at last. You're the talk of the estuary.'

Eleanor was startled. 'Am I?'

'Oh yes, quite the celebrity. Lyndon's mysterious bride.'

'There's nothing mysterious about me, I assure you.'

254

'Now, don't spoil the gossip. We don't get much excitement around here. And Lyndon Chance ... Well, let's just say he's got a bit of a chequered past.'

There was a sudden hard gleam in his eyes, despite the friendly smile. He didn't much like Lyndon, she guessed.

She smiled in return, but some rebellious impulse made her ask, 'Talking of which, I don't suppose you've seen my husband on your travels this morning?'

'Actually, yes, I have. He was down that way, towards the old chapel.' Mackenzie pointed her in the right direction, his voice suddenly enthusiastic. 'Beautiful place, that chapel, if a little rundown. The family ought to take better care of it, maybe get it restored. Early eighteenth-century, I believe. Still has some of its original pews. And the stained-glass windows are lovely ... The ones that aren't broken, that is.' He paused, searching her face. 'Have you seen inside?'

'Yes.' She shivered.

'Goodness, here's me nattering on like a fool and you're too polite to stop me but getting chilled to the bone. I'll let you get on, Mrs Chance.' The man shook her hand again, this time more warmly. 'Very good to meet you.' Then he replaced his cap and clapped his son on the back. 'Come on, old boy, time to take our treasures back home.' He glanced over his shoulder at her as they moved away, his blue eyes twinkling with humour. 'My apologies for trespassing.'

'I didn't know you were,' she said, but Robert Mackenzie didn't seem to hear her, already walking back along the track, ducking his head to avoid bare branches, hand in hand with his son.

She stared after him for a moment, still amused by his funny way of speaking, and then turned with a smile on her face to find Lyndon watching her from a few feet away.

'Oh.'

'Oh, indeed.' Lyndon came out from behind a clump of trees, his face dark and suspicious. 'What the hell was that about?'

Eleanor was taken aback by his tone. 'Nothing. He lives nearby. Some cottage. He just introduced himself, that's all.' She hesitated. 'His name's Mackenzie, he said.'

'I know who he is. I saw the two of you smiling at each other. You seemed awfully friendly for complete strangers.'

'He was nice, that's all.'

'Nice?'

'I mean, he's funny,' she stammered. 'A good sense of humour.'

He made an explosive noise under his breath. 'Don't speak to that man again. Or his son. Do you hear me?'

'But whyever not?'

Lyndon stared down into her face for a moment, his jaw working silently, and then, with an obvious effort, he managed to force a smile. 'I'm sorry,' he said in a more level tone. 'You don't understand. Why should you? But that man has a motive for speaking to you, Eleanor, and it's not what you think.'

She was baffled. 'Then explain it to me.'

'Maybe one day. Not right now.' He drew her near, his arm slipping around her waist. His intent gaze searched her face. 'Look, forget it. I've upset you, and I didn't intend to. Can you forgive me?'

Lyndon bent his head and kissed her, pulling her tight against his body. His mouth moved to her throat, and she shivered, remembering how he'd held her during the night, how they'd made love without a stitch on their bodies, the shock of so many new sensations all at once.

'One day, I promise to explain everything. Then you'll understand all this. For now, Eleanor, please try to trust me.'

Daringly, she whispered, 'I could say the same to you.'

Lyndon laughed and pulled back from kissing her, sudden humour in his face. 'Touché!'

She decided his unexpected aggression over Mackenzie was down to jealousy, however much he was trying to disguise it, and felt rather flattered. If she'd caught him chatting to another young woman out in these woods, she probably would have been just as territorial about it. Which was an odd and disturbing thought.

'You left without waking me this morning,' she said, trying not to sound accusatory. 'I woke up and you were gone.'

'Did you miss me?' He was smiling now.

'I missed ... this.'

She stood on tiptoe to kiss him back, and felt his breath quicken. He caught her around the waist, and they stood a long while, melded together, the external world muted and indistinct.

They were both gasping a little by the time he released her. His cheeks were flushed.

'Passionate little thing, aren't you?' he said unsteadily, and ran his thumb across her swollen lips. 'I knew it as soon as I saw you at the poetry reading in Cirencester. Something in your eyes ...' He frowned when she pulled away, her face quickly averted. 'What is it?'

'Nothing.'

'Don't lie.' He studied her profile. 'All right, I'll bite. What did I say to make you turn cold?'

'Nothing. I didn't get any breakfast, that's all, and I'm hungry.' Agitated, she turned to leave. 'We should get back to the house.'

'Hang on.' Lyndon wasn't letting it go. 'Is this because of what Oliver said last night? All that nonsense about Diana, and the fact that you look a little like her?'

She didn't deny it.

'For God's sake, woman.' He groaned. 'Diana was a blonde, you're a blonde. You're about the same height and figure, too. All that, it's just window-dressing. Diana was nothing like you. Not in here, where it matters.' He tapped his head, and then his heart. 'Or here, where it hurts.'

'So you aren't looking for a replacement for her?' she whispered. 'I've read your poems, remember? Is she the "lady" you mention? The one you lost and can never forget?'

'The "lady" in my poems? Good God. Not even remotely. That's just a poetic device, a way of generating new poems. Like an invocation to the Muse.'

'But a Muse can be a living woman, too. And maybe Diana—'

'Look,' he interrupted her impatiently, 'Diana was a local girl, a farmer's daughter. Sweet and loving, yes. But not an intellectual like you.'

'You think I'm an intellectual?' She was flattered and wanted to believe him, but it was difficult after the awful things his brother had said about him.

'Of course. You're smart, a real live wire. And resilient, too. You were in a bad place back in Cirencester but you refused to let it destroy you. You wouldn't let your father dictate what you did with your life. I admire that about you.'

'Why did Oliver say all that, then? He was insinuating that you only chose me because I ... I look like her.'

He ran an impatient hand through his hair, avoiding her gaze. 'Olly's jealous, that's all. He doesn't want me to be happy.'

'But why not?'

'Who knows? Because I was born first? Because I have a talent for poetry and that's given me a certain notoriety he doesn't possess?' His voice softened, becoming almost persuasive. 'Oliver's always coveted whatever I have. Trust me, if he can't take it away from me, he'll do his level best to destroy it or ruin it for me instead. That's just the way he is.'

'Why do you put up with such bad behaviour?'

'He's my twin. What choice do I have?' Lyndon looked up towards the distant house, just visible above the treetops. 'All I know,' he added, 'is that I'm not going to let you spend any more time alone with him. Not after Diana.'

His voice had hardened, his eyes chilling to dark chips of ice.

Confused, Eleanor followed his gaze up to the house. There was a blurred face at one of the upper windows, staring down at them.

Oliver.

His brother was spying on them. How long had he been there, watching from on high, like a spider at the centre of a web?

She felt coldness grip her heart.

I'm not going to let you spend any more time alone with him. Not after Diana. And she saw again Oliver's eyes, glinting in the candlelight. *She killed herself rather than live another day without him.*

Chapter Twenty-Four

Under the reeds, muscular earth.
Under the earth, a lid.
Under the lid, ultimate triumph.

— From 'Sarcophagus' in *Estuary*

News had got out about the discovery of remains under the chapel, it seemed. The first Taylor knew about it was the sound of women chanting something in the distance. She put down the book she'd been reading and wandered down to the great hall, listening curiously.

She had only recently finished breakfast – a novel experience for her since coming to Cornwall, sitting down to eggs on buttered toast at a proper table, with a knife and fork and napkin, and endless tea on tap. Not that anyone was waiting on her, but it was all so much more civilised than heating a tin kettle or frying pan over her single flame gas stove, and then sitting cross-legged on damp grass or in the cramped, interminable gloom of her tent.

Peering out through a side window, she saw a straggling line of women with placards – and one man in a blue shirt, with his sleeves rolled up, looking bored – standing in the lane, shouting through the gate.

Julius appeared behind her. 'Oh, brilliant,' he said wearily, surveying the women at the gate.

'Who are they?'

'Protesters. I told you about them, didn't I? The anti-Lyndon Chance brigade.' He drew a deep breath. 'There's a small but highly vocal number of people, and I'm afraid some of them live locally, who insist my grandfather was a murderer who was never brought to justice.'

'But ... he's dead. What on earth do they think they can achieve, coming here?'

'I'm not sure. To bring it to the attention of the national media? Instigate some kind of posthumous trial? All I know is they seem determined to make our lives a misery.'

'Have you ever asked what they want?'

'Back in the beginning, yes. But I'm not sure most of them know what they want, except to destroy his reputation even further.' He shrugged. 'They first started coming here about five years ago, after a BBC documentary about my grandfather suggested all kinds of appalling things about his character. Utter nonsense, of course. But we started getting hate mail, as did his publishers. And within weeks, these noisy demonstrations kicked off. People picketing the gate, shouting slogans, even spraying graffiti on his tombstone or down at the chapel.'

'I remember. You said they usually come here on the anniversary of his death.' Taylor grimaced. 'A bit ghoulish.'

'Well, it seems the body under the chapel has got them fairly excited. There are usually only three or four at a time.' Julius frowned, watching as one of the women unfastened the gate and pushed through, followed by the others, all still chanting vigorously and waving their placards. 'And now I shall have to call the police. That's trespass, and they know it.'

'Who's the man?' Taylor asked, noticing that the only male had not come into the garden with the others but was still in the lane, smoking a cigarette while he waited.

'One of the husbands, I believe. He drives the minibus. Picks them all up, then takes them back home again after the protest, via a pub lunch.' He caught her surprised look and grinned. 'The group has an online forum; a few years ago, I managed to register under a false name so I could keep an eye on what they're up to. But I haven't checked it in ages. I should have known this would happen once the news got out.'

He threw open the front door, and stepped out, holding up his arms. 'Good morning, ladies.'

The women stopped marching. The chanting faltered.

'I'm afraid I need to ask you to vacate my property,' Julius told them, his tone surprisingly mild given the hatred in their eyes as soon as he walked out. 'If you want to demonstrate, I can't stop you. But we talked about this last time. You can hold your demonstration in the lane. But you're not permitted on the estate, because this is private property and you're trespassing.'

'We don't care,' somebody yelled. 'Whose body is it under the chapel?'

Julius lowered his arms but didn't reply.

One of the women had pink hair and looked very young, not much older than a sixth former. 'How can you keep on protecting a murderer?' she demanded passionately. 'We all know what he did.'

'His poems are vile and should be burnt,' someone else insisted, thrusting her placard as high as she could. It read, NO MORE LIES. 'Nobody should be publishing them.'

'Everyone's a critic,' Julius muttered, though he didn't look amused.

Taylor, who had been watching all this with horror, stuck her head out of the door and demanded loudly, 'Excuse me, but whatever happened to innocent until proven guilty?'

The girl with pink hair pointed directly at her. 'Hand-maiden,' she shrieked furiously.

One of the others began to chant, 'Lyndon Chance was a murderer! Lyndon Chance should be cancelled!' and the rest took up the cry, repeating these two phrases over and over.

'Right, I'm calling the police,' Julius announced as the women began to march towards the house again. He stepped back inside, shutting and bolting the door against them, and glanced at her. 'You OK?'

Taylor was a little shaken by what she'd just witnessed, the pure, seething hostility of those women. But she nodded.

'Look, I have to call the police,' he said, running a frustrated hand through his hair. 'My phone's upstairs. I won't be long.'

While he was gone, Mrs Chance wandered into the hall and stared at her. People were banging on the door now, their angry shouts muffled. 'What's happening?' she asked, sounding frightened. 'Who is that?'

'Protesters,' Taylor said, not sure how much the old lady understood. It was possible that Julius had protected her from the worst of it. And perhaps her memory issues worked in her favour for this, at least. 'They're here because of ... well, the bones under the chapel.'

'They think Lyndon did it,' Mrs Chance whispered, backing away. 'That's why they're here. They think my husband was a killer.'

Taylor stared at her. 'What do you know?'

'Nothing, nothing.' Mrs Chance clapped both hands over her ears. 'Tell them to stop. All that banging and shouting. Oh, I can't bear it ...'

And she stumbled away, moaning something Taylor couldn't catch.

Julius came back a few minutes later, and they stood in the

hall, listening as the protesters alternately thumped on the door and marched in a small circle around the garden, furiously waving their placards and chanting, 'Lyndon Chance was a murderer! Lyndon Chance should be cancelled!'

Eventually, two police officers arrived, and the protesters sheepishly agreed to leave, though by then Taylor's nerves were fraught and she could see that Julius was in a similar state.

Was she wrong to be defending Lyndon Chance against their accusations when she still had no evidence either way?

The question haunted her.

But she had to cling to the poet's innocence; anything else would feel like a betrayal of her mother's faith in him.

'How do you bear it?' she asked as he shut the door on the police, having given them a quick statement after waiting for the protesters' minibus to pull away.

'Oh, it's all part of the Chance legacy,' Julius said, his smile crooked. 'I've been dealing with it for years. They're determined he was a brute, and until we can prove otherwise, they're going to keep coming down here, shouting the odds.' He rubbed his chin, a frown in his eyes. 'I have to admit though, this body under the chapel ... It's awful. And if it does turn out to be connected to Lyndon ...'

His voice tailed off.

'Oh, I forgot. Your grandmother heard the protesters,' she told him belatedly. 'She got pretty upset. I'm sorry, I should have said earlier.'

'I'll go and check on her.' Julius threw her a grateful look as he went in search of Mrs Chance. 'Thanks for your support, by the way.'

Taylor felt exhausted. She rubbed her arms, realising how cold she was, and headed for one of the huge, winged armchairs by the unlit hearth in the great hall. Sinking into the armchair, she drew her tatty trainers up onto the seat and wrapped both arms about her knees, hugging herself tightly, something she hadn't done since she was a child.

Talk about a stressful morning, she thought grimly. She only hoped that nothing would interrupt her afternoon, set aside for beginning to type up a rough first draft of her thesis.

The framed portrait of the Lady Elizabeth seemed to watch her with ironic eyes, as though to say that dealing with a handful of angry protesters was nothing compared to what *her life* had been ...

The next morning, as Taylor was sitting in bed in her PJs, puzzling over a map of the estuary that she'd marked out and colour-coded with various sites connected to Lyndon Chance's poems, she heard the faint sound of a telephone ringing, somewhere far off in the great house.

It continued for about ten rings while she listened, wondering if anyone would ever answer it. Then stopped.

About five minutes later, she heard quick footsteps in the corridor outside her bedroom, and there was a knock at the door.

'Come in.'

It was Julius. Hesitantly, he studied her pyjamas and bed hair. 'Is this a bad time? I'm sorry, I thought you would be up and having breakfast by now.' He checked his watch. 'It's after ten, you know.'

'I am up.' Taylor smiled. 'I'm just not out of bed yet. Anyway, I'm not really a breakfast person. Coffee is fine for me, and I'll probably grab a cup before I go out later.'

'You're going out? In this weather?' Julius glanced towards the window, where rain was steadily streaming down from a murky sky.

'To get a change of clothes from my van. I tend to leave my clean laundry stored in there until I need it.' She saw his puzzled look. 'There's a laundrette in Wadebridge. I've been taking my stuff there.'

'Well, please feel free to use our utility room while you're here. There's a washer, drier, and ironing board down there. I can show you where.'

Her lips quirked. 'I can't imagine you slaving over the laundry. It just isn't very lord of the manor-ish.'

'Well,' he admitted, also smiling faintly, 'it's true that I farm out the towels and bed linen to a service in town. And, as I said, we have a cleaner who comes in once a week. But I've been looking after myself and Gran for years. I know how to work the washing machine, trust me. And the iron.'

'Goodness me.' She folded up her map and, seeing his gaze on her head again, hurriedly smoothed down her hair. 'So, was there something particular you wanted to say? You marched up here with great purpose.'

'Oh yes, I had a call. Do you mind if I ...?'

Julius came into the room without waiting for her answer and closed the door behind him. She sat up straight and checked her cleavage wasn't showing, stupidly alarmed by being alone with him in her bedroom. But to her chagrin, he didn't even glance at her, his expression distracted as he peered absently at one of the framed poems on the wall.

'That was the local police on the phone. An officer I happen to know through the business liaison committee. He was giving me an update on the bones you found.'

'The body?'

'Yes, exactly. The body.' He turned to stare out of the window at the ceaseless rain. 'I don't know how to put this ... It's the strangest thing.'

She got out of bed and pulled a thick, hairy jumper over

266

her pyjamas, feeling a little more comfortable once shrouded in layers of wool.

'Just use short words. I'll try to keep up.'

He didn't smile. 'I'd assumed they'd be coming round to see us again any day now. To interview us formally.'

'I take it they're not coming, though?' she prompted him.

'The sergeant says it's not necessary anymore.'

'Why not?'

'Apparently, based on their preliminary findings, plus a few items buried with the body, the police don't think this woman's death was recent. That's why they're holding off on interviewing us for now.'

'*Not recent*?' Taylor felt a coldness inside and hugged her arms close in the shapeless hairy jumper. 'What does that mean?'

'I'm not sure. But they've asked me to go in and see if I can identify some of the items they found with the body.' Julius hesitated. 'I wondered if you fancied a drive out?'

Chapter Twenty-Five

At last, there was only the marrow left to suck:
Sleek, red-lipped as seduction.

— From 'The Bones of It' in *Estuary*

Gerard Chance parked his pale green, mud-spattered Land Rover in a rough turning circle at the edge of the reeds and sat looking upwards for a moment, studying the livid, overcast skies with their gleam of cold sunlight. 'Looks like a shower's on the way,' he muttered, and jumped out. 'Best not hang around.'

By the time Eleanor had climbed out, joining Lyndon on the muddy track that led towards the riverbank, Mr Chance had already marched away, cradling a shotgun in his arms, his enthusiastic wolfhound barking at his heels.

'Is he going to kill something with that awful thing?' she asked Lyndon, eyeing the long-barrelled gun with misgiving.

'Townie,' he mocked her, and seized her gloved hand in his. She'd borrowed the gloves from Jeannie, thin white leather, close-fitting and probably more expensive than anything she'd ever owned. His own gloves were sheepskin, lined with fur, quite swamping her own delicate creations. 'Come on, don't be such a coward.'

Lyndon led her down the track after his father, and now

she could see a structure ahead above the tall, waving reeds. The hut Oliver had built, presumably.

'It's about the only time Dad can shoot – when he's this side of the river. Mum won't let him hunt any nearer the house. Can't stand loud bangs, she says.' When she looked at him, surprised, he laughed. 'Mum wasn't country-bred either. A city girl. London. That's where Dad met her.'

He seemed in good spirits at last, she thought, watching him with a relieved smile. She felt better inside. All that awful business with Oliver... The story of Lyndon's ex and her mysterious drowning... It had made her feel horrible. But his father's attention had soothed his pride, and though a shower or two might be forecast, the promising glint of sunshine had lifted both their moods on rising this morning.

The hut was really quite large, she realised, as they approached it through a sea of softly rustling, waist-high reeds.

'Gosh.' Lyndon's grip tightened on hers as she stopped, staring.

She'd expected a rough lean-to. But this was more like a summer house. It had a porch with wooden decking, and a narrow chimney pipe, and it was clear that somebody – presumably Oliver himself – had started clearing the reeds in the vicinity, no doubt intending to widen the track and make it easier to park nearer.

Gerard Chance saw her impressed look. 'You like our storage hut?'

A few gentle drops of rain had begun to fall as they walked through the reeds and were now gathering pace.

'It's bigger than I expected.'

'Ah, he knows how to do a thing properly, does my Olly.' He cleared his throat, catching Lyndon's rigid expression. 'There's a padlock on the door, but the key should be on top of the frame. It saves us a tidy bit of time, keeping tools this side of the river, rather than ferrying them across every time.'

The rain was falling more heavily now, the sky darkening.

'Look, why don't you let yourself into the hut, get out of this rain?' Gerard said in a tone that was more command than suggestion. 'Us boys'll walk on down to the river; we don't mind a spot of the wet stuff.' He peered around for the dog, whistling, and then glanced back at his son. 'Come on, Lyndon. I want to show you the site for this new jetty Olly's got planned.'

'I'll be all right,' she whispered when Lyndon hesitated, and pulled her hand free from his. 'You go with your dad.'

Once they were out of sight, she reached up and scrabbled for the key on top of the frame, then unlocked the salt-encrusted padlock and let herself in.

It was surprisingly light inside the hut, thanks to a window at the back, and was split into two halves, right and left of the door. The first section was dusty and cluttered with tools, drums, and crates, the floor earthen and sandy, mostly covered with sacking and planks set over the dampest areas. One wall held shelving and she stood a moment, studying the pots and jars and boxes stored there, though without much interest, wondering how long the men would be down at the river.

The second section was darker, without the additional light through the doorway, but its narrow window also overlooked the riverbank.

She wandered across and peered out through a dirty, cobwebby pane, but could see nothing but seemingly endless reed marsh and the old trunk of a withered tree roughly halfway between the hut and the River Camel – a long, cool strip of grey in the middle distance.

She heard barking, still a way off. Then a sharp, echoing retort as a gun was fired. Finally, silence again.

Restless, Eleanor turned away from the window, and threaded her way through a series of empty crates scattered across the floor and past a dusty set of shelves, only to stop dead at the sight of a plain wooden cross, hanging on the wall in a shadowy corner.

On the patted-smooth earth below it lay a bunch of limp wildflowers, mostly green stems with a hint of white, and about the upper strut of the wooden cross something bright had been woven. Something long and silvery that glinted as she moved, unblocking the light.

She stepped closer to see it better.

A chain.

There was a fine silver chain wrapped about the cross. And not just a chain. It was a locket.

Another gunshot.

Slowly, her heart thudding, Eleanor extricated the silver chain and held it up, the heart-shaped locket swinging from her closed fist.

She could hear male voices in the distance now. Muffled, but growing closer. The sound of barking, too. The men were coming back with the dog.

The heart-shaped locket had a thick rim. A clasp, too, halfway up. Hurriedly, she unsnapped it and looked inside.

Lyndon stared back at her.

It was a cut-out from a larger photograph. Lyndon, together with a smiling blonde who looked only too uncannily like her. Just their heads, leaning together like two soulmates, and a hint of bright water behind them. The Camel estuary in summer, she guessed.

Another gunshot sounded. Louder, close at hand, and

accompanied by the crack of birds' wings as they broke cover in fright.

Eleanor stared at the photograph, and then around the dusty, dim-lit space. At the cross positioned on a nail above her. This was a shrine to the dead, she realised. And someone had been here recently. She studied the green stalks of flowers on the sandy floor, their white blooms withering but not dead yet. She thought of the silver locket left there in the darkness, hanging from the cross. The photograph hidden inside like a lover's keepsake.

They dragged the river. Her body was never found.

Her stomach clenched and roiled. She put a hand to her mouth, fearing she might be sick.

'Eleanor?' It was Lyndon calling from outside the hut. He was coming closer. 'We're back, darling.' He was almost at the door. 'Eleanor? Are you in there?'

Trembling, she thrust the necklace into her coat pocket, replaced the wooden cross roughly where she'd found it, and hurried out to meet them.

'Sorry,' she said, blinking at the daylight after the dark interior, her voice surely too high-pitched, too shaky. 'I caught my coat on a nail. No, I'm fine, no damage done.' She smiled mistily up at Lyndon as he caught her hands and hoped he wouldn't suspect how frightened she was. 'I see the rain's stopped. Did ... Did you two see everything you wanted to? It's just I've got this terrible headache. It came on suddenly. Would it be all right if we drove straight back to the house?'

'Of course,' Lyndon said at once, frowning, and after a quick glance inside the hut, drew the door shut and turned the key in the padlock.

'Go back home?' His father, a few feet from the hut, had turned to stare at them, his shotgun resting lightly on his shoulder, barrel pointing at the sky. 'Are you being funny, young lady? I've barely had any sport.'

'Dad, for God's sake.'

'I'm staying here,' Gerard told them flatly, and threw Lyndon the car keys. 'You take your wife home, if you like, and swing back round for me in an hour or so.'

'You're sure?'

But Mr Chance had already turned and was heading back through the reeds towards the river, the large, hairy wolfhound lolloping by his side.

Lyndon watched his father go, his expression torn. Then he looked down into her face. 'Eleanor, what's wrong?'

She badly wanted answers to her questions. Had he left those flowers there? Lyndon had claimed never to have seen the hut before, and not to have come home in ages. Yet who else would have turned that place into a shrine to his dead girlfriend? Was he still in love with Diana Farthing? He had made love to her so passionately, she had begun to hope he was falling in love with her, as she had fallen in love with him. But perhaps he'd been thinking of someone else all along.

Her heart was beating so hard she felt it would explode, and she guessed her cheeks must be very flushed.

Now was not the time. She needed to be alone, to think.

Somehow, Eleanor managed a smile for him. 'I told you, it's a bad headache. Probably a migraine on the way. I'm prone to them, especially when I don't get enough sleep. Didn't I say?'

'No, you didn't,' he said shortly, and she got the feeling Lyndon didn't believe a word she was saying. But he didn't press her.

With one last glance back at the silent hut, he put his

arm through hers, and together they walked back to where they'd left the car.

'So, Oliver's amazing hut,' he drawled. 'How was it?'

'A dead bore, if you must know. I've no idea why your father thinks it's such an achievement, even if Oliver built it with his bare hands. Sitting in there for half an hour is probably what gave me this headache.'

Lyndon laughed, giving her a lazy smile. He began to whistle softly under his breath.

As soon as she heard the Land Rover roar away again, Eleanor jumped off the sofa where Lyndon had left her to rest and groped her stumbling way through the dark maze of corridors to the back door. She was terrified of running into Mrs Chance or the housekeeper, and having to explain herself, as Lyndon had informed them both that she was 'ill' and not to be disturbed.

Outside under grey skies, she hurried through the formal gardens, keeping out of sight of the windows as far as possible.

Dance music drifted from an open downstairs window; she guessed that Oliver and Jeannie must be in the den again, dancing and smoking, or perhaps even making love. It was obvious those two were already lovers, despite not being married, and while that might have shocked her once, she no longer saw the harm in it. Not when she and Lyndon were sleeping together under the auspices of a sham marriage.

Life was cruel, she thought unhappily; one had to take one's pleasures whenever and wherever possible.

She'd enjoyed Oliver's company at first, finding him charming and every bit as attractive as his brother. But she realised now why Lyndon hated him so much. All the same, after what she'd seen today, she wondered if Oliver was right about why Diana Farthing died. Perhaps her death had genuinely been an accident.

Lyndon must truly regret the way he'd treated her, after all, to have written such heartfelt verse to a nameless 'lady' and built a secret shrine to her in his brother's hut. He'd even pretended never to have set foot in there before.

It was all very strange.

It occurred to her that Oliver himself might have placed the wooden cross there, and the flowers, too, perhaps out of pity for the lovesick woman who'd leapt to her death from his yacht. But she dismissed the idea.

Oliver wasn't the type, was he?

He had his feet too firmly on the ground, and it was Lyndon who had insisted on those séances and reacted so violently to the suggestion that Diana was trying to get in touch with him from beyond her watery grave.

Her fingers clutched the heavy silver necklace in her coat pocket. She needed somewhere to think, away from that dark, claustrophobic house, somewhere she could examine the locket without risk of being seen by Lyndon or anyone else.

Eleanor let herself through the gate and across the silent railway line, then ran through the scrubby patch of woodland beyond. It had already started to rain again; another quick shower, the trees soon rustling, raindrops pattering on leaves all around her, soft and musical.

Instinctively, she was making for the river and the old chapel that stood a little way from its muddy banks. She could be dry there. And alone.

The chapel door was shut. But not locked.

'Hello?'

No response.

The chapel was cold and empty.

Warily, she pushed the door to again behind her, and made for a dusty pew under the stained-glass window. A thin wind whistled through the hole in the saint's head, chill and comfortless, but the coloured glass provided enough glowing light for her to examine the silver locket in detail.

Snapping it open, she drew in a sharp breath.

Lyndon and Diana, their heads together, smiling at the camera, with the estuary shining behind them.

She traced his face with her finger, and tears came into her eyes. With difficulty, she blinked them away and tried to focus.

Was it Lyndon in the photograph? Or Oliver?

Lyndon, she decided.

But who had taken this snap?

They seemed so relaxed, so at ease, it could only have been a friend. Or a trusted family member, perhaps. She ran through all the family she knew in turn, dismissing each one. Gerard wasn't interested in much except his land and property, as far as she could see, and how it could benefit the family. Camilla clearly favoured Oliver over Lyndon, and from the meagre amount of gossip she'd gleaned from the tight-lipped Mrs Barclay, had never approved of Lyndon's close relationship with a local farmer's daughter.

Oliver was unlikely to have inspired such open smiles from both of them, and as for Iris ... Well, Iris was a possibility.

Whoever the photographer was, they'd captured the emotion of the moment perfectly. Lyndon must have loved his Diana very much indeed, she thought. It was in his eyes as well as his smile, and the protective way his arm lay along her shoulder, pulling her close.

Her heart ached. She sat a long while in the cold light from the stained-glass window, studying his face closely, poring over every faded line as though it could speak truth to her, before turning her attention to Diana Farthing instead.

Yes, they did look alike, it was true. But, exactly as Lyndon had told her, it was a superficial likeness only. Both were blonde, both had similarly shaped faces.

But Diana's eyes were doe-like and trusting. There was a softness about her that Eleanor personally felt she lacked. If she'd ever been that open towards others, perhaps when young, it had long since been beaten out of her as 'sinful', to be replaced by an angry, rebellious soul. Though she'd learned to conceal that, too, of course, to avoid further correction. An obediently lowered head had become her armour, and as much silence as she could maintain in the face of her father's watchful cruelty.

Who had obtained this locket with its hidden photograph – which must surely have hung about Diana's neck – and how?

And when?

Had Diana flung it back at Lyndon after their final, break-up row?

Or had she sent it back to him via a friend, perhaps?

She shivered under the chill light of the broken window, and not just with cold, as she imagined another horrible scenario. That Diana had not 'drowned' but been murdered by Lyndon, perhaps in one of his fits of jealous rage.

She had already witnessed first-hand how jealous Lyndon could become, and he barely knew her, despite their recent lovemaking. With Diana, the love of his life, how might he have reacted to even a little provocation?

Stirring, she became aware of laughter and voices outside. She knelt up on the pew and saw, through the hole in the window, Robert Mackenzie and Davie in a little rowboat. They had fishing tackle with them, and a lidded bucket of bait, and Mr Mackenzie was wearing fisherman's waders and a padded jacket.

As she watched, pleased to see the boy enjoying himself so much, Davie bent over to pick something up from the floor of the rowboat, and lost his cap in the water. It bobbed gently away, heading for the bank.

Mr Mackenzie grabbed an oar and tried to fish it out, but only succeeded in pushing it further towards the riverbank.

Closing the locket, Eleanor hesitated, and then, on a whim, hung it about her neck. It felt cold and heavy, but she tucked it out of sight under her woollen top and made for the door.

She had promised Lyndon never to speak to Mackenzie again. But he had not told her about his little shrine in the hut, no doubt thinking she wouldn't find it, tucked away in that dark corner. Tit-for-tat was not a particularly elegant game. But it was one of the few she knew how to play.

'Hello there, can I help?' she called cheerily, and saw both heads turn, watching as she made her way down the damp slipway to the river. 'I think I can probably reach that.'

'Thank you. Do be careful though.' Mackenzie nodded to his son to pick up the oars, and they began to row back towards shore. 'Don't fall in.'

Snapping off a prickly branch from one of the nearby shrubs, she used it to hook the floating cap and drag it to land.

'There you go.' She hoisted the cap aloft on the end of the branch, dripping but otherwise intact. 'Bit wet – just needs to sit in front of the fire for a few hours.'

They had reached the bank by then. Mackenzie helped Davie out onto dry land, and then tied up the boat to an iron ring in the slipway.

'What do you say to the lady, Davie?' he prompted his son.

'Thank you, Mrs Chance,' the boy said shyly, and took the cap from her, shaking it so violently they all got wet.

'Oi, stop that, you little scamp!' Mackenzie was laughing. He brushed down her coat, which had watery flecks on the arm. 'I'm so sorry. Are you all right?'

'Perfectly.'

'Good-o.' He hesitated, his expression turning serious. 'Look, have you got five minutes for a quick chat?'

Stay away from Robert Mackenzie.

Eleanor lifted her chin, suddenly defiant. Yes, she'd given Lyndon her word. But why was he allowed to dictate who she spoke to, who her friends were? Lyndon wasn't her keeper. He wasn't even her husband.

'Yes, if you like.'

'Bit muddy down here though. Shall we walk up to the chapel?' He turned to his son, who was messing about, twirling his cap on a walking stick. 'Tell you what, Davie. While I talk to Mrs Chance, how about you mind the boat for me? Maybe tidy up the tackle, too. I'll only be a few minutes, I promise.'

Davie looked at Eleanor a little resentfully. 'Yes, Dad.'

Chapter Twenty-Six

Dark-spelled, light-flung, each letter
A curse, a riddle.

— From 'Ouija' in *Estuary*

At the station, Taylor scrolled through social media on her phone while Julius, with apparent interest, studied a leaflet about burglar-proofing your home. The police had asked them to wait until an officer was free to show them the various items found with the unearthed bones. But fifteen minutes had stretched to half an hour, and the wait continued. Taylor was just beginning to wish she'd stayed behind and got on with her research work when a friendly-looking police officer appeared in the waiting area, her smile apologetic.

It was Leah, the officer who'd been first on the scene at the chapel that night.

'Hello again. I'm sorry to have kept you so long. Something came up.' She shook hands with them. 'If you'd like to follow me.'

They were taken through a maze of corridors to a modern, well-lit area with a series of chrome cabinets along one wall and a central examination table. There, laid out on the cold steel for their inspection, was a series of odd, discoloured and partially broken objects, along with what looked like shreds of soiled, threadbare fabric. Some of the exhibits were already bagged up and labelled.

'So,' Leah said with a frown, donning a pair of latex gloves, 'now you've had a chance to think, I don't suppose you have any new ideas about who this is?'

'Still not a clue.' Julius looked apologetic.

'No problem. That's what I thought anyway.' Leah gave him a breezy smile. 'Just wanted to make sure you hadn't turned up any additional information since last time we spoke.'

From her hiding place, she couldn't see what he was doing. But she could hear it. The sounds that would stay with her forever. At last they stopped, and she felt almost relieved. That her mother would never have to suffer such pain and indignity again. That it was over.

Julius looked at her quickly. 'You OK, Taylor? I can do this on my own if you need some fresh air.'

'Thank you, I'm fine to stay.'

Leah glanced from his face to hers, and then down at the artefacts again. It didn't take a psychic to know what she was thinking. That they were a couple.

The thought ran through Taylor like quicksilver in her veins, leaving her warm and light-headed and breathing far too fast.

'What's that?' she asked hurriedly, her attention caught by something glinting in a plastic evidence bag, partly obscured by a label.

'Ah yes. We've tried to clean it up, but ...'

Leah picked up the bag and showed it to them. It was a gold ring, dulled by time and earth, and a little scratched, yet somehow hauntingly familiar.

Then Taylor realised what it was, and felt her heart begin to thud.

'I've seen that before,' Julius said slowly.

'Me, too.' Taylor took a deep breath, nodding. 'The portrait in the hall at Estuary House. I could be wrong, but it looks like the Lady Elizabeth's ring.'

Leah raised her brows. 'You think it's a family ring?' She glanced at Julius, who was looking troubled. 'You wouldn't happen to know who wore it last?'

'Sorry.'

'That's OK.' Leah put the ring back in the evidence box and began fiddling with the shreds of fabric instead. 'I probably shouldn't say, ahead of the forensic report, but ... the body you found ... It's definitely female.' She looked at Julius, her smile apologetic. 'And I'm sorry, but we'll need to take a DNA sample from you. For comparison purposes.'

Back in Wadebridge, Julius dropped her off outside a busy tea shop not far from the River Camel, its interior cheery and unassuming, with red gingham tablecloths and framed Victorian photos of the town around the walls.

While he went off to park in the town centre, Taylor ordered a 'traditional Cornish cream tea' for two and stared out at rainy streets. A young family in shorts and T-shirts ran past, no doubt on their way to some indoor amusement, all of them laughing and soaked to the skin, the mother pushing a plastic-covered buggy.

Mack had led her, step by step, to that body under the chapel floor. She was certain of it now. But why?

Frowning, she dragged out her mobile and flicked through the photo library, trying to locate the selfie with Mack on the riverbank. She wasn't entirely surprised to find a photo of herself, smiling broadly with her head to one side as though leaning into an absent friend.

Mack wasn't there; she was alone in the photograph.

But what she could see were the waters of the estuary, stretching away behind her, sunlit and empty. And across the river, on the opposite bank, the pale, withered tree and, a little way beyond it, half-hidden in a sea of marshy reeds and shrubs, the hint of a wooden roof and walls.

Iris's shack.

Taylor favourited the photo so she could find it again more quickly, and then placed the phone face-down on the table.

Stirring the teapot to strengthen the brew, she eyed with misgiving the assorted cakes the waitress had brought while she was flicking through her photos.

After years of student life and its excesses, she'd vowed to drink less alcohol and eat less chocolate this year. But the plain scones looked innocuous enough; she broke one in half and smothered it with jam, in the Cornish way, only afterwards topping it with thick clotted cream.

The beatings hadn't stopped, of course, not even when they put her in a new place. And worse than beatings.

But she hadn't yet learned to trust, to know that a teacher could be confided in, that a social worker's smile was genuine.

She'd closed her eyes and her mind instead, and dreamed of a day when she would be free. When she could escape to a better place and live on her own, without fear, without the weight of a body over her.

The darkness threatened to overwhelm her again, but she pushed it away. The past was beginning to lose its grip on her, she realised.

Maybe one day …

Julius arrived, a newspaper tucked under his arm; he dropped his wet umbrella into the stand before sinking into the seat opposite her with a faint smile on his face. 'Ah. I see you've mastered our ways already.'

'I'm sorry?'

'Jam first, then cream.' He nodded to her scone, half-eaten on the dainty side plate. 'Proper Cornish.'

'Actually, I'm afraid I cheated.' Taylor looked pointedly at the menu, set into a spinner on the table, and then turned it to face him; one side proudly demonstrated the 'jam first' technique for which Cornwall was known. 'Though I didn't know there was another way to do it.'

'Quite right, too.'

She finished her scone in silence while he perused the local newspaper. 'Is it in there?' she asked curiously.

'Need you ask after this morning's impromptu protest?'

He held up the newspaper, showing her an inside page with a grainy black-and-white photograph of the chapel from the other side of the estuary – presumably taken with a telephoto lens – alongside the dramatic headline, BODY FOUND AT ESTUARY HOUSE, above a smaller sub-heading, *Infamous Poet's Grandson Unearths Human Remains*.

'Not terribly subtle. But I guess you couldn't hope to keep it quiet forever.' Taylor tried to read his expression; as always, she found it hard to gauge how he was feeling. 'Bad, is it? Anything you didn't expect?'

He grimaced, dropping the newspaper onto the empty chair beside him. 'The usual unpleasant suggestion that the Chance family is cursed, and that Lyndon Chance was a bad seed who's supposed to have murdered his girlfriend and his brother, and any number of other people, too,' he said, selecting a mini chocolate éclair from the cake display. 'But that's par for the course where my grandfather's concerned. I daresay they'd pin the Kennedy assassination on him if they could put him in Texas at the right time.' He laughed at her shocked expression. 'I'm kidding.'

'I'm not sure you are.'

Julius devoured the mini éclair in two large bites, and then licked his fingers. 'You'll be relieved to hear you barely get a mention, though.'

She felt panicked. 'What does "barely" mean?'

'Oh, a line or two near the bottom of the piece.' Wiping his hands on a paper napkin, Julius met her widening eyes. He sighed and picked up the newspaper again. 'Here you go.' Tapping the page, he passed it to her. 'Read for yourself.'

'Taylor Pierce, research student from UCL, was also on site when the human remains were discovered,' she read aloud, unsure whether to be piqued or relieved that her role in discovering the body had been relegated to that of a mere bystander.

To her surprise, the newspaper article included a few other facts about her, including that she was staying at Estuary House while she researched Lyndon Chance's 'dark and suspicious' history.

'Good grief.' She stared at him over the newspaper. 'They're making it sound like I came down here deliberately looking to dig up dead bodies.'

'I know,' he said calmly.

'It's inaccurate, too. My work is mostly to do with ecology.' She saw his cynical expression, and went on hurriedly, 'How on earth did they find out about my thesis, anyway?'

'Not through us, I promise you. I told Gran very specifically not to speak to any journalists about what we found in the chapel, and she never talks publicly about Lyndon anyway – it's one of her few absolute rules – so none of that nonsense came from her.'

'There was that guy taking photos at the chapel the next morning. I think he said he was a member of the press, didn't he? Maybe he overheard us talking.' Taylor scanned the rest of the article and then returned the newspaper to him, a little shaken. 'When I decided to spend the summer here, I didn't expect to end up in the local rag.'

'Or to hang out with a couple of ghosts,' he said wryly.

She looked at him closely. 'So, you believe now that I actually saw Mack and Davie? That I didn't *imagine* them?'

'I don't know what you did or didn't see. But I'm aware that you believe in such things. The mind is very good at playing tricks on us.'

She considered that for a moment, and then turned her mobile over, found the photo of her on the riverbank, and passed it over to him.

'What do you make of this photo, then? I took a selfie with Mack and Davie, just before ... Well, before Davie was stung by a wasp and I ran for the epi pen. Only there's nobody in the photo now except me, as you can see.'

He studied the photograph and then handed it back. 'Respectfully, it's a selfie of you alone on the riverbank. I'm not sure what that proves.'

'He asked me to raise the phone higher, to get more of the estuary into the shot. I think there was something Mack specifically wanted me to notice.' She pinched the photo to narrow in on the distant shack and showed it to him again. 'Like that, for instance.'

He gave her a blank look. 'Iris's hut?'

'I don't know, I'm just throwing out ideas. But there were odd things on the wall when I visited her hut, remember? Tarot cards, old drafts of Lyndon's poems. And Mack more or less sent me over there.'

'He did what?' Julius sounded thunderstruck.

'That day when I borrowed the boat and rowed over to the other side of the river. That was Mack's doing. He told me where your rowboat was moored. He even gave me the false impression the boat was his.' She looked at him apologetically. 'Or I would never have borrowed it.'

'You didn't mention any of that at the time. Or him, in fact.'

'Mack asked me not to say anything to you about him. He said there was bad blood between him and your family. I realise now he simply didn't want me to discover he didn't exist.'

'Sounds like an intelligent ghost.'

Ignoring this sarcasm, Taylor studied the selfie again and then put the phone away, frowning. 'I can't work out the connection, but I'm sure there must be one. Otherwise, why keep pointing me towards Iris's place?' She picked up the teapot, belatedly realising it had probably brewed to death by now. 'Thirsty?'

'God, yes. Thank you.' He watched her pour him an exceptionally strong cup of tea, and then took a deep gulp of it. 'Are you annoyed?'

'About what?'

'You found the body. You were the one who uncovered her grave. But the way that newspaper article tells the story, it was me. Your role in this has been all but erased.'

'I don't mind. Far from it.'

'I'm not sure I want to take the credit though, either. Feels like bad luck to me.' He drank some more tea, gazing out at the rainy day. 'So, it's not my great-uncle down there. You heard her. The bones belong to a female. But if that turns out to be a family ring, as you seem to think...' He shook his head, his expression grim. 'Maybe the Chance family really is cursed, after all. I mean, what kind of monster does something like that to a woman? Whoever she was, it looks like she was murdered, and then her body dumped under the chapel floor to prevent anyone discovering their crime.'

A cold shudder ran through her, and she put down her cup. She felt faint, the blood rushing from her head, leaving her face cold and clammy, her fingers tingling, a strange buzz in her ears…

'Taylor?'

She swallowed hard before managing a curt nod, forcing herself to speak. 'It's a possibility, yes.'

Julius said nothing for a moment, watching her. Then he leant back in his seat, patterns of streaming rain from the windows reflected on his lean face.

'Of course,' he said softly. 'I'd forgotten about your mother. That was incredibly insensitive of me, I'm sorry.'

Her heart contracted painfully, and she closed her eyes, unable to look at him anymore. Tears squeezed out from under tightly shut eyelids.

She felt his hand touch hers across the table. 'Hey,' he said. 'I really am sorry. I'm an idiot.'

He squeezed her hand and then released it.

There was a long silence.

Slowly, the buzz in her ears receded and Taylor felt able to open her eyes again. She still couldn't look at him, but nodded, wiping away her tears. People claimed words didn't matter, but sometimes words were all she had to stave off the darkness.

Before she could find the strength to speak, the waitress appeared beside their table with awesomely bad timing and beamed down at them, her round face cheerful. 'How are the cakes, m'dears? Looks like you enjoyed those éclairs. Can I get you a fresh pot of tea, perhaps? Refills are included in the price.'

Taylor shook her head wordlessly.

'Thank you, we're finished.' Julius got out his wallet to pay. 'No, it's my treat,' he insisted when Taylor tried to protest.

Much to her relief, he never returned to the subject of the body under the chapel, and Taylor was able to hide her momentary panic behind a lively debate over the tip. But she was shaken by what had just happened. Nobody had ever got through her armour like that before. And with a passing remark, too.

What kind of monster does something like that to a woman?

Delicately, painstakingly, she began the task of rebuilding and reinforcing her mental shield. But she knew it had been weakened. Next time, it might crumble altogether...

Rain was still falling when they left the café; they hurried back to the car park, jostling beneath his umbrella to avoid getting soaked.

'Bloody Cornish rain,' Julius said, holding the dripping umbrella over both their heads while he unlocked the car. 'Isn't it meant to be summer? Or did we miss the memo?'

He glanced down at her, smiling, and in that warm, intimate space, she thought for a moment that he intended to kiss her again. But he merely inclined his head and opened the passenger door for her.

'My lady,' he said, that mocking note back in his voice as he ushered her inside, 'your carriage awaits.'

Chapter Twenty-Seven

Through arched rivulets, a sand bar for an altar,
The bridal gown of Cornish weather.
Let no man put them asunder...

— From 'River Marriage' from *Estuary*

'Davie's a lovely boy,' Eleanor told Mackenzie, rubbing and clapping her gloved hands as they entered the chapel. It felt even chillier in there now, shadows lengthening along the west wall as the day wore on. No doubt Lyndon would have got back with his father by now and must be looking for her. Well, he wouldn't find her. Not up at the house. 'Such nice manners. You must be very proud of him.'

'I am,' Mackenzie agreed, smiling.

Eleanor turned, surprised and a little alarmed to find him close behind her. 'So,' she said, 'what did you want to say to me?'

'Shall we sit down?'

She chose the same wooden pew as before, and Mackenzie sat down beside her on the hard bench seat, both of them facing front as though waiting for a service to begin. It must be fifty years or more since this place had seen its last service, she thought.

'You'll probably think me impertinent,' he added sharply.

'Feel free to tell me to mind my own business. And perhaps I should.'

She stared ahead at the altar end, which lay in thick, cobwebby shadow. 'Is this about Lyndon?'

'In a roundabout way.' Mackenzie grimaced, pulling off his cap and running a hand through his fair hair, smoothing it down. 'Actually, it's about my sister.'

Eleanor turned her head to stare at him, bewildered. Of all the things he might have said, she could not have predicted that.

'I beg your pardon?'

'Stepsister, I suppose. Though we never paid that any heed.'

'I'm sorry, I don't—'

'Her name was Diana,' he said abruptly, and nodded when her face changed. 'Diana Farthing. I see you know the name.'

Her eyes widened and she felt her heart thud, for a moment almost too shocked to speak. 'I ... I don't understand. Diana Farthing was your *stepsister*?'

'My mother died when I was a boy, and my father remarried. She was a widow from Rock, further up the estuary, and Diana was her child from her first marriage. Dad brought us up the same way, like we were brother and sister. I certainly loved her like a sister. You never met a kinder nor a sweeter soul.' He drew a deep breath. 'But Diana kept her father's name, she didn't take ours. She was proud of him, you see, and rightly so. Flight Lieutenant John Farthing. Shot down in the war. He was a hero to some in these parts. But not to the Chance family, of course.' His voice had turned bitter. 'To them, he was probably just another peasant.'

'Oh no, I'm sure that can't be true.'

'How would you know?'

Eleanor looked away, embarrassed by the ringing condemnation in his voice.

'I'm sorry, Mrs Chance,' he said. 'I ... I shouldn't have spoken to you like that. It's not your fault. You're new to all this. To *them*.' Mackenzie replaced his flat cap and tugged on the brim, his face restless, his eyes moving about the chapel. 'I'll try to explain.'

'Please do.'

'My parents were pleased when my little sister and Lyndon started courting. Before all the trouble started at any rate. They thought it was a step up in the world for her. Dad's a tenant farmer, you see; his land belongs to the Chance family.' His face hardened. 'When I got married, I moved into my own cottage, just down the way here. But I made sure it was nothing to do with them. I rent it from a Mrs Hibbert, whose husband bought it from the family years ago. I won't be beholden to the Chances.'

'I see.' Her heart was thumping hard, and she felt light-headed again. The cold of the silver locket seemed to burn into her skin, hidden beneath her top. 'You said, before all the trouble started ... What trouble? What did you mean?'

'The trouble between the Chance boys. Over Diana.'

Eleanor caught her breath. She understood at once and saw how it must have happened. Lyndon, bursting with pride over his new love, and Oliver, watching from the shadows as usual.

'They fought over her?'

He looked at her grimly. 'More than fought. They tore each other apart, and our Diana with them.'

What had Lyndon said? *Oliver's always coveted whatever I have.* So they'd naturally fallen out over the lovely Diana Farthing. Perhaps Oliver had tried to flirt with her, as he'd done with Eleanor herself. And Lyndon had been furious when he found out. No doubt he'd decided to finish it, to end the relationship before he could be humiliated in that way.

And Diana had been left heartbroken.

There was a noise outside. Footsteps, a deep male voice, and Davie answering in a puzzled tone. She turned, a sudden fear striking her heart, and saw Mackenzie half-rise from the pew.

The chapel door was thrown open.

Lyndon stood there in the doorway, blocking out the light. For a strange instant, she felt a sense of déjà vu, thinking it was Oliver there, as it had been the last time she was here ...

But then he spoke, and she knew by the voice which twin it was. 'What the hell are you doing here with him, Eleanor? My God, I don't believe this.' Lyndon's voice was hoarse. 'I told you to stay away from him.'

Mackenzie took three steps up the aisle towards him. 'Maybe if I'd said the same thing to my sister about you, Diana would still be alive today.'

There was a terrible silence in the chapel as the two men squared off against each other. Nobody moved.

'Eleanor, go back to the house, please. I want a word alone with Mr Mackenzie.' Lyndon stood waiting, hands bunched into fists by his side.

'I'm not going anywhere,' she said.

His eyes warred with hers, then he glared at Mackenzie instead. 'Very well. You want this to happen inside or out-side?'

'Go to hell, Chance.'

'Fine by me.'

Lyndon lunged forward and his large fist swung hard and fast, catching Mackenzie like a hammer-blow on the jaw.

The lighter of the two men, Mackenzie was sent reeling backwards by the punch; he stumbled into one of the pews and was righting himself with a dazed expression when Lyndon grabbed him up by the jacket lapels, bending close to his face.

'How dare you go near my wife?' Lyndon demanded. 'How dare you speak to her without my permission?' He was almost strangling the poor man.

'Lyndon, please stop,' Eleanor cried, dragging on his sleeve, but he ignored her.

Mackenzie was saying something unintelligible, choking and gasping. It could have been an apology. But when Lyndon let him drop, he swore viciously, and then rolled onto his hands and knees before clambering back to his feet. His cap had fallen off, lost somewhere under the pews, and he was red in the face.

'You arrogant bastard,' he snarled, and threw a punch at Lyndon – who had half-turned in that instant, looking at Eleanor with concern – that caught him in the side of the head.

Lyndon staggered sideways, blinking, but recovered quickly. 'Not exactly Marquess of Queensberry rules, that,' he said thickly, spitting out a mouthful of blood, 'was it?'

'These are estuary rules, Chance.' One eye already bloodshot, Mackenzie swung another punch, this time connecting heavily with Lyndon's cheek, who'd failed to move away in time. 'No holds barred. Last man standing.' He hit out with his left fist, too, but missed and stumbled.

Before he could recover his balance, Lyndon hit him flush on the nose. 'All right. How's that, then?'

With a grunt of pained surprise, Mackenzie put a hand to his nose; thick red blood had begun trickling down his face.

Eleanor, horrified and intent on the fight, heard a sobbing noise at her back, and turned, risking a quick glance at the chapel door.

Davie stood in the doorway, his eyes wide, his face white, one small fist pressed to his mouth. His whole body was trembling.

'Oh no, don't look!' Eleanor hurried towards him. 'Here, let's go outside ...' She caught him as Davie flailed against her, trying to get to his father. 'No, better not, darling. You can't do any good in there. Come with me.'

But the young boy wasn't trying to reach his father, she realised. He was struggling to breathe.

That was when she remembered his asthma.

'Davie?' She took his hands and rubbed them. 'Davie, stay calm. Try to take deep breaths.' But he was gasping, his chest heaving spasmodically. 'Hush, it's all right. There's no need to be afraid.'

His hands were stiff, the fingers bent inwards like little claws. So cold, too; she couldn't bear it. She looked round, calling urgently, 'Mr Mackenzie!' but his father wasn't listening.

Swaying like a drunk, Mackenzie scrabbled blindly for the back of the nearest pew, trying to stand his ground.

'Stay down,' Lyndon told him.

'I'm not done yet,' Mackenzie muttered, and wiped the blood from his face with the back of his hand. 'Not by a long shot. You killed my sister. It's time someone made you pay for that.'

'I had nothing to do with her death.'

'So you keep saying. You may fool the rest of them, but you don't fool me, Chance. She's dead because of you. Can you deny it?'

'I was in love with Diana. Why in God's name would I kill her?'

'You tell me. And even if you won't tell me, at least tell your wife. She deserves to know the truth.'

'Mr Mackenzie, please,' Eleanor cut across this exchange, 'your son can't breathe. I think he's having an asthma attack.'

Mackenzie barely glanced at her. Perhaps he hadn't even heard her, his whole being still focused on his opponent. He lurched forward again, ungainly, both fists raised, but Lyndon knocked him back with one quick blow to the chin. Even at that distance, Eleanor heard the crack of that contact, and shuddered.

This time Mackenzie fell and did not get up again, his face bloodied, pain and defeat in his eyes as he lay panting...

It was obvious all the fight had left him.

'Mr Mackenzie, for the love of God, your son needs you!'

Lyndon's fists dropped, and he turned, noticing the boy at last. 'What?'

Slowly, Mackenzie sat up and stared her way, uncomprehending. Then the mist seemed to clear from his eyes, and he struggled back to his feet.

'Davie?'

Lyndon was there before him, frowning. 'Eleanor, what's wrong? Is the boy hurt?'

'It's asthma,' Mackenzie said roughly, pushing past him. 'Davie, listen to me. You know what to do. Come on, son.' He cupped his hands around the boy's mouth. 'Breathe deep. Nice and slow.'

'Does he have any medication?' Eleanor asked him.

'An inhaler. Back at the cottage. The doctor said it's the new way they're treating asthma upcountry, so I decided to give it a try. But I didn't think he'd need it... It's been weeks since his last attack. I thought he was on the mend.' He squeezed the boy's shoulder, bending close to his face. 'Davie? You need to get your breath back, and then we'll take you home. Slow, deep breaths, remember?'

But Davie's condition was getting worse. He didn't seem

aware of what was being said. His eyelids kept fluttering open and shut, and he was making a horrible rasping noise, deep in his throat.

Eleanor was terrified. 'We have to do something. And quickly.'

'Maybe some fresh air ...' Mackenzie's voice faltered; he looked lost, crouched helpless by his son's body. 'I don't understand. I've never seen him so bad.'

Lyndon scooped the boy up in his arms and carried him outside, paying no attention to Mackenzie's furious protests. 'Come on, Davie,' he said heartily, striding up the path back towards the house. 'It's all right, your dad's fine. We just had a bit of a disagreement, that's all. But he needs you to breathe. Can you hear me?'

'Put him down,' Mackenzie snarled.

Lyndon stopped, swinging round with a sympathetic expression. 'Look, we should take him up to the manor house. I can carry the boy; he barely weighs anything. And it's a good deal nearer than your cottage. My father can ring for an ambulance once we get there.'

'I said, put him down!'

Lyndon hesitated, and then, with a frustrated look towards Eleanor, lay the boy gently on the cold, grassy track.

Mackenzie pushed him aside. 'He's my bloody son. I'll be the one to look after him, all right?'

Lyndon stepped back and watched in silence as Mackenzie dropped to his knees beside his son, and began talking to him, trying to help him breathe freely again. Davie was still making the rasping noise, but more faintly now, his eyes rolling up in their sockets, his chest barely moving.

Mackenzie bent low over his son, urging him, 'Breathe, Davie. In and out, in and out. Deep and slow.' His voice cracked. 'Like the doctor showed us, do you remember?'

Davie didn't respond.

'I'm going to call an ambulance,' Lyndon said flatly, and set off at a run back to Estuary House.

Mackenzie was chafing his son's limp hands. 'Come on, Davie, stay with me. Oh God... Please, Davie, you've got to try...'

'Mr Mackenzie, tell me where your cottage is,' Eleanor urged him, desperate to do something to help. 'I could run there and see if I can find this inhaler. You'll have to tell me where to look for it though and give me the key.'

Robert Mackenzie made no reply, not even looking her way. She might as well not have been there for all the notice he took of her. But that was hardly surprising. Davie was no longer making any noise. The boy lay still and silent on his back, his eyes closed, mouth open.

'Davie, for God's sake, wake up!' Mackenzie shook him, but there was no response. 'Christ Almighty.'

He tilted the boy's head back and began blowing into his mouth, as though his son had drowned and needed to be resuscitated.

Eleanor realised her own hands were clenched into fists, her fingernails digging into her palms, as though she, too, had been fighting.

Was this her fault?

Lyndon had warned her not to speak to Mackenzie; she'd known how angry he would be if he found out, yet she hadn't cared, not at the time. And perhaps if she'd stepped between the two men sooner, tried more forcefully to intervene in their fight, broken it up before it got so far, before the boy had seen his father being beaten to a pulp...

Mackenzie continued to work, alternately breathing for his son and exhorting him to 'Breathe, Davie, breathe!' as he pressed rhythmically on his chest.

The rain had begun to fall again, pattering with a thin sound on the chapel roof, cold against her cheek like icy tears.

Eventually, Lyndon returned, out of breath as he ran down the track, accompanied by his father. A slight bruise was swelling across his left cheek, and he looked flushed and dishevelled, but otherwise he seemed to have come out of their fight more or less unscathed.

Gerard Chance crouched, a hand on Mackenzie's shoulder. 'How is he?' There was no response; Mackenzie's face was still turned away from them, all his focus on breathing for the boy and pumping his chest. 'Ambulance is on its way. Shouldn't be too long now. My wife will direct them from the house.'

Lyndon glanced at her, but Eleanor folded her arms, unable to meet his eyes.

Gerard hesitated, watching Mackenzie work for a moment. Then he plucked Davie's wrist from the wet grass and felt for a pulse. After a moment, he looked up at them grimly and shook his head.

'Oh God.' Eleanor turned away in grief and Lyndon caught her as she wept, pulling her face against his chest.

Mackenzie didn't look up or acknowledge their presence. He could only be persuaded to abandon his efforts when the ambulance men arrived with their stretcher, though he was careful to explain about Davie's asthma, how long he'd suffered from it, and how they hadn't brought his medication out with them today. All this as calmly as though the boy were still breathing or could be brought back to life.

The two men bent over the boy for a few minutes, talking to each other in low voices. Eleanor waited, a creeping horror on her skin. Then one of them straightened and gave Mackenzie an apologetic look.

'I'm very sorry, sir,' he said. 'But there's no point taking him back for treatment. He ... He's gone. There's nothing to be done.'

Mackenzie gave a great groan and covered his face with his hands.

The ambulance man shuffled his feet, hesitated, and then glanced around at the rest of them. 'I'm afraid the police will have to be informed before we can move him. Sudden death like that. I know it seems wrong, but we don't make the rules. If we could use your telephone, sir?'

This question had been directed at Gerard, who nodded. 'Of course, of course. I'll show you where.'

'Thank you.' The man repeated, 'I'm very sorry for your loss,' to Mackenzie before following Gerard back up the track.

Discreetly, the other ambulance man moved a little way apart from them, taking the rolled-up stretcher with him.

The rain wet Eleanor's hair. She'd lost her hat somewhere in the kerfuffle, she realised. She felt cold, unable to stop shivering.

Mackenzie stood looking down at his pale, lifeless son, and then said clearly, 'Get out of my sight, Chance. And take your bloody wife with you.'

'I'm really sorry,' Lyndon began, but Mackenzie interrupted him.

'You should be sorry. My God ...' He ran a hand over his face. 'This was your fault. All your fault. First Diana, now my boy. My lovely boy. I'll never forgive you for this, Chance.' His voice thickened and broke. 'Never.'

Lyndon made no reply but drew Eleanor away, leaving Mackenzie to wait with his son for the police.

'It's just awful,' she said as they crossed the railway track. Tears rolled down her cheeks as the full enormity of it began to hit her. 'Davie was such a sweet, good-natured child. It all happened so quickly, too. One minute he was fine, messing about by the river, and the next...' She put a hand to her mouth. 'I can't believe he's gone.'

Lyndon made no comment.

Eleanor looked up into his face, unsure what his silence meant, and read condemnation there.

He blamed her for Davie's death, she suspected, just as Mackenzie had blamed him. And perhaps it was her fault. She'd played with fire today, not caring about the consequences, but an innocent child was the one who'd been burnt.

She would never forgive herself.

Chapter Twenty-Eight

Ultimately, this is what you gave to the world –
Not the blind seething of spirit
Wracked by a second birth.

– From 'Ascendant' in *Estuary*

'A *woman*? You think those are a woman's bones under the chapel floor?' Mrs Chance sat down abruptly, staring out of the window. It was late afternoon. The last shower of rain had been patchy, the clouds beginning to clear away to the east, and shafts of late sunlight were gleaming through the trees below the house. 'Oh.' She looked blank rather than shocked, but Taylor guessed it was simply too much for the old lady to take in. 'That's awful.'

'They wouldn't let us take the ring away,' Julius told her. 'But it did seem very like the family ring in that portrait in the hall.'

'Which portrait?'

'The one of the Lady Elizabeth,' Taylor said helpfully.

Mrs Chance made a noise under her breath and tightened her clasped hands in her lap, almost wringing them, but said nothing.

Iris, who'd been pacing restlessly up and down the cosy sitting room Mrs Chance used during the day, came to a halt in front of Taylor. 'And what do you think?' she asked, jutting a finger towards her. 'You *feel* things, don't you? You sense them.'

Surprised that Iris had somehow understood this without being told, Taylor nodded. 'Occasionally, yes.'

'And these remains? What did you *feel* about them?'

'I don't know.' Aware of Julius's gaze on her face, Taylor added quickly, 'I had a strong emotional response in the chapel. But nothing concrete. It's not always immediate, you see; sometimes my ... my visions, if you want to call them that, take time to come.'

'I see.' Pale-faced, Iris gripped the back of an armchair as though to steady herself. 'A rare gift. A little unpleasant, too. Can you sense other things?'

Julius frowned. 'What do you mean?'

'I was talking to her, not you,' Iris hissed.

'I can't read people's minds, if that's what you mean,' Taylor said, and saw Iris narrow her eyes.

Yes, that had been what she meant, she thought warily. And now she'd just signalled that, actually, she *could* read minds.

Not that it ever worked like that.

'My apologies.' Stiffly, Julius folded his arms. 'I thought this was a family conference. Not a private conversation.'

'I'm not one of the family.' Taylor looked at him, feeling awkward now. 'I should go. I really don't mind; there are things I should be doing, anyway.' She started heading for the door.

'Stay where you are,' Julius told her. 'You found the body. This involves you, too.'

Iris made a noise under her breath and stalked from the room, leaving the door wide open.

'What's the matter with Iris today?' Julius asked, clearly irritated.

'She probably hates being cooped up here with the rest of us, instead of across the river in her shack.' Taylor looked out at the lush, wet treetops, aware herself of a pressing sense of restlessness. 'I know how she feels. As soon as this rain has cleared up, I'll be heading back to my tent.'

'So soon?'

'Tomorrow morning, I expect,' she told him. 'The weather forecast is for drier weather by then. And they've finished down at the chapel, haven't they? There'll be no need for me to stay in the house any longer.' Seeing Mrs Chance grope for an absent hanky up her sleeve, Taylor handed her a box of tissues from the coffee table. 'Thank you both for your hospitality. I'm really very grateful. But I need to get back outside tomorrow. To clear my head.'

As she made for the door, Julius called after her, 'Hang on a tick,' and after bending to give his grandmother a quick kiss on her cheek, followed her into the corridor. 'Can I have a word with you before dinner, Taylor?'

There was a darkness hovering about him today that seemed to grow as he hunched his shoulders, looking away.

'Sure.'

'Maybe we could talk now, in your room?' he said, surprising her. 'There's something I need to show you.'

'It's not really convenient right now. I have to start packing. I seem to have strewn my books and papers all over the bedroom; it's a bit of a mess up there, I'm afraid.' She caught a flicker of impatience in his face. 'But you're welcome to talk to me while I tidy up.'

Upstairs, her bedroom window was open; she hurried to close it, aware that midges might slip in and cling to the walls once dusk began to creep along the estuary. She hated midges with a passion.

'So,' she said, picking up her empty rucksack and throwing it on the bed ready for packing, 'what did you want to show me?'

Grimacing, Julius pulled out his smartphone. 'After some research, I finally found this on the net tonight.' He flicked through a few website screens with his thumb, and then handed her the phone. 'It was on the local history archive.'

She stared, uncomprehending, at a grainy black-and-white photograph of a man holding up a fish. The man was wearing a flat cap and a thick fisherman's jacket, and smiling proudly at the camera, a rosette pinned to his lapel bearing the words Second Place.

It was Mack.

Underneath the photograph, a caption read: *Robert Mackenzie in 1962, Runner-Up at the Camel Annual Anglers' Championship.*

Stunned, Taylor scrolled to the archive text below, and blanched.

'Mr Mackenzie,' she read out loud in a whisper, 'pictured above, hanged himself at home in Riverside Cottage, December 1963, just days after his young son's funeral. His body was discovered by his landlady, Mrs Hibbert.' Swiftly, she scanned the rest of the short paragraph, which gave only scant details. Davie had died of an asthma attack, according to the coroner's report. 'Oh no, poor Mack.'

She had stood over the simple gravestone for hours, re-reading the name and dates, her heart heavy and bitter.

If only she had done something. But she had done nothing.

This was her fault, her fault, her fault.

'I'm sorry to be the bearer of bad tidings. But at least this proves that your Mack existed. So, I need to make you an apology.' He dug his hands into his pockets. 'He wasn't, after all, a figment of your imagination.'

'I never thought he was.'

He nodded to the phone. 'It says the boy died of an asthma attack when he was only ten years old. Robert Mackenzie couldn't bear the grief and hanged himself. At least, that's what the local coroner decided, ruling it suicide. Case closed.' Julius looked at her sympathetically. 'I was just wondering ... This whole Mack thing. It could just have been in your head. Not a ghostly encounter but something you dreamed up.'

'Right.' She glared at him. 'For a minute there, I thought you were apologising for having disbelieved me. But what you're actually saying is, I'm insane.'

'Not insane,' he said quickly. 'Just suggestible.'

'Thanks, that's much better.'

'But isn't it possible you may have come across Mackenzie's name and history during your research?'

'No.'

'OK.' He studied her thoughtfully. 'Before coming here, did you ever look through the local history archive online for mentions of Lyndon Chance?'

Taylor frowned, thinking back.

'Now you've said that, I do recall reading through that archive,' she admitted. 'But I never saw anything to do with a Robert Mackenzie or his son. I would have recognised the name instantly.'

'Would you? And what about this landlady of his? Mrs Hibbert. You mentioned her to my grandmother, do you remember? I checked the family records, and her husband bought a cottage and some land from us back in 1950. That's obviously where Mackenzie was living when he died. You might have seen his name in passing during your research and noted the Chance family association. It's quite a moving story, after all. Single father commits suicide after son's death ... Maybe you scribbled it down in a notebook and forgot about it. But then, walking along the Camel Trail, reading Lyndon's poems to yourself, trying to place them within the landscape, maybe you ...'

'Saw dead people?'

Julius half-smiled. 'Something along those lines.'

'You think I'm a fraud.'

'Nothing so clumsy. Please don't take this the wrong way, but ...' He hesitated. 'I think you have a wonderful, creative imagination. Not unlike my grandfather's, in fact. But the estuary can be a lonely place, especially if you're sleeping outside on your own after dark, night after night, the way you do in that tent.' He paused. 'The very thing that makes you so sensitive to Lyndon's poetry is what also leaves you open to suggestion.'

Taylor looked away, a faint heat in her cheeks.

'As someone who works in the sciences, I have to concede that I may have imagined the whole thing. I am very conscious of atmosphere, and I have been known to see things that aren't there.' She drew a deep breath, trying to keep her voice level. 'Will I find Robert Mackenzie's death in my original research notes? Or Mr Hibbert's purchase of land from the Chances? I won't know for sure until I check. Most of my early research is back in London though. And I certainly don't *remember* reading about his son's death or his suicide or seeing that photograph of him.' She handed back his phone. 'But I hear what you're saying, Julius, and I accept it's possible that my own past traumas may have left me susceptible to ...'

Her voice broke on a compulsive sob, and she hid her face in her hands.

'Hey,' he said, and took her awkwardly in his arms. 'Please don't get upset. It's perfectly natural. You're a sensitive soul.

And that boy died very young. His death was appalling and unnecessary, as was his dad's. Maybe, by reinventing them, you were trying to save them. To rescue them from history and give their story a new ending.'

She wept against his chest. The darkness hovered just above their heads, waiting for her to be alone, to be defence-less. 'But I can't believe I imagined them,' she said indistinctly. 'They were so real to me.'

'I know.'

'Davie was such a sweet boy. What happened to him ... To Mack ... It's so bloody unfair.'

'I know.'

She gulped. 'I don't think I can do this anymore. I need to go home.' Taylor wiped her wet cheeks and looked up at him; his face was startlingly close. 'Back to London, I mean.'

'Must you?'

Their eyes met. Taylor jerked backwards, her heart thud-ding, suddenly keen to be free, and he released her at once.

'I'm sorry,' she whispered.

Julius stood a moment, unmoving, and then gave an abrupt nod and left.

She sat at her bedroom window for several hours after-wards, watching the dusk thicken into night above the estu-ary, and trying to pick a path through what was happening to her. But it was too difficult. She kept coming back to her past, like an ugly great rock in the stream, parting the waters.

An odd sound disturbed her just as she was getting ready for bed – a soft rhythmic thudding sound, accompanied by sobbing.

Taylor opened her door to peer along the unlit corridor. She couldn't see a damn thing.

But she could *feel* something. Something fierce and un-relenting, coming at her in waves through the darkness.

Hurriedly, she shut her bedroom door again and leant against it, breathing hard, staring at nothing.

In her dream, Taylor was walking in the gardens at Estuary House. Only the ornamental plants and palm trees were taller and more exotic-looking than in real life; towering over her in the midday sun, they cast bizarre shadows on the gritty path under her feet. Glancing down, she realised that her feet were bare, the tiny stones in the path digging into her soles.

She stopped and balanced on one leg, lifting first one foot and then the other to discover diamond-shaped in-dentations on the sole of each foot. The stones had cut deep, the wounds bleeding and dirty from the path.

As she brushed off the grit, her tender flesh stung.

Taylor sucked in her breath, staring at her hand; there was soil as well as blood on her fingertips, as though she'd been digging in the earth. Yet she had no memory of doing so.

'Thank you,' Mack said.

She turned, shielding her eyes against the sun. There was Mack, and behind him, playing with a large black cat, was Davie.

'Oh, Davie, you're alive,' she said thankfully.

'Because of you,' Mack said, nodding.

'I didn't do anything.'

'But you wanted to save him. You tried your best. That means a lot.' He smiled gently. 'Thank you.'

She blinked, dazzled by the light, squinting at him. She could barely see Mack and Davie now, their outlines had become so faint ... The sun beat down with an intense, bright-white heat. Everything seemed bleached by it, all the colours draining from the world.

'Mack?' She shielded her eyes with her hands, half-blinded. 'Mack? Davie? Where are you?'

But the gardens were empty. All she could hear now was birdsong. Mack and his son had gone.

She felt incredibly tired. But there was nowhere to lie down in this part of the gardens. No bench, no restful patch of grass. Only a gravelled path weaving between formal flowerbeds and artfully arranged rock gardens.

A summer pavilion stood a short way ahead, a small, wooden structure she'd never noticed in the gardens before, pleasantly shady and nestled among trees. The colours looked stronger there too, out of the heat of the sun.

With a grimace, Taylor began to limp towards the pavilion, eager to get off the path and rub her aching feet.

In the distance, she sensed rather than saw a long, green sea of rustling reeds, almost shoulder-high, and the estuary beyond. Which was odd, as she couldn't recall any reeds growing in the formal gardens. It seemed a bit out of character. But perhaps Mrs Chance was trying something new.

She looked up, surprised to find a withered tree growing right in the middle of the gravel path, blocking her way so she couldn't go any further. Its bark was strangely pale and discoloured, even peeling off in places; several starved, wizened branches twisted about its trunk like mad arms.

'That's where they used to meet,' someone said behind her.

Startled, Taylor turned.

It was Iris, wearing a soft grey nun's habit. She was younger though, maybe in her twenties, her face a smooth, cool oval.

'Sorry?'

'At the dead tree,' Iris told her calmly. 'They left coded messages tied to the branches. And sometimes, on hot afternoons, they would creep into the reeds over there,' she added, nodding to the summer pavilion, 'and make love where they thought nobody could see them. But they were wrong.'

'Who?' Taylor asked, bewildered.

'X marks the spot.'

With this cryptic comment, Iris turned away, and Taylor realised there were angry red stripes torn through the back of her nun's habit, as though she'd been mauled by a tiger.

The sky turned dark and shadowy. Taylor shivered, hugging herself. But no, the sun was still shining outside, as hot and bright as ever.

Iris had gone, and she was inside the pavilion, looking out.

Except it was no longer a summer pavilion. Staring through a shuttered window, she saw reeds glint in the distance and heard the cry of seabirds over the estuary.

This was Iris's shack on the other side of the river, she realised. The familiar wooden slats loomed about her, tarot cards and fluttering scraps of poems pinned to the walls everywhere she looked.

Except there was a hole in the sandy ground where the floor ought to have been. A yawning hole, long and deep enough for a grave.

She was standing above the hole, looking down into it like a mourner at a funeral. A few red and white petals lay scattered in the bottom of the hole, as though shaken from a bouquet of flowers. As she watched, perplexed, the petals began to grow and merge, slowly spreading into a sticky red pool that seeped into the mud walls. It looked like blood.

Then someone gave her a shove from behind, and Taylor lost her footing, toppling forward into the damp grave.

'No,' she cried, struggling to climb out again, her arms flailing wildly. 'I'm still alive. Please, somebody help me!'

But though her mouth moved, no sound came out.

Thick clumps of earth began to shower down on top of her, great spadefuls of it shovelled across her face and body, clogging her nose and throat with dirt so she couldn't breathe. Finally, her entire body was covered with soil, weighed down with it, and everything became dark and still.

Chapter Twenty-Nine

Samphire, glasswort, springing verdant
Under muddied fingers...

– From 'Glasswort' in *Estuary*

The knocking at the front door had become a hammering now, and still nobody was answering it.

Eleanor threw aside the pillow she'd been using to cover her ears for the past ten minutes and stumbled reluctantly out of bed.

She'd stirred soon after dawn to find Lyndon gone from their bed without waking her, but had rapidly gone back to sleep, her dreams unhappy and confused. She'd had a long and difficult night, broken by alternate bouts of weeping over Davie's senseless death and staring dry-eyed into the darkness, so perhaps it wasn't surprising that she'd gone back to sleep so readily.

Now, though, somebody was at the door of the manor house, furiously demanding entry, and apparently the house-keeper was not on hand to open the door. There was a washing line in the backyard, and she imagined Mrs Barclay must be outside, hanging out the washing.

Eleanor wrapped a dressing gown about her nightie, shoved her feet into slippers, and hurried downstairs.

The brass knocker on the door thundered deafeningly

against the wood, again and again, the sound booming through the manor house.

'All right, I'm coming.' Wearily, Eleanor dragged the heavy front door open, peered outside, and froze in shock.

'So it's true.' It was her father on the doorstep, looking like a man who'd spent the night in his car. His usually smart jacket and shirt were both rumpled, his black tie slightly askew as though he'd been wrenching at it. He looked as though he hadn't shaved recently either, his pointed chin rough with stubble. 'You wicked, wicked girl … I knew you'd never come to any good. Too much of your mother in you. She was a worthless slut, too.' He glared past her, his angry gaze restless, his chest heaving. 'So, where is he, this poet, this godless man you've married? If you're even married to him at all?'

Eleanor couldn't speak, her heart pounding. But she knew the guilty flush on her cheeks must be giving her away.

'Get out of my way, girl.' Her father knocked her sideways into the door and barged inside. 'Your grandfather sent me a cutting from the newspaper. You and all those evil men in that place of sin. You'll burn in hell for this, mark my words.' He strode to the bottom of the stairs, and shouted up, 'Chance? I want a word with you. And then I'm taking my daughter home.' He paused. 'Did you hear that? She's mine, Chance, not yours. You had no right to marry her without my permission, and you'll *never* have my permission.'

When there was no sound from upstairs, her father swung to face her again. 'Where is he?'

'I d-don't know,' she stammered, and didn't get out of the way quickly enough as his hand came sweeping down across the side of her head.

She dropped to her knees, half-stunned by his blow, her

ears ringing. She'd forgotten how much it hurt to be struck like that.

'Get up.' He grabbed Eleanor by the arm, dragging her back to her feet. 'We're leaving. The car's parked in the lane.' He jerked her forward. 'Hurry up. You're going to your grandfather's and I want to be in Plymouth before dark.'

She tried to get away, but he hit her again and shoved her out of the door. She stumbled down the front steps in her slippers, still dizzy from the blow, moaning, 'No, no, no,' over and over.

'Hold it right there,' said a voice, coldly.

'What the . . . ?' Her father just managed to stop himself before blaspheming.

Iris was blocking the path to the lane, holding a pistol loosely in her hand, its ominous, gleaming muzzle pointed towards them.

'Put that gun down, woman,' he blustered. 'Where on earth did you get that?'

'It was my father's service revolver.'

'And what do you think you're doing, waving it about like that?' His voice rose in outrage. 'You could kill someone with that thing.'

Iris looked at her. 'Are you all right?'

'Yes,' Eleanor managed to gasp, a hand at her mouth. Her lip was bleeding, she realised.

'Who is this horrible little man?'

Her father began to rage, 'What did you call me? How dare you speak to me like that?' but fell silent when Iris cocked the pistol and levelled it directly at his chest.

The belt to her dressing gown had come undone. Embarrassed, Eleanor dragged the two sides shut. 'This is . . . my father.'

'I see.' Iris looked her father up and down, her thin brows

raised in faint hauteur. 'He doesn't seem like a very pleasant person,' she remarked at last. 'But one can't choose one's relatives. Do you want to go with him?'

'No.'

'Then you'd better go back inside,' Iris told her, and motioned him with the pistol to go past her down the path. 'You. Leave. Now.'

Eleanor's father folded his arms and shook his head. 'I'm not going anywhere without my daughter.'

'You can leave dead or you can leave alive. Which do you prefer?'

His eyes bulged. 'You can't be serious. I'm going to report you to the police.'

'Go ahead,' Iris said coolly. 'I'm sure they'll be interested in why you've beaten your daughter and are now trying to abduct her in broad daylight from her husband's home.'

Eleanor's father opened his mouth, and then closed it again, his expression furious. He jabbed a finger round at Eleanor. 'Don't think you can get rid of me that easily. I'm still your father and I don't believe a word of this Mrs Chance nonsense. No man would marry a slut like you. I demand to see your wedding certificate. Who were your witnesses?'

'I'm going to start counting to three, and then I'm going to make a nasty hole in your chest,' Iris said. 'One ... Two ...'

Her father turned and ran through the formal gardens before she reached 'Three,' and was soon out of sight. A moment later, they heard the car start up in the lane, and then pull away up the hill.

Soon, there was silence along the estuary again, broken only by the faint tweeting of birds and the soft, distant lap of water.

316

'Thank you for helping me,' Eleanor said shakily. 'Where did you get the gun?'

Iris lowered the pistol and followed Eleanor back into the house. 'I told you, it's my father's. He keeps the shotguns locked up but this one's just kept in a drawer. I heard a fox this morning, going after the chickens … Thought I'd scare him off with a few pot shots. But he was long gone by the time I got out there.' Placing the pistol almost reverently on the hall table, she ran a fingertip along its narrow barrel before turning to look at Eleanor. 'Your lip is bleeding. You should see to that.'

'I don't know what I would have done if you hadn't come along. My father was so angry. I've never seen him like that.'

'Some people are like animals. Like that fox this morning. They have no control over their desires.' Iris glanced at herself in the hall mirror, her oval face empty of emotion. 'And some people are just better than others at knowing when those animals need to be put down.'

Eleanor shivered. 'Everyone seems to be out,' she said, wishing they weren't alone. 'Do you know where Lyndon's gone?'

'No idea, sorry.' And Iris walked away into the gloomy maze of rooms as though nothing out of the ordinary had occurred.

Eleanor hurried upstairs to splash water on her face, put on her makeup and get dressed. She was still shaken, unable to believe what had just happened. Her father, here at the manor house?

If Iris hadn't intervened, he would have dragged her to her grandfather's house in Plymouth. To a life of slavery and imprisonment, and God alone knew what else.

That photograph in the newspaper ... Lyndon had been right, it had revealed her whereabouts to her family.

No doubt her father had wasted no time in discovering where Mr Lyndon Chance lived, and then driven straight down here to hunt for the property, perhaps sleeping in his car when it got too late to keep travelling. She imagined his fury as he drove along the estuary, searching for the right place, for where his runaway daughter was hiding, and her hands trembled as she applied her makeup and made her hair look more presentable.

The sound of raised voices downstairs in the hall made her freeze, her heart thudding wildly, body tensed for flight. Was her father back again? Had he fetched the police as he'd threatened?

She tiptoed to the head of the stairs and stood, listening.

To her relief though, it was Oliver and Jeannie she could hear arguing downstairs. Oliver sounded furious, shouting something like, 'Do what you're told,' and even though Eleanor wasn't the one on the receiving end of his temper, the note in his voice still made her shiver.

Poor Jeannie. What had she done to deserve such wrath? Nothing, probably.

Abruptly, the voices ceased.

A door slammed.

Then she heard the sound of sobbing and feet running lightly upstairs. Not this staircase, though. The other one, above the breakfast room.

Eleanor came to a decision. She waited several minutes, to make certain that Oliver had left the house, and then went in search of Jeannie's room.

She wasn't quite sure which room Jeannie had been given – though she was fairly certain the two lovers had

318

been sleeping together in Oliver's room without his parents' knowledge – but followed the sound of crying.

Coming to a closed door near the end of a long, gloomy corridor, she knocked tentatively. 'Jeannie? It's Eleanor.' The weeping stopped, to be replaced by sniffing. 'May I come in?'

The door opened.

Jeannie stood there in a simple, white, knee-length dress, a wet cloth pressed against one cheek, her black hair dishevelled, her eyes bloodshot.

'Oh my God.' Shocked, Eleanor slipped into the room, quickly closing the door behind her. 'Are you all right? What happened?'

'You can see for yourself.' Jeannie lowered the cloth to display a bruised cheek, her face damp with tears. 'That bastard ... I really thought Oliver was different. A nice boy from a posh family, you know? But, as usual, I got it all wrong.'

There was a washstand in one corner of the prettily decorated bedroom. Gently, Eleanor took the cloth from her, soaked it in cold running water again, wrung it out, and then handed it back to the girl.

'I don't understand. I thought the two of you were happy together.'

'Me, too.' Jeannie sat down on the soft mattress, her mouth pouting, a faraway look in her eyes. 'But he always knew I wanted a career. I never tried to hide it.'

'As a model?'

'That's right. And it's going well for me. I've been offered a photo shoot in London next week. Vogue Magazine. I knew he wouldn't be happy, so I suggested a walk down to the old chapel this morning. He loves that place; I thought it might soften the blow. But when I told him I had to leave, he got so angry.' Jeannie shivered. 'He said I couldn't go to London, that we had to get *married*, for God's sake.'

'Married?' Eleanor stared at her.

She hadn't realised Oliver was the marrying kind. But she hadn't known he loved the riverside chapel either, like his brother.

Perhaps the twins were more alike than she'd thought.

It was a sobering thought.

'I told him where he could stick his marriage. I told him I'm going to be a famous model. Only I'll never get that photo shoot now, will I?' Jeannie started to cry again, great heaving sobs that shook her slender frame. 'Look at me, I'm a mess.'

Eleanor sat next to her on the bed, putting an arm about her shoulders. 'Hey, of course you will. Maybe not this time. But once it's healed—'

'If it ever heals. He used his bloody *fist*.' Jeannie shook her head; her eyes were brimming with tears, mascara running in streaks down her face. 'Olly did this to me deliberately, you know? He marked me. He said if I wasn't going to marry him, he'd make sure I couldn't have a career either. Said he was going to ruin my looks ...' Her voice tailed away into weeping.

'Honestly, it's not that bad. A few weeks, I daresay nobody will even notice.' Eleanor gave Jeannie's shoulders a quick squeeze, hoping she was right. 'Though I don't understand. Oliver actually asked you to marry him?'

'I said so, didn't I?'

'But you told him no. You refused.'

Jeannie looked at her as though she were an idiot. 'Of course I did. Some men are for keeps, Eleanor. Others are just playing around. Olly was never serious about me. He likes the package, yes. But any woman would do.'

'Sorry?'

'He just wants a wife so he can get her pregnant and

inherit this place. The house, the grounds, all of it.' She got up and limped over to the mirror above the washstand. There, Jeannie leant heavily on the basin and examined her bruised face, turning her head from side to side. 'I'm not going to be any man's brood mare. I'm going to have a career.'

'So it's true.' Eleanor put her hands to her cheeks, feeling hollow inside as she realised the horrible, startling truth. 'Mr Chance plans to leave the house to whichever brother has a child first.'

'For sure.' Jeannie nodded, her face weary. 'Sick, isn't it? These rich people ... They think they can do whatever they like. And they usually can,' she added bitterly.

Downstairs, Eleanor could hear more doors slamming. More raised voices. And a dog barking joyfully as it ran about. 'Sounds like Lyndon and his father are back,' she said.

'You go.' Jeannie looked round at her. There was pity in her face. 'I'm free of this place; I can walk away. I've got a taxi coming in an hour. Go be with your husband.'

Eleanor bit her lip. 'He's not my husband,' she whispered.

For a moment, Jeannie said nothing, staring at her fixedly. Then she threw her head back and laughed throatily.

'Oh, for the love of Christ ...' She chucked the wet cloth into the sink and grabbed a suitcase from inside the open wardrobe. 'Good luck, Eleanor. That's all I can say to you, girl. Good luck.'

Leaving Jeannie's room, Eleanor leant over the banisters, listening. More raised voices, but this time it was Lyndon and his father arguing somewhere below her. Something about taking a gun without permission. Presumably they weren't aware Iris was the one who'd taken it.

She considered going downstairs and showing them where Iris had left the pistol, on the hall table next to the front door. But after everything that had happened, she didn't think she could face Lyndon right now. She would have to tell him about her father's visit at some point, of course. But she knew he would immediately insist on them getting married. And, like Jeannie, she wasn't sure that marriage was what she wanted from life.

Marry Lyndon?

Out of the frying pan and into the fire was the expression that came to mind. No, she needed time to think. And some fresh air.

Eleanor followed the corridor of dark, polished wood along to the servants' stairs, a dangerously steep, enclosed set of steps that led down into the kitchens. There was a door off the stairs at the next landing that would take her directly into the garden.

Carefully, she descended the stairs, wishing she could shake off the aching pain in her head, and eventually came to the side door, letting herself out into the gardens.

It was peaceful outside, almost idyllic.

The river, its white gleam glimpsed here and there through autumnal tree branches, looked tranquil and unruffled today. But the stillness only seemed to mock her. She kept thinking of Davie's body on the ground, and Jeannie's bruised face, and her own father's enjoyment of doling out pain, how he had often taken his belt to her for some minor infraction of the rules. The world was so beautiful, she thought. Why did there have to be so much cruelty in it?

She hadn't walked very far towards the riverbank when she heard a twig crack behind her in the trees.

Turning in surprise, she found Lyndon a few feet behind her. He was smiling and seemed happy, despite the row with his father.

'Darling,' he said softly, and took her hand, bending his

head as he raised it t⟨...⟩
you come with me? ⟨...⟩

Eleanor was perple⟨...⟩
'If you insist. But I tho⟨...⟩
Jeannie and Oliver?'

'Hmm?' His dark hea⟨...⟩
lips warming her skin.

'She refused to marry h⟨...⟩
hit her. Left a nasty bruise ⟨...⟩

He made a noise under h⟨...⟩
saying anything.

Eleanor pulled her hand fre⟨...⟩ ⟨...⟩nce and
lack of response. Didn't he c⟨...⟩ ⟨...⟩is brother's cruel
behaviour?

'Lyndon, are you ... Are you still in love with Diana?
Please tell me the truth. Is that why you and Oliver are
forever arguing? Because she went out on his yacht the day
she drowned?' She heard the pain in her voice, the anguish
tumbling out unrestrained, and put a hand to her mouth. 'Do
you suspect her of having an affair with your brother? Is that
what it's all about, this thing between you and him? That
awful Ouija board ... It was you that night in the den, wasn't
it? Moving the planchette, trying to get him to admit—'

'Admit to what?' he asked sharply, looking at her directly.
His eyes met hers, cold and mocking, and in that instant, she
realised her mistake.

It wasn't Lyndon.

She took a quick step back, horrified.

How could she have been so stupid? But he'd been careful
to keep his face partly hidden, of course, and to speak in the
same deep voice that Lyndon used when speaking to her,
not Oliver's light tones.

He'd tricked her.

323

...t answering, raising his brows in

...ed in playing games with you,' she said ...mbled away, not sure where she was going, ...e that she needed to put some distance between ...Lyndon's brother.

...he'd only gone a few steps when a black hood dropped over her head, blocking out the daylight. Eleanor gave a cry of fright and felt a hand clamp down hard across her hooded face, silencing her.

'Do be quiet, Mrs Chance, there's a good girl.'

Paying no attention, she continued to resist and cry out against the large hand blocking her nose and mouth, but the sound was too muffled to be effective, and she soon became light-headed, unable to breathe. As her senses swam, she felt herself being dragged along the path, and struggled to be free, but received a blow to her stomach that left her winded.

'You want another like that, just keep it up.' Oliver spoke hoarsely into her ear. 'Yeah, I smacked Jeannie. And I'll hit you too if you don't shut up and do exactly what you're told. Is that clear?'

She managed a nod, and he released her mouth.

'Good,' Oliver said, and she was sickened to hear triumph in his voice. 'Now walk, and don't give me any more trouble.'

It was hard going, blinded by the hood over her face, stumbling along an overgrown track with a hand on the back of her neck, guiding and steering her forward.

Where on earth was Oliver taking her? And for what purpose? He must have gone mad if he thought he could get away with this.

Then reality slowly dawned. She'd left the house without telling anyone where she was going. If Oliver killed her, and then buried her body somewhere out here among the woods, there was a good chance nobody would ever discover what had happened to her. And anyway, who would believe that Oliver – charming, suave, handsome Oliver – would abduct a woman?

Lyndon might believe it.

But Iris would tell everyone about her father's visit, and Lyndon would then assume he'd come back when Iris was no longer around and taken her away with him.

By the time he realised his mistake, it would be too late.

There was no one to save her from Oliver, she realised, except herself.

It was a chilling revelation.

'I ... I'm sorry I shouted before,' she said after a moment, having calmed down enough to realise that struggling and antagonising him further would be futile. He was in too dangerous a mood. She had to humour him somehow, stall for time. 'But you took me by surprise. Please let me go, Oliver. I promise I won't try to run away.'

'Just keep going.' His voice was urgent, and she had the impression he was constantly looking back over his shoulder. 'Not far now.'

Eleanor obeyed, her heart thumping, her breath coming fast. She couldn't see anything but blurry daylight through the black cotton of the hood.

'Oliver,' she whispered, 'why are you doing this?'

'I told you to shut up, bitch.' He hit her again, this time in the side of the head, and she was knocked sideways by the blow, her ears ringing.

There was no mistake.

He's going to kill me, she thought groggily.

She tried to raise her head, but it hurt like hell, so she kept still. She was lying on damp and chilly ground. There was grassy mud under her fingertips. She could smell the River Camel nearby, and hear it too, the steady, pulsing lap of water against the banks, the estuary's life blood flowing out towards the sea.

Oliver bent over her, muttering, 'For God's sake ...'

Eleanor felt herself being unceremoniously picked up and slung over his shoulder like a sack of spuds.

Oliver began moving faster, and her body thumped up and down over his back. She screamed for help but knew in her heart that nobody would be able to hear her; they were too far from the house by now.

A moment later, she was being jerked violently through the air, and hit her head and shoulder on something hard. She gave a yelp, but lay still, too terrified to move. The whole thing rocked under her as Oliver kicked her legs to one side and sat down heavily. Then she heard the sound of oars creaking and dipping into water, the distinctive splash as they rose and dipped again.

They were in a boat.

A small rowboat, already shifting uneasily against the prevailing current, bobbing on the lively waters of the estuary.

Oliver intended to row her across the River Camel, she realised. To the desolate waving reeds and the withered tree. To the dark storage hut, with its shrine of flowers ...

Chapter Thirty

Lord Ten afflicted in the Eighth House. The mouth
Still grimacing after the head's lopped off.

– From 'Execution' in Estuary

'Taylor? Are you awake?'

Taylor woke to a bulky shadow rearing over the sunlit roof of her tent. She knew the voice at once. Julius Chance.

'Just a minute,' she called out, still a little groggy from sleep.

She sat up, tidied her hair, and scrambled out of her sleeping bag in her pyjamas.

When she finally unzipped the entrance and poked her head out of the opening, she found Julius standing a short way from the tent. Arms folded, he stood with his back to her, staring out across the estuary.

He turned when she came out.

'Sorry to have disturbed you; I know it's early.' He was looking grimmer than usual, dressed entirely in black and with his hands clasped behind his back. He glanced down at her bare feet, and then at her face. 'You haven't gone back to London, then.'

Taylor belatedly remembered what she'd told him about needing to leave the estuary, and Cornwall, too.

She'd been so upset that night, and then he'd thought

about kissing her, she felt sure of it. And that had unnerved her horribly. Because she wasn't sure how she felt about him either.

'I need maybe another day or two here,' she said. 'There are still a few things I have to sort out. I haven't finished my research.'

'Which part? The ecology or the poetry?'

He was sounding cold and cynical again, more like the man she'd met on her first day at Estuary House.

'Both, actually.' Taylor straightened her pyjama top, which was decorated with brown teddy bears and slightly askew, and wished she'd stopped to pull on jeans and a T-shirt before coming out of the tent. He was looking her over in an odd way. 'If you must know, I've discovered something unusual about your grandfather's poems.'

He sighed. 'What now?'

Diving back into the tent, she fetched out her mother's paperback of the estuary poems, which she'd been marking up the night before with new notes.

'I've been studying his *Estuary* book again. No, don't make that face. Because I noticed something odd. Something that could be important.' She flicked through the poems, pointing out where she'd marked each title with a bright orange highlighter. 'The first letter of each poem title in *Estuary* ... Please stop looking at me like that. Willing suspension of disbelief, OK?'

He grimaced. 'OK.'

'Thank you,' she said, still fearing he might think her mad, and blurted out, 'So, if you take the first letter of each poem title, and put them together in chronological sequence, they spell out a sentence.'

'Like an acrostic, you mean?'

'Exactly like an acrostic. Thirty-three poems. Thirty-three

letters.' Taylor paused. 'You see, I'd been thinking about an interview Lyndon gave to London Magazine, where he talked about poetry being a way to control things that are otherwise impossible to control. That writing poetry is about trying to impose order on a disordered world.'

'So?'

She showed him the sheet where she'd written each letter down in sequence. 'So, this is what I came up with when I tried to impose order on his poetry titles.'

Frowning, Julius took the sheet and read aloud the sentence she'd written out, 'THEY LIE TOGETHER UNDER THE STORAGE HUT.' He handed the sheet back to her. 'Seriously?'

'I know it seems weird. And incredibly prosaic, I grant you that. But Lyndon *was* prosaic. He was never one of these dreamy, lyrical poets who wants to make everything beautiful, to spin straw into gold. He was a believer in material reality and in calling a spade a spade.' Eagerly, she took back the sheet. 'This is definitely a code, don't you see? Come on, what are the odds of the titles spelling out a full sentence, otherwise? I was right all along. There's a secret message buried in these poems.'

'You were *right*? What does that mean?'

'I've always had this suspicion about *Estuary*, a nagging feeling that it was put together for a specific reason. And I think this message is it.'

'For God's sake ...'

'No, listen to me. It's not as impossible as you might think. Lyndon absolutely believed in the idea of poetry as a code. According to his own writings, Yeats was the master symbolist, and Lyndon references all sorts of Yeatsian things in his essays on poetry ... Symbols, ciphers, mysteries, cryptology, the Kabbalah.'

329

'My grandfather wrote poetry. Not crossword puzzles.'

'But to Lyndon, poetry could be both.'

He made an exasperated noise under his breath. 'Let's say I humour you for a minute, and there really is a secret message buried in the poem titles. What is, "*They lie together under the storage hut*" supposed to mean?'

'Exactly what it says.'

He laughed, incredulous. 'What, that somebody, or two somebodies, are buried under a storage hut?'

'I think he means the old hut where Iris lives now.'

'That's just nonsense.' Julius shook his head, his voice cracking. 'Look, sorry to drag you back down to earth, but I came here for a reason. It's urgent and I need your help.'

She saw the strain in his face and was instantly contrite. 'No, I'm the one who should be sorry. Given what we found under the chapel, all this stuff about bodies must seem pretty insensitive.' She put down the sheet. 'Please go on. What's happened?'

Julius unclasped his hands, pushing them into the pockets of his black jeans instead, his shoulders hunched. His aura today was frazzled – dark and bitty, almost crackling in places.

'Great-Aunt Iris has gone missing,' he admitted. 'And her mobile isn't picking up any calls. It's a long shot, but I was hoping you might have seen her.'

'I'm afraid not. I overslept. I haven't been out all morning.'

'Damn.'

'Have you been across to the hut?'

'No, but I checked the rowboat, and it's moored on this side. So, unless Iris walked back—'

'Maybe she got a taxi.'

'She doesn't have enough money,' he said bluntly. 'Iris has never worked; she gets a small allowance from the estate instead. I doubt she'd blow it on a taxi.'

Taylor folded her arms, feeling prickly and defensive, and not really knowing why. Unless it was because he'd rejected her theory about the secret code, which seemed a bit childish of her.

'Well, I haven't seen her. Sorry.'

'Ordinarily, I wouldn't bother you, but Gran ... She's not feeling well today, and I don't want Iris's disappearance to make things worse.' He ran a hand through his uncombed hair. 'There's a chance she's still in the house somewhere, and just not answering me. But it's a big place and it would take a long time to search it alone.'

Taylor remembered her strange dream two nights ago, before she'd moved out of Estuary House and back into her cosy tent. She'd found herself standing before a sandy hole, deep as a fresh-dug grave, and had fallen into it, only to be buried alive. Iris had featured in that dream, too, hadn't she?

Perhaps it had been a premonition, not simply a nightmare.

'You think Iris may have hurt herself?'

'I hope not. But anything's possible.'

She gave up. 'All right, I'll come and help you look. Give me a few minutes to get washed and dressed.'

'Thank you.' His gaze skimmed her pyjamas again, suddenly awkward. 'I'll wait in the house for you. Just let yourself in.'

Taylor watched Julius trudge back down the field, and then darted into the safety of her tent.

Speaking the truth about him – and witnessing its consequence – had been the sweetest moment ever. Though painful, too.

Afterwards, she'd made a vow never to let anyone get that close again. Affection, yes. Company, definitely. But never love. Not the bond that annihilates the heart when it's finally, irrevocably broken.

★

331

She found Julius gently remonstrating with his grandmother in the entrance hall; Mrs Chance was wrestling with a pair of wellies, determined to go outside and search the grounds for her sister-in-law. But it was clear from her pallor and trembling frame that she was not feeling well.

'I'm going to take you back to your sitting room, Gran, and then I'll bring you a nice cup of tea,' Julius told her calmly, linking his arm with hers. 'No, leave the wellies. I'll deal with them when I come back.' He glanced at Taylor as he led his grandmother away, and mouthed, 'Sorry.'

'I'll have a quick sweep around, see if I can find any clues to where Iris might have gone,' Taylor called out as the two figures vanished into gloom, but there was no response.

She hesitated, and then headed up the stairs, as it seemed likely that Julius would already have searched comprehensively for her downstairs.

Iris had been staying in her old room, Mrs Chance had told her earlier, the one she had occupied when she lived here before her strange remove to the hut across the river. But Taylor had only the vaguest idea where that might be.

She wandered slowly along the confusing corridors and landings on the first floor, not really sure what she was looking for or why she had chosen to come and help.

Peering into empty rooms and occasionally calling, 'Iris?' she eventually found a narrow, enclosed staircase, probably once intended for servants to use, and went slowly up it, entering a part of the house she had never visited before.

There was a long corridor with a faded carpet runner down the middle. Most of these rooms were empty, their doors standing wide open. The recent rains had cleared up, and where the curtains were drawn back, sunlight lay in deep golden patches under each window, the air warm and still.

There was a feel of summer everywhere, and yet a curious darkness, too, like the kernel inside a glossy nutshell.

She found another staircase at the far end and followed it down to a broad landing with a diamond-paned window that overlooked the east side of the house. The way forked there. There was another corridor leading away into gloom, and a further set of stairs that would presumably lead her down to the kitchens and garden door.

About to head down the stairs, Taylor stopped, hearing an odd noise along the corridor. There was something she recognised about the sound, something that caught at her heart.

That soft rhythmic thud, and the tiny sobs, like a woman catching her breath at the end of a cry ...

It was the same sound she'd heard one night while staying in the house. Abruptly, she realised what she was hearing, yet in the same instant dismissed the realisation as impossible, unthinkable, horrific.

It had to be Iris.

She turned away from the stairs and followed the corridor instead. At the far end was a pointed archway, and a closed door beyond it. The floorboards were old and polished to a high sheen. Taylor tiptoed towards the door, trying to be as silent as possible, but the floor creaked beneath her, and the sobbing stopped.

Taylor stiffened, holding her breath, about to move away.

She had no right to be here, eavesdropping. She should fetch Julius instead and tell him where to look for his great-aunt. That was the right thing to do. Anything else would be an intolerable intrusion.

'Who's there?' a shaking voice called out from inside the room.

Taylor groaned inwardly. 'It's only me, Taylor,' she said quickly. 'I'm sorry, Iris. I'll go away.'

'No, come in.'

Taylor hesitated, surprised. Then she pushed the door and went inside.

It was a large, dusty and untidy room, cluttered with old-fashioned furniture, like an auction room on sale day: chairs, tables, stacked picture frames, glass-fronted cabinets, even a vast mahogany wardrobe. There was no sign of a bed. A storage or junk room, perhaps. Long velvet curtains covered the tall windows, except for one pair, which had been opened a little, and light streamed brightly through that gap, dust motes spinning in the sunshine.

An old, free-standing mirror stood opposite the door.

For a split-second, Taylor saw the reflection of herself opening the door, a blank look on her face, and a half-naked Iris kneeling in the centre of the room, her back towards the door, head bent, and a mass of terrible red stripes across her back.

As though she'd been mauled by a tiger.

Taylor recalled her dream – a young Iris dressed as a nun, the grey back of her habit torn and stained with blood.

She was accustomed to bizarre dreams, and even to predictive dreams; she had often woken knowing what was about to happen, especially as a child. But those dreams had only concerned herself before, or occasionally one or both of her parents. Never someone outside the family, someone she barely knew. The unexpected correspondence between her dream and this startling reality shook her.

There was something on the floor beside Iris.

A cat o' nine tails, Taylor thought instinctively, glancing that way. It was a black whip with a short, stubby handle, and a flail-like end made up of leather strips. The vicious-looking strips accorded to the red, weeping marks on Iris's back. Only they were not merely fresh wounds. They lay over a mass of old, pale, crisscrossed scars, as though her back had been brutalised in this way again and again over the years.

She stepped back. 'I'm sorry,' she said again, her voice high with embarrassment.

'No,' Iris said, and bent forward for a loose grey shirt that she pulled over her head. It formed a seamless grey with her skirt, which covered the rest of her almost to the ankles. 'I wanted you to see. To understand.' She stood and turned to her, looking almost hopeful. 'Did you?'

But Taylor could only shake her head, horrified. 'Why do that to yourself?'

'Because I'm a sinner,' Iris said simply. 'I sinned and I needed to be punished. And yet I've never been punished.' She picked up the whip and put it away in a drawer, her movements gentle, almost reverent. 'So I punish myself.'

'How long?' Taylor's voice had silted up; the words came out as though she were underwater. Clearing her throat, she tried again. 'I mean, how long have you been doing that? Punishing yourself?'

'Since it happened. Since the day of my fall.'

'I don't understand.'

'Really?' Iris looked amazed, and then disappointed. Perplexed, too, her brow furrowed. 'I felt sure that you … That first day, when I saw you across the river, I thought you must be my executioner, come at last.'

'God, no.'

Iris blinked. 'But I saw your wings. Like a great white cloud behind you. You came to judge me, didn't you?'

'Never.'

'How strange, I was so sure …'

Iris walked to the dusty mirror and looked at herself

searchingly, turning her head from side to side as though she could still see sin in her face. Or perhaps was astonished that she couldn't see it there either, because she felt the stain of it so strongly inside.

She turned and held out her hands to Taylor at waist-height, palms turned upwards in a stylistic gesture, as though displaying stigmata.

'Look,' she urged her. 'Look hard. Do you understand now why I need to be punished?' Iris gave her a strained smile. 'I have blood on my hands. Do you see it? Can you smell it?'

Chapter Thirty-One

You called it Johnny Jump Up, three-faces-in-a-hood
Or love-in-idleness. The joker's wild card
Easing the heart's sorrow with dark pansy eyes,
Its promise of tomorrow.

– From 'Heartsease' in *Estuary*

Inside the damp-smelling storage hut, Eleanor lay on her side, hooded and trembling, wondering if these would be her last moments, her final memories. The ground was damp and chilly. There was a smell of sulphur and a faint tang of salt. She lay still, as ordered, and listened to the mournful cries of seabirds along the estuary, and to thick reeds bending and rustling in the wind outside, while her unseen captor paced the hut, feverishly muttering to himself and smoking his third cigarette.

She had no idea what Oliver planned to do with her. Of course, maybe he didn't know either. That was possible. He'd been eerily silent since leaving the boat, barely addressing a word to her.

But she knew he must intend something desperate, even if his plans were still formless. Why abduct her otherwise? Why bring her here of all places, to this remote, unpromising spot, unless Oliver was prepared to face the consequences of discovery?

No, this was an act of last resort.

His family might indulge his strange moods and even his rages, but none of them would condone this behaviour, she felt sure. This would finish him. So, he had nothing to lose by treating her as badly as he liked, a thought that struck cold terror into her.

She'd fought him at first, flailing about and reminding him loudly what Lyndon would do when her disappearance was discovered. But Oliver had been unmoved even by the prospect of his brother's wrath.

He'd struck her again, bound her hands behind her back with a length of cord he must have brought with him specially for the purpose, and then half-dragged, half-pushed her from the riverbank to the hut, ignoring her protests and struggles.

Oliver crouched at last, dragging off her hood. 'Why did you have to come to Cornwall?' he demanded, his eyes wild. 'I had the whole thing sorted out. I had Jeannie eating out of my hand. She would have said yes if I'd proposed next summer, once she'd got used to the idea. But you and Lyndon ... It's ruined everything.'

Eleanor blinked up at him, her vision blurry, having grown accustomed to the soft, dusky interior of the black hood.

Her mouth was dry, but she wet her lips, tasting dried blood. 'What do you mean?' she whispered, fearing he might strike her again if she spoke too aggressively. Like her father, he had a heavy hand.

'You're such a little innocent, Nell,' he said contemptuously, and ran a hand across his mouth. His eyes grew cunning. 'Exactly how innocent, though? I could have sworn when I first met you that he hadn't even touched you yet. His own wife! Though that's Lyndon all over. He never could get past that image in his head of a chivalrous knight, rescuing damsels but never helping himself to the spoils.' Deliberately, he stroked her cheek and laughed when she shrank back. 'But the way he's been looking at you these past few days ... Did my pathetic brother finally consummate his wedding vows?'

She flushed and looked away.

'That's a pity.' Studying her hungrily, Oliver took a last deep drag on his cigarette, which had almost burnt down to the stub, and then threw it aside. 'I would have enjoyed being your first.' She looked back at him, scared then, and he showed his teeth in a humourless smile. 'But I suppose he learned his lesson after Diana. Though I must say it took him long enough. Poor slow old Lyndon. His head too full of poetry to notice a woman smiling at him.'

How long would it take for the alarm to be raised back at Estuary House? She hadn't been gone that long, maybe an hour or so. But if Oliver was missing as well ...

Would Lyndon quickly guess where his brother had taken her? She would have to hope so and play for time. She'd feared at first that Oliver meant to rape her, but the look in his eyes was murderous. Though the one didn't preclude the other.

He propped her up against the wooden slats of the hut wall, leaving her hands still bound behind her back. Her dress had ridden up her thighs; she saw him look that way a few times, leeringly, and wished she could drag the hem down, or cover herself. But he would only laugh if she did.

She had no defence against this man.

Only her wits.

Avoiding his predatory gaze, Eleanor glanced about the hut instead; they were in the main room of the structure. The opening to the second, smaller section with its crates and barrels yawned in the shadows to their right. That was where she'd found Lyndon's shrine to the dead Diana Farthing, hidden away in a corner behind shelving. Was that why he'd brought her here? No doubt Oliver had found the shrine, too, and been enraged that his brother had tried to make this place his own, the hut that Oliver had built, as his father had so fondly called it.

I would have enjoyed being your first.

She caught her breath, suddenly realising what a fool she'd been. Of course, of course, she thought, and looked back at him.

I suppose he learned his lesson after Diana.

Her heart thumping with terror, she asked rather daringly, 'Oliver, were … were you in love with Diana?'

Oliver stood abruptly and drew his packet of Player's from his jacket pocket again. He lit another cigarette with hands that were not quite steady, and then glanced her way.

'Want a drag, darling?' He gave a cruel laugh but removed one from the packet and crouched to lodge it between her lips. 'One last cigarette for the condemned woman, and all that.' He lit it, the lighter flame dancing in his dark eyes. 'In love with Diana? God no, what a thought. But she was mine, not his. She was always going to be mine.'

Eleanor dragged on the cigarette, unable to remove it from her mouth, and the acrid smoke drifted upwards, making her eyes water.

'I don't understand,' she mumbled. 'I thought she and Lyndon—'

'I couldn't stand idly by and watch him inherit everything, just because he'd happened to catch Diana's eye. Besides,' he added grimly, 'you don't know about the pact.'

'Sorry?'

'Lyndon and I made a pact early on, when Dad first told us he had to choose one of us to inherit. A pact never to marry, never to have children. It was the problem of twins, you see. Dad couldn't bear the thought of Estuary House being sold, if we jointly inherited and then split the proceeds.' Oliver stared gloomily into the shadows. 'It was our bloody fifteenth birthday. He said we were "men" now and had a right to know who would inherit. So he told us, it would be whichever of us had a child first. A son to carry the Chance name into the future.' He made a dismissive noise under his breath. 'As if anyone would have a future in that crumbling heap of stones.'

That was much the same thing Jeannie had told her; Eleanor hadn't quite believed it before, but Oliver seemed perfectly serious.

'Why didn't you just get married first, then?'

'We made a pact, I told you. Anyway, I didn't take the old man's threat seriously. And marriage seemed a long way off for both of us. Career first, earn some money, and then ...' Oliver shook his head. 'I was away on the continent that year, enjoying myself with some well-heeled friends who were happy to pick up the tab. We had a great time: the Med, the Greek islands, Turkey, sunbathing on the beaches, taking in the sights ... Much better than dreary England, I can tell you.' His smile died. 'But then Lyndon came home after university and started to court Diana. Mum sent me a letter. Said I had to come home and do something about it, pronto. Find myself a girlfriend and get her pregnant, basically.'

Eleanor stared at him. 'Your *mother*?'

'Mum can be very determined when she wants something. And she wanted me to inherit, not Lyndon. I've always been her favourite, you see.' The corner of his mouth quirked. 'She was the only one who could tell us apart when we were little. She said it was because Lyndon was always frowning. But I was a smiler. "Her little snake-charmer," she called me.' Oliver looked at her sharply, frowning. 'There was never anything unnatural in it, if that's what you're thinking.'

Eleanor, whose skin had been creeping, quickly shook her head. 'Of course not,' she tried to say, but the cigarette lodged between her lips fell out and she jerked away with a cry as the hot tip glanced against her thigh, burning it.

Oliver moved swiftly, crushing the fallen cigarette beneath his heel. 'Are you hurt? Let me see.' He crouched, throwing aside his own smoke. He pushed back the hem of her dress, staring down at her bare thigh. She moaned and cringed away at his touch. His eyes narrowed, lifting to her face. 'What's the matter? Don't tell me you're not interested. Because I won't believe it.'

Eleanor looked away, blushing. He did look so uncannily like Lyndon at times, it was hard not to feel the tiniest flicker of sexuality at his touch. But he wasn't Lyndon, and it was strong revulsion she felt for him, not desire.

'I fooled you before,' he said softly, and she held her breath, unable to resist looking round at him again, her gaze locked to his. 'Down by the trees. Do you remember? I kissed your hand and you enjoyed it, I could tell. Yes, you guessed it was me, not him. But only because I allowed you to see that. I grew bored of playing charades with you, Nell. But I definitely had you fooled there.'

Contradicting him would be dangerous, she decided, aware of a kind of madness in his eyes, so she said nothing.

His smile grew sensual. 'I could have kept on pretending to be Lyndon, and taken you to bed, and you would have been none the wiser. But that would have spoiled it for me, darling. Because I want you to know which of us is inside you when it happens.'

Seeing her look of shocked horror, Oliver laughed, seeming to find her response almost pleasurable. 'Oh yes, why do you think I brought you here? To talk you to death?' His hand slid more seductively across her thigh again, his gaze speculative. 'I felt sure you'd be a screamer, so I figured this hut would be the best place for it. Nobody around for miles.' His smile was repellent. 'Nobody to hear when I lay my brother's soft little wife down in the dirt and show her what a real man feels like.'

'Is that the … the only reason?' she stammered desperately, hoping to distract him. 'Because I know about the cross and the flowers, Oliver. I … I found them the day your father brought me and Lyndon across to see the improvements to the river defences.'

It was a gamble. But she was convinced now that Oliver had been in love with Diana, and had made that shrine to the dead girl.

I could have kept on pretending to be Lyndon, and taken you to bed, and you would have been none the wiser.

He'd raped Diana, she realised with a shudder of genuine horror. Only the poor girl hadn't known it; Diana had assumed she was in bed with Lyndon, while all the time …

'You say you weren't in love with Diana,' she added hurriedly. 'But I think you were. You must have been, to keep a shrine in her memory for so long. Did you seduce her, pretending to be Lyndon? Is that when you fell in love with her?'

Oliver was frowning fiercely. His hand had stilled on her thigh. 'Shrine?' he repeated, ignoring the rest of what she'd said. 'What shrine? What flowers? What are you talking about?'

'In the other room,' she whispered, scared by his expression, and jerked her head towards the gloomy opening. 'In the far corner, behind the barrels and the shelves. You don't need to deny it. There's no shame in wanting to preserve her

343

memory. I found the cross hanging on the wall. And your flowers beneath it.' She hesitated. 'And a locket. There was a photograph of them inside it. Lyndon and Diana, together.'

Abruptly, Oliver straightened, staring into the other room of the hut.

'I took the locket with me, I'm afraid,' she admitted, and hoped he wouldn't be too angry about the theft. 'It's in my bedroom back at the house. I wasn't stealing it, honest. I would have brought it back, only I wanted ... That is, I intended to confront Lyndon with it. I thought he'd left it here, you see. I thought he must still be in love with Diana.' She could hear her own heart beating so loud in the silence, it seemed almost deafening. 'But it was you, wasn't it? It was you who made the shrine. And laid the flowers in her memory.'

'Get up.' Oliver dragged her to her feet and pushed her ahead of him into the shadowy compartment next door. She stumbled, pins and needles in her legs after being made to sit still on the damp earth for so long. But he was relentless. 'Show me,' he growled in her ear.

She took him to the place. The cross was still there on the wall. The faded flowers lay even more withered on the sandy earth, now bare husks.

'There,' she said, and was thrust aside while he examined the spot. 'But I thought ... I don't understand.'

A locket, with a photograph of them inside it. Lyndon and Diana, together.

Eleanor gasped, her own stupidity dawning on her too late. Why on earth would Oliver, who loathed and despised his twin brother, who had seduced Lyndon's girlfriend, make a shrine to the girl after her death and hang up a necklace that contained a photo of his brother and Diana, for God's sake?

He would have ripped that photograph out and torn it up, or at the least folded it over so that only Diana was showing.

But now she was more confused than ever. If Oliver hadn't made that shrine to Diana, who had?

'Somebody knows,' Oliver muttered, staring from the cross to the flowers with his eyes wide and bulging. There was a vein standing out in his forehead. 'Somebody bloody well knows.'

'Knows what?'

He was silent for a moment. Then he gave a terrible roar and knocked her to the ground. Eleanor hit her head on a barrel and lay dazed. There was a dull noise in her head, a kind of buzzing, almost like the sound of an engine. Was she concussed? she wondered.

Oliver was cursing under his breath, calling her all kinds of vile names. He bent his head and kissed her, though there was nothing loving about it, his lips grinding cruelly against hers. His hands dragged her skirt higher up, exposing the tops of her bare thighs, then moved to unfasten his belt.

With a shock, she realised what he intended, and tried to crawl away, to cry for help ...

Then Oliver was gone, miraculously plucked away from her as though by a giant hand, and she was staring up into a thin, intense face, a pair of dark, wary eyes fixed on her.

'Are you hurt? Can you get up?' It was Iris. 'You shouldn't be in here,' she said, almost scolding. 'Turn around, let me cut you loose.' Eleanor stared, not understanding. Then she saw the knife in Iris's hand, and her eyes widened. Iris gave her a thin smile. 'Bread knife. Took it from the kitchen on my way out. Thought we might need it. And I was right.'

Iris sawed at the cord until it snapped. Eleanor heard Lyndon's voice outside the hut, deep and furious. And Oliver was there, too, responding wildly, mentioning her name ...

'I have to see Lyndon,' Eleanor said, panicking at the thought of what Oliver might be saying about her. 'I have to explain—'

'Lyndon knows this wasn't your fault.'

Iris adjusted Eleanor's dress and helped her back to her feet.

'How?'

'I saw Oliver take you. I was down at the chapel, and I saw him rowing you across the estuary. I went straight back to the house, but Lyndon was still out. It took me ages to find him. But he knows you didn't come here willingly.' Iris looked round at the cross hanging on the wall, as though checking it was still there; she certainly didn't seem surprised to see it in this dark corner of Oliver's hut. 'Nobody would come here willingly. It's a place of evil and sinfulness.'

Eleanor suddenly understood. 'You put it there. You hung the cross on the wall, and the locket on the cross. You brought the flowers.'

'Somebody had to. The dead must be remembered.'

'The dead?'

'At least I was in time to save you from the same fate.' Iris studied her closely, then reached out to touch Eleanor's cut lip. 'Though you look awful. Did Olly ...' Something flickered in her face. A kind of revulsion. 'I mean, were we too late?'

'Your brother didn't rape me, if that's what you're asking.'

'Thank God.' Iris crossed herself piously.

Eleanor, who had nothing to say to that, left the young woman standing alone there in the shadows.

She stumbled out of the hut and found the twins facing off against each other in the sandy, reed-fringed clearing in front of the hut. Like two faces of the same coin, she thought, glancing from one to the other, looking uncannily similar today in the same all-black clothes.

She wanted to run to Lyndon, to make him understand it hadn't been her choice to come here with his brother. But one look at his forbidding face told her it would be pointless. Oliver had already been filling his head with poison, that was clear.

'And here she is now,' Oliver drawled, 'your ever-loving wife. She's a good kisser, I'll give her that.'

Standing stiffly, hands clenched into fists, Lyndon turned his head without actually looking at her. 'You all right, Eleanor?' he asked, and she heard the fear in his voice.

'He forced me to come here,' she said hurriedly. 'It wasn't my fault.'

'I know, Iris told me. She saw Oliver rowing you across the river. She said he put a hood over your head? I'm sorry it took us so long to get here. We came round by the road. I drove as fast as I could.'

'Lyndon to the rescue,' his brother said, and gave a harsh laugh. 'Pity you couldn't have made it in time for Diana, isn't it?'

There was a terrible silence.

'What's that supposed to mean?' Lyndon turned back to his brother.

'You know what it means.'

'I've got my suspicions. So why don't you tell me the truth, Oliver? For once in your miserable life.'

'She didn't know it was me, the first time. But afterwards, of course, I had to tell her.' Oliver's mouth twisted in a fleeting smile. 'Couldn't have the silly girl mentioning it to you, thinking you were the one who'd made love to her out there, on a picnic blanket, hidden from the world by all the reeds.' He pointed beyond the hut towards the riverbank.

'There was no hut here that summer, of course. Only the old tree. That's where we met, after that first time.' His face grew dark. 'That's where I brought her, the last time I ever saw her.'

'I knew it.' Lyndon was leaning forward as though in a high wind. 'You killed her, you bastard. Rather than see me inherit, you murdered an innocent girl.'

'No,' Oliver said thickly. 'I was in love with her. It was a summer madness. It wouldn't have lasted. And yes, I did it to take her away from you. But when she told me about the baby—'

Eleanor put a hand to her mouth. 'Baby?'

'She was pregnant when she died,' Oliver said grimly, looking at her for the first time since he'd knocked her down in the hut. 'And yes, it was my child. Lyndon never touched her.'

'We were waiting,' Lyndon said, 'until after we were married. Diana told me that's what she wanted.' He shook his head. 'And I don't believe you about a baby. Why would she do that? Maybe once, because you tricked her. But keep sleeping with you behind my back? You're lying.'

'No, I'm not. She preferred me to you. She was just too scared to come clean and tell you, that's all. And I have proof.' Oliver pointed to Iris, who had come out of the hut, cradling the withered flowers in her arms. 'She knows what happened. Don't you, Iris?'

'I know you're a sinner,' his sister said coldly.

'But you know I'm not a murderer.'

Iris said nothing.

'So, let me get this straight. You're saying you had nothing to do with her death.'

'That's right.'

'You expect me to believe that Diana killed herself because

she was carrying your child while engaged to me? That she couldn't live with that and drowned herself out of… what, a sense of shame?' Lyndon's voice was erratic and disjointed. 'That makes no sense. You're insane.'

'Maybe. But I still had her,' Oliver said with deliberate, goading emphasis, 'and you didn't. Diana was mine, not yours. And so is your wife now.' His smile was pure evil. 'She's a screamer, isn't she? Not that I'm complaining.'

With a maddened roar, Lyndon rushed at him at last, like a wild animal released from a trap; the two brothers clung together, fists swinging and flailing, and then wrestled each other to the ground.

'He never touched me, he's lying,' Eleanor shouted, but Lyndon wasn't listening. 'We have to stop them,' she told Iris.

'There's no stopping them. Not anymore.' Iris lay the flowers down on the wooden porch, ignoring the vicious fight unfolding only a few feet away. Her expression was oddly contemplative. 'I'll have to fetch fresh flowers from the gardens next time. Her grave should always be marked.'

Eleanor felt a rushing in her ears. 'Her grave?' she faltered.

She turned to look at Lyndon, but he wasn't listening. He'd struggled free of his brother's bear-like grasp and rolled away. But Oliver crawled after him and began laying into him with both fists.

'That was my child in her womb,' Oliver spat. 'It should have lived. She was in love with me. Her death was your fault. All your fault.'

'I wasn't the one who made her desperate,' Lyndon threw back at him. He whipped round and punched Oliver full in the face, and his brother fell backwards with a thick cry, blood streaming from his nose. 'I wasn't the one who drove her to kill herself.'

349

'Diana didn't kill herself,' Oliver yelled back, and birds rose noisily from the reeds at his shout. 'Our mother killed her.'

Lyndon stopped abruptly, panting and staring. 'What?' He ran a hand over his sweating forehead, and then repeated in shock, 'What?'

'It was Mum. She took Diana a cup of coffee in bed, laced with rat poison. Watched her drink it, and then came to find me.'

'I don't believe you.'

'Then you're a fool.' Oliver wiped the blood away with the back of his hand. 'She'd guessed Diana was pregnant, and she thought ... Well, Mum thought it was yours. That you were going to inherit Estuary House instead of me. So she killed Diana for me.' He gave an odd little laugh. 'I never had the heart to tell her the baby was mine. She thought she was doing me a favour.'

Lyndon looked round at Iris, his eyes wild. 'And you knew about this? And never breathed a word to me?'

'I knew Mummy had killed her,' Iris admitted. 'She told me herself and made me promise not to repeat it. So I couldn't say anything. Not even to Oliver. Mummy wanted forgiveness, to have her sins heard and to pray afterwards. And you can't break the seal of the confessional. It's a sacred trust.'

'God in heaven,' Lyndon cried; his eyes were bloodshot, and there were tears on his cheeks. Eleanor couldn't bear to see him so broken. 'But why tell everyone she drowned? Why put us through that? And her family, too. Her brother, Mackenzie. He hates me because of it. And I can't blame him. Never knowing where her body was ...'

Iris looked faintly surprised. 'Oliver did it to save Mummy from going to prison, of course. And you don't need to

350

worry about where her body is. He laid Diana to rest here, where she was happiest. And built the hut over her body.'

Oliver was staring at his sister. 'You knew?'

'I've always known.'

He gave a cracked laugh. 'Of course you did.'

'Oh, Diana...' Lyndon stood a moment with his face buried in his hands, his shoulders shaking with grief. Then he straightened and spun to face Oliver, his fists up again. 'This is all your fault. If you hadn't been so greedy, if you hadn't seduced her to spite me, Diana would still be alive today. We'd be married now, perhaps with a child of our own.' His throat convulsed, and he fell silent, not looking at anyone but staring dully at the ground.

'What are you going to do?' Iris asked him.

'I'm going back to the house to call the police,' Lyndon told her, moving away wearily at last. 'I'm not leaving her in the dark under that vile little hut. Diana deserves a proper burial. She deserves to have her name on a stone, and for her family to know what happened to her.'

'Lyndon, come back. Don't be stupid. Think about what you're doing.' Oliver followed him back towards his Land Rover, which stood a few hundred feet away, reeds smashed and crushed under its tyres. 'You can't go to the police. You'll be condemning our mother. Dragging the family name into the dirt.'

'I don't care.'

'Stop right there, or I'll shoot you.' Oliver had drawn a pistol out of his jacket pocket. 'I mean it, Lyndon.'

It was the same pistol Iris had used to scare off her father earlier, Eleanor realised, staring at it horrified. Oliver must have spotted the gun on the hall table where Iris had left it and decided to take it with him.

Iris, who had also been trailing after her brothers in a despondent way, stopped and stared at Oliver's back.

Eleanor, just behind them, saw Iris's hand steal towards her pocket and produce the long kitchen knife she'd used to cut her free. Instinctively, she opened her mouth to call out a warning, and then closed it again.

She wanted Lyndon to live.

Lyndon had turned in disbelief, his car key already in his hand. He stared at the pistol. 'What the hell is that?'

'You know what this is. It's Dad's service revolver from when he was demobbed. And yes, it's loaded. I checked.'

'Come on, Olly. You're not going to shoot me with Dad's old Webley.'

'I'll do whatever it takes to protect our mother.' There was an intensity in his voice now. 'Mummy doesn't deserve to go to prison. She could be hanged for what she did, for God's sake. Or hadn't you thought of that?'

'Of course I thought of it. But Diana didn't deserve to die.'

Oliver raised the pistol, pointing it straight at his twin's heart. His hand was shaking, his face contorted. 'I don't want to shoot you. But I can't let you go to the police, Lyndon. This is our *mother* we're talking about. You may not love her, but I do. And she trusts me.' There was a pleading note in his voice now. 'I have to do this for her, don't you see?'

Lyndon said nothing, his gaze on his brother's face.

Suddenly, Oliver dropped the pistol and crumpled to the ground, a long-handled kitchen knife sticking out of his back. Iris, having plunged it into him, turned away.

'Olly,' Lyndon cried, starting forward as though to help him, but then stopped. His tortured gaze rose to meet Eleanor's.

Oliver Chance gasped and writhed in the dirt while his

blood bloomed thickly around his body like a strange, red-petalled flower.

'Oh my God,' Eleanor whispered, watching him in horror. 'Quick, we ... we ought to do something.'

'Like what?' Iris asked, clearly baffled by this suggestion.

'I don't know. Try to stop the bleeding?'

'But why?'

'Because he's going to die.'

'Well, that was the idea.' With a shrug, Iris kicked the pistol away and then stooped to remove the knife. Oliver gave a terrible strangled groan, his fingers rigid now, digging into the soil. 'I don't think that made any difference,' she said, holding up the knife, which was dripping blood.

'Olly ...' Lyndon collapsed to his knees next to his dying brother and bent his forehead to the earth. His body shook with silent sobs.

Eleanor ran and put her arms around him.

It was soon over.

Once Oliver had finally stopped moving, Iris crouched to check his pulse. 'He's dead,' she said without emotion, and straightened up, studying the terrible gash in his back. 'That was surprisingly quick. I must have hit an artery. Or maybe his heart.'

Eleanor felt numb inside. She wracked her brains for something she could say that would ease Lyndon's suffering. But what could she say? His twin was dead; his life would never be the same again. Nonetheless, she wanted Lyndon to know she was there for him, and that she would always be there for him, whatever happened.

'You ... You were right,' she whispered into his ear. 'I should have said yes when you asked me. Next time, I'll say yes.'

Lyndon lifted his head to stare at her, uncomprehending.

'We should marry for real.' Eleanor stroked the back of his neck. 'And never be apart again.'

He took her hand and pressed it to his shaking mouth. 'My darling Eleanor,' he said hoarsely. 'I love you.'

'You know, we should probably bury Oliver under the hut, too.' They both looked round at Iris, who was still gazing down at his body. 'He can lie beside Diana. She'd like that, after being alone there so long. And I think Olly was in love with her, in his own horrible way. He just didn't know how to say so.' She bent to wipe the knife clean on the grass, oddly calm despite having just murdered her brother. 'Does this mean they'll hang me, do you think?'

Chapter Thirty-Two

The bug wriggled in its silken chrysalis –
Once, twice – and was still.

– From 'Unborn' in *Estuary*

After Iris had finished confessing to the murder of Oliver Chance, they gave her one of Mrs Chance's sleeping pills and put her to bed, though she was still muttering feverishly to herself that she needed to be punished for her sins.

Taylor and Julius trailed downstairs in stunned silence.

Mrs Chance was in her sitting room, staring out of the window. She had come upstairs at one stage to see how Iris was doing, but left in distressed confusion when she realised her sister-in-law was confessing to murder.

She turned when they came in and put shaky hands to her face. 'I never thought Iris would speak of it again … That awful day.'

'Gran, what's all this about?' Julius asked, still incredulous. 'Did she really kill my great-uncle, or is this another of her mad fantasies?'

If Julius had been hoping his grandmother would refute the whole thing, he was going to be disappointed, Taylor thought. She could see in the old lady's face that it was true and found herself wishing she could protect Julius from what lay ahead.

But there was no way to protect him from the truth.

'I ... I'm not sure I should say anything. The three of us agreed to keep quiet about it. Lyndon made the decision, and we all stuck by it. Until now ...' Mrs Chance gave a frightened moan. 'Oh, it's too horrible to think about. And it all happened so long ago, what does it matter now?'

Julius put an arm about her shoulder and led her to the sofa. He sat down with her and patted her hand. 'It's all right, Gran. There's no need to get upset. But I think the truth has to come out. Why not just tell us in your own words what happened?'

'Must I?' She wrung her hands in her lap. 'Could I at least have some brandy first, do you think?' Her laugh was high-pitched. 'Dutch courage. I'm a bit wobbly.'

Julius hesitated, then said, 'Very well,' and left the room.

While he was gone, Mrs Chance looked up at Taylor, giving her a lopsided smile. 'I knew you would sort it all out in the end,' she said, with an odd kind of satisfaction. 'You're the investigator. You were sent here to make things right. Lyndon always knew you would come one day. He told me to look out for you.'

Taylor was startled. 'He did?'

'Oh yes, my dear. He saw you in the cards.'

The investigator.

Taylor couldn't imagine what Mrs Chance had been through as Lyndon's widow, keeping this huge secret all these years, aware that her sister-in-law would be arrested for murder if she ever revealed what she knew about Diana's death and Oliver's disappearance.

Eleanor, she reminded herself. She had to start thinking of Mrs Chance as Eleanor.

It had all seemed so far away and forgotten before, divorced from the real world around her. But she knew the woman standing before her now was the closest she'd ever get to the truth of Lyndon Chance's life.

'I didn't do anything,' she said.

'I think you did everything you were supposed to. You see things, don't you, dear? Things other people can't.' Eleanor's smile faded, and a troubled look took its place. 'Long dead things from the past. Things that probably ought to have stayed buried forever.' She shivered. 'Iris warned me it was time to come clean. To let the light in. And she's right, of course. But that doesn't make it any easier.'

Taylor looked at her, uneasy. Was Mrs Chance right? Was this all her fault? Had she stirred up the darkness simply by coming here to Estuary House?

Murder seems to follow you about, Taylor. You were born with death in your heart, girl.

No, that isn't true, she told herself. Her father should never have said that about his own daughter. He was a cruel and evil man. Anyway, he'd only said it to make her feel worthless and beyond saving, to keep her under his control.

It was hard to silence that ugly voice in her head. But she had to do it, for the sake of her sanity.

Julius returned a few minutes later, bearing a silver tray before him, for all the world like a butler. There were three brandy glasses on the tray, and a decanter. He set the tray on the coffee table.

'Let me,' Taylor said, and bent to pour them a small helping of brandy each, while Julius sat next to his grandmother.

'So,' he said, frowning, 'just to be clear, did you really see my great-aunt murder Oliver Chance with a kitchen knife?' He passed a glass of brandy to his grandmother and took one for himself. 'Or has Iris finally cracked?'

'Oh no,' Mrs Chance told him, sipping at her brandy, 'she really did kill him. I was there. Saw the whole thing.'

Falteringly, with many exclamations and shakes of her head, the old lady told them exactly what had happened that day. How Oliver had rowed her across the river to the storage hut, with rape and murder in his heart, and Iris and Lyndon had come after them to save her. And just as Iris had said, Oliver had threatened to shoot his brother, so she had no choice but to stab him. In the back. With a kitchen knife.

'This is appalling.' Justin knocked back his brandy and swiftly poured himself another. 'But if it's true, why on earth has nobody ever told me about it? And why weren't the police involved?'

'Lyndon made us promise not to tell anyone. For the sake of the family. Though it was hard, having to live with Camilla afterwards, knowing what she'd done.'

'Hang on, *Camilla* . . . You mean my great-grandmother?' Julius interrupted, looking horrified. 'What's she got to do with it?'

'Didn't I say? Camilla was the one who caused it all. That tragedy over Diana Farthing. The girl who drowned off Oliver's yacht. Or rather, who didn't.'

'I'm sorry, I don't understand.'

Mrs Chance finished her brandy and looked longingly at the decanter until he reluctantly poured her another couple of fingers.

'Well, why should you, dear? It was all hushed up.' She sipped at her brandy, cradling the glass. 'Even Diana's own brother didn't know how she died, poor man. He thought Lyndon killed her. Most people did, of course, though there was never any proof. They just thought it made a good story. And when Oliver disappeared, people said Lyndon must have killed him, too.'

'Sorry . . . Diana's brother?' Taylor asked, confused.

'Robert Mackenzie. After his little boy died, he couldn't

live with the grief. Not after losing his sister, too.' Mrs Chance sighed. 'Such a pity. Robert was a nice man, the kind you could really trust. I liked him.'

'Mack,' Taylor said wonderingly, and Julius glanced at her with an arrested look on his face.

'OK, that's … weird,' Julius said. 'But Grandma, I still don't understand why you kept quiet all these years. Didn't you care about the truth? Or justice?'

'Of course I did. It was awful, not being able to tell the truth and shame the devil. But Lyndon swore us all to secrecy, to save Iris and his mother from the hangman.' Seeing their stunned expressions, Mrs Chance explained, 'They were still hanging people for murder back in those days. Can you imagine what that would have done to the family?'

'Sorry, but what on earth did Lyndon's mother have to do with the death of Diana Farthing?' Taylor asked. 'You said she didn't drown, as people supposed. So, what happened to her?' She gasped as a horrible thought struck her. 'Were those Diana's bones I found under the chapel floor?'

Mrs Chance put down her glass, seeming almost affronted. 'Of course not. Diana was buried under the storage hut.' She shrugged. 'Whoever that woman was under the chapel, she's nothing to do with this.'

Julius stared at his grandmother, nonplussed, and then turned and looked at Taylor without speaking. But she knew what he was thinking. Of the strange acrostic she'd found hidden in Lyndon's poem titles.

THEY LIE TOGETHER UNDER THE STORAGE HUT.

'Oliver agreed to bury Diana across the river,' Mrs Chance continued in a matter-of-fact way, 'so nobody would know his mother had poisoned her.'

'Poisoned her?' Julius exclaimed.

'Please don't interrupt, dear. Then Oliver very cleverly built the hut over her grave to conceal it. Except Iris had been aware of their affair all along and knew exactly what had happened to Diana. She was like a ghost about the house in those days. Nobody paid much attention to her, but she saw and heard *everything*.'

'I feel like I'm going mad,' Julius said.

'It's really very simple,' his grandmother said kindly, and reached over to pat his hand. 'Oliver seduced Diana behind Lyndon's back and got her pregnant. Only he didn't tell his mother. Camilla must have realised Diana was expecting a baby, or maybe the silly girl told her in confidence. Anyway, Gerard had insisted he was going to leave the whole estate to whichever son produced an heir first.' She stared into the distance, as though reliving those days. 'They may have been twins, but Camilla liked to play favourites with her children. And she wasn't about to let Lyndon inherit, instead of her *darling* Olly. So, she murdered Diana, and asked Oliver to cover it up for her.'

'Good God.' Julius jumped up and paced to the window and back, his face agitated. 'And then Iris killed Oliver?'

'Yes, but only to save Lyndon. He'd found out about Diana, you see, and said he was going to tell the police. He'd been suspicious from the start, of course. Even tried to flush Oliver out using a Ouija board and pretending to be Diana, accusing him from beyond the grave. He didn't know it was his own mother who'd done the deed.'

'But Oliver tried to shoot his brother,' Taylor said slowly, 'to stop him going to the police. And that's why Iris killed him.'

Mrs Chance nodded. 'We buried Oliver under the hut alongside Diana. Fetched spades and torches, dug a deep pit ... All three of us. Then Lyndon filled in the pit and put down floorboards. Quite simple, really.'

'*They lie together under the storage hut,*' Taylor quoted softly.

'Next day, Lyndon told his parents he and Oliver had argued again, and Oliver had left in a rage. Gone abroad for good, he said.'

'And they believed him?' Julius raised his brows.

'I think Gerard always suspected the truth. But he kept quiet. Maybe he knew, deep down, that Camilla had killed Diana, and this was the price they had to pay for keeping the family intact.' Mrs Chance shrugged. 'Anyway, Camilla never recovered from losing her favourite son. She died of lung cancer about five years later, and Gerard had a heart attack the following year.'

'And you and Lyndon?' Taylor asked.

'Lyndon and I got married, of course. We hadn't officially tied the knot before then, you see, but I'd fallen pregnant that summer ...' She smiled mistily at Julius. 'I had your father. Gerard left the estate to Lyndon. No questions asked.'

'And Iris went slowly mad,' Taylor said.

'She was always a strange girl, to be honest. A thwarted nun. They're the worst.' Mrs Chance reached for the decanter and poured herself another glass of brandy, her hands steadier now.

Groaning, Julius buried his face in his hands, before emerging a moment later, flushed and dishevelled. 'OK. What do we do now?'

Mrs Chance shrugged. 'Iris has finally confessed. So we dig them both up, I suppose.' She gulped at her brandy and gave a violent shudder. 'Face the music at last.'

Taylor and Julius drove over to the old storage hut that afternoon, with Iris in the back seat, her face haunted. She pointed to the spot where they'd buried Oliver, though she wasn't sure of Diana's exact position, and they marked the floorboards with chalk so they could show the police when they arrived. Then Iris began to collect her belongings from the hut, agreeing it was time to move back to Estuary House full-time. Though they all knew it was likely she'd be going to prison once the truth was out.

As Iris trailed around the hut, slowly gathering up her meagre possessions, Taylor tried not to think about what – or rather, who – lay beneath their feet. Instead, she began to unpin the tarot cards and poem drafts from the wall.

It made sense to her now: the tarot cards, the poems – all of them taken from Lyndon's *Estuary* sequence – even a faded old photo of the withered tree and the river beyond.

'All the answers lay in his last work. That's why she pinned these poems up. As a reminder of what she'd done.' She held up the tarot cards, showing them to Julius one at a time. 'The Lovers first,' she explained, 'that's Lyndon and Diana. Or perhaps Oliver and Diana. Then the Wheel of Fortune turns, and look what happens ...'

'Somebody falls and someone else rises,' Julius said.

'Exactly. But then you get The Tower.' She showed him the card. 'Lightning strikes. The building tumbles down. Defeat, sudden reversal, the end of the old order. Eleanor's arrival at Estuary House, perhaps? She "broke" the family. But it was a dynamic reversal, not merely destructive. Her arrival freed Lyndon to be the famous poet he was destined to become and paved the way for your father to be born, and then you. A new beginning from the ashes of the old.'

'OK.' He peered at the other cards. 'The Hanged Man. That's sacrifice, right? Odin, the god in the tree. I suppose Oliver was "sacrificed" in a way. His death meant the family could continue as they were. But what's this one?'

He flicked The World with his finger; the card depicted a

naked woman floating mid-air, surrounded by four creatures – man, ox, eagle, lion.

'I looked it up; it's about becoming one with the universe, sharing or giving back what you've gained.'

'Atonement,' Iris said gloomily from behind them. 'I had to atone for my sin, and Lyndon knew that. So he let me live over here. To be their guardians until the time came to reveal their resting place. He understood about penance.'

'I'm sorry,' Taylor grimaced, holding out what she'd taken down from the wall. 'I shouldn't have touched these. They're yours.'

'No,' Iris told her, 'they were Lyndon's. I brought them here after he died. You should have them now. You're writing about Lyndon. Take them, use them in your work.' Iris nodded to the dog-eared card of The Magician, which depicted a young man with a wand, conjuring and pointing to the sky. 'That's Lyndon. He was a conjuror, making poetry out of thin air, out of memories. Write the truth about him,' she said earnestly. 'Explain what happened here – why Lyndon didn't deserve his evil reputation.'

'I will,' Taylor promised.

'He knew someone would come one day to clear his name.' Iris looked Taylor up and down. 'Though I'm surprised it was you. I'd imagined someone quite different.'

Julius was still troubled. 'Iris, when we tell the police about the bodies, you'll be arrested for murder. You understand that, right?'

'This place has been my prison for longer than I can remember.' Iris stared about the shadowy, damp-smelling hut without affection. 'I'd like a new cell now.'

A mobile phone rang, loud in the silence.

'Sorry, I need to take this.' Julius answered it, heading

outside into the sunshine for a better signal. When he returned a few minutes later, he looked stunned.

'That was the police,' he told Taylor slowly, 'calling about the bones you found under the chapel floor. The pathologist's results are in.' He put his phone away. 'You're not going to believe this. But that body has been there since the mid-eighteenth century.'

'*What?*'

'They used the DNA sample I gave them, and there's a strong likelihood it's a match.' He took a deep breath. 'Given that, and the provenance of that signet ring they found with the body, using the portrait for comparison, they think it's possible those remains were of the Lady Elizabeth herself, and that she died by strangulation.'

Iris crossed herself, muttering in Latin under her breath.

'You mean, she didn't run off with a pirate and live happily ever after? That was all a lie?' Taylor thought of the woman in the portrait, her bold eyes and daring smile, and felt like weeping. 'Who do you think killed her?'

'The report says she was pregnant. And her murderer was probably one of the family.' He looked grim. 'Who else would have unrestricted access to our private chapel?'

Taylor buried her face in her hands, feeling nothing but pain for that spirited young woman, murdered hundreds of years ago.

'Hey, you OK?' Julius put his arm around her, and she looked up at him gratefully, pushing aside the dark echoes of her past.

'Yeah, I just ...' She exhaled shakily. 'That poor girl. It's so like what happened to Diana Farthing. It would have been a major scandal in those days, carrying a child out of wedlock. According to your grandmother, the Lady Elizabeth's father

364

was a brute with a series of wives who died young.' Taylor felt sick. 'You don't think he did it, do you? Her own father?'

'All we can ever know for sure is that somebody strangled her, and that somebody was most probably a man.' Julius grimaced. 'At least now she can be reburied in the parish churchyard with a proper headstone.'

'I think she just wanted to be found,' Taylor whispered, remembering the waves of darkness and emotion she'd always felt on the threshold of the chapel.

'She *did* want to be found.' Iris had fixed Taylor with an intense stare. 'Eleanor told me the Lady Elizabeth spoke to her once.'

With clear restraint, Julius asked, 'And how did she manage that feat, given she's been dead for the past few hundred years?'

'Through the Ouija board. She said her *brother* killed her. Eleanor thought perhaps Lyndon was manipulating the planchette, trying to scare Oliver into admitting what he knew about Diana's death. But after this, I'm not so sure.'

Taylor nodded. 'That is curious,' she agreed. Once she might have dismissed it as superstitious nonsense. But after meeting Mack and Davie ...

'All these dead bodies.' Iris fingered the heavy cross about her neck, her face gloomy. 'Murder runs in our family. It's the Chance curse. We are all sinners. None of us can be trusted.'

'Speak for yourself, Aunt Iris,' Julius told her. 'I have absolutely no intention of murdering anyone, thank you.'

His great-aunt shot him a sour look and then headed outside into the sunshine with her bundle of belongings, muttering, 'I need to look for my cat.'

Once she'd gone, Julius turned to brush a finger gently across Taylor's cheek. His gaze met hers, a little troubled. 'You believe that, don't you? That we're not all cursed?'

She looked into his face and decided in that instant to take a chance on him.

'Of course I do.'

He bent to kiss her, and for a few seconds Taylor felt curiously light, as though she were floating.

'I've always hated this place,' Julius said, looking around with a shudder. 'Now I know why.' He took her hand. 'Let's get out of here.'

Epilogue

Forever, like the sea, like the river.

– From 'Totem' in *Estuary*

It was raining by the time they put the finishing touches to the chapel interior, and the walk back up to the house looked like being a wet and muddy one.

'I wish I'd thought to bring an umbrella,' Taylor said, peering out at the dark skies massing above the estuary.

Julius, who was busily hammering paint lids shut with the handle of his brush, gave an impatient shrug. 'So we'll wait until it stops. It's just a passing shower.'

'I hope so.'

Taylor glanced down towards the river. The bushes had been cut back, and the slipway swept clean of debris, and there was a warning sign, freshly erected, warning visitors of deep water ahead.

Another sign indicated that Lyndon Chance had often walked along this stretch of the river when looking for inspiration, and that one of his favourite haunts in his youth had been this disused family chapel, now fully restored and open to visitors.

'We've done a good job.' Julius appeared in the doorway behind her, drying his hands on a cloth. 'And I need to thank you, by the way.'

She looked round at him, surprised. 'What for?'

'Persuading me not to sell up.' He, too, gazed down towards the river, a faraway look on his face. 'It was an excellent idea, turning Estuary House into a museum.'

'A lot of hard work though. And that huge bank loan...'

'It'll get paid off in time. All we need is for the audio tour walkie talkies to be delivered, and the flower displays for the entrance hall, and we'll be ready for the grand opening. Preliminary bookings are looking very healthy, I have to say.' Gently, he touched her arm. 'Hey, come back inside, you'll get cold out there. It's still only March, remember.'

Taylor followed him back into the chapel. She collected her coat and bag from one of the beautifully polished old pews. The stained-glass had also been lovingly restored by a local artisan, its saints bright again, with no holes for the wind to blow through.

She stood a moment, looking up at the stained glass, and recalled how she'd stood here in Mack's kitchen once, and laughed with him and gazed out over the estuary, never knowing she was sharing the company of the dead, her feet all the time hovering above the bones of the Lady Elizabeth.

'Mack wanted me to find her, you know,' she said softly, and turned to study the slate floor plaque they'd had installed, marking where her body had lain undiscovered for centuries. 'That's why he brought me here, I'm sure of it. And that's why he kept showing me the hut where Iris lived, nudging me to go there, too, to find the other two.'

Julius put an arm about her shoulder. 'It sounds like you were half in love with your charming ghost. Should I be jealous?'

'Maybe.' But she was smiling.

He bent his head to kiss her, and although they'd been sleeping together for some months now, she felt again the

368

same dreamy urge for love warring with an abject fear of intimacy.

He must have sensed that internal struggle, because he pulled back at once, searching her face. 'Bad memories?'

'Maybe a little,' Taylor admitted. 'But we're making happier ones all the time, aren't we? Restoring this place together, opening Estuary House to the public. I've loved seeing my own research form such an integral part of that, too. It was about time the world had a museum dedicated to Lyndon Chance and his poetry.' She heard the emotion quiver in her voice and didn't try to suppress it. He knew how she felt, both about him and about his grandfather's work; there were no more secrets between them. 'I owe you and Eleanor so much, Julius.'

'I think it's we who are in your debt, actually. You coming down here, finding out what really happened to Diana and Oliver ... Well, you've heard what Gran says on the subject. You've been a blessing to the Chance family.'

She raised her eyebrows. 'What, getting your great-aunt arrested? Bringing all that scandal down on your heads?'

'But at least the judge saw sense and acquitted Iris of murder,' he pointed out, 'and Gran of aiding and abetting. Neither of them had to go to prison. OK, it was a bit of a shock for Gran, especially not being able to remember all the details. But Diana and Oliver have been laid to rest at last. And the Lady Elizabeth, too, with a memorial plaque inside the parish church, which she hugely deserved. So, yes, I'd call it a blessing.'

Taylor said nothing.

She'd finally told him the story of her childhood. Most of it, anyway. The bits she could bear to tell. The rest could wait for another time. Or remain locked in her heart forever. Not every dark and sordid secret had to be spilt out just because a person had fallen in love.

'You got another letter from him yesterday, didn't you?' Julius asked suddenly, once again plucking her thoughts out of thin air.

'My father?' Taylor felt her hands clench into fists. 'Yes.' It was hard not to say the words without baring her teeth. 'He wrote to me again.'

'And will you write back?'

'He murdered my mum in front of me, Julius. I was ten years old, for God's sake. Of course I'm not going to write to him.'

Julius reached out, stroking her hair. 'I'm sorry.'

'He only wrote because he saw my name in the news-papers, anyway. That was one consequence of finding the Lady Elizabeth's remains that I wasn't expecting.' She tried to keep her voice light, but inside she was struggling. Every time she thought of her father, she could see her mother's face as she died. 'His first parole hearing is due later this year. If he gets out on licence, which I hope he doesn't, then he wants me to go and visit him.'

'Do you think you will?'

'I don't think I could,' she said frankly. 'It would be too upsetting. I never expected to hear from him again, and I've certainly never wanted to *see* him again.'

'Does he know about your foster father?' he asked quietly. 'The years of abuse you suffered after you went into care?'

She couldn't find the words to reply but shook her head. It was only recently that she'd found the courage to tell Julius about the abuse, late one night after too many brandies.

Her childhood had been the stuff of nightmares, and she wasn't ready yet to discuss it openly in the daylight. Even when she'd finally been given a safe refuge by Tom and Sheila, the lovely couple who'd fostered her from age fourteen to eighteen, and encouraged her love of books and poetry as well as sciences, even helping her apply for a place at university, she'd still been unable to talk about that part of her life except in therapy sessions. And they'd accepted that reticence as just part of who she was.

Maybe one day, she thought grimly. But not today.

'Well, whatever you decide, I'll stand by you.' Julius put an arm about her waist, but loosely, aware of how difficult she still found physical intimacy. 'I love you very much, Taylor. You know that, don't you?'

Taylor heard the uncertainty in his voice and turned, smiling against the pain in her heart. Julius wasn't to blame for it, any more than he'd been to blame for the way his own history had made him wary of outsiders – his father's early death and his mother's abandonment, his family's dark reputation. But it took one survivor to recognise another. And they were both survivors.

'I know,' she reassured him, 'and I love you, too. Like you said on our first night together, we dysfunctional types have to stick together.'

'For safety?' Julius was only half-joking.

'For love,' she said softly, and took his hand, quoting from Lyndon's final poem, *Totem*, 'Forever, like the sea, like the river.'

THE END

Acknowledgements

This novel was written at the height of the Covid-19 pandemic in 2020. Accordingly, it's had a turbulent genesis, from first conception through writing to acquisition and now to market. I initially wrote it as an escape, going back in time to avoid the big problem facing writers of contemporary fiction in 2020 – whether to include references to coronavirus, or pretend all our stories take place in a world untouched by the pandemic?

By the time the book was finished, it was clear that the publishing industry was in turmoil. We'd had almost a year of furlough, offices unstaffed, editors working from home via Zoom, bookshop closures, followed by paper supply and delivery driver shortages. Many readers were too distracted by working from home or handling boisterous kids in permanent residence to settle down with a book, or else were choosing different kinds of books to their usual tastes, making reading trends unpredictable. Not surprisingly, publishers had become nervous about which and how many books to acquire, and that shifting landscape continues as I write this in January 2022, for we are not out of the pandemic yet.

All of which makes me doubly grateful to my editor Rhea Kurien at Orion Dash for loving this book as much as she did on first seeing it, and for nursing it through the pandemic speed bumps. I also thank the whole Dash team, who have been exemplary, and I hope this year sees a return to business as usual for the beleaguered publishing industry.

My heartfelt thanks also to my wonderful editor, Alison Bonomi at LBA. You believed in this book right from the start, and understood its origins better than anyone, and I thank you for it. These past two years have been horrendous, but we are nearly out of that dark tunnel and back into the light. Just a little further …

Finally, as ever, I thank my family, who have been so supportive. I possibly had Covid while writing this book – testing was not yet a thing – and while I coughed in self-isolation, they brought me meals and endless cups of tea. Writing occupied my time, and my husband Steve, to whom this book is dedicated, kept me sane with Facetime calls. So, a huge thank you to Steve, and to my three youngest children Morris, Dylan and Indigo, all of whom came of age during the Covid pandemic. May the universe bless you and keep you, and may you never face another global catastrophe in your lifetimes!

Lastly, thank you to my readers, without whom none of this would be possible. Thank you for continuing to believe in me and to read my stories. Bless you all.

Printed in Great Britain
by Amazon